"This novel has all the funny banter and sexy feels you could want in a romantic comedy—and, of course, a terrific grand gesture before the happy ending."   —NPR.org

"[An] enticing debut."   —She Reads

"*The Marriage Game* is a hilarious blend of humor, romance, and family."   —The Nerd Daily

"Desai has done a wonderful job showcasing Indian culture—it informs every aspect of the book and makes for a complex and entertaining story. The humor and banter in this book are superb—they had me in stitches in parts."   —Frolic Media

"Desai's delightful debut is a playful take on enemies-to-lovers and arranged marriage tropes starring two headstrong Desi American protagonists. Rom-com fans should take note of this fresh, fun offering."   —*Publishers Weekly* (starred review)

"This witty and delightful story about family, forgiveness, and letting go is utterly satisfying. Desai's first book will be a hit with fans of Sonya Lalli's *The Matchmaker's List*."   —*Library Journal*

"*The Marriage Game* is the most delicious read! From the humor to the heartwarming family bonds to the off-the-charts chemistry, it's impossible for me to love this book any more. I can't wait for more from Sara Desai!"   —Alexa Martin, author of *Intercepted*

"I fell hard for *The Marriage Game* from the moment I read Layla and Sam's dynamite meet-cute. It's a hilarious, heartfelt, and steamy enemies-to-lovers romance."   —Sarah Smith, author of *Faker*

THE

Dating Plan

· SARA DESAI ·

JOVE
NEW YORK

A JOVE BOOK
Published by Berkley
An imprint of Penguin Random House LLC
penguinrandomhouse.com

Copyright © 2021 by Sara Desai
Penguin Random House supports copyright. Copyright fuels creativity,
encourages diverse voices, promotes free speech, and creates a vibrant culture.
Thank you for buying an authorized edition of this book and for complying with
copyright laws by not reproducing, scanning, or distributing any part of it in
any form without permission. You are supporting writers and allowing
Penguin Random House to continue to publish books for every reader.

A JOVE BOOK, BERKLEY, and the BERKLEY & B colophon are
registered trademarks of Penguin Random House LLC.

Library of Congress Cataloging-in-Publication Data

Names: Desai, Sara, author.
Title: The dating plan / Sara Desai.
Description: First Edition. | New York: Jove, 2021.
Identifiers: LCCN 2020034224 (print) | LCCN 2020034225 (ebook) |
ISBN 9780593100585 (trade paperback) | ISBN 9780593100592 (ebook)
Subjects: GSAFD: Love stories.
Classification: LCC PR9199.4.D486 D38 2021 (print) |
LCC PR9199.4.D486 (ebook) | DDC 813/.6—dc23
LC record available at https://lccn.loc.gov/2020034224
LC ebook record available at https://lccn.loc.gov/2020034225

First Edition: March 2021

Printed in the United States of America
1   3   5   7   9   10   8   6   4   2

Cover art by Marina Muun
Cover design by Katie Anderson
Book design by Kristin del Rosario

To Mum,
for giving me the gift of stories.

Daisy Patel had no issues with besotted lovers hiding away in a toilet cubicle for a little covert tongue gymnastics. For the most part, technology conferences were stressful and boring, and if someone could find a little lip loving between networking, speakers, and seminars, she didn't begrudge them their happiness.

In this case, however, the gold medal winner of the twist 'n' tangle in the women's restroom at the Oakland Convention Center happened to be her ex-boyfriend, Orson Fisk.

And the woman in his arms was her former boss, Madison Montgomery, CEO of Activize LLC.

"Ahem." Her attempt to draw their attention fell on deaf ears. Or maybe they didn't care. Maybe Orson had been bespelled, and when he was finally released from Madison's clutches, he would realize he'd made a mistake breaking up with a neurotic software engineer and her *pakora*-loving pup. Daisy and Max came as a package; dog haters be warned.

Curiously numb at the sight of her ex wrapped around her old boss like the most tenacious of invasive species—she'd caught a glimpse of them in the mirror before they'd closed the stall door—Daisy slid a quarter into the disposable menstrual product dispenser.

She'd been under no illusions when Orson had asked her out after they'd met in a Developer Week hack-a-thon in Oakland,

California. Clearly he was desperate for a hookup. After all, not many men were interested in a woman who lived by plans and quantifiable results and could do one compile a day in C++ in a POSIX environment with zero errors. They wanted the prom queens, not the class valedictorians; the women who wielded fashion as a weapon, and not a shield. So she'd been thrown off her Manic Pixie Dream Girl game when Orson had called after their one-night stand and asked her out again.

Thirty-five going on sixty-five, devoid of any body fat, and possessing a wispy goatee, Orson had introduced her to long walks, black coffee, art house films, slow jazz, gourmet cooking, and the benefits of intellectual over physical relationships. They worked in the same field, attended the same conferences, and shared the same interests in the online world. It should have been perfect. And yet she'd never once, in the four weeks they'd been seeing each other— making it the longest relationship in her life—thought of introducing him to her family. Serious relationships were not in a life plan that involved working hard, looking after her dad, and growing old alone in the house where she'd been born.

Orson tugged on Madison's blouse, tearing the top button to reveal the secret treasures of a woman seriously lacking in discretion. There was nothing intellectual about his frenzied pawing. If Daisy had known tearing off clothes was one of Orson's skills, she might have put a ring on it right away. But she'd been plagued with doubt. Why didn't she feel the flutters in her chest that were supposedly indicative of love? Where were the birds that were supposed to be tweeting around her head? Did she have some kind of chemical imbalance, or was something else wrong? Only when she caught Orson and Madison doing the nasty in Madison's office late one evening did she finally feel something.

Relief.

As she had always suspected, she was meant to be alone.

Turning the crank as slowly as possible to minimize the decibel level of menstrual product release, she glanced over again at Orson and Madison pawing at each other like horny teenagers. She should make a quick exit before she said something awkward that would make the situation infinitely worse. Her tendency to blurt out whatever was on her mind had gotten her into trouble too many times. She was happiest alone in her cubicle at work, fully immersed in a screen of code, her favorite dance beats playing over her headphones. There was beauty in the simplicity of programming. If something was illogical, it simply wouldn't work.

Maybe there was a message here that wasn't getting through. She assessed the situation as if it were code and came up with: <<Connection Failed>>. It was the story of her life all over again.

The menstrual pad dropped into the dispenser with a soft thud. Her new boss, Tyler Dawes, CEO of Organicare, only needed one of the competitor's pads for the demonstration, but what if something went wrong? If they didn't secure more venture capital funding soon, the company would shut down and all of Organicare's employees would be out of work.

It didn't help that Tyler was a terrible salesman. A professor at Caltech, with a Ph.D. in chemical engineering, he had become involved in developing sustainable, organic menstrual products after his daughter, Kristina, realized there was a gap in the market. With hard work and millions in venture capital funding, they had built a successful subscription-based, direct-to-consumer business with an app-based product for lifestyle health and wellness. And then everything had gone wrong.

Daisy pushed another quarter into the slot and yanked on the dial. If Tyler had asked her to pitch with him when he first signed up for the conference, she wouldn't have been in the restroom at all. Daisy didn't go into meetings unprepared. Instead of sweating it out as she tried to dispense a pad in silence, she would have been seated in the air-conditioned conference room, sipping homemade chai from her thermos as she mentally rehearsed a demonstration she would have practiced for weeks.

Still oblivious to her presence, Orson and Madison continued to make out in the toilet stall, shaking the metal walls as they grappled and groaned. The toilet flushed—not once or twice, but three times in quick succession. Daisy hoped it was from an excess of passion and not because they'd had the dodgy seafood at the buffet lunch. She'd told herself to avoid it, but those prawns had been so tempting . . .

In any event, it was all very disappointing. When she and Orson had been together, he had been an efficient, no-nonsense lover, expressing the satisfactory outcome of their coupling with a whoosh of air followed by glass of Rioja and a deep dive into Aristotle's science of logic envisioned through the syllogism. There had been no moans or panting, no bras falling on the filthy tiles (thank God!), and no automatic toilets flushing a symphony of germs into the air.

The second pad dropped out of the machine, followed by another and another. Boxed pads shot out of the machine, hitting Daisy in the chest like bullets. She dropped to a crouch, scrambling to catch them before they touched the floor.

"Is someone there?" Madison called out.

Oh the huge manatee. Programmer slang for a catastrophic data failure, or in this case, a malfunctioning menstrual pad machine. Panicking, Daisy grabbed the boxes and bolted out of the restroom.

"Daisy! I was looking for you." Salena Auntie, her father's sister, ambushed her only a few steps from the door.

"What are you doing here, Auntie-ji?" Chest heaving, she

looked over her shoulder to make sure she hadn't been followed. The last thing she wanted was for Madison and Orson to think she'd been spying on them. Although she'd been devastated by their betrayal, she wasn't the type of woman who wanted revenge, nor would she ever stoop to begging Orson to take her back. She wasn't that pathetic. One unfortunate drunk dial had cured her of that.

"I was having lunch with my friend Anushka and her son, Roshan, and they mentioned he was looking for a wife." Salena Auntie gestured to the tall, handsome man behind her. "I thought you'd be perfect for each other. I called your office and they said you were here, so we thought we'd drop in."

Daisy bit back a groan. Her aunties had been on a mission to get her married ever since her cousin Layla had gotten engaged, approaching the task with military precision. They showed up unannounced and unexpected at her home, her gym, grocery stores, and malls, always with an innocent bachelor in tow, and always on the pretense of "just being in the neighborhood" even if the "neighborhood" was an hour away.

"I'm so sorry." Daisy shot what she hoped was an apologetic smile at the dark-haired stranger. "I don't have time to chat. I'm about to go into a pitch session, and I have to get these product samples to my boss."

"But you haven't even met Roshan!"

"Another time!" She bolted away, clutching the boxes of pads as she wove in and out of the crowd, her heart pounding in her chest. When she'd woken up this morning, she would never have guessed she would be pulled away from her cozy workspace and dragged to a tech conference, only to wind up on the run from her ex, with an armload of pads and her matchmaking auntie hot on her heels.

Maybe she hadn't woken up. Maybe this was just a dream and any moment now she would open her eyes and . . .

"Ooof." She hit a slab of something rock hard and teetered back on red Mary Janes that were slightly too high for comfort but looked fabulous with her red flowered minidress. Daisy didn't care that her feet were usually hidden away under her desk all day. Shoes made an outfit. Whether they were kitten heels with kitten faces, funky flats decorated with embroidered bananas, or even her blinged-up biker boots, her shoes were always the finishing touch to her somewhat eclectic sense of style.

Off-balance, she dropped the pads, her hands flailing for purchase, her Marvel Universe tote bag swinging from her shoulder. Tyler was going to kill her if she didn't die from the cerebral hemorrhage that would be inevitable once her head hit the tile floor. At least Salena Auntie was there. One text and the entire Patel family would know when and how she died, and the funeral would be arranged before the ambulance arrived to take her to the morgue.

Time slowed and she squeezed her eyes shut as she fell, trying to remember every moment of her twenty-seven years on earth—happy family, sad family, small family, big family, heartache, heartbreak, Max . . .

She was so preoccupied with reliving her most poignant memories that it took her a moment to realize she was no longer airborne. Strong, warm hands encircled her waist, holding her safe.

"Are you okay?"

Deep, warming, and as delicious as liquid caramel, the voice sent a tingle of electricity down her spine, and a jolt of recognition through her body as hard as the strong arms around her.

She knew that voice. She had heard it almost every day for ten years. Her gaze lifted, and for a moment she forgot to breathe.

Liam Freaking Bastard Murphy.

Her brother's onetime best friend. Her undying preteen crush, teen obsession, and still the object of her nightly fantasies. The man who had broken her heart and disappeared from her life never to be seen or heard from again . . .

Her pulse kicked up a notch, as the still-functioning part of her brain cataloged his appearance. Time had worn hard lines and chiseled planes into what had once been a slightly rounded face, tipping the balance from simply handsome into breathtakingly gorgeous. A five-o'clock shadow darkened his jaw, and his lips— God, his lips—were firm and curved into the familiar smile that had once made her weak in the knees.

"Daisy?!" His voice rose slightly in pitch, and her gaze snapped up to eyes as blue as the ocean she had wanted to drown herself in after Liam stood her up on the night of her senior prom and scurried off into oblivion like the lowly night-crawling scumbag he had turned out to be.

She opened her mouth to speak but nothing came out. How did she express the maelstrom of emotions coursing through her veins? It had been ten years since she'd stood alone on the front steps of her house—in a bright pink prom dress, the corsage her father had bought her pinned to her shoulder—waiting for Liam to take her to the prom. Ten years since he'd disappeared, never to be seen again. How many times had she imagined this moment?

Should she slap him or kick him between the legs?

· 2 ·

LIAM'S arms tightened around Daisy's waist in a grip he seemed in no hurry to break. "I can't believe it's you."

Of course he couldn't. The Daisy he knew was young and innocent and had fully embraced her position on the high school geek squad. Her clothes had been quirky and weird, a mix of accessories, colors, patterns, and fandoms that she'd combined into a unique geek-chic style. She'd tied her long, dark hair in a ponytail so it didn't get in the way when she was helping the freshmen with their computer programs, mixing chemicals for science fair projects, or studying for the latest math competition. Prom night was the first time she'd ever dressed up, and even then she'd had to ask her cousin Layla to help with her hair and makeup. Not that it had done much good.

"Let me go, Liam." How ironic that she'd spent her teen years dreaming of being in Liam's arms, and now it was the last place on earth she wanted to be.

"For a moment there, I thought you didn't recognize me." He slowly relaxed his grip and she pulled away, feeling instantly bereft.

"I wish that were true." She looked back over her shoulder for an escape route only to see Orson and Madison walking her way, hand in hand, hair slightly mussed, clothes askew. Behind them,

Salena Auntie battered her way through the crowd with her enormous red purse, poor Roshan following in her wake.

Just what she needed. A lifetime's worth of humiliation descending on her all at once.

Liam studied her intently as if he hadn't heard the burn. "How long has it been?"

"Ten years, eleven months, thirteen days, thirteen hours, forty-seven minutes, and sixteen seconds." The clock behind him had a bright red second hand for precise calculation.

She realized her mistake when his lips tugged into an infuriating smirk.

"You haven't changed."

Hadn't changed? Was he serious? She'd grown up the night she had to go to the prom with Layla instead of with the most infamous bad boy in their high school. It was supposed to be the defining night of her high school life—the moment when she showed everyone she wasn't the geek they thought she was. Someone wanted her—someone handsome and charming who had insisted on being her escort when he found out she didn't have a date.

A senior when she was a freshman, Liam was the boy every girl wanted and every guy wanted to befriend. He had spent more time in the principal's office than he did in class. With a new girlfriend every week, a permanent gang of hangers-on who followed him around the school, and the legendary pranks he'd played etched on the restroom walls, he was still remembered years after graduation. It would have been perfect. But now, as she took in those sparkling blue eyes and thick dark hair, the chiseled planes and angles of a face that had morphed from good-looking into devastatingly handsome, she couldn't believe she had fallen so hard for someone who had always been completely out of her league.

"I have changed. No glasses. No frizzy hair. Better clothes. Bigger boobs . . . Not that any of that matters. You made it clear what you thought about me."

"That was a long time ago." His voice was rough, strained. "I don't feel good about what happened."

"What a coincidence. Neither do I."

He let out a ragged breath. "Don't tell me you're still upset."

"'Upset'?" She wanted to scream. Angry. Hurt. Humiliated. Disappointed. Crushed. Bitter. Wrecked. Destroyed. There were so many better words to describe her devastation when the man of her dreams stood her up for her senior prom and then disappeared from her life.

But what had she expected? Her own mother had abandoned her, too.

"No," she lied, letting the pain and hurt she'd been harboring for the past decade wash away any thoughts of forgiveness. If she clung to it, embraced it, maybe she wouldn't think about her pathetic teenage fantasies, the embarrassing ways she'd tried to catch his attention, the dreams of kissing him and living happily ever after with the only boy she'd ever loved.

"I'm totally over it," she continued. "High school prom? What's that? I never think about it. Or you. I never think about you. When I bumped into you right now, I couldn't even remember your last name."

He raised an incredulous eyebrow. "That's hard to believe since you probably know the details of every meeting that's going on in every room, the location of every exit, the number of attendees, and how long it takes to walk from one end of the conference center to the other."

She did know all those things. Her brain had an irritating habit of working even when she wasn't conscious it was processing information. Over the years she'd found a way to shut it down. Unfortunately, her mental tricks only worked when her life was under control, and right now she was caught in a maelstrom of contradictory emotions that threatened to tear her apart. Why did he have to look so breathtakingly gorgeous? Why couldn't he have worn a boring suit and tie instead of a badass leather jacket that made him look like a young James Dean?

"I only remember important things." She bent down to pick up the pads, tearing her gaze away as she tried to control her instinctive reaction to him. Although she desperately wanted to escape, she couldn't return to Tyler empty-handed.

"You're angry with me." A pained expression crossed his face.

"I thought that was obvious."

"Let me help." Liam crouched down beside her and picked up one of the boxes.

How irritating. She wanted him to act like the bad guy he was. Saving her from a fall and crouching on the floor of a conference center to help her stuff pads back into boxes were not the actions of a villain.

"That's a lot of . . ." His faced reddened and he cleared his throat. "Products."

She snatched the box from his hand. "My boss needed one for a pitch and I accidentally got too many."

"Who do you work for?"

"Organicare. We're in the personal care business." After leaving Madison behind, Daisy had taken some time off from her work as a software engineering consultant to help Layla start up her new recruitment business. Office management involved too much social interaction and hadn't given her the intellectual challenge she craved, so she'd responded to Tyler's ad for a senior software engineer who could support his rapidly hemorrhaging engineering department. He'd been up front about the financial state of the company, but Daisy didn't mind. She'd spent her career hopping from start-up to start-up, moving on before she made attachments that would make it difficult to leave.

"I haven't heard of them."

"Why would you?"

"I'm with Evolution Ventures, a venture capital company based in New York. I moved out here a few weeks ago to head up our new West Coast office. We mainly fund start-ups in the food services industry, but we've been expanding into tech so I'm here for the pitch sessions."

Even more irritating. Hopefully Tyler hadn't put Evolution on the pitch list. Bad enough that he'd dragged her along to answer questions about the software system and pour blue liquid onto pads to demonstrate the superior absorbency of Organicare's products. But to have to beg Liam Murphy for money to save the company . . . She couldn't imagine anything worse.

"I'm glad things worked out for you, Liam, but honestly, if we weren't in public, I'd slap you across the face."

"That's very considerate of you." He held out a hand to help her up, but she waved him off as she stood, cradling the boxes in one arm.

"I'm surprised you even know what that word means."

His behavior on her prom night had been all the more devastating because Daisy had seen another side of Liam when he had first started coming to her house to hang out with her older brother, Sanjay. He joked with her, teased her, even played video games with her if Sanjay had homework to do. Although he'd become more distant after she turned sixteen, he was more protective of her than her own brother, volunteering to pick her up from late-night study sessions, and showing up to drive her home on the few occasions Layla managed to drag her to a party.

"Let me take you for a drink after the conference." He handed her the last box. "We can catch up, and you can tell me about your dad and Sanjay . . ."

Her anger finally peaked, crashing through her veins in a tidal wave of emotion. Every moment of her prom night was etched into her mind—from the heartfelt emotion in her father's eyes when she walked down the stairs in her dress, to the tears on her pillow as she cried herself to sleep. Liam had been a fixture in her life for eight years, and he had disappeared without even saying goodbye.

"Are you serious?" She rounded on him, now grateful for the heels that put her a few inches closer to his eye level. "I don't want to have a drink with you. I don't even want to breathe the same air as you. I don't want to catch up or talk about the fun times we had. And you don't deserve to know about Sanjay and my dad because you didn't just leave me; you left them, too."

Liam went utterly still, his eyes intense, brows knitted together in a puzzled frown. She moved to step past him, but he caught her arm in a gentle grip.

"Daisy . . . wait."

She spun to face him. "I don't owe you anything."

"What if I beg?" He tipped his head to the side, his seductive smile so achingly familiar her heart squeezed in her chest. This was the Liam she'd fallen for when she was ten years old. Reckless. Charming. Handsome. Charisma flowing off him in waves. Despite her antipathy toward him, it was impossible not to still feel the pull of attraction.

"Daisy!" Madison waved from the crowd, tugging a reluctant Orson along; in the distance, relentless like the tide, came Salena Auntie and poor Roshan.

There was nowhere to run. No graceful way to extract herself from the situation without losing face. Daisy tipped her head back and groaned.

Liam frowned. "What's wrong?"

Gritting her teeth she gestured to the left. "That's my aunt coming toward us with the man she wants me to marry. And in three seconds, we'll be accosted by my old boss. She's with my ex, Orson. I got him a job at my last start-up, and the next thing I knew, she'd stolen him away. This day is getting worse by the second."

Liam twisted his lips to the side, considering. "I can see why you—"

"Shh." She held up a warning hand. "I'm praying for a natural disaster—earthquake, flood, tornado, murder wasps, even a plague of locusts will do."

"How about a kiss?"

Daisy frowned. "How is that going to fix anything?"

His gaze dropped to her lips. "You can't get married if you're seeing someone else, and you'll be able to show your ex and your boss that you've moved on. It's a perfect solution."

It would have been perfect ten years ago at the senior prom. She'd imagined it night after night. The shock and awe in the faces of her classmates. The jacket he would place over her shoulders when she shivered. The gentle squeeze of his hand as he walked her to the dance floor. His arms around her, warm and strong. The slow, steady beat of the music. His whispered declaration that he'd loved her since the moment they met. And then his lips on her lips . . .

"You are the last man on earth I want to kiss."

His voice dropped to a low rumble that vibrated through her body. "I would do the kissing."

Daisy looked back over her shoulder at the approaching storm.

It *was* a perfect solution. She would have her fantasy prom kiss, show Orson and Madison she was no victim, and shut down her matchmaking aunties all in one fell swoop. And after they'd gone, she'd be close enough to knee Liam in the groin.

"Fine. Just one kiss," she gritted out through clenched teeth. "And there are rules."

"I wouldn't expect anything less." He stepped closer, sliding an arm around her waist, crushing the boxes of pads between them.

All her nerves fired at once and she drew in a calming breath, desperately trying to regain her sense of self-possession. "No tongue. No pressure. No open mouth. No roaming hands . . ." Her voice trailed off when his lips moved over her hair. She drew in a sharp breath, inhaling the scent of him—leather and the ocean breeze and something so deeply familiar, longing stirred inside her, melting the ice in her veins.

Bristling, she stiffened against him. She needed that ice. Needed the walls that kept her safe. It had been easy to hate Liam when he was gone, but now that he was here, only a whisper away, it was almost impossible to hold back the feelings that she had buried along with her heart.

"I'll try not to throw up in your mouth."

Liam chuckled. "Is that your idea of foreplay?"

"It's my idea of getting this over with as quickly as possible so I can go back to pretending you don't exist."

With a soft growl of amusement, Liam gently cupped her face with his free hand, filling her vision with the face that still haunted her dreams.

Daisy's heart pounded a staccato beat. "Hurry."

His lips brushed over hers in a featherlight caress, so gentle and unexpected she forgot to breathe. There was no passion in the kiss. The earth didn't move, time didn't stand still, fireworks didn't fill the sky, not even a single bird twittered around her head. But it was tender and sweet, his lips were soft and gentle, and for the briefest second she was tempted to give in to the heat of sensation and kiss him like she was a lovelorn teenager all over again.

"Daisy! How nice to see you." Madison's voice grated over her nerves, pulling her out of the moment. Her defenses slammed back into place and she jerked away.

"Madison." Turning, Daisy forced a smile and slid one arm around Liam's waist. He was broad and solid and mouthwateringly hard, like he spent his days pumping weights in the gym. "Nice to see you, too."

"We're together." Liam slid his arm around Daisy's shoulder and pulled her to his side.

"You're with *him*?" Orson's bushy eyebrows flew up like two dancing caterpillars.

"Oh, Orson." Daisy leaned into Liam's side, feigning surprise. "I didn't see you hiding there behind Madison."

She made the introductions. Orson glared as he shook Liam's hand. Madison was too busy checking Liam out to notice that her new boyfriend had spiked a jealousy fever.

"How sweet. Daisy has a new boyfriend." Madison licked her lips like a predator about to feast.

Daisy's pulse kicked up a notch and panic fuzzed her brain. She had no interest in Liam. That ship had sailed ten years ago on a tide of tears. But she wasn't about to let Madison steal another man away.

"We're actually . . . engaged." The word dropped from her mouth before she could catch it, and she shot Liam a frantic sideways glance silently begging him to play along.

"Engaged?" Orson's voice cracked. "We only broke up a short while ago."

"When you know, you know." Liam pressed a kiss to her temple, jumping on the bandwagon without hesitation.

"'Engaged'?" Salena Auntie pushed past Orson to stand right in front of her, red purse clutched to her chest. "You're engaged? Does your father know? Who is this boy?" She turned and squeezed Roshan's arm. "I didn't know. I thought she was available."

"Um . . ." Lying to her aunt wasn't part of her impromptu plan, but Orson and Madison were watching with avid fascination. "This is Liam."

"Lemon?" Salena Auntie's forehead wrinkled.

"Liam."

"Limb?"

Seemingly nonplussed by Salena Auntie's inability to say his name, Liam held out his hand. "It's a pleasure to meet you."

"Salena Patel." She shook his hand, mollified by his warm smile and easy charm. "What kind of name is Limb?"

Daisy sighed. "His name is Liam, but it doesn't really matter—"

"'It doesn't matter'?" Salena Auntie staggered back, hand over her heart as if she were about to collapse. Her matchmaking aunt put the *queen* in *drama queen*. "You are secretly engaged and it doesn't matter? When did this happen? What does he do? Who is his family? Your poor father . . ."

Madison mouthed a sympathetic goodbye and turned away, tugging Orson behind her, as a slew of questions tumbled from Salena Auntie's lips: *Who? Why? Where? What? When?*

"It only just happened today." Daisy interrupted her aunt with an apologetic shrug. "You're the first to know. I'm going to tell the rest of the family when dad gets back from his trip." Her dad had flown to Belize with his new girlfriend, Priya, and they weren't due back for another three weeks. By then, she hopefully would have come up with a story about how she'd been engaged and then unengaged and have found another way to put her matchmaking aunties off the scent.

Salena Auntie's eyes narrowed. "Why not tell him now? Marriage is a family affair. You shouldn't have done this without speaking to him first."

"I didn't want to bother him on his holiday with something so . . . trivial."

"An unmarried woman of your age left alone to roam the streets is no trivial matter." Salena Auntie shook her finger. "Look what happened. Your father goes away and this Limb boy took advantage. It isn't right."

"I'm not old!" Daisy protested.

Liam lifted an eyebrow. "In some countries, you'd have been put out to pasture by now."

She shot him a sideways look. "Stay out of this."

"I don't think you're old," Roshan countered.

"Such a good boy." Salena Auntie patted his arm. "Don't worry. I have another niece for you. Her name is Sonam. Beautiful girl. Very smart. She's a lawyer, but don't hold it against her. Her office isn't far." She narrowed her eyes at Daisy. "And you . . . We'll speak later after I've talked to your aunties. Everyone will need to meet Limb."

"It's Liam."

Her aunt waved as she turned away. "Goodbye, Daisy and Limb."

After bidding farewell to Roshan and her aunt, Daisy lifted Liam's arm from her shoulders. "Thanks. You didn't have to play along."

"Anytime you need a fabulously handsome fake fiancé, my lips are at your service." He made a theatrical bow. "It's the least I can do after you managed not to throw up from my kiss."

Daisy shook her head, unsettled by his teasing warmth. He didn't act like a man who would stand her up and disappear for ten years without a word. He acted like the old Liam, the one who'd made her feel like her quirks and lists and plans were perfectly normal, the one who'd made her laugh and kept her safe and filled the hole in her chest that her mother had left when she moved to New York, leaving her young family behind.

"Nothing has changed, Liam." She heard the chill in her voice. "I don't want to see you ever again."

He flinched the tiniest bit, but a slight smile still played on his lips. "So the engagement is off? I'd say it was a pleasure but . . ."

"It wasn't." Daisy finished his sentence.

A shadow of sorrow flickered across his face so quickly she wondered if she'd seen it. "See you in another ten years." His softened tone, unwanted and unexpected, rippled gently over her senses like a warm summer breeze.

Disconcerted by the flare of heat that flooded her skin, she stumbled over her final words. "That will be too soon."

She left him in the foyer and hurried down the hall. After so many years, she'd finally gotten her closure. So why was her heart still pounding? And why did her lips still tingle from his kiss?

LIAM Murphy had to hand it to the cocky entrepreneur standing in front of him: the dude didn't waste time. And in the world of venture capital funding, time was everything.

"Disposable, biodegradable, edible, sustainable sex toys made with kombucha slime." The thin weasel-like man with slicked down hair and a peach-fuzz moustache held up a thick ring made of what looked to be amber-colored plastic laced with oil.

"What's our scorecard for sex toys this afternoon?" Liam murmured to his junior associate, James Sunjata. After scrambling to be noticed in New York, James had jumped at the chance to move to San Francisco to help Liam open the new West Coast office, with a view to taking over when Liam joined the partnership.

Evolution's management had all but promised Liam a seat at the partnership table, and that would mean a permanent return to New York. It would be the pinnacle of his career. He would show the world that a high school delinquent could rise to the top of his profession, even without a college degree.

If only his grandfather were alive to share in his success. It was life's cruel irony that only a few weeks after Liam had moved back to San Francisco and reconnected with his grandfather after an almost twenty-year estrangement, the old man had passed away.

Between the houseful of Irish relatives, the funeral arrangements, the wake, and the pressures of working in a temporary space while he and James tried to find a new office, he hadn't had time to properly mourn.

"This is pitch number five," James said quietly. "But it's the first sex toy made of slime."

Liam had made up his mind after the word *slime*, but this was supposed to be a learning opportunity, and after bumping into Daisy, his head wasn't fully in the game. He handed the reins to James. "First impressions?"

"Honestly, it sounds kind of exciting," James said. "Biodegradable sex toys? Do you know how many of those things wind up in landfills?"

"We call it King Kom." The inventor handed the sample to James. "I've tested it extensively. Six hours and I was still going strong. Eight hours and it just melted away."

While the inventor set up his slideshow and James examined the product, Liam flipped through the conference brochure searching for Daisy's company. Although Daisy had made it clear she didn't want to see him again, he was desperately curious about her life. What did she do at Organicare? No doubt something high level. She'd been a straight A student, and one of the smartest people he'd ever known—capable of work way beyond her grade level. Hell, the only reason he'd graduated from high school was because of her.

Although he had been capable of doing the work, he just hadn't been interested. He'd had too much on his plate, dealing with his dysfunctional family, to waste time adding up numbers or drawing diagrams of food chains. But any time he had "accidentally" left an assignment on the Patels' kitchen table, he'd found it completed and tucked into his backpack, all ready to be handed in. Daisy had never mentioned it directly, and he'd never thanked her, but it was clear she had understood that admitting he needed help was a weakness he couldn't afford to show. The feelings of unworthiness that he had tried so hard to keep buried could never have been spoken out loud.

Turning his attention back to the pitch, he asked James, "What do you think?"

"Um . . ." James cleared his throat. "It's . . . uh . . . Interesting . . . uh . . . Slimy."

"'Interesting' isn't good enough. If you think it's worth going through due diligence, you have to try it out. Would you use a kombucha slime ring in the heat of passion?"

James grimaced. "No, sir."

"That's a problem," Liam said. "The dude wants five million for a five percent stake in his company. That means you have to think of five million reasons why it's a good idea before we can put the proposal to the partners, and one of those reasons has to be that you believe in it and you've seen it work."

"It's pretty much all I can see." James tucked the ring back into its plastic packet.

"Do you believe in King Kom?" Liam persisted. "Would you be happy to go to trade shows and Costcos extolling the virtues of the product to convince distributors to put it on their shelves? Are you ready to save the environment one King Kom slime ring at a time?"

James paled. "Not when you put it that way."

After the slideshow presentation and a show-and-tell of the various products, Liam thanked the inventor and offered the usual platitude. "It's an interesting concept. We'll be in touch."

"We've got the guy with the instant sobriety pill next," James said after he'd gone. "I'm looking forward to this one!"

Liam checked his phone while the next inventor set up at the front of the room. He could still smell Daisy's perfume on his shirt, a soft, sensual floral scent that brought back memories of the evenings he'd spent with the Patels when things were too difficult at home. What were the chances of running into her again after all these years? Granted he had only been back in San Francisco a few weeks, but with almost eight million residents in the Bay Area, the chances of seeing her again had been slim.

And yet, fate had brought them together again. She was everything he remembered and much, much more, from the softly rounded curves to the beautiful oval face, and from her keen intelligence to her sharp wit. He'd spent years resisting the siren call of his best friend's little sister, but now that he'd found her again . . .

Don't go there. With a shake of his head, he pushed those thoughts away. His father had made sure Liam knew he wasn't good enough for anything or anyone, much less a girl like Daisy. Even though he'd made something of his life, inside he was still his father's son—unworthy and unwanted, a ticking time bomb waiting to explode. Daisy deserved so much more.

And then there was the fact that she hated him.

"He's ready," James murmured, pulling him out of his reverie.

"This pill is the miracle cure everyone has been looking for." The inventor handed Liam a small plastic packet. "You drink all night, take one of these, and boom, fifteen minutes later you're legal to drive."

"This could be our unicorn," James whispered as the inventor scribbled chemical formulas on the whiteboard at the front of the room.

Every junior associate wanted to find the elusive unicorn—the product or company that was an instant success. Even Liam, Evolution's most successful senior associate of all time, had only ever found one.

"Possibly, but I recognize his name. He has a reputation in the industry for falsifying his results." Not only that, the moment the inventor had opened his mouth, Liam's instincts had screamed a warning. In the end, investment decisions came down to people, and no idea was worth the headache of trying to work with a difficult CEO. Ideas were easy. Running a business was hard, and running a business with a venture capital firm breathing down your neck took a strength and commitment not many people had.

James sighed. "I knew it was too good to be true."

Even if his gut hadn't told him something was off, Liam would have turned the inventor down. Big and broad, with a thick beard and thinning hair on top, the dude looked too much like his dad, right down to the vodka bottle on the table beside him.

Liam would never have considered moving back to San Francisco when his dad was alive. The city wasn't big enough for both of them. The birth of his nephew, Jaxon, and his grandfather's poor health had finally brought him back, but only for brief visits when he had business in the city. It was only last year, after his father had died in a drunk driving accident, that Liam had offered to move to San Francisco to set up a West Coast office that would give Evolution access to the Silicon Valley market. Six months later, the partnership had agreed, affording Liam the opportunity to reconnect with his family in a meaningful way.

"Thank you," Liam said at the end of the pitch. "We'll be in touch."

The inventor's face morphed from hopeful to furious in a heartbeat. "You're passing up the greatest opportunity of your life," he spat as he stormed out the door.

"I passed up the greatest opportunity of my life a long time ago." Memories of Daisy's prom night twisted his gut. "Which is how I can wish you the best of luck and feel no regret."

James checked the schedule after the door swung closed. "We're done for the day. Do you want to go for a drink? Maybe test out the product?"

Liam shook his head. "You can take it. Let me know how it works out. My family is getting together tonight for the reading of my grandfather's will, and one last party before some of our overseas guests head back to Ireland. A traditional Irish sendoff involves copious amounts of booze. One pill won't be enough."

After parting ways with James, Liam wandered past the conference rooms checking the schedules posted on the doors until he found Organicare listed on a pitch session. Pushing the door open he slipped inside and leaned against the back wall. Daisy was seated at a table beside an older, slightly rumpled man who was passionately explaining the company's products. He introduced Daisy as one of the company's senior software engineers and she stood to give her demonstration, pouring blue liquid on the pads set out on the table in front of her. Not a task one usually gave a software engineer, but maybe her boss had her lined up for a project manager promotion.

With one hand in his pocket, toying with the penknife his grandfather had given him when he was a boy, he watched Daisy field questions about the company website and sourcing software without even a hint of the shyness or awkwardness she'd had as a girl. Calm, competent, and quietly confident, she was clearly the star of the show.

His phone vibrated in his hand and he glanced at the screen. Brendan was texting yet again to find out what time he would be at their grandfather's house. His older brother just couldn't help himself. Despite the fact that Liam had found success, Brendan still acted as if he expected Liam to let him down.

He texted Brendan to let him know he was on his way. With one last, lingering look at the only woman he had ever wanted, he slipped out the door and walked away.

· 4 ·

"UNCLE Liam!" Jaxon raced down the hallway of Liam's grand-father's house, his small voice barely audible above the cacophony of sound coming from the living room. No matter what the occasion, when his Irish relatives got together, there was always music, laughter, whiskey, and usually a fight.

"How's my favorite nephew?" He lifted Brendan's son into his arms, grateful for the distraction. Still shaken by his unexpected meeting with Daisy, he had spent the drive trying to think of a way to see her again so he could try to make things right between them. Ten years was too long to leave unfinished business, especially when that business involved a woman he'd desperately wanted and couldn't have.

"I'm Uncle Liam's favorite nephew!" Jaxon beamed. At five years old, fair-haired Jaxon was the spitting image of his dad, right down to the blue eyes.

"You're his only nephew." Liam's sister-in-law, Lauren, leaned up to kiss Liam's cheek. "Thanks for coming."

Tall and slim, her hair a glossy chestnut, cut in soft, long layers that flattered her tanned skin, Lauren was a corporate lawyer and the least likely person Liam would ever have expected his brother to marry. After three failed relationships with women whose physical attributes outshone their common sense, Brendan had married smart, sensible Lauren in a small ceremony at her parents' house in Santa Cruz, and six years later they were still going strong.

"I only came because Brendan thought I wouldn't." He dug around in his pocket for the toy plane he had brought for Jaxon. His nephew shared his love of planes and motorcycles, and they'd had many days out at the airport, watching planes together.

"Whatever the reason, it will mean a lot to him," she said. "Things haven't been going well with the company. Maybe you could talk to him."

Liam frowned. "I've never been involved in Murphy Motors so I'm not sure why he would tell me anything. You know how Brendan feels about me."

"It's about the distillery—"

"Is that for me?" Jaxon snatched the plane from Liam's hand. "Mom, look!"

Lauren smiled and turned her attention to the new toy, while Liam tried to puzzle out what interest Brendan could have in the run-down distillery that his great-grandfather had built in Napa Valley after emigrating from Ireland. A replica of the original Murphy & Sons Distillery that had been in the Murphy family since 1750, it had been handed down from father to oldest son, until Liam's father had turned his back on tradition to found Murphy Motors, tearing the family apart. Brendan had joined the car business after graduating from college, eventually taking over the company when their father died.

"Daddy, look what Uncle Liam gave me!" Jaxon held up the toy plane when Brendan joined them in the narrow hallway. "It's a 747."

Brendan's face softened. A taller, heavier version of his son, Brendan resembled their father, whereas Liam took after their mother. But they both shared the Murphy blue eyes of their father, grandfather, and the Murphy men before them. "That was very nice of him. I hope you said thank you."

"Thank you!" Jaxon lifted his arms for a hug.

An unexpected warmth filled Liam as he bent down for Jaxon to wrap his arms around his neck. He'd never allowed himself to imagine having kids of his own, but sometimes with Jaxon . . .

"You're so good with him." Lauren smiled as Jaxon ran into the living room. "You talk to him like he's an adult and not a kid."

"He's got interesting things to say."

"You'd be a great dad. Don't you ever want—?"

"No." It wasn't just that he'd seen so many marriages fail and so many people suffer. He'd never met anyone who'd made him want to try. There was only one woman he'd ever imagined a future with, and now that she'd rejected him, it was clear he'd made the right decision the night he'd walked away.

"I see you came dressed for the occasion." Brendan gestured vaguely at Liam's leather jacket. "Couldn't you have left the motorcycle at home just this once? The lawyer will be here in twenty minutes, and we should look like we at least made an effort—"

Christ. Five minutes with Brendan and his hands were already clenched into fists. The dude was so uptight, Liam was amazed he'd ever been able to have a son.

"I don't do suits." Venture capitalists dressed only a step above the inventors who were the bread and butter of their business. Liam followed the crowd with button-down shirts, khakis, and dress pants, but he drew the line at North Face jackets and fleece vests. If he had to cover up for warmth, it was his leather motorcycle jacket or freeze. As for shoes, he wouldn't be caught dead in white lace-up sneakers. His worn black leather boots took him from motorcycle to work and back again.

"My mistake. I thought you were a professional." As usual, Brendan was dressed in a dark suit, white shirt, and bland-as-hell tie.

"Knock it off, you two." Lauren squeezed between them. "You have a house full of relatives to entertain. Don't let them see you like this or they'll lay on the Catholic guilt and you'll get another lecture about being good brothers."

"I don't have to deal with the guilt trips since I converted to atheism." Liam followed Lauren down the hallway. "It just washes right over me."

Brendan snorted, unwittingly taking the bait. "People don't 'convert' to atheism."

"I did." He shot a sideways glance over his shoulder at his very conservative, religious big brother. They had been at odds since the day Liam's parents brought him home from the hospital and four-year-old Brendan tried to drown him in the bath. Brendan was a typical firstborn. He was a rule follower, cautious and conservative, and very ambitious. He had never been able to understand Liam's wild, reckless, and rebellious nature.

"I unbaptized myself," Liam continued, unable to resist the temptation to wind up his brother. "Now I'm a free agent. No hellfire. No threat of eternal damnation. No church on Sunday. No Hail Marys or Our Fathers. And no guilt. It's very liberating."

"If you were any more liberated, you'd be—"

"Tell him about the company, Bren." Lauren interrupted with a gentle hand on his arm. "I'm sure Liam will want to help."

"Are you kidding? The only person Liam helps is himself."

Liam shot Lauren a sideways look. What did she see in his brother? Brendan was rigid, controlling, self-absorbed, and often abrasive. He had never been there for Liam when they were kids, and Liam couldn't imagine he was there for Lauren now. Not that he was complaining. If it weren't for Lauren, he would never have had a relationship with Jaxon.

"Lauren mentioned the distillery . . ." Liam offered, curious about what was going on.

Brendan sighed. "I hate to say it, but Grandpa's death came at the perfect time. I desperately need the cash to keep the family business going."

"The *distillery* is the family business," Liam spat out. "And that's a damn cold thing to say. I know you and Grandpa weren't close but . . ."

"He didn't mean it that way," Lauren said quickly. "He's just stressed. Aren't you, Bren?"

"Liam's right," Brendan said. "Grandpa never liked me. He said I was too much like Da and he never forgave Da for turning his back on the distillery to start Murphy Motors. But the joke's on him. Tradition says it goes from oldest son to oldest son. Unless he decided to change the legacy, the distillery will be mine, and I'm going to knock it down and sell the land to save Murphy Motors. How's that for irony?"

Bile rose in Liam's throat. He had spent his early childhood working with his grandfather in the distillery, learning everything there was to know about the business. Everything changed, however, when he was thirteen and his father discovered he was "fraternizing with the enemy." He'd beaten Liam and forbade him from visiting the distillery or his grandfather ever again. Only thirteen and distraught at the loss of one of the most important relationships in his life, Liam had found solace with his best friend, Sanjay, and his welcoming family.

"I can't imagine that's what Grandpa would have wanted." He pulled out his penknife and rubbed his thumb along the smooth wood surface. It was his touchstone, his connection to the grand-father he had only just found and lost again.

Brendan leaned against the wall, arms folded. "The equipment is fifty years out of date, everything is falling apart, and output has been dropping every year. It's a mercy, really. I'm just putting ev-eryone out of their misery."

"He put his life into that distillery," Liam protested. "As did his dad and his dad before him. And what about the staff? And Joe?" He lowered his voice when he caught a glimpse of the distillery manager in the living room. "He's been managing things for thirty years. There must be another way." Joe was seventy-five years old, half Scottish and half Mexican, his grandfather's good friend, and the most experienced distiller Liam knew. As far as Liam was con-cerned, Joe was family, and if Brendan was just going to cut him loose . . .

Brendan shrugged. "Joe's a good guy, but he's getting on in years and he can't run it alone. And as for staff, my priority is my own employees. Murphy Motors has hit a few road bumps, and without a cash injection, we might go under."

Liam was about to invite Brendan to take the heated discussion outside, but before he could open his mouth, their great-aunt Dinah waved them into the stuffy living room, still decorated with the same dark wood furniture, threadbare woven rugs, heavy green velvet curtains, and framed paintings of Irish landscapes that his grandmother had bought fifty years ago.

"Here they are!" Short and round, with a thick Irish accent and pearl-gray hair, his great-aunt greeted them with a smile. She had come for the funeral from Ireland with her brother, Seamus, and planned to stay for a few months in the now vacant house.

"I almost thought you were your da for a moment there when I saw you." She gave Brendan the once-over, not easy to do at only five-two and Brendan just shy of six feet. "You're just missing the big belly." Turning, she called over her shoulder. "Seamus! Doesn't he look more and more like his da every day? He's even lost more of his hair since we got here."

"Sure enough he does," Great-Uncle Seamus called out from the makeshift bar he'd set up in the corner. "And the wee boy's the spitting image of Brady O'Leery."

Liam had no idea who Brady O'Leery was, but the last week had been one conversation after another about relatives he didn't even know he had. He'd quickly learned not to ask unless he had a few hours to spend listening to the complicated history of the Murphy family.

"Och. Don't compare the boy to Brady," Dinah said. "He was always in his cups."

"He's not the only one," Seamus retorted.

"Away with you." Dinah made a shooing motion with her hand. "All I ever have is a wee drop of Baileys in my fecking tea."

"That old lady swore." Jaxon's eyes were wide with admiration. "She's fecking awesome."

"Jaxon!" Lauren raised her voice in warning. "Watch your language."

"But Dad swears all the time. He said he was only here for the fecking money and he was fecking not leaving without it."

"Out of the mouths of babes." Dinah shook her head.

"At least I have a son," Brendan huffed. "And a wife. Liam's got no one."

"He's only thirty." Seamus settled on the worn, flowered couch. "Let him sow his wild oats. A Murphy never turns down the chance to take a woman to bed."

"*That's* why there's so many wee babes at home with your big nose," Dinah said. "I was thinking it was something in the water."

Liam greeted his father's sister, Aunt Fiona, and her husband, Uncle Fitz, as well as the other relatives who had come to hear his grandfather's bequests. He had never been close with his father's side of the family. Although many of his relatives lived in the area, not one of them had tried to save his mother from his father's abuse and he hadn't been able to forgive them.

When the doorbell rang, he took the opportunity to escape the bickering and welcome Ed McBain, a junior lawyer from the law firm that was handling his grandfather's estate. After everyone had found a seat, Ed shuffled through his briefcase to find the will.

"I'm sorry Mr. Murphy's regular attorney, Mr. Abel, couldn't be here." Ed tugged at the collar of his shirt. "I've never actually done a will reading before." He gave a nervous laugh. "This is my first estate file."

"You just have to read it out loud," Lauren offered, not unkindly. "It's not something that's usually done anymore, but there's not much more to it than that. Mr. Murphy's daughter, Roisin, isn't here, and neither is his grandson, Ethan, but you can send them a letter."

Ed cleared his throat and read out the list of bequests. Liam, Brendan, and their cousin, Ethan, received generous financial gifts, as did most of the other relatives and the distillery manager, Joe. The rest of the estate was divided between Seamus and Fiona. Roisin inherited the house.

"What about the distillery?" Brendan asked impatiently. "The land is worth a small fortune."

"I was just coming to that," Ed said. "He set up a conditional trust for the distillery. It says: 'I leave the Murphy & Sons Distillery to my grandson, Liam Patrick Murphy, provided that he is married by his next birthday, following the date of my passing, and stays married for at least one full year in the hope that he will finally find the love of a family, and have a child to pass on the legacy. If Liam is not married by his next birthday, or if his marriage does not last one year, then I leave the distillery to my grandson, Brendan Colin Murphy.'"

Silence.

"He named our law firm as the trustee," Ed explained. "It will be our responsibility to manage the distillery until the gift vests, and to determine whether or not the marriage meets the terms of the trust so we can honor Mr. Murphy's intent."

A smile spread across Brendan's face. "So I get it after all."

"Well . . . uh . . . only if Liam doesn't get married before his birthday," Ed offered. "Or doesn't stay married for a year after that."

"His birthday is in two months." Brendan barked a laugh. "He doesn't even have a girlfriend."

"Don't write him off yet," Seamus interjected. "He's a good-looking young man. Who knows what can happen."

"Marriage fraud can happen," Lauren pointed out. "A fake marriage to defeat the will-maker's intent can be challenged by the trustee or even in court."

Liam took one deep breath and then another. How could his grandfather do this to him? Although he'd never expected to inherit the distillery, he was certain his grandfather knew how much it meant to him.

"I just wish Da were alive to see how I saved Murphy Motors," Brendan said quietly. "It would make him smile."

Liam couldn't understand why Brendan was still seeking the approval of a man who had physically abused their mother and had been nothing but cruel and unkind to his youngest son. But then,

Brendan had stayed with their dad even after Liam had finally gotten their mother out of a marriage that had almost destroyed her.

"What's it worth?" Brendan asked Ed. "Ballpark?"

Ed closed his file. "We'll be sending someone out to value the land and buildings for the estate in the coming weeks."

"Send me the details and I'll be there." Brendan shot Liam a smug look. "I'll bring my construction guys to get an estimate for the demolition."

Every muscle in Liam's body tightened. Brendan was going to destroy the Murphy legacy and put twenty good people out of work. And there wasn't a damn thing he could do about it. He couldn't even remember the name of the last woman he'd slept with, much less find someone who would agree to marry him and stay married for a year.

"I need another drink." Liam crossed the room to the bar where Joe was refilling his own glass. Behind him, his relatives chattered, asking Ed details about the bequests.

"I'm glad your grandfather isn't here," Joe said quietly. "He would have been sick at heart to know this was the end of a three-hundred-year legacy."

Still reeling, Liam shrugged. "I'm not sure about that. He knew how I feel about relationships, and he must have suspected what Brendan would do with the distillery."

"You sure you can't find someone to marry?" Joe poured Liam a glass of whiskey. "How about an ex? You've got more than a few of those kicking around. You could mend fences and give it a go . . ."

"They are exes for a reason. I couldn't live with any of them for a few weeks, much less a year."

"What about paying someone? Maybe an actress. I'm sure there are lots of girls who need money. Or what about one of those mail-order brides?"

"I couldn't lie to someone like that." Liam shook his head stiffly. "And I wouldn't want to lead someone on. It would have to be someone who has no interest in a relationship with me."

"Someone who hates you, then?" Joe seemed almost desperate. "You piss off any girls in your day?"

Something niggled at the back of Liam's mind. The scent of wildflowers. Warm curves. Soft lips. A face almost as familiar as his own . . .

His fake fiancée. And the making of a plan. "Joe, you're a genius." He tossed back his drink. "You've just given me an idea."

"Well, thank God for that." Joe finished off his glass. "Even with your grandfather's generous gift, I need the work. Keeps the mind and body active. And besides, who's going to hire a man my age?"

"Sorry to tell you this, Bren," Liam called out, "but I'm engaged." It wasn't entirely a lie. He had been engaged for the duration of his encounter with Daisy.

Brendan snorted. "What a load of bullshit."

"*Fecking* bullshit, right Dad?" Jaxon looked up at his father, his face aglow with innocent adoration.

"You're absolutely right," Brendan said to his son. "It is fecking bullshit."

Lauren stared at him, aghast. "Brendan!"

"I'm not going to pretend it's anything other than a bogus story," Brendan spat out. "Who here believes that Liam is actually engaged? The guy had to get another phone because he had so many women in his address book he maxed out his storage. And where is she? Why isn't she here? Why did he never mention her before?"

Liam shrugged. "I like to keep my private life private."

"Why doesn't Liam bring her for dinner?" Lauren suggested. "We can meet her."

"Good idea." Brendan smirked. "We can ask her the going rate for a fake fiancée."

"You really got a fiancée?" Joe asked quietly as he refilled Liam's glass.

"Yes." Liam sighed. "But the problem is . . . she really does hate me."

· 5 ·

DAISY'S cell phone woke her out of a dead sleep. Max jumped up from the pillow beside her, barking like there was a five-alarm fire. No one ever called this early unless it was an emergency, and she wasn't awake enough to deal with whoever was waiting on the other end of the phone.

Pushing aside the pink duvet that she'd had since she was fourteen years old, she swung her legs over the side of her white four-poster bed and checked her clock. Five minutes until her alarm. Only one caller knew her schedule that well.

"*Beta*. It's Dad." Daisy's father's voice crackled over the phone.

"You don't have to tell me who you are." A smile tugged her lips. Even though he was an economics professor at Berkeley and handled complicated software every day, her father was old school when it came to phones. "I recognize your voice."

"It's been seven days. I thought you might have forgotten your old dad."

Daisy shoved her feet into a pair of fluffy pink slippers, preparing herself for the coming storm. He wouldn't have called from Belize if something wasn't up, and she knew exactly what it was. The early call. The hitch in his voice. The incident on Friday at the conference center. Put together, it smelled suspiciously of auntie involvement. "I thought you were on an 'Extreme Jungle' trek with no phone reception for five days."

"We hiked back as soon as Salena called with the news." His voice tightened. "She says you didn't even meet the boy we chose for you. That you are"—his voice cracked, whether from emotion or a bad line, she couldn't tell—"engaged."

Daisy groaned. News traveled faster on the auntie underground than by any other mode of communication. "How could she possibly have contacted you in the middle of the jungle? Did she send a pigeon?" She opened her closet door and pulled out the outfit she had planned for the day: flowery skirt, vintage T-shirt, leather jacket, and her favorite biker boots. One of the benefits of working as a software developer was that no one ever expected her to wear boring clothes.

As if sensing the hostile turn of the conversation, Max barked and jumped on his hind legs. A gift from her cousin Layla at a very down time in her life, her Westie wasn't just a pet; he was an emotional support dog who knew just when she needed him.

After giving Max some assurance that she was okay, she pulled off her Captain America nightshirt and proceeded to dress for work while her father talked over speakerphone. She'd been a Marvel superhero fan ever since her tenth birthday, when her father had given her his old-school comic book collection, the pages tattered and worn from use. Unlike Sanjay, who admired the superheroes for their otherworldly powers, Daisy loved how they were committed to saving the world, even though they were all broken inside.

"Salena has a cousin in the travel business," her father continued. "He knew someone at a travel company in Belmopan, who knew someone at the embassy, who knew someone at the company that was running the tour. He contacted our guide on his emergency radio."

"Seriously, Dad?" She rubbed Max's fluffy head as she pulled on her boots. "He got an emergency call that your daughter in San Francisco did not want to meet some random guy you chose for her to marry because she was with someone else? I can't imagine what he thought about that. And what about Priya? Is she happy to have her vacation interrupted by your family crisis that isn't a crisis at all?"

"Priya understands," he said firmly. "Also one person in the tour group broke his arm abseiling, and another twisted his ankle portaging the kayaks, and the helicopter had just come back for the woman who almost drowned when we were cave tubing, so we were already three people down. Plus, Priya didn't like staying overnight in the caves. The bats kept her awake, and after a snake got into her sleeping bag she said she would prefer a hotel."

"Very sensible." Daisy moved the phone to her shabby chic dresser. Her father had found it at a thrift store and they'd fixed it up together and painted it robin's-egg blue, a contrast to the sea of pink in her room.

"Not everyone shares your enthusiasm for extreme activities," she added. Her father had a thirst for adventure that meant family holidays had never been mundane.

"Who is this boy? Salena couldn't remember his name. She said she thought it was Limb. What kind of name is that? Limb. What parents name their boy after body parts?"

"He's . . . umm . . ." Definitely not someone her father would approve of, since he'd cursed Liam in three different languages after he'd stood her up, and cursed him again after he disappeared. "It's not what you think, Dad." She pulled her long, thick hair into a ponytail, and fixed it with three hair ties to keep it in place.

"Not what I think?" His voice rose in agitation. "You're engaged to a man I haven't even met and has a strange name. A man you never mentioned or brought to meet me and now you're planning to marry him? That's what I think, and the thinking is making my heart ache and my brain sore with worry. And what about Roshan? He is your perfect match . . ."

Only half listening to the list of Roshan's virtues as she tried to figure a way out of the mess, Daisy picked up her phone and made her way downstairs in their cozy Bernal Heights home. She'd been reluctant to leave her father alone after her older brother, Sanjay, left to go to college, so she'd stayed to keep him company, completing her computer science degree at Stanford and taking jobs in Silicon Valley. They'd rattled around in the house together until her father had started dating Priya, neither of them able to admit that the house was too big for two, because that would finally mean accepting that her mother was never coming home.

"Everyone has met Roshan and liked him, and even your horoscopes were good," her father continued. "Salena was so excited. She took him to see you as a surprise . . ." His voice tightened. "And then . . ."

"And then she discovered that I managed to find someone on my own." Daisy took a blueberry muffin out of the freezer and popped it in the microwave. Priya owned a small bakery in the Marina District and had filled the freezer full of treats for Daisy before the big trip. She hadn't had to make breakfast once since they'd been gone.

"I don't believe," her father said abruptly. His English always became worse when he was emotional. "How could you meet someone and make such an important decision so quickly without consulting your family? No. I don't accept."

Daisy could almost imagine him waving his hands in the air, dismissing what he didn't want to hear. He'd said almost the same thing when Liam had disappeared, acted almost the same way.

"I thought you were done with men after that Orson boy," her father continued. "That's why I found someone for you."

She was done with men. Life was easier without the messy entanglement of emotions. Orson had been a mistake, a rare foray into the relationship wilderness brought on by having to witness Layla falling in love. If she was honest with herself, Daisy had known from the moment Orson first asked her out that he would leave her. Everybody did.

"I was done, but the aunties wouldn't leave me alone. Every time I stepped out the door I was afraid one of them was going to pop out of a bush, so I handled it myself." She bit into the muffin, silently cursing Priya for her incredible skill as the fresh pop of blueberries woke all her taste buds in a sugar-sweet burst. One wasn't going to be enough.

"Your aunties are worried for you," he said. "Twenty-seven and unmarried. It's like a red flag for them. They don't want you to fall for the wrong man or wind up with no man at all. Now I fear they didn't act fast enough."

Holding out her fingers, Daisy let Max take a little lick. Only rarely did he get human food, but when he did, his preference was for Jana Auntie's pakoras over anything sweet.

"He's not the wrong guy. He's just . . ."

Absolutely the wrong guy. Without a doubt Liam Murphy was the last man on earth she should marry. Her aunties were right about that.

"Did you know that eighty-five percent of young Indians prefer to marry the boy or girl chosen by their families?" Her father rattled off a slew of marriage statistics like he'd purposely memorized them for this very kind of conversation, which he probably had. "The divorce rate of arranged marriages is only one out of one hundred."

"This is what I get for having an economist as a father," she muttered, half to herself. "Where did you dig up those conveniently biased statistics?"

"It doesn't matter," he said. "What matters is that in the West, when couples choose their own partners, the divorce rate is fifty percent. Don't you agree that a one percent chance of divorce is better than fifty?"

"If I don't get married, my chance of divorce is zero." She grinned at Max, and he barked in approval.

Usually when she won a point in an argument, her dad would laugh, but this time he was quiet for so long, her skin prickled. "I don't understand, beta. Do you love this Limb boy? Are you getting married to him or not?"

"It's complicated. Can't we just say I'm engaged so no one needs to worry about finding me a man? And if we're still together when you get back, you can meet him." Hopefully, by the time he returned she would have a new decoy to keep the aunties at bay.

"Fine." Her father sniffed. "Make your own decisions. In twenty years I'll be gone, and you won't have to worry about your old dad trying to make you happy by finding you the perfect man."

"Dad . . ." She didn't have a chance when he pulled out the Indian parent guilt.

"No. Be engaged to a stranger." He gave a dramatic sigh. "Who am I to know best? Only your old dad with a lifetime of experience who cares only for what's best for you and just wanted you to meet the boy I knew would make you most happy."

"Dad . . ." Daisy groaned. "Don't do this."

"I have to go," he said sadly. "Maybe Priya and I can make it back to the jungle before they do the bungee jumping into the gorge. She didn't want to try it because the elastic looked frayed, but what does it matter if my life is cut short a few extra years? My job as a father is done. You don't need the ol' man's advice."

"Okay, Dad." She tipped her head back in frustration. "You win. I'll meet him."

"Salena Auntie will call you to set something up." His voice lightened in an instant. "You will love him. I hear the roar of wedding bells already."

"I think that's a helicopter."

"So it is. Time to lift off. A new adventure awaits!"

· 6 ·

TRIPLE shot latte on her right, another one of Priya's muffin creations on her left, Daisy settled in at her workstation and turned on her computer. Tucked away at the back of the engineering floor, she could enter and exit each day with minimal human interaction. Since she was an introvert at heart, socializing with her colleagues was something she tried to avoid. It was better not to make connections when you knew you weren't there for the long haul, and Daisy never usually stayed with any start-up longer than it took her shares to vest.

Unlike the rowdy second floor where the sales, marketing, finance, and design teams were based, the third floor was generally calm and quiet. Everyone understood the need to protect the programmers' flow state. Programming required focused mental concentration and that meant no interruptions, no conversations, no ringing phones, no deliveries, no noise of any kind. The floor was serene and silent, and her little shadowed corner was the most peaceful of all.

As soon as her screens flickered to life, she put on her headphones, flicked to her playlist of dance music, and read over the cliff-hanger—a set of notes written in the form of code comments—she had written the night before to remind herself where she was in her thinking process when she had stopped coding for the day.

The code bug that had been frustrating her since the night before had been solved by her sleeping self—a miracle given that every crack and creak of the too-empty house had made her jolt awake. Sure enough, she was right. The test dates were causing the problem. She slid easily into her flow state, ignited by the cliffhanger and fueled by caffeine and music. After three intense hours of coding, she joined the other project engineers for the morning stand-up to discuss the project with the team.

Josh Saldana, another senior software engineer, joined her as she refilled her Avengers mug at the coffee bar. Despite her attempts to keep to herself, Josh had latched on to her from the very first day—pulling her away from her desk at lunchtime, chatting with her over the office messaging service, and trying to drag her out for Friday night drinks. A fellow Marvel superheroes fan, he was friendly and upbeat, and now he was a permanent fixture in her otherwise impermanent life.

"No muffins today." He looked sadly at the empty basket. "I'm going to starve. I know things are tight, but how I am supposed to work without sustenance?"

"There's fruit." Daisy pointed to the display.

"Fruit isn't food." Blessed with strong, even features, full lips, and eyes almost as dark as his thick, wavy hair, even a frown on Josh looked sexy. He was six feet of tall and lanky and a favorite with the staff on the second floor, but not so much with the other programmers. He had a tendency to roll his own code and would magically find his way off a project if he wasn't permitted to build in his preferred language.

Daisy laughed and handed him a plastic container. "I might have brought a few of Priya's muffins in case of a shortfall."

"This is why I love you." He took the container and peeked

inside. "And I especially love you today because the blueberry ones are the best."

"The stand-up was supposed to start three minutes ago." Daisy glanced over at the door. Their project manager, Andrew Daly, was even more particular about time and schedules than her. Not once since she'd started working at Organicare had a stand-up ever started late.

"I heard a rumor something big was going on." Josh took a healthy bite of muffin. "My guess is that Tyler either got funding, and he sent Andrew out to buy gourmet muffins, or he didn't get funding and I should steal all the apples and sugar packets so I have something to live on when I get laid off."

"I thought you said fruit wasn't food."

"It isn't." His nose wrinkled in disgust. "I'm going to sell the apples. I'll tell people they're organic, free range, grain fed, and watered with melted snow from Everest. I'll make enough money to buy at least three months' worth of muffins."

"Nice." She lifted an eyebrow. "You're going to lie."

"And steal." He slipped a sugar packet into his pocket.

Daisy folded her arms. "If I'd known you were such a moral degenerate, I would have thought twice about agreeing to let you be my emotional support person."

Josh laughed through another bite of muffin. "It's too late now. You need me and all my moral corruption."

"I need the stand-up to start." She glanced down at her limited-edition Captain Marvel watch, a gift from her father when she got her first job. "I was deep into the flow and I don't want to lose it."

"You're in luck." He gestured to the door. "Our supreme leader has arrived."

Dressed in pair of red flip-flops, baggy blue shorts, and a purple shirt bearing the words *Byte Me*, Andrew held up his coffee cup to quiet the noise as he walked to the front of the room. Cranky and prone to using profanity, the veteran software engineer had been with Organicare since its inception, and chewed through product managers as quickly as Max chewed through squeaky toys. He was perpetually in need of a haircut, and his thick brown beard and moustache were streaked with gray.

Silence descended instantly on the room. Andrew didn't tolerate interruptions and no one was willing to get on his bad side, especially when the glare in his eyes was a clear warning that he was in a bad mood. Even Tyler was afraid of Andrew.

"I have bad news . . ."

Josh grabbed a handful of sugar packets and stuffed them in his pocket.

"You all know Organicare has been trying to secure additional funding, but it's a long process and the time has come to cut some costs."

Daisy's heart sank. She'd never expected to stay at Organicare long term, but it was the only start-up she'd ever worked at where she'd been excited about the company's products, admired the company's mission, and—she glanced over at Josh—started to make friends.

"To try and save jobs, Tyler has decided to sublet the second floor," Andrew said. "That means Finance, Marketing, and whoever the hell else works downstairs will be moving up here with us. We tried something like this when we first started the company and it was a total failure. But no one had any other bright ideas, so we're stuck with it."

"We're going to have to barricade ourselves in the corner and throw sugar packets at anyone who comes near us or we'll never get into the flow state with all the noise." Josh tore open a sugar package and poured it into his mouth. "At the very worst, we'll leave here on a sucrose high."

After answering a few questions, Andrew moved straight into a war story about how the project before this one had been messed up and how management couldn't handle the stress. Daisy only half listened, her mind churning over the news. How many people were going to move upstairs? Where were they going to sit? Would she have to leave her cubicle and where would she go? What if they put her in the middle of the office?

By the time the stand-up was over, her anxiety had ramped up so high she could barely breathe. She returned to her desk, but couldn't get into her state of intense flow. The problems seemed harder, her hands were shaking, and even that second cup of coffee wasn't enough to fuel her brain now that she was stressed about the imminent invasion. This was the exact situation she tried to avoid. Unplanned and uncontrollable. It was why she had Max.

She pulled out her phone and flicked to a picture of Max on her bed, staring up at her with his adorable fluffy face. Mehar Auntie had offered to look after him during the day while Daisy was at work. A middle school teacher who taught Bollywood dance classes on the weekend, she was happy for the company during her summer vacation.

Daisy sent a quick text to her aunt to tell her she was going to pick up Max early to take him for a walk on Ocean Beach. He loved to play in the off-leash areas, and the soothing sound of the ocean would help take her stress away. Andrew didn't care what hours they worked so long as the work got done.

After letting Josh know she was leaving, she took the elevator down to the bright, modern lobby. Located in the South of Market district, her office was in start-up central with some of the biggest tech companies in the buildings around them.

Hand wrapped tight around the giant multicolored Marvel tote bag that served as both as a handbag and a dog carrier, she stepped out of the elevator looking forward to a relaxing afternoon. Her moment of anticipatory pleasure was cut short when she saw Liam standing in the lobby, looking like he'd just stepped out of *Sons of Anarchy* in his worn leather jacket, thick leather boots, and black *Destructor* T-shirt, a motorcycle helmet in one hand.

Their eyes met and something shifted inside her, loosening the knot of tension in her chest. Liam had always had that effect on her. No matter how bad her day, the moment Liam had walked in the door with Sanjay, she had felt like she could breathe again.

"I was just coming up to see you." He walked over to her, his smile fading as he studied her face. "What's wrong?"

Damn. He knew her so well. For the briefest second, she was tempted to share. Liam had always been a good listener, especially when she was upset.

Steeling herself against the urge, she scowled. "Ten years didn't last very long."

"I wanted to talk to you, and I had a feeling you wouldn't take my calls."

"You were right." She walked past him, focused on the door where a security guard was posting a sign advertising the vacancy on the second floor. She could do this. Walk away, keep a physical distance between them, because in her current emotional state she didn't trust herself to get too close.

Liam followed her into the sunshine. "I just need five minutes."

"And I needed a prom date."

He jogged ahead of her, blocking her way. "I'm sorry, Daisy. Things happened that I couldn't control and I was in a bad place that night. What can I do to make it up to you?"

"Nothing."

Liam opened his hands. "If you'd give me a chance . . ."

"That's not going to happen." She dropped her gaze, trying to keep her composure under that intense blue stare.

His gaze flicked to the door behind her. "I've been looking for office space," Liam mused. "We're in a temporary location right now. Maybe I could . . ."

"Absolutely not."

"The location is perfect, and it would give us a chance to see more of each other. I could explain, and you could forgive me. And you could invite me to have dinner with you and your dad . . ." He trailed off when she shook her head. "Is he away on a new adventure?" A wry smile slid across his face. "I'll bet he is."

Daisy pressed her lips together and studied her boots. Unlike Liam's boots, which were worn and faded, hers were polished to a shine with chrome button top rivet details. They made her feel badass while she pounded away on her keyboard. And they were waterproof. Not that she was planning on riding a motorcycle in the rain, but it didn't hurt to be prepared.

"I'll take that as a yes." She heard, rather than saw the amusement in his voice. "What is it? Volcano boarding in Nicaragua? Downhill mountain biking on Bolivia's Death Road? Freshwater cave diving in the Yucatan Peninsula?"

"Jungle expedition in Belize," she muttered under her breath.

Liam chuckled. "I'm only surprised you aren't with him. You two did all sorts of crazy things together."

That had been before Liam had disappeared. Before her mother had returned, knocking out the foundations of her carefully ordered life and destroying what little self-esteem she had left.

"I don't go with him anymore." She lifted her gaze and forced her face into a tight smile. "He has a new girlfriend, Priya. She's the one who gets dragged out on all his adventures now."

"How about Sanjay? Is he around?"

Her heart swelled with pride for her older brother, and she couldn't help but share. "He's a doctor now, working with Doctors Without Borders. He goes from one war-torn country to the next. He hasn't been home for three years, but he stays in touch over Skype when he's in a city with Internet access."

Liam's face softened. "I always knew he could do great things."

"He'll be happy to know you're alive," she said dryly.

"What about you?" He tipped his head to the side and gave her the puppy dog eyes that once had her giggling and snorting milk through her nose at the dinner table.

Classic Liam. He could charm his way into anything, and had never been above capitalizing on his wicked allure.

She gave a half shrug. "I don't care one way or the other."

"And yet here you are talking to me." He opened his hands in a placatory gesture.

"I wouldn't be talking to you if you weren't in my way."

He stepped to the side and gave a gentlemanly bow. "Can I walk with you?"

"No." She walked away, conscious of his gaze on her ample behind. Fighting back a smile, she gave a little wiggle. Ten years later, she wasn't the girl she'd been at eighteen; she was so much more.

"Dinner?"

"No."

"*Jalebi* ice cream sandwich?" he called out, referring to one of her favorite childhood treats.

Her betraying lips quivered at the corners. "No."

"How about a snack? French toast crunch? Scooby Snacks? Trix with extra sugar? Pakoras and pretzels? Roast beef on rye with mustard and three thinly sliced pickles with a side of chocolate milk?"

Laughter bubbled up inside her. He had done this almost every day to guess the after-school snack even though she had always taped the weekly family meal plan to the refrigerator door.

"*Pav bhaji, chaat, panipuri* . . . ?" Liam had loved her father's Indian dishes.

"I'm not listening." But of course, she was.

"Two grilled cheese sandwiches with ketchup and zucchini fries? *Masala dosa* . . . ?" His voice grew faint as she neared the end of the block.

"Cinnamon sugar soft pretzels, tomato basil mozzarella toasts . . ." His voice faded away when she turned the corner. With a sigh, she leaned against the rough brick wall and let her laughter escape with a soft chuckle.

Peeking around the corner, she watched him take a picture of the vacancy sign. That didn't bode well if she wanted to keep her distance. Bad enough he knew where she worked, but to have him downstairs?

Still, her vantage point behind the wall allowed her a few moments of unadulterated gazing at her teenage crush. His hair was brown, streaked with gold in the sunlight, tousled and just long enough to betray the rebel inside him. He was at once wild and civilized, and she could see him both in a boardroom and on his motorcycle, burning up the road as he sped down the coast on his next great adventure.

He looked up, head turned in her direction. Daisy's pulse kicked up a notch and she shrank behind the wall. He hadn't seen her. Or had he? He didn't know she was there. Or did he?

"Goodbye, Daisy!" His raised voice was clearly audible even though she was half a block away.

Her face flushed and she took off down the street as fast as her boots could carry her. She needed to keep her distance from Liam Murphy. Falling for him had never been a choice. Losing him had almost destroyed her.

She couldn't go through that emotional roller coaster ever again.

·7·

LIAM pulled open the door to the Rose & Thorn, an Irish pub in the Mission. Managed by his cousin, Ethan, it was a great little neighborhood dive bar first, Irish pub second, and had been his favorite place to relax when he visited the city. Now that he was back permanently, it had become a second home.

He paused on the threshold to check out the small stage where he could find anything from a barbershop quartet to a Marilyn Manson cover band belting out the tunes. Tonight, a small jazz band was performing their set, creating the perfect mood with the dimmed lights and cozy atmosphere. Exposed brick walls, plank wood floors, Irish décor—everything from carved Celtic Trinity knots to historical maps—and a big stone fireplace gave the pub authentic charm.

Breathing in the scents of hops and barley, he felt the tension ebb from his body as he grabbed the last seat at the bar. Sounds from the crackling fire and clinking glasses thrummed like a pulse beneath the low hum of chatter. For a few blissful hours he could forget about Brendan and the will, the houseful of relatives he didn't really know, the end of the distillery, and the emptiness in his heart from the loss of his grandfather.

"Hey, stranger." Rainey Davis, the head bartender, looked up from the dishwasher where she was stacking glassware. She was wearing her usual *Kiss Me I'm Irish* tank top so people would overlook her Texas drawl, her red-gold hair a tumble of curls down her back. "Ethan got in a shipment of Middleton Very Rare this afternoon. You want a taste?"

"Fill up a glass and keep pouring until I fall down."

"Bad day at the office?" She pulled a bottle from the case on the floor.

"Bad week overall."

"Then I'd better drink with you." She poured two glasses and passed one over to Liam. "What should we toast?"

"To John Murphy, founder of Murphy & Sons Distillery, who died doing what he loved after he drowned in a vat of partially distilled spirit . . ."

"My kind of guy."

"And to my grandfather, Patrick Murphy, who is soon to be turning in his grave."

They clinked glasses and Liam took a sip of the smooth, rich liquid. Peppery spices slowly began to soften, followed by a sweetness that was a mix of licorice, barley sugar, and a hint of honey, edged with a touch of sherbet. The finish was slow to fade. As he savored the spices, he added a drop of water to the glass.

"My grandfather taught me that trick," he said when Rainey frowned. "He said it mutes the alcohol and allows the other flavors to come forward."

"Ethan told me your grandfather passed away." Rainey refilled his glass. "Were you guys close?"

"We'd just reconnected," Liam said. "He owned a whiskey distillery in Napa and I spent a lot of time there with him when I was a kid."

"You never mentioned it before." She took another sip of her drink. "What's the name? I'll make sure I have a few bottles for you next time you come in."

"Murphy & Sons." He drained his glass. "It's mine now. Or at least it would be if I had a wife."

"I guess he didn't know you very well." Rainey had seen Liam leave with a different woman almost every time he'd come to the pub. She didn't judge, but she didn't pull any punches, either.

"He did know me," Liam said. "After we reconnected it was like we'd never been apart. We had a lot in common—same sense of humor, same political views, and even the same taste in whiskey. We had some issues—mostly because of my dad—but we were able to put them aside. I thought I'd found someone in the family who actually understood me."

"Are you talking about Grandpa?" Ethan joined Liam at the bar. Two years older, tall and broad-shouldered like all the Murphy men, his dark hair was long, tethered in a loose ponytail, and his blue eyes were set in a rough, craggy face. He was the only son of Liam's uncle Peter, who had died when Ethan was young. "I got a letter that he'd left me some money. I'm going to use it to fix up the bar, maybe take another trip to Ireland."

Liam nodded. "He left me the distillery on the condition that I'm married by my next birthday, and stay married for a year. Brendan is furious. The distillery usually goes from eldest son to eldest son. I guess Grandpa decided to change the tradition because our father turned his back on the family business. Not only that, he expressed a wish that I continue the legacy by having kids."

"I guess he wanted to make sure there were some little Murphys running around to carry on the family name." Rainey snickered. "Maybe you should find yourself a wife real quick."

"I've been through all my contacts." Liam pulled out his phone and placed it on the counter. "Unfortunately, I've burned a lot of bridges." He sighed. "I can't do mail-order brides or green-card marriages in case something goes wrong, or they get attached, or they take half of the distillery when we get divorced after the year is up. The risk of involving someone I don't know is just too high."

"You need someone you trust," Ethan mused. "What about someone you work with? Or a childhood friend?"

Liam swirled his drink around his glass. "I bumped into a woman from way back the other day at a conference. Her name is Daisy. She's the sister of my best friend from high school. I thought maybe she could help me out, but we parted on bad terms ten years ago, and she made it clear that she still hates me." He drained his glass and pushed it across the counter for a refill.

"I thought most of the women you'd hooked up with in the city hated you," Rainey said.

"Not like this." Liam sighed. "I stood her up for her senior prom, then left town without telling her and never got in touch again."

Without warning, Rainey leaned over the counter and slapped him lightly across the face.

"What the hell?" His hand went to his cheek. He looked to Ethan for support, but his cousin was doubled over with laughter.

"How could you?" she demanded. "You stood her up for her high school prom? What kind of scumbag are you? It was her PROM for chrissakes!"

"I know it was her prom," he spluttered. "I was supposed to be her date."

"If you'd stood me up for my prom, my dad would have hunted you down and used you for target practice." She took an order from a new customer at the end of the bar, then returned to Liam. "And you thought you'd ask her to marry you? I'm surprised you got out of there with your balls attached."

Ethan frowned at Rainey. "I thought you didn't have a dad."

"Well, of course I have a father." She pulled two bottles of Budweiser from the cooler and slammed them on the counter. "That's basic biology. The question is: Which of the dozens of men my mother brought home is the one? I like to imagine he's the protective type—*Don't hurt my baby girl!* and all that—and one day he's going to walk through that door and ask what the hell I'm doing working here when he's got a big house out in the country with a stable full of horses and a loving family who have all been looking for me since the day I was born."

"That's a nice dream," Liam said as she flipped off the tops with her bottle opener.

"We all need a dream." She carefully poured one bottle into a glass. "What's yours?"

"I want to save the distillery." Liam pulled out his penknife and rubbed his thumb absently over the surface. "My happiest memories are from the time I spent there with my grandfather. It's my only real connection to the Murphy side of my family." And wouldn't that just stick it to his old man? His dad had never accepted that Liam was truly his son.

Ethan raised his glass. "Let's drink to broken families and damaged souls."

"How about you?" Liam asked Rainey after she had served her customer and poured herself a drink. "Do you want to marry me? Quick civil ceremony. A meeting with the legal trustee. Maybe one appearance in front of the family. We live our separate lives for a year. Then get divorced. I'd be willing to pay."

"Tempting as it is, I'm allergic to marriage," Rainey said dryly.

"Also, I'm running the Canadian Death Race in Grand Cache, Alberta, this weekend so a quickie marriage doesn't fit into the schedule." She held up a toned arm, covered in tattoos. "One more banner and I'll have a full Death Race set."

"Impressive." He was relieved she'd turned him down. Of course he'd had to ask—he'd regret leaving no stone unturned—but he and Rainey together were a disaster waiting to happen. "I guess Daisy is still my best option."

Ethan refilled their glasses. "I think you should just move on. Forget Daisy. Forget the distillery. I washed my hands of all that Murphy crap a long time ago. Your family. My family. There are no good Murphy relationships. No good Murphy businesses. You're making a fresh start here in the city. You've got a good job. You're going to meet new women. Why complicate things by dredging up the past?"

Liam didn't speak for a few moments as he mulled over Ethan's suggestion. "I can't let Brendan destroy it," he said finally. "Besides the family legacy, there are jobs at stake. And Daisy would be a perfect fake wife. We know each other, so it wouldn't be suspicious if we got together. And she hates me so there would be no relationship issues and no expectations."

"That's the stupidest thing I've ever heard." Rainey shook her head. "I almost want to slap you again. What does she get out of it, other than an easy opportunity to slit your throat in your sleep?"

Liam took a moment to consider. "Her family is trying to set her up in an arranged marriage. She's not interested."

"Not worth it." She grabbed a cloth and wiped down the already clean counter. "A year with a guy you hate versus just telling your parents to get the hell out of your life. I know which one I'd pick."

"It's not that simple," he said. For the Patels, he knew, there was no life without family. Every weekend there was a family gathering, dinner, or celebration. When Sanjay had a soccer game, thirty or forty relatives would show up to cheer him on. If Mr. Patel couldn't make it home from work on time, an aunt or uncle would bring over a full cooked dinner. If someone had a problem, everyone rallied around to help. By contrast, Liam had rarely seen his relatives. His mother's family lived in Florida, and his father's family hadn't wanted to be around his dad.

"Sure it is." Rainey brushed back a loose strand of hair. "If she tied herself to you for a year, she'd be giving up the chance to find that one person in the world who thinks you're worth throwing down for when things go wrong. Don't you want to find that person, too?"

"I'm not relationship material." He pushed his glass across the table.

"You just told me you're trying to find a wife."

"A fake wife."

She finished her drink in one gulp, a waste of good whiskey considering the cost. "I think I'll get one of the bouncers to come over and pound some sense into you."

"I thought you already did that." He looked to Ethan again for help, but his cousin just held up his hands in mock surrender.

"I don't even try to control her."

"That was a just a love tap." Rainey narrowed her eyes. "If you do something stupid, like propose to a woman who hates you to get a distillery you don't need and have no time to run, that's when things really get rough."

· 8 ·

"Good morning, Mrs. Liam Murphy."

Layla's voice crackled over the speaker in Daisy's Mini Cooper. They usually caught up in the mornings on the way to work if they hadn't talked the night before. It made the drive from Bernal Heights to Organicare's offices in SoMa almost bearable.

"That's not funny."

"You're right. It's not funny," Layla said. "But now that the family knows you're engaged, everyone wants to know who he is. Some of the aunties even tried to bribe me to divulge his last name—special jewelry for my wedding, snacks from India, saris they were keeping for their daughters . . ." Layla was engaged to Sam Mehta, and with the wedding only ten months away, they were well into wedding planning.

"I trust you," Daisy said, laughing. "I know you won't break."

"I was tempted by Nira Auntie's offer of a ten percent discount on a wedding *lehenga* at her store. You know how she overcharges."

Daisy slowed the car for the usual traffic jam. She preferred taking the 280 for the occasional glimpse of the Bay, but her map app had shown the 101 route could get her to work in substantially less time.

"At least you're free now," Layla said. "Until you break up with your fictitious fiancé, they'll leave you alone. You just better hope no one realizes that Liam is the same guy who stood you up for our senior prom."

"I'm not totally free. I still have to go out on a date with Roshan." Daisy sighed. "Dad guilted me into it. He thinks he knows me better than I know myself." She lifted a hand to brush her hair back from her cheek and mentally checked herself. Her hair instantly frizzed if she touched it with anything other than her fingers at any time other than in the three seconds after she stepped out of her shower.

"You might want to go on that date," Layla said. "My dad said he was the 'real deal.' And it would be good to have an accountant in the family."

Daisy groaned. "I don't want to get married, but if I ever did, it would be to someone interesting, someone who takes risks."

"Accountants take risks."

"Adding numbers by hand instead of using a calculator? I'm not talking about that kind of risk. I'm talking take-your-breath-away risks. Unexpected risks." She popped a fluffy *pav* in her mouth. The delicious breakfast treat was one of her favorites, and no one made them like Layla's mom, who often dropped by with food when her dad was away.

"You're talking about Liam." Layla knew all about Daisy's recent encounters with Liam and had not been impressed.

"You should have seen him . . ." Daisy allowed herself a small smile. "He looks like Hrithik Roshan in *Mohenjo Daro*."

"If I had seen him, especially when he showed up at your office after you told him you never wanted to see him again, he wouldn't be standing."

"The first time I saw him was straight out of Bollywood," Daisy continued. "One minute I'm ordinary me, stressing because Tyler dragged me to the pitch session even though he knows I'm an in-

trovert at heart, breaking the pad dispenser, watching my ex-
boyfriend and my old boss going at it in the restroom, running
through the conference center with an armload of pads, and the
next I'm kissing the man I hate most in front of the man who broke
my heart and the man I'm supposed to marry."

"Orson didn't break your heart," Layla countered. "You weren't
into that relationship at all. You were just tired of bad dates and
Orson was—"

"Nice."

"I was going to say available. But 'nice' will do. Also the word
'boring' comes to mind. After our first double date, Sam said he
couldn't handle another. He said he wanted to shoot himself when
Orson described his favorite art house film as a two-and-a-half-
hour phantasmagoria of bourgeoisie misery, and then proceeded to
outline it for us miserable scene by miserable scene."

"It was a good film." Daisy drummed her thumb on the steering
wheel, willing the traffic to start.

"You texted me 'help' twenty times from the theater. You said
you wanted to stick needles in your eyes."

Daisy bristled. "We all have to make sacrifices in the name of
love."

"But that's the point. You didn't love Orson. If you did, you
wouldn't have come out with me to Larry's Liquid Lounge the
night after you broke up. You wouldn't have hooked up with that
dude who said he was about to be deployed and it was his last night
in the city."

"I thought I was doing something good for my country," Daisy
retorted. "What if he never came home again?"

"If you'd really loved Orson you would have been sitting in
front of the TV in your pajamas, eating ice cream, feeding Max
pakoras, and watching a Marvel movie marathon. Look what hap-

pened when Sam and I broke up. I spent a week eating dal and drinking vodka until I passed out in a pool of vomit on the floor of my parents' restaurant. That's true love."

"You're not selling it very well," Daisy said dryly.

Finally the car in front of her started to move, and her Mini kicked into gear. "Love takes commitment. You know I have issues."

"I know you do," Layla said gently. "Every time I come to your place and see you and your dad kicking around in that big empty house, I feel your pain. But he's finally moving on. Don't you want to move on, too? Maybe the perfect apartment is out there, or even the perfect man—someone who makes you happy, who cares for you, and makes you laugh." She hesitated. "Maybe Roshan is the one."

Liam had made her laugh, but she suspected Layla wouldn't want to know that. "My dad thought my mom was the one, and look how that turned out. I'm happy to stay single, but I am going to string out the fake fiancé thing at least until Dad is back from his trip. I haven't been accosted by any aunties since the conference. It's been positively peaceful."

"You'd just better hope no one puts two and two together. If your dad thought you were with Liam after what he did . . ."

"I'd just tell him it wasn't real. Who would believe Liam and I would ever get together?"

DAISY was in the zone. At least she was in the zone until someone tapped her on the shoulder and she felt, rather than heard, the rumble of a voice behind her. With an irritated huff, she pulled off her noise-canceling headphones.

"Yes?"

Hunter Cole, CFO—a man so blond and beautiful he had no business being in a company filled with geeks—held out his computer. "My laptop isn't working. Someone said you were in IT. The screen froze, and I've got the spinning wheel . . ."

Daisy's mouth opened and closed again. She didn't do well around people like Hunter—confident, beautiful, popular people who were spatially aware and had never once tripped going up stairs, stumbled over a crack in the sidewalk, or bashed their head on a cupboard door. With their perfect bodies and toned muscles, they made her feel clumsy and awkward, the ten pakora pounds she could never lose a glaring signal that she was not one of them, if they hadn't guessed that already from the nonsensical words that came out of her mouth when they were around.

Liam was one of *them*, but she'd never felt the same way around him, like the clumsiness and the lost words vanished the moment he walked in the door, and all that was left was the Daisy inside who was smart enough to do the puzzles he brought her, funny enough to make him laugh, and interesting enough that he would blow off Sanjay to listen to whatever she had to say.

"Seriously, man?" Josh shot out of his chair in the nearby cubicle. "Asking her to fix your computer is the equivalent of asking a Michelin starred chef to wash the dishes." He frowned at Hunter, folding his arms across a chest that was only half the size and lacking any of Hunter's definition. "I thought Finance had its own IT people downstairs. What are you doing up here?"

Hunter gestured behind him at the slow parade of people walking through the door, hands filled with boxes, bags, and laptops. "The move just started." His deep voice rumbled so low Daisy could feel it in her bones.

"I was told this was where IT would be." He tipped his head from side to side, making his neck crack, then grabbed his collar, like he was about to rip the shirt off his massive shoulders and throw down with Josh right there on the cubicle floor.

"It's okay, Josh." Daisy took the computer, fumbling with it before she got it to the safety of her desk. "I do this for my relatives all the time." She turned it off and on again and the computer hummed to life. She tapped a few keys and looked up at Hunter. "Looks like it's working now."

"Thanks." Hunter lifted the laptop off her desk—as if he knew she'd probably drop it if she picked it up again—and walked away, his broad shoulders swaying above his tight-as-a-rock ass.

"He didn't even know to turn his computer off and on." Josh sneered. He was in a savage mood. "No wonder the company is going under."

"Be nice," Daisy scolded. "It's not his fault."

"How can I be nice when we're being invaded? How are we going to . . ." He trailed off as Mia Hart, the marketing director, placed a box in the empty cubicle beside him. Daisy knew Mia, with her expressive green eyes and thick auburn hair, from project meetings and the occasional elevator ride, but they'd never had more than a passing conversation. Josh, however, knew everyone.

"Look what the cat dragged in." He glared at Mia.

"Sorry, guys." She shrugged off the insult. "Marketing and Design is moving in beside you, but I brought donuts!"

"You can stay." Josh took the donut box from the top of her pile. "But only until they're gone."

Mia gave Daisy a sympathetic smile. "I know you guys like to be left alone. It sucks for everyone."

"Not Hunter," Josh said. "He thinks anyone with a screen is Help Desk."

"Aren't we in a bad mood today." Mia pulled a bundle of files out of her box. "What's wrong with you?"

"We can't work like this," Josh said. "I refuse to be diminished to 'IT.' I'm going to speak to Tyler."

"Maybe give him some space right now." Mia leaned over to turn on her computer and Josh tracked her movements with a less-than-subtle shift of his eyes. "He's not in good shape. He looks like he's just stepped off *Survivor.* Any moment now, I expect him to call a Tribal Council and vote one of us off."

"I heard a rumor that he's letting ten percent of the staff go." Josh's expression turned serious.

Mia snorted. "You hear rumors about everything. Day-old muffins instead of fresh, spyware in the computers, corporate espionage—"

"The corporate espionage rumor turned out to be true," he protested. "Some dude wanted the secret to super absorbent tampons so badly, he was prepared to go to jail for it. That's probably why we lost market share."

"It was never proven in court," Daisy pointed out. "I think we're in financial trouble because we expanded out of our core market, at least that's what Tyler told the VCs when we pitched at the tech con."

"How did the pitch sessions go?" Mia asked. "I did a marketing proposal for Tyler to hand out, but he never gave me any feedback."

Daisy shrugged. "A few of the VCs said they'd be in touch, but we didn't get any requests for a meeting. I told Tyler they were probably overwhelmed with all the pitches, but he said that was VC speak for 'F-off, loser.'"

Mia's face softened. "He reminds me so much of my second stepdad. He was a scientist at an aeronautics company who could spend hours just staring into space as he contemplated how many quarks were in the universe."

"How many dads have you had?" Daisy asked.

"Three, but none of them stuck around. My real dad died in a car accident and my mom drove the next two away with her drinking. She never got over my father's death."

Daisy's heart squeezed in her chest. It had taken her father twenty years to get over her mom. As far as she knew, he hadn't dated anyone until Priya. They'd both believed that one day Daisy's mom would come home. And she had, but it hadn't turned out as either of them expected.

"It must have been very hard for both of you," Daisy said.

"Tyler's been an incredible support." Mia pulled a file from her box. "He got her on my medical plan as a dependent."

When Josh tipped his head in a puzzled frown, she explained. "She has a lot of accidents when I'm not at home—fires, falls, alcohol poisoning . . . She's a disaster waiting to happen." She retrieved the donut box from Josh and offered it to Daisy with a smile, as if she hadn't just spilled her dark and painful family secrets. "All Star?"

"No, thanks. I had breakfast this morning."

"I'll take it." Zoe Banks thumped her box in the cubicle beside Daisy and settled in her chair. A skilled graphic designer and a single mom, she had worked with Daisy on the website design. "I missed breakfast this morning when Lily had a tantrum and threw her cereal all over the floor. Don't let anyone tell you the toddler years are the best of times."

Daisy laughed. "I've got lots of cousins that age. I know what it's like."

"What's going on with you?" Zoe leaned back in her chair so she could see Mia. "You're wearing your serious face this morning."

"Daisy said we're doomed."

Daisy's eyes widened. "No I didn't."

"She said the VCs told Tyler to fuck the hell off. That means dust off the old résumé and start pounding the pavement."

"That's not what happened." Daisy looked from Mia to Zoe and back to Mia. "I'm not saying it's a lost cause."

"All of us squeezed onto one floor?" Josh gestured to the now bustling office. "Constant chattering? Boxes of donuts with the chocolate ones missing? I'd say it is. And this is only the start of the budget cuts. Next thing you know, Tyler will be pulling all the free sample condoms and lube. What am I going to do? Colossal is the only size that fits."

"They're only called 'colossal' to pander to the male ego." Mia gave him a withering look. "They're actually tiny size."

"Well, no wonder he's cutting staff," Josh retorted. "The marketing department can't tell the difference between six inches and ten."

Zoe shot a sideways glance at Daisy. The tension between Josh and Mia shimmered in the air between them. "We just need to find an investor," she said. "How hard can it be? Does anyone have a connection or know a VC with money to burn?"

I do! The thought crossed her mind and she quickly dismissed it, just as she'd tried and failed to dismiss all thoughts of Liam since she'd bumped into him again. Why did he have to look so damned gorgeous? And why did his voice sound deeper and his eyes look bluer than she remembered? And why were his lips so soft and his hands so firm when he'd held her?

"I think we should go for drinks and brainstorm ideas to save the company," Josh said. "Friday night after work. Who's in? Daisy is, of course, because she absolutely *loves* going out with her work colleagues to party." He gave her a hopeful grin, even though she always turned him down.

Before she was forced into an awkward explanation, Tyler walked into the office looking more unkempt than usual, in a rumpled shirt, baggy jeans, and sock feet. His thick graying beard and uncombed hair were a decided contrast to the clean-shaven look he had sported until things started to go downhill.

Tyler had never been interested in running the company. He'd left the business side to Kristina and her then-boyfriend, Derek, who convinced them to expand the product line to include diapers, adult incontinence undergarments, and sexual health products. Unfortunately, their new slogan, "From Cradle to Grave, Top to Bottom," didn't translate well internationally—"Baby Bite My Grandfather's Ass" not being the optimal message for foreign consumers. Funding dried up. Derek took his money and ran. A jilted Kristina left the company to do outreach in developing countries. And poor Tyler was left holding the bag.

The noise quickly died down and Daisy pushed her chair into the aisle to hear what he had to say.

"As you might have guessed from the move, our last round of fundraising didn't go well," Tyler said. "I'm still not giving up, but I know many of you have families and financial commitments, so I want to tell you where we stand so you can make informed decisions about your future . . ."

Daisy stifled a gasp when he outlined the cuts that were about to come. Josh had been right about the layoffs, but that was only the beginning. If things didn't pick up after one month, another 20 percent of the team would have to go. Travel and conferences were canceled. All tech purchases were frozen, and there would be no more new hires.

Should she start sending out résumés right away? Where would she go? What if she couldn't find a job she liked as much as this one? Her hands shook as anxiety sent tendrils of worry through her veins.

"Tyler . . ." Rochelle, the company receptionist, walked through the open-plan office, stilettos clicking on the tile floor. Her long blond hair was swept back from an elegant oval face dominated by wide blue eyes. She'd been Derek's executive assistant until he'd disappeared from the company. Good-hearted Tyler had offered to keep her on as a receptionist. Another woman might have turned down what was effectively a demotion, but Rochelle carried on, as officious and condescending as she had ever been.

"We have a visitor." She smoothed her hand down her pearl-white sheath dress, drawing attention to the curve of her slim hip.

Tyler's gaze flicked to her, slightly annoyed. "I'll be there in a minute. I'm making an important announcement."

"You'll want to come now. He's from Evolution Ventures. His name is Liam Murphy."

Daisy sucked in a deep breath. It couldn't be him. Liam wouldn't dare come to her office. Not after she'd made it clear he wasn't welcome.

Or would he?

"*THE* Liam Murphy?" Visibly shocked, Tyler staggered back. "From Evolution Ventures? Here?" He waved his hands frantically in the air. "Everyone. Calm down. Don't get excited. We're right in the middle of start-up central. He probably got lost on his way to see Google or Twitter. I need a clean shirt. And my tie. Where's my jacket? Where are my shoes? And just in case it is the miracle we've been hoping for, who has the pitch deck?"

"What's Liam doing here?" Daisy whispered, half to herself.

Mia leaned toward her. "Do you know him?"

"He was my brother's best friend."

"Did you miss the part where Zoe asked if anyone knew a VC with money to burn?" Josh spun around in his chair. "That was your chance to say, 'Why yes, I know one of the senior associates in one of the top VCs in the country who found a unicorn when he was just starting his career.'"

Daisy shrugged. "We're not close."

"Who cares if you're close?" He grabbed the arms of her chair and gave it a gentle shake. "Look around you. People are scared about losing their jobs. Tyler looks like a caveman. The snack bar is going to be permanently closed. And you and I will never get into the flow until all these people go back downstairs."

"He's not here to save us," Daisy said. "He wants to rent the second floor. I saw him the other day and I told him not to. I guess he didn't care what I thought." The words poured out of her in a tidal wave of anger, flushing her anxiety away. "But then that's the kind of person he is. He stood me up for my senior prom and then disappeared without a word after practically living with my family for eight years."

"But he has money to invest," Josh protested. "So he wasn't a nice guy ten years ago. People change."

"Don't be an idiot." Mia glared at him. "He stood her up for her prom. That's huge for a teenage girl, Josh. Huge. And then just bailing on her family? Unforgivable."

"Thanks." She gave Mia a smile, feeling a lightness in her limbs. Mia understood her pain in a way not many people did.

Josh grabbed his phone. "Evolution Ventures have ten million in assets across four funds, locations in New York and Silicon Valley, over eighty investments, and they've done three IPOs and two acquisitions. What's not to like?" He turned the phone around to show them a picture of Liam. "And check this guy out. I wouldn't mind having that eye candy walking around."

"Damn, he's fine," Zoe said. "A bastard, of course, but a good-looking one. I'd fight you for him."

"You sprained your finger pushing the elevator button," Josh said. "I'm not afraid of you."

"I am totally unaffected by his breathtaking good looks." Mia waved the phone away. "It's what's inside that counts."

"Exactly." Daisy nodded. "I'm going to tell him to get lost—"

"Everyone get back to work," Tyler called out. "Don't let him think we're slacking. Rochelle, bring him to my office."

"I took him to the conference room," she said. "But—"

"Good. Conference room. Bring him coffee. Or muffins. Or avocado toast. Or how about those little Linzer cookies from the bakery down the street?" He pointed at the nearest employee. "You. Get cookies. Rochelle, tell him I'll be there in five minutes. In the meantime, get him whatever he wants."

"He wants Daisy."

A smile spread across Josh's face. "He wants you, Daisy. Think of Mia's mom and Zoe's daughter. Think about my rent increase and Hunter's inability to use basic tech. Do you really want us all out on the street, foraging for muffins in back alleys?"

"Daisy. Hallway. Now." Tyler raced out of the room before she could object.

"I've never seen him so panicked," Mia said. "He's barely functioning. You'll need to calm him down."

Tyler was still buzzing with excitement when Daisy joined him and Rochelle in the hallway. "This is it, Daisy. Our big chance. I saw him watching our pitch to Alliance Ventures at the con last week. He must have seen something he liked."

Daisy's words of warning died on her lips. "What do you mean he was watching?" She quickened her pace as Tyler strode down the hallway toward the conference room.

"He was at the back of the room. I hadn't put Evolution on our pitch list because I didn't think we were a good fit, but I guess I was wrong, because here he is! He must have questions for you about the software system or he wouldn't have asked for you by name." Tyler smoothed down his hair. "Keep him busy. I'll be back as fast as I can with the pitch deck."

"We might as well throw in the towel now." Rochelle gave a dramatic sigh as she followed behind them. "She's going to bore him to tears with her monosyllabic answers, stilted conversation about coding bugs, and weird facts."

Ignoring Rochelle's insult, Daisy scrambled for a reason to

avoid meeting with Liam. "She's right. Maybe you should send in someone else—"

"Don't bail on me now," Tyler warned. "He wants you. I need you. Get in there and kick some VC ass."

Daisy took in his disheveled appearance and reached for his tie. "You need to get yourself together if you're going to pitch. Tuck in your shirt. Find your shoes." She tied the tie for him, a skill she'd learned after years of helping Sanjay and her dad. "Josh said you've been sleeping at the office . . ."

"There are so many good people here. I don't want to let them down. I've reached out to everyone . . ." He tucked his shirt into his pants and straightened his shoulders. "We can do this. We're going to give him the best pitch we've ever done. It's going to blow him away." Taking a deep breath, he threw open the door to the boardroom.

"Mr. Murphy. So nice to see you. I'm Tyler Dawes, Organicare's CEO." He pumped Liam's hand. "I've brought Daisy Patel, our senior software engineer, as requested. Daisy can answer any questions you might have about our system software or our direct-to-consumer platform."

Liam smiled and held out his hand. "Ms. Patel."

Gritting her teeth, Daisy shook his hand, eyes widening as electricity sparked between them. Had she picked up a charge on her shoes on the way in? "Mr. Murphy."

"I'll just gather the rest of the team," Tyler said. "Rochelle will be in with coffee and snacks in a moment."

Daisy waited until the door had closed behind Tyler before ripping her hand away. "What are you doing here? I told you not to rent the second floor. Poor Tyler thinks you're here to save the company."

"I needed to see you." He fumbled in the pocket of his sleek, dark suit—the kind that fit in all the right places. She'd never seen Liam in a suit before, but it added another dimension to his cool, confident persona—a dangerously sexy one.

"If you aren't interested in offering funding to Organicare, then your visit here was ill conceived. Tyler is apoplectic with excitement. He's sending people out to buy you special cookies, and in about five minutes, he will have the entire pitch team assembled. I wouldn't be surprised if he shows up with a throne for you to sit on."

"I do like a good throne." Liam stroked his chin. "And I did wear a suit for the occasion . . ."

"Liam!" She glared. "Be serious. What are you doing here?"

He shoved one hand in his pocket. "I need a wife."

"And you came here . . ." She searched for an explanation for his outlandish statement. "Because you thought a company that sells feminine care products might also have a supply of women available for marriage? I can go to the stock room if you want and see what we have on the shelf. Are you looking for a blonde or a brunette? I guess it doesn't matter whether she likes you or not."

"It's not just for me," Liam explained, pulling his hand out of his pocket. "I need a wife to preserve my family legacy."

"So you want to breed her? Good to know. That takes Margie and Joan out of the running. They're both in their sixties."

He dropped to one knee and held out a blue velvet box. "I want you. Marry me, Daisy."

Of all the things she'd expected him to say, "Marry me" did not even make the top thousand. For a long moment, all she could do was stand and stare.

"I think you have me confused with someone who would even want to be in the same room as you, much less wed you after such a romantic proposal." She moved to leave and Liam held up his hand.

"Daisy. Wait. I've handled this wrong. Let me explain."

"You have two minutes, and only because Tyler needs time to get his pitch deck together."

"My family owns a whiskey distillery in Napa." Liam pushed to his feet, still holding out the velvet box. "It was handed down from father to son for three hundred years until my father turned his back on tradition to focus on his dream of building cars. My grandfather continued to run the distillery until . . ." Liam's voice caught, broke. His head dropped and his hand went to his forehead. "He passed away two weeks ago."

Daisy's throat tightened when his blue eyes glistened. She'd never seen Liam so emotional. Or so open. "I'm so sorry, Liam. I know you didn't have much family."

"He left the distillery to me in a trust on the condition that I marry before my next birthday," he continued, clearing his throat. "Family meant everything to him and he told me before he died that he was worried that I'd wind up alone. His lawyers are administering the trust. If I don't marry by that time, the distillery goes to my brother, who intends to knock it down and sell the land to save his business."

"I'm sure you can find *someone* to marry you," Daisy said, trying not to be too harsh in light of his circumstances. "You're not hard to look at. Actually, Rochelle is single. I think you two would make a great match."

"There's a catch."

Daisy groaned. "There always is."

"I have to stay married for a year to show the marriage is legitimate," Liam said. "I don't want to involve friends or exes or lead anyone on because I have no interest in a real marriage, and our arrangement will be over when the year is up. I also don't want to marry someone I don't know and can't trust. There's a lot of money at stake, and at the end of the day, I can't risk a stranger turning around and demanding fifty percent because we're in a no-fault divorce state. That's why I need you."

"You should write that on a greeting card," she said dryly. "I can barely contain myself."

"But that's why it's perfect," he said. "You don't like me, and I have no interest in a relationship, so there would be no expectations either way. Except for a few events to establish the legitimacy of the marriage, we could continue to lead separate lives. No one will know."

"I'll know," Daisy said. "Every time I look at you, I'll wonder if you're just going to disappear again. You were part of the family, and then you were gone, like you didn't care about us at all."

"I did care." He paced in front of her, irritating her even more because now she caught a glimpse of his tight ass and the strong thighs that carried him across the room and back.

"It wasn't easy to leave. I thought I was doing the right thing for me and for your family."

Ah yes, her family. They now thought she and Liam were together. And here he was with a fake marriage proposal that would save her from matchmaking aunties and boring blind dates. Superstitious Lakshmi Auntie would call that karma. Or she might assume that Daisy had seen a fox when she'd woken up in the morning, which signified a productive and fruitful day.

"There has to be something you want," Liam pleaded "Something I can offer you."

"Your head on a spike?" She'd always envied Liam's relaxed attitude, his impulsiveness and disregard for rules. He was chaos. She was order. Even if she agreed to his crazy plan, it would never work. They'd destroy each other before they could say "I do."

· 10 ·

Sᴡᴇᴀᴛ beaded on Liam's brow. He'd spent the weekend think-ing through the options. Aside from the fact that Brendan would see through the ruse, there were significant emotional and finan-cial risks involved in marrying a stranger. Daisy was his only hope. Maybe he shouldn't have winged the proposal, but planning just wasn't his style.

"I could pay you." He regretted the words as soon as they dropped from his lips.

Daisy's face shuttered, and for a moment he thought she'd throw something at him. Lucky for him, the coffee hadn't arrived.

"I'm not a hooker, Liam."

"Jesus Christ. I don't think you're a hooker."

"And just for your information," she continued. "I don't need to sell myself to get sex. Lots of guys want to have sex with me. For free. I don't even let them pay for my dinner. That's how free it is."

"Daisy . . ." His voice cracked. Was it possible to screw this up any more? What the fuck had he been thinking? If he'd seriously wanted to convince her to be his wife, he'd just blown it all to hell.

"I have free sex all the time," she mumbled, half to herself. "I don't pay them. They don't pay me. You missed out at the prom. Big time."

"I shouldn't have offered to pay you," he said contritely. He shouldn't have done a lot of things, starting with pulling her braids when she was ten and encouraging her obvious crush with smiles and winks behind Sanjay's back. By the time he had realized she had real feelings for him, it was too late. He'd fallen for her, too. But she was his best friend's little sister, and worthy of a man far better than him.

She gave an indignant sniff. "Definitely not, but it just goes to show what a degenerate you are."

Undeterred, he kept talking. "I thought the idea of a business arrangement would appeal to your logical nature, and since most business transactions involve money . . ."

Daisy held up a hand. "If you have that much money, why don't you just buy the distillery yourself? Or finance it? Or get your company to invest? You are in the food business, after all."

Of course she'd think of all the logical options. "Brendan would never sell it to me, nor would he allow my company to get involved. We have issues going way back. He's the kind of guy who would take a hit just to spite me."

"Fancy that."

"But you and I have a history together," he continued. "It would be entirely plausible that we reconnected, fell in love, and I proposed when my grandfather was ill because it made me realize that life is short."

"Let me stop you right there." She held up a warning hand. "You are clearly not understanding how things work in my world. Marriage isn't just about two people; it's about family. There's no possible way we could get married without them being involved. I would be disowned if I showed up at the next family dinner and announced I was married. And then, if I got divorced? No good desi boy would ever want me."

"I thought that was the goal," Liam said. "You said you wanted them to leave you alone."

She hesitated for a heartbeat. "That's true. If I were almost thirty and divorced, my aunties wouldn't even try to find a husband for me. I would be a lost cause."

Hope bloomed in his chest. "Just say the word and I will happily ruin you."

"It's not just up to me," Daisy said. "My family would have to approve of the engagement. Imagine sitting in front of twenty or thirty of my relatives and being grilled about every aspect of your life, your every word and every move analyzed to death. One wrong word, one misstep, and you would be deemed unworthy, and that would be the end of it for you." She drew her finger across her neck.

His eyes widened. "They'd kill me?"

"Worse."

Liam shuddered. "Torture?"

"That's another word for Taara Auntie's cooking."

He had a vague memory of Sanjay warning him never to eat food from a plastic container he'd been given by one of his aunties. "So, what would happen if I didn't get their approval?"

"You would walk away without a bride. There are no second chances."

"Sounds harsh."

She shrugged. "Patels have a very low divorce rate."

"Are you ready for us, Mr. Murphy?" Tyler knocked on the door.

"One more minute," Liam called out.

Daisy's smile faded. "Tyler thinks you're here to save the company. He's going to be devastated to find out you only came here to find a wife."

"I'm not sure why. I asked for you."

"We're in financial trouble, Liam." She twisted her hands in front of her. "The former CEO cashed out after an ill-conceived decision to expand the product line. That's why we were pitching at the con. It's such a shame. Organicare is a great company with amazing people, good products, and wonderful outreach programs for young women in developing countries. It's the first start-up I've worked at where I've really wanted to stay, but Tyler just told us we should start looking for new jobs. He thinks you're a miracle, come to save us."

Damn. He hadn't even considered how his presence could be misconstrued. "Most start-ups fail. It's the nature of the business."

"Well, it shouldn't have happened to this one," she said vehemently.

"Clearly I miscalculated," Liam said. "I'll do him the courtesy of listening to his pitch."

"But you won't give him the funding, will you?"

He made the mistake then of looking at her. Between them lay memories of a time when he would have done anything she asked. "I don't think—"

"What if I agreed to marry you?" She blurted out. "Would you save Organicare?"

Even now, he couldn't deny her. "I can put together a proposal, but the partners have the final say. I'll be honest, though, personal care isn't really our thing, and from what you've told me, it sounds like the company has been mismanaged." Not only that, a proposal to finance a dud company might make the partners question his judgment and destroy his chances of joining the partnership.

"Marriage isn't my thing," Daisy said. "But this would not only get my matchmaking aunties off my back and make me totally unmarriageable when we get divorced, it would mean Organicare could be saved, my colleagues can keep their jobs, and they can move back down to the lower floor so I can be left alone to work in peace."

It was what he'd come here for, what he wanted. Not only that, spending time with Daisy would give him time to make amends. He'd made many mistakes in his life, and leaving her had been one of them. "I can't make any promises," he said. "But I can have my team analyze the business and help Organicare put itself in the best possible position to get funding, if not from us, then from another VC. But you would have to agree to stay here and see it through."

She was silent for so long, he thought she'd changed her mind.

"Fine." She sighed. "I'll marry you."

It wasn't the acceptance a man dreamed about, but it was a "yes" just the same. He pulled out his phone.

"I'll tell my assistant to get us on the first flight to Vegas tonight."

"Vegas?" Daisy's brow furrowed in confusion.

"We can get married tonight," Liam said. "I know a good chapel. Some of them are tacky, but this one has class. We can fly out after work. The Elvis wears a three-piece suit and a tie . . ."

His spider senses tingled, warning him that something was wrong. Or maybe it was the scowl on his fake fiancée's face. "If you don't like Elvis . . ."

"Are you kidding?" Daisy walked over to the whiteboard and picked up a marker. "We're not going to Vegas. We need a plan for this whole thing."

"I don't do plans."

"Well you're going to do one now because otherwise you won't have your marriage of convenience." She turned to the board, giving him a perfect view of her lush behind. His thoughts immediately went somewhere the thoughts of a fake fiancé shouldn't go, a small indication that this was going to be harder than it looked.

"We can't just jump into a marriage," she said as she wrote on the board. "It won't be believable, especially if the trustee is a lawyer. We'll have to plan out some dates to legitimize our relationship before the wedding. We have to be seen together, Liam." She turned around and pointed to the board. "This is what we need."

Liam read the heading and laughed. "A dating plan? I don't plan dates, sweetheart. I go where the wind takes me."

"When Orson and I used to go out with friends, we'd talk about restaurants we'd been to, or an interesting documentary we'd watched on Netflix, or an art exhibition we'd seen, maybe an energetic walk along the coast. Those are the stories that make a relationship sound real."

Liam faked a yawn. "Orson sounds like a boring guy."

"He was easy to be with. We didn't have to talk much."

"My kind of relationship." He gave a sly smile.

Daisy raised an eyebrow. "If you are suggesting that all we did was have sex, you would be very wrong. It was an intellectual relationship. We saw thought-provoking films. We discussed philosophy, religion, politics, programming issues . . ."

Liam dropped his head and then jerked it up again. "Sorry. I fell asleep after you said you and Orson never had sex."

"I didn't say . . ." She trailed off, her eyes narrowing. "It's none of your business."

"I'm your fiancé. I think your sex life is very much my business. I need to know what kind of woman I'm marrying."

"The kind that doesn't kiss and tell," she snapped.

Thoroughly enjoying her discomfort, he leaned back in his chair, hands crossed behind his head. "Who is a better kisser? Me or Orson?"

Daisy's eyes widened and she froze, her hand hovering in midair. Liam remembered that look from the afternoons he'd spent at her house, when she'd been caught doing something wrong.

"I have my answer." He puffed out his chest. "The old Murphy charm wins again."

"That was the only kiss you'll ever get from me," she said firmly. "My feelings for you haven't changed. This is a marriage in name only. That means no physical contact except for holding hands or a peck on the cheek for appearances." She turned back to the white-board. "I'll write that down so you don't forget."

"I'm liking this plan less already," Liam grumbled. "Write that down, too."

"How long do we have before your birthday?"

"Six weeks. June twenty-fifth, to be exact. I'm surprised you don't remember." He'd looked forward to his birthday every year because the Patels had always made it into a big celebration. He hadn't needed the decorations, treats, or gifts, although he appreci-ated their thoughtfulness. It was the fact that they had cared enough to make the day special for him—something his family never did because his father wouldn't allow it.

Her gaze dropped and she turned back to the whiteboard. "Ty-ler's waiting, so I'll fill in the details tonight and send you the spreadsheet. Basically we have time for six mini dates, two big fam-ily get-togethers, and then we'll elope and get married at city hall the day before your birthday. Afterward, we'll rent a two-bedroom apartment, live our separate lives, and one year later we'll get a divorce. I'll be ruined. You'll have the distillery. We'll be set." She put down her marker. "I'll need a list of close relatives from you and places we could possibly meet them. Our first date will have to be at Layla's aunt's clothing store to shop for your wedding outfit. She is practically family, and it's usually the first thing people do when they get engaged because of the length of time it takes to get the clothing made."

Stunned, Liam just stared. "You came up with all that in five minutes?"

"It's just the bare bones of a plan, Liam. The only problem is: Who do we tell outside of the family?"

"I'll have to tell Tyler that we're engaged," he said. "There may be conflict of interest issues. And if I do send the pitch to my partners, I'll have to tell them, too. As far as business goes, it will be a real engagement. A stable relationship can only help my chances of partnership. I can't think of anyone else who needs to know the truth."

"Same here, except for Layla. I can't lie to her."

"What about your dad?" he asked. "I know you two are close."

Her face crumpled, and for a moment he thought it was the end of their arrangement.

"I've never lied to him about anything important before." She twisted her hands together. "But he's the one spearheading this matchmaking frenzy. Just this morning he guilted me into meeting some guy he picked from a matchmaking site. He just can't accept that I'm not interested in having a serious relationship, so it will be easier if he believes our engagement is real. The bigger problem is that it's you. Somehow we'll have to convince him you're not the guy you used to be."

There was an easy way to solve the problem. He could tell the truth about that night. But that would mean letting Daisy's father know that his own son wasn't who he thought he was. Even if he had to lose the distillery, Liam wasn't prepared to betray his best friend.

"So you plan to be alone forever?" Liam asked. "No sex?" He immediately regretted his words when her expression tightened.

"Just because I'm not interested in having a long-term relationship doesn't mean I plan to be a nun."

"What about when we're married?" He looked away, as if not seeing her would change her answer.

"Fake married. And yes, I plan to have sex then, too. I'm a single woman with a healthy sex drive. A year is too long to wait."

Liam's pulse kicked up a notch at the thought of Daisy sleeping with other men. "How many?"

Affronted, she sniffed. "I beg your pardon?"

"How many guys are you planning to sleep with while you're married to me?" he asked.

Daisy folded her arms across her chest. "It's none of your business."

His eyes narrowed and he pulled out the ring box and tossed it to her. "I'll be your husband."

"Fake husband." She tossed it back. "And the day I accept a ring is the day I start believing in love."

"Well, I'll be sleeping with people, too," he said with an unexpected surge of jealousy. "Lots of them. When we're living together, you might want to find a place to spend the night if the noise bothers you."

"You're disgusting."

"That's not what the ladies say." He had no idea why he was being such an ass, except that he was still struggling to get his mind around the fact that Daisy was a woman now—a woman other men wanted.

Daisy closed her eyes and drew in a deep breath. "I think we need to be clear about one thing." She underlined the words she'd written on the board. "No physical contact means no sex."

"Ever?" Liam didn't like ultimatums. "What if you beg for it?"

"I have never begged for sex in my life."

A slow, sensual smile spread across his face. "You've never been with me."

"I'm not sleeping with you, Liam," she said firmly. "And no developing feelings, either. This is solely a business arrangement. I'll include my terms and conditions when I send you the final plan." She took a picture of the whiteboard and then wiped it clean. "I'll go get Tyler."

"Daisy?"

She looked back over her shoulder as she reached for the door. "Yes?"

"What if *I* beg?"

"I'll throw you a bone."

· 11 ·

Wednesday, 5:48 A.M.

DAISY: Confirming Date #1. Wed. 5:30 p.m. Krishna Fashions, El Camino Real. Objectives: discuss dating plan, shop for wedding outfit, meet Layla and her relatives.

LIAM: Shh. I'm sleeping.

DAISY: Obviously not.

LIAM: This is an autoresponder. I use it for people who wake up at ungodly hours and send messages about dates they already scheduled in my calendar.

DAISY: Clearly not an autoresponder, since your responses suggest sentience.

LIAM: Definitely not sentient. Why aren't you asleep?

DAISY: I get up every morning at 5:45 a.m. to work out.

LIAM: I don't get up at 5:45 a.m. to sleep as long as possible.

DAISY: That's why we would never work in real life. We're too different.

LIAM: I could turn you to the dark side. Come and sleep with me.

DAISY: Read the dating plan I sent you. No sex.

LIAM: ZZZZZZZZZZZ

. . .

"A<small>RE</small> you crazy?" Layla turned from the mirror in the changing room of her aunt's clothing store. She had taken the afternoon off to check out the latest shipment of bridal lehenga and to give Daisy moral support for her first fake date with Liam. Layla ran her own recruitment firm and enjoyed the flexibility that came with being her own boss.

"Yes, but you've always known that about me. I like plans and quantifiable results, but the rest of my life is a disaster." Daisy adjusted the bright green silk *dupatta* on Layla's shoulders. With her radiant complexion and rich brown hair, Layla could wear almost any color and look amazing. By contrast, Daisy avoided autumn colors after a makeover from one of her work colleagues at an online fashion start-up showed that those colors made her look sallow and pale.

"You can't marry Liam after what he did to you," Layla spat out. "We hate him. Also, he thought we were brats."

"We were brats. How much time did we spend spying on him and Sanjay? How many 'secret' valentines did I put in his school bags over the years? It makes me cringe to think about how I used to follow him around and giggle every time he looked at me."

Layla frowned. "Why are you defending him? He utterly broke your heart. I'll never forgive him for that."

Born within two weeks of each other, Layla and Daisy had always been close. Their fathers were brothers and had immigrated to the U.S. together, Daisy's dad to study accounting at Berkeley and Layla's dad to study engineering. They had both had arranged marriages, but where Layla's parents had fallen in love and stuck by each other through decades of marriage, Daisy's mother had left her family to chase her dreams and her heart in New York.

Daisy fisted her fifties-style black pleated skirt. She'd been in a pinup mood when she'd planned her outfit the night before, color coordinating the pink edging on the skirt with a fuzzy pink sweater and bright pink streaks in her hair. However, the feet-pinching three-inch Mary Janes with pink bows had put a damper on her enthusiasm for the quirky retro outfit.

"This marriage means the aunties will leave me alone. My dad will stop wasting time trying to find me a husband. I'll be ruined, and I'll be able to save Organicare. Everything will go back to the way it used to be."

"You barely know the people you work with," Layla protested. "And I thought you were thinking of moving on because you can't get into the flow with all the noise." She turned back to the mirror and ran a hand over the intricate gold embroidery on her skirt. They'd been close for so long that Daisy could tell she didn't like it just from the set of her mouth.

"Organicare is a good company. I like their commitment to seeking sustainability and celebrating diversity, and their out-reach is—"

"Since when did you become Organicare's spokesperson?" Layla frowned at herself in the mirror, and Daisy slid the dupatta off her cousin's shoulders. This clearly wasn't her style.

"Why don't you try the red one?"

"Yeah, you're right. This one is a bit too much." Layla squeezed into the changing room. Nira Chopra, owner of the clothing store and Layla's maternal aunt, had left no hook unfilled in her quest to find Layla the perfect dress.

"I've gotten to know some of the Organicare employees over the last few days," Daisy said through the curtain. "We're all squished onto one floor, so I'm never alone. Zoe is a single mom with a little girl at home and she lives from check to check because her ex doesn't make his support payments. Tyler lets her bring her daughter to work when her childcare falls through. And Mia's mom is an alcoholic who spends a lot of time in the hospital. Tyler got her on Mia's medical insurance to help pay the bills. And then there's Josh, whose dad kicked him out after finding out he was bisexual. Tyler gave him an advance to—"

Layla poked her head around the curtain. "What happened to not getting too involved with your work colleagues?"

"It's hard not to get to know them when they are all around me. I knew Tyler was passionate about the company and that he was a good guy, but I didn't know all the things he's been doing to help his employees. And I didn't know about all their difficulties."

"I hear these kinds of stories every day." Layla disappeared behind the curtain again. "It's hard times all around. If things don't work out, send them to me. I'll do my best to get them placed quickly."

"But that's just it. They love the company and don't want to leave."

Layla pushed back the curtain, a wide smile on her face. "What do you think about this?"

No thinking was involved. The red and gold embroidered skirt and matching top were perfect, and from the smile on her face, her cousin knew it.

"You look beautiful."

"I feel beautiful." Layla spun around, checking herself out in the large three-way mirror. "This is it, isn't it?"

Daisy gave her a wistful smile. She had agreed to Liam's crazy proposal in part to avoid putting herself in this very situation, but seeing Layla's joy, she couldn't help but imagine herself in a wedding outfit, twirling around the changing room. "I don't think I've ever seen anything so exquisite."

Layla hugged her in delight. "I can hardly wait to negotiate the price with Nira Auntie."

Better Layla than her. Daisy hated bartering. Why not just put a fair price on something and the customer could decide whether they were willing to pay it or not? But bartering was a big part of shopping on El Camino Real and some storeowners were insulted if you didn't even try to negotiate the price, which was why Daisy never shopped without Layla.

"I'll hide behind one of the racks."

Layla laughed. "You should stay and learn a few tricks. My mom taught me everything I know."

Skills a mother taught her daughter if she wasn't busy living her dreams on the other side of the country—dreams that didn't include her children.

After Nira Auntie had pinned the outfit for alterations, and Layla had bargained her down to the point of being disowned from the family, they searched the racks for something for Daisy to wear, both to Layla's wedding and her own fake ceremony.

"No saris," Daisy said. "I need to be able to run after you when you come to your senses and see Sam for who he really is."

Layla chuckled. "I think you guys are too much alike. He's very logical and practical like you."

"I wish I wasn't so logical. Then I could just make up a history with Liam instead of having to go out on pretend dates. I sent him a spreadsheet this morning and told him we'd be discussing the dating plan. I hope he doesn't want to change anything."

"You've scheduled a date to go over the dating plan." Layla laughed. "I think you're marrying the wrong guy. This is Liam we're talking about. Every time I saw him at school he was in the principal's office. He spray-painted 'Anarchy' on the street. He lounged around your house in ripped jeans, heavy metal T-shirts, and leather jackets, and hung out with a dangerous crowd. I think at one point his hair was longer than mine. He is not a schedule kind of guy. That's what you liked most about him. He was your opposite when it came to managing life, but you both had that little bit of rebel inside."

"Or maybe we were just both messed up," She flipped through a rack of brightly colored *salwar* suits. "But he has a good job now, and he was even wearing a suit and tie. He wouldn't have gotten as far as he has if he couldn't make it to meetings on time."

"He showed up at your office unannounced and smooth-talked you into a fake marriage." Layla's voice rose in exasperation. "That tells me he hasn't changed, and the part of you that was attracted to his Rebel-Without-a-Cause self is attracted to him now. You didn't even call me when he proposed." She whirled around, dropping her hands to her hips. "Since when do you make spur-of-the-moment decisions? It takes you twenty minutes to decide what kind of coffee you want to drink, and yet you decided to marry him in less than ten minutes."

"Twenty-two minutes, fifty-three seconds." Daisy pulled out the lone *salwar kameez* on the rack, an offensively florescent orange number with green and brown embroidery. "And I didn't call you because it wasn't real. Besides, it's only for a year. The company will be saved. I'll have my space back. My friends will have their jobs. Dad and the aunties will think I'm a lost cause, and they'll leave me to a peaceful single life."

"Life isn't that neat and tidy," Layla warned. "You have to be prepared for curveballs. Look what happened to me. I came home from New York thinking I'd be single forever and instead I married the man who irritated me most in the world."

"I have control over this situation," Daisy said. "You didn't. Nothing unexpected is going to happen."

"Ladies." A deep, loud, familiar voice boomed through the store and Daisy turned to see Liam walking toward her clad in head-to-toe black leather, the only white face in a sea of brown.

"As I was saying . . ." Layla smirked. "You get involved with Liam, you need to be prepared for curveballs."

"Layla." Liam inclined his head. "Nice to see you again. It's been a long time. You look just as pissed at me as I expected you would be, but no less beautiful."

"That's exactly how I feel," she retorted. "It's funny how, after ten years, my loathing for you has not faded in the least, so you can turn off the charm."

"This is all me, sweetheart." He held his arms wide, a motorcycle helmet in one hand. "The charm doesn't get turned on. It's just there." He winked as two young women passed by, sending them into a fit of giggles.

Daisy finally found her tongue. "What are you doing here? You're twenty-three minutes early."

Liam pulled out his phone and turned it around to show her the spreadsheet she'd sent him. "I received your draft dating plan and I was so overwhelmed with excitement at the prospect of discussing it with you, I just couldn't wait. I swung by your office and asked Rochelle if she knew where I could find you."

"Of course you did," Daisy muttered under her breath making a mental note to find out how Rochelle knew where she was when she wasn't at work.

"She's a *very* accommodating woman." He shrugged off his jacket.

Daisy recoiled in horror. "Did you sleep with her?"

"Of course not. I don't fish in the company pond." A slow, sensual smile spread across his face. "Not unless the fish bite."

"How delightfully crass." Layla slung a few outfits over her arm. "You picked a real winner, Daisy. Congratulations."

Daisy bristled. "It's not real."

"Thank God for that."

Her muscles tensed, and she bounced a curved knuckle against her mouth. "Is there a problem with the dating plan?"

Liam scrolled through his phone. "Date #1: Buy wedding outfits. Not my favorite thing, but okay. Date #2: The Dosa Palace restaurant. Not a problem. I like to eat and I like Indian food. But Date #3 . . ."

Daisy let out the breath she hadn't known she was holding. "What about Date #3?"

"Dinner at Puke. That's a big no."

"It's pronounced the way it's spelled," Daisy said coldly. "Pewque. And what's wrong with it?"

"I checked out the menu," Liam said. "I can't get excited about a faux-rustic meal of fromage-frisée, bone-gel bream, and liver-sauced jowl."

"I see you haven't changed." Layla's voice dripped sarcasm. "Once an ass. Always an ass."

"That's what I thought when I read the house special for this week," Liam said. "It doesn't matter if you house-ferment, dehydrate, and then pulverize your eel. Sprinkle it on your pigeon roulade and it's still going to be eel."

"I'm going to check the racks near the front." Layla narrowed her gaze at Liam. "Try and be nice. I know it's an effort, but if you hurt her—"

"Are you threatening me?" Liam's lips quivered at the corners. "You're only half my size."

"There are many ways to hurt a man," Layla said quietly. "And our choir does need a new soprano . . ."

"She's changed," Liam said, after she'd gone. "She used to be so . . ." He shrugged. "Actually, she hasn't changed at all."

"You could have just sent me a message to let me know you wanted to change some things around." Daisy moved to look at the beautiful lehenga, glistening with beads and jewels.

"I thought it would be better to say 'no fucking way' as soon as possible." He leaned against a pillar, his biceps bulging in a most distracting way beneath the sleeves of his T-shirt.

"Do you swear to shock me, or are those words part of your normal vocabulary?" She couldn't let him know his physical presence was doing strange things to her stomach, so she feigned an intense study of the beading on the nearest salwar suit.

"I swear when I get a list of dates that includes things I would never do at places I would never go." He leaned in, so close she could smell the leather of his jacket and the rich scent of his cologne. "For example, Date #4 is a movie. Two hours of sitting in the dark not getting to know each other. What about a bar or club? Somewhere fun."

Heat flooded her face. "It's not just any old movie. If you'd looked at column *J*, you'd see I'd planned for us to see *Pufferfish*, an acclaimed Belgian absurdist dystopian black comedy that challenges us to be bored while refusing to be boring."

"Yawn." Liam tapped his hand over his mouth. "I'm bored already. No need to be challenged."

"Clearly I expected too much."

Far from being insulted, Liam just laughed. "The only reason men agree to movie dates is so they have a chance at getting to second base in the dark. So unless you want a little loving between the seats—"

"I'll cross the movie off the list," she said quickly, although her mouth had gone dry and all she could think about was Liam in the dark with his hands under her clothes.

"Appreciated."

"What about Date #5: coffee?" She pulled out her phone to make the necessary adjustments.

"People don't get to know each other over coffee," Liam said. "It's like trying to get to know someone while they're brushing their teeth. It's a non-activity. You walk into the café. You order your venti seven-pump vanilla soy twelve-scoop matcha 180-degree no-foam green-tea latte. I order a simple filter coffee with cream and sugar and send the world of overpriced designer drinks into a tailspin. We make awkward, banal conversation with the fifty other people who are waiting for the newbie barista to figure out how to steam the milk while her colleagues gossip over at the panini press. By the time we get our drinks, there is nowhere to sit. So we say goodbye and drink our now cold coffees alone. Fun."

"When did you become so hard and bitter?"

"When I realized I didn't fit in. So, around three years old."

He wasn't joking, she realized, but his absent expression made her wonder if he even knew what he'd said. She decided against sharing that she also knew what it felt like to be an outsider, and brought him back to the plan instead. "Fine. No coffee. What would you like to do instead?"

"Oh. I get a choice?" He feigned shock, thudding his hand against his chest. "In that case, let's have a sports night, and don't even think about shaking your head because I know for a fact that you like sports."

"I like to *watch* sports, not play them. If you remember, I'm lacking in body awareness."

Liam's voice dropped to a sensual purr. "I'm very aware of your sexy body, so that's not a problem."

He thinks I'm sexy. She shoved that delicious little nugget away to savor later. "Fine, you can have your sports. What about Date #6? You can't possibly have any objection to a walk."

"We're walking now. What amusing anecdotes will this delightful date provide?"

"Daisy, who is this?" Deepa Rao, Layla's cousin on her mother's side, and second-in-command at the store, intercepted them between the salwar suits and the *sherwanis.*

"This is Liam." She didn't give his last name in case his identity got through to her father in Belize before she could share the big news that she was engaged to the man who had broken her heart. The Patel gossip mill worked faster than the Internet. "My . . ." She stumbled over the word. "Fiancé."

Liam reached out to shake Deepa's hand after Daisy introduced them, turning up his megawatt smile. Daisy bit back a laugh when his charm offensive didn't produce the usual results. Deepa was resistant to anything except the sound of money.

"This must be the boy Salena told me about." Deepa's eyes glittered. "I was wondering when you'd be coming in to buy your wedding outfits." She pulled out her tape measure and wrapped it around Liam's chest.

Daisy felt a sudden irrational stab of jealousy as Deepa's hands slid over Liam's pecs. Why did Deepa get to touch him, and not her? "Actually, Deepa, he just needs a tux. He's not—"

"I have the perfect outfit for you," Deepa said, cutting Daisy off. "Quiet and understated, yet powerful and strong. It's Burma ivory with Banarasi silk, yarn-dyed and hand-spun to create a soft and luxurious quilt. The Bengal-tiger buttons are circled with Japanese cultured pearls. Perfect for a man of your size and stature. It's got a magnificent shawl made of the highest quality *chikankari* with a *zardosi* border. And, of course, you'll want a sword."

"Sword?" Liam brightened.

Deepa's eyes gleamed. "I'll go get a sample. I know the perfect one."

"The sword won't go down so well at city hall," Daisy muttered under her breath. "They don't think too highly of concealed weapons. You'll probably get arrested. Although, I have to admit it sounds kind of exciting being married to a criminal."

A maelstrom of emotions flickered across his face, and then they were gone. Moments later he was back to his teasing self. "I have a concealed weapon in my pocket I could show you," he whispered.

"Don't you dare . . ." She trailed off when he pulled a small penknife out of his pocket. Small and sleek, it had a wood inlay that had been worn smooth in the middle.

"My grandfather gave it to me when I was a boy." His face softened and his eyes misted the tiniest bit. "I always keep it with me."

She was touched by his fondness for his grandfather and the rare glimpse into his more serious side. "It's a lovely memento."

Deepa returned a few moments later holding up an exquisite sherwani, the material of the long, coatlike garment so soft and fine it glittered in the overhead light.

"It's beautiful," Liam said. "I'll try it on."

"I'll get a pajama pant and shoes," Deepa said.

"I didn't bring you here to buy an expensive sherwani for a ten-minute civil ceremony," Daisy said as they walked over to the changing room. "It was more for Layla and her relatives to see you so they could spread gossip about our engagement. You can just rent a tux."

Liam's jaw tightened. "It's my fake wedding. I want to dress how I want to dress."

Five minutes later, Liam was out and preening in front of the mirror. "How do I look? Amazing, right? Why do men always wear tuxes when they could wear something like this?" He waved Layla over. "Take a picture of us. Let's see how we look together. We can use it for our fake dating portfolio."

Daisy stood stiffly beside Liam for the picture, trying to resist the urge to run a hand over the hard biceps bulging beneath soft embroidered silk. With an exasperated grumble, Liam wrapped his arm around her and pulled her into his side. He was warm and solid, his arm firm around her waist. Something inside her loosened and sighed.

"Don't you look like the perfect fake couple." Layla took the phone Liam offered. "I'll try to take a picture before Liam runs away." She managed to snap a few shots and glare at the same time.

"Don't forget your sword." Deepa returned with a curved thirty-five-inch sword in a decorated gold and red velvet scabbard, the handle of which depicted a golden leopard mid-roar. "This sword signifies the true glory of a king of the jungle who is brave, courageous, fearless, and protective of his family."

Liam grinned. "It's perfect."

"She's laying it on pretty thick," Daisy whispered to Layla.

"It's because she knew she had a sale the minute she said 'sword.'" Layla shook her head in exasperation. "The same thing happened when I came here with Sam to try on shoes. He already had a wedding outfit, and yet the moment she said 'sword,' another five hundred dollars was gone. What is it with men and weapons?"

"The scabbard is ornamentally decorated to demonstrate masculine vigor." Deepa pulled the sword from the sheath. "As you can see, the blade is beautifully etched with intricate designs."

Liam took the blade, hefting it as if he were an expert swordsman. "It's lighter than it looks."

A sly smile spread across Deepa's face. Daisy could almost hear the cash register ring. "If you want something larger and more substantial, I have just the thing."

Liam's breath hitched. "You have a *bigger* sword?"

Before Daisy could protest, Deepa was heading to the storeroom, leaving Liam armed and dangerous.

"*En garde!*" He took up a fencing position, knees bent, legs apart, sword tip resting at the nearest mannequin's throat.

"Oh my God." Daisy covered her burning face with her hand. "Kill me now."

Layla shook her head. "It's not you he's planning to kill."

Daisy looked up in time to see Liam attack the mannequin, slashing at its clothes with the edge of his blade. He danced around, thrusting and slicing from all sides, muttering to himself as if the mannequin were alive.

"You dare to look at my lady? Cower before me, you dog, before I slit your throat."

"What's going on here?" Layla's fiancé, Sam, joined them in the aisle. Tall, dark, and deadly handsome, he and Daisy had butted heads when they'd first met, but he'd won her over with his love for Layla and the respect he'd shown their family.

"That's Daisy's—"

"On the left!" Sam shouted. "He's got a knife."

"Don't encourage him." Daisy glared at Sam. "Liam. Stop. What are you doing?"

"He insulted your honor." Liam lifted the sword high and sliced down in a long arc. The mannequin crashed to the ground, its head rolling across the floor and under a rack of clothes.

"Yes!" Sam held up his hand and Liam gave him a high five with a loud slap.

Laughter bubbled up in Daisy's throat. She'd never seen this side of Liam. Although part of her was cringing, another part was drawn to his delight.

"Sam, this is Daisy's fake fiancé, Liam Murphy." Clearly unimpressed, Layla scowled. "Liam, this miscreant is my real fiancé, Sam Mehta."

"You won't be fake for long." Sam shook Liam's hand. "Once you're part of the Patel family, they don't let you go, and I mean that in the best possible way."

"Liam was my brother's best friend. He's got some idea about the Patel charm." Daisy tugged Liam away when she saw Deepa coming, but she was too late. Liam had seen her, too.

"Now that's a sword!"

"The larger one is more effective against unarmed foes." Ever the consummate salesperson, Deepa neatly stepped over the fallen mannequin and handed Liam the sword.

Liam drew the blade from its pearl-encrusted sheath and inspected the design. "I'll take it."

"It's almost as long as my sword." Sam said smugly.

"Seriously? Now you're comparing sword lengths." Layla grabbed Sam's arm. "You do not need a new sword-wielding best friend. Come and try on your shoes."

Daisy followed Liam to the cash register. "This is crazy. First of all, you didn't follow the plan. Second, you don't just walk into a store and buy a sherwani. You need to research them first. You have no idea what it's worth or how much it might cost at another store, and you didn't ask the price. That's like shouting from the rooftops that you have money to burn, and I can guarantee Deepa will be more than happy to accommodate you."

"If you were really getting married," Liam said, "is it something you would want your groom to wear?"

She didn't have to look at the sherwani. When she'd imagined her wedding, it had always included the beautiful and elaborate Indian wedding outfits she'd admired as a girl. "Yes."

"Then I'll wear it."

She felt a curious, melty sensation inside but quickly pushed it away. Time to change the subject because she definitely didn't want to remember *that* Liam—the Liam from before who'd been kind and thoughtful and caring. "Whatever." She waved a dismissive hand. "It's your fake wedding."

Liam's face shuttered, and in a second he wore his bad-boy persona again. "It comes with a sword, I'll be happy to pay whatever she asks."

"Don't say that so loudly," she warned.

"Why? Nothing is too good for my fake bride."

Wednesday, 6:49 P.M.

DAISY: Confirming Rescheduled Date #2. Wed. 7:00 p.m.
The Dosa Palace restaurant. El Camino Real. Objective:
finish discussing dating plan, meet my cousin Amina.

LIAM: Why are you texting a confirmation when I'm
standing beside you in line?

DAISY: I'm annoyed. We were supposed to finalize the plan
in the clothing store.

LIAM: I can't help that I got hungry and Sam mentioned
there was a great restaurant right across the street. I call
that killing two birds with one stone.

DAISY: I'd like to kill something right now and it's not a bird.

LIAM: I like this new dark and violent side of you. What
would you do if I marked up your spreadsheet?

DAISY: You wouldn't dare.

Liam looked up from his phone. They were standing in line
inside the restaurant and Daisy hadn't spoken to him since she'd
agreed to have their Date #2 dinner right after Date #1.

Run-down on the outside, with the ambiance of a noisy cafete-
ria inside, the Dosa Palace had no ostentatious decorations, and no

fake statutes or paintings on the wall. Sam had said the restaurant was all about the food, and since Liam was all about eating, it was a perfect place for a starving man.

"Did you seriously just say that to me?" he teased.

Daisy had dared him to do lots of things over the years, from jumping off the roof to hiding under Sanjay's bed, and he'd never failed to do them.

"I didn't say it," she snapped. "I texted it."

"Since you're so quick with the texts, you could have provided me with a little help when I was negotiating the price of my sherwani. I can't believe how badly Deepa tried to rip me off."

"Are you sulking?" She stared at him, incredulous. "The big venture capitalist who just closed the company's fourth fund at $350 million is sulking because he was bested at negotiating the purchase of a traditional Indian wedding outfit for a fake wedding that will last ten minutes by a frail sixty-year-old woman for whom English is a second language?"

"She wasn't frail." Liam hadn't given much thought to what he would wear for their quick civil ceremony. Good Irish boys wore a three-piece suit or a tux to their wedding with a green cravat or tie and maybe the addition of gold harp cuff links. But he'd never been a good Irish boy—at least not according to his father—and although the marriage was a sham, he liked the idea of honoring Daisy's culture. The sword was just a bonus.

"What are you going to have?" Daisy asked as they approached the cashier. "I recommend the *dosas* and *uthapams*. The *upma* is a little bland, but the *idli*, *vada*, *sambar*, and chutneys are all good. The *kesari* is quite good, too, if you want sweet instead of spicy."

"I'll have the pork vindaloo. Extra hot." He puffed out his chest. He'd acquired a taste for Indian food after the years he'd spent sharing meals at the Patel home, although he hadn't had food as good in many years.

"It's too hot for me the way they make it," Daisy said. "I wouldn't even consider asking them to raise the heat."

"I ate at your house every night and your dad made his curry extra hot. I miss that burn."

Daisy's lips quirked at the corners. "He said it was extra hot so he didn't crush your ego, but in fact he kept the heat down when you were around. What he called 'extra hot' is actually a restaurant mild. His real extra hot would blow your mind."

"You don't scare me," Liam said. "I'm not changing my mind."

"Stubborn and ungrateful." Daisy smirked. "I'm going to enjoy listening to your screams of pain."

"Is that your idea of a good date? Screams of pain?"

She smiled, amused. "I don't date often. I usually just hook up with someone for the night. Orson was an unfortunate aberration that happened when I was feeling emotionally fragile after Layla and Sam got engaged."

They reached the cash desk and Daisy placed her order with the cashier, a young woman of around eighteen with long, straight dark hair.

"So you hook up with strangers?" Liam asked in a hushed whisper as the cashier rang up their order. "Were you with someone last night?"

"Yes. His name is Max." She pulled out her phone. "I have a selfie of us together." She held it up for the cashier to see, keeping the screen away from Liam's line of vision.

"Oh, he's gorgeous," the cashier said. "He's got the nicest eyes."

"Let me see." Liam felt his protective instincts rise. "Who is he? Max who?"

"He doesn't have a last name."

"Jesus Christ, Daisy," he spluttered. "Does Sanjay know you do this? What about your dad?"

"They know all about Max," Daisy said. "In fact, my dad took a picture of us cuddled together in bed the night before he left on his trip, and the cutest one of Max on my pillow. I bought Max some pajamas but he refused to wear them. He likes to sleep au naturel."

Bile rose in Liam's throat. "And your dad took . . . pictures?"

"Photography is his new hobby. He took some great shots when I was giving Max a bath . . ."

"Stop." Liam held up a hand. "Just . . . I can't. I don't know what's happened to you, but it ends now. We're engaged and that means no more random hookups, no pornographic pictures, and no flashing pictures of strangers in the nude."

"Amina doesn't mind. She's my second cousin." Daisy introduced them before turning her phone around. "And this is Max."

Liam was a heartbeat away from shutting his eyes when his brain registered the picture of a fluffy white dog on a pink duvet.

His tension left him in a rush. "Max is a dog."

"He's a Westie. Layla got him for me as an emotional support dog at a bad time in my life."

Liam bit back the urge to ask Daisy about a time so bad she'd needed extra love. It was her business, and he could only hope she would tell him when she was ready so he could offer his support. "That wasn't funny."

"Amina and I were amused."

"I heard you were engaged." Amina's gaze flicked to Liam and she blushed. "He's almost as cute as Max." They had a brief conversation in Urdu that Liam couldn't follow, but from the way Amina's eyes kept shifting his way, he knew it was about him.

"You should add some raita," Daisy suggested when Liam

handed his credit card to Amina. "Maybe two or three bowls—yogurt and cucumber are the perfect way to soothe the burn."

"I don't need raita," Liam scoffed. "I have a tongue of steel." He flipped his card over his fingers—a party trick he'd learned in high school—making Amina giggle.

"This promises to be an interesting date," Daisy said after he'd paid for his meal. "First, you try to seduce my second cousin, then you're going to burn your mouth out of stubborn pride. What other surprises do you have in store for me?"

Liam gave her a slow smile. "You'll just have to wait and see."

After waiting only five minutes, they were seated at their table. Liam munched on the free *poppadums* while Daisy chatted with the waiter. He'd forgotten how well the Patels were connected. It had been the same with Sanjay. It was a rare occasion that they were out and didn't meet someone his friend knew.

"I took the liberty of ordering you a Kingfisher beer," Daisy said after she finished her conversation. "This date will be a waste of time if you can't talk."

He lifted an eyebrow in censure. "So, what should we discuss since we've already talked about the first half of the dating plan?"

"The second half of the dating plan."

Liam pulled out his phone and sent her the spreadsheet he'd amended while they'd waited in line. "I've sent my changes to you so you can have a visual of what I do and do not like."

Daisy studied her phone, eyes narrowing. "I don't appreciate all my hard work being defaced with juvenile comments." She read off the screen. "'Seriously?' 'Yawn.' 'Snoozefest.' 'WTF.' 'OK Boomer.' And my personal favorite, 'Kill me now.'"

"I tried to be creative." He took a crunchy poppadum off the plate and nibbled the edge.

"I thought I was very accommodating," Daisy said. "I even allowed you to have a sports night. But Magowan's Infinite Mirror Maze? Alcatraz?" She drew in a ragged breath. "We're supposed to be going on dates to get to know each other. How can we talk if we're focused on solving a maze? And who takes a date to Alcatraz?"

"I've always wanted to see the inside of the world's most infamous prison. What if I wind up there one day?"

Daisy snatched a poppadum off the plate and bit into it with an angry crunch. "It's closed."

"Then it won't be hard to escape."

"What about the textile exhibition that's going on right now?" she asked. "Or the Nerd Nite talk on metagrobology? I thought you liked puzzles."

"I liked doing puzzles with you because you could finish them before I could even find the corner pieces," Liam said. "Now my interests veer toward drinking, dancing, sports, motorcycles, gaming, and sex."

She lifted an eyebrow. "We discussed sex."

"I'd like to discuss it some more," he said. "Talking about sex is my second favorite thing next to actually having sex."

Daisy sighed. "We agreed on sports. I'll put that in as Date #3."

"Date #3 has to be meeting my family," he said. "I have relatives who came here for my grandfather's funeral and they'll be leaving soon. It's probably best if you meet everyone at once."

Her face softened. "Of course. I'll put that in. Sports will be Date #4. We should try to get tickets to see a hockey game at the SAP Center. My aunt and uncle and their boys have season tickets and we can arrange to accidentally bump into them, like we just bumped into Amina."

"Go Sharks!" Liam pumped his fist in the air. "I'll handle the tickets."

Daisy's lips curled in a smile. "And since you got what you want, how about a lecture on tamale-making for Date #5?"

Liam shook his head. "No tamales."

"But it would be so interesting. Did you know that San Francisco residents ate twenty-five thousand tamales a week in 1890?"

God, he loved this. If he closed his eyes, he could imagine himself back in the Patel kitchen as Daisy told him all sorts of weird and wonderful facts. Even now, he could remember the height of the world's tallest man, and the size of the world's biggest ball of string.

"I'd eat twenty-five thousand tamales right now if it meant we didn't have to go to the lecture. How about going to a bar for Date #5 instead, and then a motorcycle ride for Date #6?"

"I don't know anything about riding." She bit her bottom lip. "And I don't do that kind of stuff anymore."

"Exciting stuff?"

"Risky stuff. I like to play it safe."

Liam wanted to know why she'd given up the fun things she used to do with her father, but this wasn't the time to ask. Still, there was nothing he loved more, and he desperately wanted to share it with her.

"What if I take you to a motorcycle shop and you can quiz my friend Hamish about safety and bike mechanics, wind velocity, and safety gear? If you're still not comfortable after that, I'll go with you to listen to one hundred years of tamale-making history."

Her face lit up with a smile. "One hundred and thirty-one to be exact, and I agree to both #5 and #6. For Date #7, we'll be meeting my family and my dad to get their approval. And Date #8 isn't really a date, but it can be our wedding. I'll book a time at city hall."

"Vegas," Liam said firmly. "I can't do city hall, even for a fake wedding. It's not me. If I'm spending a small fortune on an outfit and I'm carrying a big-ass sword, I want to get married somewhere it will be appreciated. And I want an Elvis."

"An Elvis?" she repeated.

"He'll be in full costume, and after he says 'You may kiss the bride,' he'll break out his guitar and sing 'A Big Hunk o' Love.'" He sighed and gazed into the distance. "Men have wedding fantasies, too."

Daisy's eyes widened. "Seriously?"

"No." He fought back his laughter. Sometimes Daisy was so literal, it was almost too easy to wind her up. "I think 'Just Pretend' or 'Return to Sender' might be more appropriate."

Daisy stared at him, her expression blank, but he knew what was going on behind those narrowed eyes. She was amused, but afraid to show it.

"'Heartbreak Hotel'?" He was determined to make her smile. "'Crying in the Chapel'? 'Jailhouse Rock'?" He pushed a little harder. "Or how about 'Hard Headed Woman'?"

"'Don't Be Cruel.'" Her lips quivering at the corners, Daisy picked up her phone and tapped on the screen. "One Vegas wedding plus one Elvis. Song: TBA. I'll send you the final spreadsheet."

"Your cold, detached, and calculating approach to dating is a huge turn on," Liam said dryly. "You're lucky we're in a public place. I can barely contain myself."

Their food arrived and Daisy tucked in to her dosas. Liam studied his plate and frowned at the unfamiliar presentation. "Is this—"

"Pork vindaloo. Extra hot. Just the way you wanted it."

Liam scooped up a mouthful of pork, taking a moment to savor the rich, delicate flavors on his tongue.

"Delicious," he said. "And not too hot at all. I might even ask for some extra cayenne."

Daisy stared at him, her lips quivering at the corners. "Wait for it . . ."

Liam lifted his fork for another bite, but even after the warning, he was totally unprepared for the flaming inferno in his mouth.

He gasped, sweat beading on his forehead, pain screaming across his tongue. "Water!"

"Water won't help you." Daisy pushed her raita across the table, clearly trying to contain her laughter. "You need yogurt."

Liam grabbed the bowl and gulped down the yogurt in frantic slurps.

"It's a dip. Not a drink." Laughing now, she snapped a picture of him. "How's the asbestos tongue now?"

"What the fuck was that?" He was at once embarrassed and angry with himself for his stubborn pride.

"Extra hot. Just the way you ordered it. Instead of being so stubborn, you should listen to people who know what they're talking about. It doesn't make you less of a man."

"That's not what my father thought," he said, half to himself. His father never took advice if he thought he could do something himself, whether it was filing false tax returns with the IRS, forging applications for disability benefits, or screwing investors out of their hard-earned cash.

His father also never thought his youngest son was his own flesh and blood. Liam was worthless, stupid, no good, and most definitely less of a man.

He pushed his plate away and soothed his tongue with the remaining spoons of raita. What the hell was wrong with him? He didn't think about the past, and he never talked about his father. "I don't need advice," he said abruptly.

It had taken him a long time to move past his father's emotional abuse, to learn to disregard people's opinions and rely only on himself, to actually feel the confidence he projected to the outside world. But sitting here in front of the smartest, prettiest, sexiest woman he'd ever known—a woman he would never be worthy of having except in a world of pretend dates and fake marriages—he wasn't feeling it at all.

Daisy paused mid bite and frowned. "I just didn't want you to burn your mouth."

"I know what I want," he snapped. "And I wanted it like that."

Her mouth firmed into a straight line and she shrugged. "Okay."

They ate in uncomfortable silence for the next few minutes. Liam mentally cursed himself, and his father, and the chef who had made the dish so spicy he had needed to be warned.

"I'm an ass," he said finally.

Daisy looked up, a pained expression on her face. "I won't disagree with you."

"I'm sorry."

"Apology accepted," she said stiffly.

"My dad passed away a few years ago, but just thinking about him . . ." He hesitated, not wanting to wind himself up again, but desperately needing to clear the air. "Triggers me."

Her face softened. "I can't even imagine how hard it must be. I know a little about what he was like."

Of course she did. She'd been there when his mom had brought him over to her house, his arm in a cast, his face swollen from the worst beating he'd ever had. He'd seen her on the stairs while their parents talked, her bare feet peeking out of her pink nightdress, a stuffed rabbit in her arms. He'd found the rabbit on his bed when her father had taken him up to Sanjay's room, and it had been a great comfort in the darkest hours of the night.

He took another bite of his vindaloo, savored the punishing burn. "I've ruined our second date," he said, his eyes watering.

Daisy offered him his beer. "It's okay. Talking about triggers and personal issues was one of the objectives for our dates. We're just ahead of schedule."

He waved away the glass. "I'm going to eat the entire dish. No raita. No beer. I deserve the pain."

Daisy laughed. "I didn't know you were a masochist. Lucky for you, I don't enjoy seeing you suffer. I ordered extra food in case we needed it."

"If this were a real second date, would we have had a third?" He leaned forward, studying her intently for even the faintest sign of forgiveness. "I thought I did pretty well at the beginning. On time. Scintillating conversation. Objectives not just fulfilled, but exceeded because now we're ahead of schedule. Abject apology when I screwed up—many men have trouble with that—and I was willing to inflict mortal injury to my tongue to make it up to you."

"Liam?"

"Yes?"

She pushed her plate of dosas toward him. "It doesn't matter if it isn't real."

But it did matter. More than he cared to admit.

· 13 ·

DAISY'S Thursday morning was taken up with sprint plans, bug counts, and daydreaming while Andrew droned on during the weekly team meeting.

Last night's dinner had almost been a total disaster. She'd let her guard down, and for a while she'd almost forgotten it wasn't real. Liam's antics with the sword in the dress shop had made her laugh and she'd enjoyed teasing him in the restaurant. His sudden change in demeanor had been the wake-up call she needed. It would be too easy to fall for Liam, too hard to get hurt again.

Liam had never once indicated he felt anything more than brotherly affection for her. She was still the nerdy geek who'd spent lunches in the science lab, and Liam was still the guy who'd dated the most beautiful girls in the school. Daisy had watched them from the window when he came to pick up Sanjay, and wondered how it felt to be so thin you could disappear between two blades of grass, and what they would do when faced with a summer of desi weddings where you had to starve yourself at the beginning of the week so you could eat for three straight days.

Not that she wasn't attractive—she was comfortable with her body, right down to the chipped front tooth that had come from taking a line drive to the face on the baseball diamond—but she and Liam were from two different worlds. Except for their childhood wounds, they shared nothing but memories, a love for video games, and good taste in black leather boots.

Stop thinking about him. She shifted in her chair, trying to push away the memory of how warm and solid he'd felt against her when he'd kissed her at the conference, and his sharp intake of breath when she'd kissed him back . . .

"Daisy." Josh gave her a nudge. "The meeting's over."

She sighed and pushed the fantasy away. "I need another coffee. Andrew's talks always put me to sleep."

"He told us to stay put. Tyler's having a meeting with Marketing and Design and he wants us to be here. He said something about another website redesign."

"Not again." She tipped her head back and groaned.

Mia and Zoe joined them as the rest of the marketing team filed in, taking the empty seats beside Daisy.

"I hope this doesn't take long." Zoe checked her watch. "I have Lily at an emergency day care in the Mission. Our babysitter was sick again. I need to find something else."

"I talked to my aunt about Lily," Daisy said. "She's an elementary school teacher and she's off for the summer. She looks after my dog, Max, and she said she'd be happy to help you out until school starts again. I'll give you her number."

"Oh my God. That would be amazing!" Zoe waved a hand in front of her face as her eyes teared. "You can't imagine the stress. Tyler's been so good to me, but I feel like I'm taking advantage."

"And I've got a number for you, too." Daisy handed a business card to Mia. "I've got a cousin who works at an addiction center. They do really good work with addicts and their families. They have a long waiting list but he owed me a favor, so if you're interested you can give him a call."

"I've tried pretty much everything to help her," Mia said. "But I'll definitely get in touch. You've got some family."

"I've got a lot of family." Daisy laughed. "Sometimes it's a good thing, but sometimes they can be too involved."

Tyler cleared this throat to quiet the room. He had trimmed his beard, cut his hair, washed his clothes, and even put on a pair of shoes. "I have exciting news. Evolution Ventures has expressed an interest in Organicare. They haven't offered us funding, but they did a business analysis and suggested that we do a rebrand. Liam Murphy has generously offered us the services of Brad Assard, from Assign Design Consultants to make it happen. I'll turn the floor over to Brad to outline his plan, and Liam will be joining us later."

Brad was at least twenty years older than most of the marketing team, and the only person in the room wearing a suit and tie. His dark hair was thinning on top, and his salt-and-pepper sideburns needed a trim.

"Zoe and I recommended a rebrand," Mia whispered as Brad connected his laptop to the projector. "We wanted to move away from the peach packaging to something more edgy."

"Peach." Josh chuckled. "There's some subliminal advertising right there."

Mia groaned. "Do you think about anything other than sex?"

"I like peaches." Josh smiled. "I also like bananas. Does that make me a bad person?"

"Shh. He's going to start."

Brad held up a box of Rapture tampons and the chatter in the room died down. "You have great products here. These pads have the best adhesion and longevity in the market . . ."

"We're off to a bad start if he doesn't know the difference between tampons and pads," Mia murmured. "I definitely don't want tampons with maximum adhesion."

Brad clicked to a picture of Organicare's products on a store shelf. "To gain traction from the younger end of the market we need to bring your packaging into the new millennium. The question is . . ." Brad raised his voice. "What do women want at that time of the month?" He clapped his hands together. "We have the answer."

"Oh yes, please," Daisy muttered. "Mansplain to us what we want at that time of the month."

"We've done some preliminary market research," Brad said. "Women want to feel excited about pulling out a box of menstrual products each month, something to distract them from the unpleasant side effects." He clicked to a slide of a woman standing on a beach with a huge smile on her face and a box of pads in her hand.

Unpleasant side effects. Daisy choked back a snort.

"This is our vision." Brad's next slide featured a woman with long blond hair, dressed only in a piece of pink chiffon, straddling an unsaddled white horse with a pink horn attached to its head. Ribbons fluttering from its mane, the horse galloped through a field of flowers toward a rainbow in a purple sky.

Is he serious? Mia mouthed.

Brad cleared his throat. "What we've come up with is an image, a feeling. It encapsulates the pleasure of having a product that makes a woman feel confident and secure. We'll take a ten-minute break so you can have a good look at the handouts, and then we'll move on to the new logos and website redesign."

"I wouldn't feel secure dressed in a shredded tissue and riding bareback on a horse that's about to jump over a cliff," Mia said as Brad handed out the design packages. "And is she on her period or in heaven? I think he's confused that they're the same thing."

"It's a unicorn." Zoe snorted a laugh. "Or did you think that long thick cylinder on his head was something else? Maybe it's subliminal advertising."

"This is ridiculous." Mia slumped in her chair. "What about the women of color? Or plus-size women? And what about teenagers and young women? Market research shows they don't buy in to the idea of menstruation as taboo. They talk about it. They own it. They aren't ashamed. They need real facts and real products."

"You need to say something," Daisy urged Mia. "You and Zoe are going to be a big part of the redesign and no one knows the products and the market like you."

Mia shook her head. "We can't afford to rock the boat. Tyler wasn't interested in our ideas before; he certainly won't be interested now. He's still talking about making staff cuts. I don't want to give him an excuse to let me go."

Daisy glanced up at Brad and Tyler, busy distributing the handouts. What was Liam thinking sending in this guy? Organicare was supposed to be a forward-thinking company that would make a difference in women's lives.

"I could talk to Liam," she offered.

"Yes!" Mia's face brightened. "I forgot you knew him. Definitely talk to him. See what he can do."

Tyler offered them each a design package featuring additional pictures of nymphlike women and their unicorns. "I haven't had a chance to say congratulations on your engagement," he said to Daisy. "You and Liam . . ."

Oh my God. Daisy froze, her heart pounding so hard she thought she'd break a rib. She'd forgotten Liam was going to tell Tyler about their engagement.

"Wait. What?" Josh scowled. "You're engaged to Liam Murphy and you didn't tell me? You said he used to be your brother's best friend. You said you weren't close."

Daisy's pulse kicked up a notch. She wasn't good on the fly. "We were . . ."

"On a break?" Mia offered.

Daisy shot her a grateful look. "Yes. On a break. A long break. Very long. Years. And then we bumped into each other and it just happened."

"I can't thank you enough," Tyler said. "You saved us. I was at the end of my rope. Total despair."

"I didn't really do anything . . ."

"No need to be shy. Liam told me everything. How you begged him to step in, cooked him his favorite dinner so he would listen to the pitch . . ." He pressed a fist to his lips, overcome with emotion. "That story about spilling the wine was classic. Classic!" He patted her shoulder. "We'll talk later. I have to finish handing these out so Brad can get on with the presentation."

Zoe gave her a hug after Tyler had walked away. "Congratulations!"

"You're engaged!" Mia clapped her hands together. "I'm so happy for you, I could cry."

"You cry at everything," Josh said dryly. "An extra pickle at lunch? Here come the waterworks. Baby shower? River of tears. Someone comes back from vacation? Hysteria. I can't imagine what you'd be like if you watched *My Little Pony*. That scene where Tempest sacrifices herself . . ."

"Don't." Mia held up her hand. "I can't even think about it."

"I still don't understand this." Josh turned his attention back to Daisy. "Last month you hooked up with a fireman and the weekend before that was the car salesman from Freemont. And now, you're getting married? To Liam? Has he seen the collection of Marvel Funko Pops on your desk? Does he even know what the Marvel Universe is?"

Sweat trickled down her back and her throat constricted. She thought she'd assessed all the angles of their fake engagement, but she hadn't even considered her colleagues finding out. "It all just happened so fast. When you know, you know."

"Want to know what I know?" Josh's voice wavered. "A person who schedules everything down to the minute, and is totally allergic to commitment of any kind, does not get married on a whim. It doesn't make sense."

"It's love," Zoe said gently. "Of course it doesn't make sense."

Josh shook his head. "Something doesn't add up."

He was right. Her behavior was inconsistent, and if Josh could see it, her family would see it, too. She needed to think through her plan again. Clearly there was something she'd missed, and the fewer people she had to lie to the better.

"It's not real," she murmured.

"What do you mean, 'it's not real'?" Josh's frown deepened.

"He needs a wife to get an inheritance. I need to get my matchmaking aunties off my back. We made a deal, and part of it was that he would try and help Organicare. It's only for a year, and then we'll be done."

Josh's expression blanched. "Are you serious? You're going to tie yourself to this guy for a year? The one who broke your heart?"

"She's doing it for us," Mia said. "To save the company. Why are you giving her a hard time? She's the best!"

"You said what he did was unforgivable," Josh retorted. "And yet here you are forgiving him."

"It's so romantic." Zoe clasped her hands together. "I love it."

"I didn't forgive him," Daisy rubbed the back of her neck. "We both benefit from this arrangement. That's all there is to it."

And that's all it would ever be. He hadn't wanted her before and he didn't want her now—not the way she'd always imagined. No one wanted someone "weirdly smart" who preferred action figures to dolls, and math puzzles to fairy tales. Her mother had come back after a twelve-year absence to tell her so.

A disturbance at the door caught her attention. Rochelle had just brought Liam into the meeting and was eating him up with her eyes as he shook hands with Brad and Tyler.

Why was it so unbelievable that he would want to marry her? Why did she still hear her mother's voice in her head?

Fake or not, he was her fiancé, and in this game of pretend, a man like him loved a girl like her, and it wasn't okay for Rochelle to be slithering over to steal her man.

Gritting her teeth, she joined him near the door. "Hi . . . ah . . ." What did she call him? Honey? Babe? Darling? ". . . *Humraaz*." The Urdu term of endearment came out before she could stop it.

Liam's gaze shifted to her, and his face softened. Before he could ask her what it meant and ruin the performance, she rose up on her toes, pressed her hands against his chest, and kissed him.

Without hesitation, Liam wrapped one arm around her waist, pressed his mouth against hers, and bent her over backward in a full-on movie kiss.

Her breath hitched and her lips softened. His lips were firm and cool and tasted of coffee and something sweet. He slipped his tongue into her mouth and for a moment she thought her heart had stopped. But it didn't matter. Upside down, in front of her work colleagues, she was the woman she always wanted to be.

Then she was up and back on her feet, lips tingling, an ache of desire between her thighs.

"What does it mean?" he murmured gently.

"The one with whom we share our secrets."

"Then I am your humraaz," he said. "And you are mine."

·14·

Friday, 11:06 P.M.

DAISY: Confirming Date #3. Saturday 6 p.m. Liam's grandfather's house, Richmond. Objective: Meet Liam's family.

LIAM: Why are you home at 11 p.m. on a Friday night?

DAISY: Why are you assuming I'm home? Maybe I'm out having sex with a hot MMA fighter.

LIAM: Who the hell is this guy? Did you tell him you're engaged?

DAISY: I thought that might scare him away.

Friday, 11:20 P.M.

LIAM: Is he still there?

DAISY: Who?

LIAM: The MMA fighter who's having sex with my fiancée.

DAISY: There was no MMA fighter. Max and I are watching Fight Club on Netflix.

LIAM: Will I get to meet Max?

DAISY: Yes. If Max doesn't like you, it's all over.

LIAM: I'll bring treats.

DAISY: He can't be bribed.

LIAM: Everyone has a weakness.

DAISY: What's yours?

LIAM: You.

Friday, 11:30 P.M.

LIAM: You forgot to call me humraaz.

DAISY: I just said it for show. No one is around to hear it now.

LIAM: Say it anyway.

DAISY: Good night, humraaz.

"YOU haven't touched your drink."

Liam looked up from his phone, momentarily disoriented. He'd come to the Rose & Thorn after work with James and their three new staff hires for a little get-to-know-each-other drink, but now he was sitting at the end of the bar alone.

"Your drink." Rainey pointed to the pint of Guinness in front of him. "You wasted a good head and it's getting warm."

Liam looked around and spotted James and their new employees on the dance floor, swinging each other around as the live band played a fifties jive.

"Who were you texting? Never seen you so focused." She cleared away the empty glasses from the counter beside him.

"The woman I told you about. Daisy."

Rainey froze. "Not the one you stood up for prom?"

On instinct, Liam threw up a hand in case Rainey decided to slap him again. "She agreed to be my fake fiancée."

"Did she hit her head or something? Does her father need medical treatment and you agreed to pay the bills? Was the bank about to foreclose on the house that's been in her family for generations and you talked to the bank manager who's a friend of yours? Or did you just pay her a shitload of money?"

Liam half rose from his seat, Daisy's own words on his lips. "She's not a hooker, Rainey."

"Well, you must have offered her something pretty amazing because last time you were here, you said she hated you, and now she's agreed to be your wife."

He settled back down, still wary of a sudden attack. "She gets her matchmaking relatives off her back, and I help her company get back on its feet. It's purely a business arrangement."

"Are you sure about that?" Rainey gestured to his phone. "You've been smiling at your phone for the last half hour. Your team hit the dance floor and you didn't even know they'd gone. Maybe you've fallen for your fake fiancée."

Liam took a breath to speak, then released it. Considered a dozen different explanations for why he'd been more focused on texting Daisy than getting to know his staff, then rejected them. "I'm sure." He took a sip of the rich, thick Guinness, letting the malty sweetness and hoppy bitterness slide over his tongue. Usually he drank his Guinness as a whiskey chaser, but James had ordered the first round before he arrived. "We're meeting my family tomorrow and she was just confirming the details."

Nothing had changed in the last ten years. Daisy was still Sanjay's little sister. She was still smart, beautiful, and funny, and her ability to bring order to chaos still made him feel like his world wasn't spinning out of control. She'd taken his half-baked idea to save the distillery and made it real. She got his jokes, and nothing made him feel as good as when she smiled. He just hoped that the man who would one day win her heart would be both worthy and appreciative of what he had.

"How was the Death Race over the weekend?" he asked into the silence of her stare.

"You're changing the subject, but I'll tell you anyway." She held up her arm and pointed to a fresh, white bandage. "I finished it in record time. Got my tattoo from *the* Bobby Tam. He doesn't just do ink, he creates masterpieces. I'm keeping it hidden until it's perfectly healed. I can hardly wait to show it off."

"I look forward to the big reveal."

Rainey poured two shots of whiskey and pushed one toward him. "How does she feel about you?"

Of course Rainey wouldn't let it go. Once her curiosity was piqued, she'd keep at him until he told her the truth—if he even knew what that was. "I don't know."

Two weeks ago, he would have had a different answer. But two fake dates later, he wasn't so sure. They'd laughed together, swapped stories about the past, and teased each other like they'd done before. And that kiss. So unexpected . . . so sweet . . . and so damn hot. He'd felt passion in her kiss, awakening a longing inside him that had never truly died. And from the flush in her cheeks when he'd finally let her go, he knew she'd felt it, too.

"Well, she obviously doesn't hate you, or she wouldn't have agreed to your crazy plan." Rainey sipped from her glass and licked her lips. "And you very clearly don't hate her. The question is: Are you doing this to appease your conscience, to save the distillery, or to get the girl?"

Liam tipped his head back and groaned. "It doesn't matter. Even if I wanted something more than a fake relationship, at some point she'll want an explanation for what happened between us in the past, and it will all be over. I made a promise to keep a secret, and the truth would tear her family apart."

"I wouldn't be so sure." Rainey pulled down a bottle of Glenmorangie. "Families are stronger than you think."

"How would you know?"

She unscrewed the bottle. "I've seen it on TV."

"YOU'RE spoiling him." Daisy shook her head when she saw a plump pakora in Max's bowl. "What am I going to do when Max has to go back to Doggie Daycare in the fall? He'll turn his nose up at normal dog food."

"Spoiling pets and nieces and nephews is an auntie's job." Mehar Auntie handed Daisy a plate of Indian sweets. She had finished the choreography for one of Layla's wedding dances, and Daisy had offered to help them rehearse before her date with Liam.

"Try these." Mehar Auntie plucked a jalebi from the plate. "I've been in the kitchen all afternoon. I thought I'd bring some treats to our dance class." Short and round, and blessed with an amazing sense of rhythm, Mehar was the family dance queen, hogging every *sangeet* pre-wedding party with her well-rehearsed dance moves. She and Daisy taught Bollywood dancing together at the local recreation center, both as a fun cardio workout and a way to connect to the Indian culture.

"I'm meeting Liam's family tonight." Daisy nibbled the jalebi. Fragrant with rose water and spices and dripping with heavy, sweet syrup, the spiral-shaped orange treats were her favorite Indian dessert. "Can I bring some to share?"

Mehar Auntie sniffed her displeasure. "The boy should meet the girl's family first."

"I couldn't have a family gathering without Dad."

"I'm with you two times a week," she huffed. "You didn't say anything about him." Mehar Auntie turned away. "I thought I was the favorite auntie, but you let Salena meet him first."

Daisy put down the plate and her treat to give her aunt a hug. "Don't be like that, Auntie-ji. Of course you're my favorite. Meeting Salena Auntie was an accident. If I hadn't bumped into her, I would have told you first."

Slightly mollified, Mehar Auntie sighed. "Take some sweets then. Maybe they will like them; maybe not. Who knows? We know nothing about this family. Not even their name."

Layla arrived while Mehar Auntie was packing up the sweets. She shooed them into the living room with steaming cups of chai while she cleaned up, and they settled on the couch with Max curled up between them. Mehar Auntie's taste veered toward the traditional, with dark wood furniture and brightly colored fabrics.

"How are things with the fake fiancée?" Layla asked.

"I kissed him."

Layla froze, her cup halfway to her mouth. "Are you serious?"

"It was just for show." She gave an absent shrug. "Tyler told my friends at the office that we were engaged. Mia and Zoe were happy for me, but Josh couldn't believe someone like Liam would want to marry someone like me. I got a bit irritated, and then when Rochelle brought him in and was clearly just waiting to make a move, something snapped inside me."

Layla sighed. "Stories like this never end well."

"So I kissed him," Daisy continued. "But he took it a step further and bent me right over backward like they do in the movies . . ."

"Oh no." Layla put down her cup. "Do not fall for that. You saw what he was like in high school. You know that move. Remember Becky Evans? And Maria Lopez? He dipped them, slept with them, and dropped them. Even after he broke it off, they hung around his locker like lovesick sheep."

Daisy stroked Max's fluffy head. "I'm not a lovesick sheep. It was just . . . He understood that I needed to make a point and I didn't have to explain."

"All he understands is how to get a woman into bed. If he has to bend you over in the middle of your office, then that's what he's going to do."

"We have rules," Daisy said. "No sex."

"Be careful with him," Layla warned. "That's all I'm saying. He broke your heart once. Don't let him to do it again."

· 15 ·

LIAM slowed his motorcycle outside his grandfather's ranch-style house in Richmond, pulling up to the curb where Daisy was waiting beside a bright red Mini.

She tapped her watch as he pulled off his helmet. "You're two minutes and thirty-seven seconds late."

"I wanted to make an entrance."

Daisy laughed. "If you want to make an entrance when we meet my family, you'll need to do better than that. Two minutes would be considered ill-mannered and early. An hour late is right on time."

In her family, people didn't just get together for weddings and funerals. They were involved in each other's lives. They would know if someone was being abused and would step in to help, unlike his father's side of the family, who had never once reached out to his mom. It was one of the reasons he hadn't made an effort to reconnect with them after his dad passed away. Forgiveness wasn't easy when he couldn't forget.

"I brought Indian sweets." She held up a pink cardboard box. "Mehar Auntie made them this afternoon. I was tempted to eat them all myself, but Layla convinced me to share."

"How is Layla?" He secured his helmet to the back of his bike.

"Very skeptical of you and your motives."

He bit back a chuckle. "I would expect nothing less. She always had your back."

"So this is your motorcycle." Daisy walked a full circle around his bike.

"That's my baby." He patted the dark brown seat. "It's a Ducati XDiavel S in liquid concrete gray with black mechanics."

"It's beautiful."

"You're beautiful." The words dropped from his lips before he could stop them. She was wearing a cherry red dress with white polka dots that hugged all her curves and dipped low at the top, giving him a delicious glimpse of the soft swell of her breasts.

"Thank you." Her gaze dropped and she pulled her phone out of a small red purse that matched her shoes.

Liam had never thought much about a woman's shoes before, but Daisy's shoes demanded to be noticed. Curvy and round with bows on top and a high, graceful heel that made his mouth water, they were sweet and sexy all at once—the kind of shoes a man could admire when his lover was bent over his table in her fancy dress, skirt flipped up, and . . . fuck, why had he locked his helmet to his bike?

Shrugging off his leather jacket, he held it discretely in front him and forced his mind back to the conversation because, holy hell, when had he ever let his Daisy fantasies get this out of control?

"Not bad reviews for the XDiavel." She read off her screen. "'Brave, irreverent, and unconventional.' 'So good to be bad.' 'Powerful.' 'Muscular.' 'Imposing front.' 'Strong and restless.'" She snorted a laugh. "Did you match the motorcycle to your personality or was it the other way around?"

Liam's chest puffed with pride. "It called to me in the showroom."

Daisy laughed. "Imagine that."

It was the laugh he remembered, the deep, throaty chuckle that warmed him inside. For a moment he allowed himself to imagine her on his bike, arms locked around his waist, chest pressed up against his back, her thighs curved against his hips. He imagined riding with her until they ran out of road, leaving the past behind them.

Maybe Rainey was right. Maybe he had fallen for his fake fiancée. And there wasn't a damn thing he could do about it except keep playing the game.

"Who are we meeting today?" Daisy asked. "I like to be prepared."

"A mix of great-aunts and great-uncles who came from Ireland for the funeral, and relatives who live nearby." He rattled off a list of names. "You'll know my aunts Roisin and Fiona right away because they're always fighting, and usually they'll drag my uncle Fitz into it. Great-Uncle Seamus is a bit of character. He was only here a few days and managed to stir up trouble flirting with the neighbor's wife. Brendan will be there with his wife, Lauren, and his son, Jaxon, and there might be a few others . . ."

"Don't look so concerned." Daisy tapped her head. "I've got this. Every name is in the mental vault, and I've got our talking points on my phone in case you didn't read them."

Puzzled, he frowned. "What talking points?"

"They're going to ask us questions about our relationship," Daisy said. "I was caught off guard at work when Tyler blurted out the news of our engagement, and I don't want it to happen again. I wrote out the story of how we met in an e-mail, as well as the answers to other questions they might ask, and sent it to you. As I suspected, you didn't read it."

Liam grimaced. "I get a lot of e-mails . . ."

Her free hand found her hip. "Is that supposed to be an apology?"

"Yes?" Despite Daisy's obvious annoyance, he felt a curious

sense of peace wash over him. He'd been worried about this get-together, but Daisy clearly had everything under control. Just as she had done in the past, she took all the chaos and made it calm.

"It better be or you're suddenly going to find yourself without a fiancée." She pressed her lips together and glared. "You should read it before we go in so you know how we met."

"I thought we met at a tech conference a few weeks ago after you bumped into me with an armload of stolen pads," he teased.

"I didn't steal them," Daisy gritted out. "And we can't say that because we're supposed to have met months ago. I came up with a story about how we met at a bus stop during a rainstorm. Kissing in the rain is the ultimate cinematic symbol of uncontrollable passion. It's the moment when the audience willingly accepts that the characters' love is so intense that they don't even notice they are getting wet."

"Someone has been reading too many art house film reviews." With one hand on her lower back, Liam walked her to the front door. "Just so I understand, we met again after ten years, and instead of the usual catch-up, we threw ourselves at each other in a passionate kiss, so instantly and intensely in love we didn't even notice the rain?" He shook his head. "It doesn't make sense."

"No kiss. I'll make it clear in the story." She handed him the box of sweets to type on her phone.

Liam leaned over to look at her screen. "Also make it clear that I don't take the bus, so I would never be at a bus stop."

"You were sheltering there."

Liam frowned. "Why would I run to a bus stop instead of going into a building?"

"Because there were no buildings." She tipped her head back in exasperation. "Why are you making this so difficult?"

"Where is this bus stop in the middle of nowhere?" Liam continued, enjoying the chance to ruffle her feathers. "Why would I be somewhere that only has a bus stop and no buildings? And why am I out in the rain?"

"I don't know." Daisy's voice rose in pitch. "You're supposed to be the one with the imagination. Not me. I can't make things up on the spot. That story took me hours to create."

"Why don't we tell people the truth?" he suggested. "After losing touch for ten years, we met at a work conference—they don't need to know which one. You realized who I was and—"

"I ran away." Her lips curved in a smile as they reached the door.

"Then I chased you," Liam said. "I caught you because I am bigger and faster . . ."

"And I called for the security guard and had you arrested." She tucked her phone away, her eyes sparkling with amusement. "They took you to the police station and charged you with threatening behavior and assault. They stripped you down, gave you an orange jumpsuit and put you in a holding cell with a bunch of thugs. Things didn't go well for you because the thugs took issue with your handsome face. Vengeance was served. The end."

Liam stared at her, aghast. "For someone with no imagination, that's a pretty detailed story."

"Actually, it's not mine. It's a scene from the Bollywood film *Jail*. I put you in the role of Parag Dixit, who gets jailed for false possession of narcotics and evidence tampering. He is mentally and physically tortured for the entire movie. It's one of my dad's favorites."

Liam's smile faded. "Does it have a happy ending?"

"No." She was laughing now, her eyes sparkling, so beautiful he couldn't resist the urge to touch her.

Gently, he brushed her hair back, his fingers skimming over the soft skin of her shoulder. "Maybe we should practice . . ."

Her lips quivered at the corners, and she closed the distance between them, her voice husky and low. "For authenticity?"

"Exactly."

She slid her free hand over his shoulder, soft breasts crushing against his chest. All his blood rushed down to his groin, taking with it the last vestiges of his rational thought. He locked his arms around her, pulling her so close he could feel each gentle breath as an exquisite stroke on his cock. Raw desire coursed through his veins as his hands skimmed over the sweet softness of her curves.

"Someone is watching us through the window," she murmured, her breath warm on his cheek.

"All the more reason to put on a good show." With one hand on her nape, he tipped back her head and covered her mouth with his own.

A moan escaped her lips, filling his head with thoughts of tangled sheets, banging headboards, sweat-slicked skin, and the realization of a fantasy that had consumed him night after sleepless night since she'd turned sixteen and he'd realized she wasn't a little girl anymore.

He parted her lips with the gentle slide of his tongue, touching, tasting, savoring, pausing between heady sips to let her essence dance over his taste buds. With every breath he inhaled the fresh scent of wildflowers in a rain-soaked meadow, the grassy lawn where they'd played catch in the summer sun. He'd known she was smart and fun and beautiful. But this kiss. These feelings. The throbbing heat of desire. It was all completely new.

With a force of will he didn't even knew he had, he pulled away, focused on the twitter of birds, the soft hum of an electric car, the faint laughter from inside the house—real sounds, safe sounds, grounding him in the moment instead of the past.

"I think we've got it down." He gave a half laugh, trying to process what had happened. He'd kissed dozens of women over the years. Why was he so shaken?

For a long moment, Daisy didn't move, face soft, plump lips swollen from his kiss. She swallowed hard and her gaze dropped below his belt where the evidence of his desire was barely hidden beneath his jeans. He draped his motorcycle jacket over his arm, creating a discrete shield and a barrier between them.

"Do you have something to hide, Liam?" All cool and calm like she hadn't just blown his mind with her kiss, she gave him a teasing smile.

Yeah, he had something to hide . . . the truth. "Don't want to scare the ladies."

"This lady isn't scared."

He heard a cough and saw Aunt Fiona watching them through the glass door.

"Let's go with the bus stop in the rain story," he said, reaching for the door. "Does it have a happy ending?"

"We'll have to wait and see."

· 16 ·

DAISY made a last check in the hallway mirror for anything that would reveal her inner geekiness. She'd decided to play it safe with a fifties-style dress and matching shoes. Although she'd hated to do it, she'd washed out her pink streaks and let her thick, dark hair fall loose and full around her shoulders. Still, an undercurrent of tension knotted her stomach. Working in Silicon Valley and being part of a large, vibrant desi community, she didn't often find herself in places where she was the odd one out, and she didn't do well in groups of strangers.

"You look perfect." Liam caught her gaze in the mirror. As usual he looked mouthwateringly hot in his leather jacket, a blue sweater that matched his eyes, and a pair of jeans that was tight in all the right places.

"I didn't want to give your family a reason to doubt our relationship was real. You're not the kind of guy who would date someone who dresses the way I usually do."

"I like how you dress," he said softly.

Music and laughter echoed down the hallway. She could isolate at least a dozen voices. Her pulse kicked up a notch and she stared unseeing at the painting in front of her. Why had she agreed to this? Without even a pair of patterned tights, colored sunglasses, or a quirky hat, she felt utterly exposed. Panic slid icy fingers up her spine and she tightened her grip on the box of sweets Mehar Auntie had given her.

"Uncle Liam!" A little boy with a shock of blond hair ran down the hallway toward them. "I got a new plane!"

Liam knelt down and swept the boy up in his arms. "This is my nephew, Jaxon. He just turned five. And this beautiful lady is my friend Daisy."

"She has a flower name," Jaxon said.

Liam glanced over and smiled. "It's pretty. Just like her."

"Do you want to see my plane?" Jaxon wiggled down. "It's in the living room."

"Of course we do."

"Smile," Liam whispered as they followed Jaxon into the living room. "Pretend you're on stage doing the dance that won you first prize in the high school talent contest."

"You saw that?"

"After watching you and Layla practicing for months, I felt obligated to provide moral support for the performance."

Before she could process that statement, they were in a large, bright living room, decorated in pink and green and furnished with what had to be antiques.

"Liam, I was wondering when you two were going to come in." A woman with curly brown hair and hazel eyes greeted them with a smile.

"Aunt Fiona, this is Daisy Patel." He glanced around and raised his voice. "My fiancée."

Daisy held out Mehar Auntie's box, a sinking feeling in her stomach when Liam's declaration got no response. Maybe they'd miscalculated. After all, she was the only person of color in the room. "I brought sweets."

"How lovely." Fiona moved forward to take the box. "It's so nice to finally meet you.

"Liam! You didn't even mention you had a girlfriend the last time I saw you." A tall woman wearing a colorful woven dress walked toward them, her long auburn hair braided down her back. "Or maybe you did and I don't remember." She gave Daisy an apologetic smile. "I've been at an ayahuasca retreat in Costa Rica. I needed to get the hell out of my head."

"That's Aunt Roisin," Liam murmured.

"And, boy, did your retreat deliver," Fiona muttered, putting the box on the coffee table. "You're still not all back."

"Don't be unkind," Roisin said. "Just because you're unable to let go of your fixed self doesn't mean you should put down those of us who were able to achieve enlightenment."

"You spent a month taking psychedelic drugs and living in a hut in the jungle," Fiona said. "You missed Da's funeral. I had to hire a security company to hunt you down and drag you out. How enlightened is that?"

"The drugs were a shortcut to glimpsing a higher truth," Roisin retorted. "It was like a decade of therapy packed into a night. And this isn't about me. It's about Liam and his new fiancée."

"I don't think anyone believed you when you said you were engaged," Fiona said to Liam. "It was such a surprise."

"It all happened very quickly." Liam clasped Daisy's hand and gave it a squeeze. "Daisy is the sister of one of my old high school friends. We reconnected recently, but with Grandpa sick, I didn't think it was the right time to introduce her."

"I thought he was like you, Uncle Seamus." Fiona nudged the old man beside her. He had the same round face and hazel eyes, but his hair was gray, and he was tall and lean where Fiona was short and round. "Sowing his wild oats until it was too late."

"It's never too late," Seamus said, puffing out his barrel chest. "I'll be sowing oats until I'm lying in my coffin."

Liam introduced Daisy to his relatives one by one. Aside from a few polite questions about her job, they were more interested in their own snarky banter than getting to know her. Unlike her family in a "meet the potential partner" situation, she didn't have to sit in the middle of the room and field questions about everything from her favorite foods to her religious and political views. Liam's relationship with her was clearly Liam's business and they accepted his choice.

It was refreshing, but at the same time she had a feeling that if something went wrong, Liam would be on his own. By contrast, when Nasir Uncle had been recovering in the hospital from heart surgery, the entire family had gone to see him. She'd often found her family suffocating, but would it really be better to be left alone?

"Brendan!" Fiona called into the kitchen. "Forget the booze. Come and meet Liam's new fiancée."

Daisy turned as Liam's brother walked into the room. Shorter than Liam by about two inches, with the same wide shoulders but on a stocky frame, Brendan was an older, more rugged version of his brother. Individually, his features were rough, but together, with his thick blond hair and the same intense blue eyes as Liam, he had a dangerous appeal.

Brendan's gaze flicked from Daisy to Liam and his voice was pure disdain. "Christ, I can't believe you are actually carrying out this charade. What total bullshit."

"Bullshit," Jaxon repeated, his eyes wide with delight. "Fecking bullshit."

Brendan puffed out his chest. "See, even a child knows it's a load of cr—"

"Brendan!" A slight, fair-haired woman ran out of the kitchen and scooped Jaxon up. "Not in front of Jaxon."

"Is this true?" Fiona asked after a protesting Jaxon had been quickly carried upstairs.

"We are engaged." Liam put his arm around Daisy's shoulders. "I've known Daisy for almost twenty years, but it was Grandpa's death that made me realize life is too short to waste."

Damn, he was impressive. Daisy had never mastered the art of lying on cue. Deceit required imagination and improvisation and she leaned toward logic and planning.

"That is so true," Roisin said. "The world is a lonely place full of lonely people. If you find someone you can connect with, someone who can take you out of yourself and bring you joy, you can't let it go. My shaman felt that connection with me after we drank our ayahuasca brew."

"I'm sure he did," Fiona muttered. "A close and intimate connection."

"Then why wasn't she at the funeral?" Brendan challenged. "Or the wake? Why did you never bring her to meet any of us? You didn't say anything until you found out Grandpa had given the distillery to me."

"We were . . ." He trailed off and Daisy panicked, terrified he wouldn't be able to wing this one. What could she say? What made sense? She wasn't good with making things up. Maybe something close to the truth.

"He cheated on me." She blurted out the words, her heart pounding so hard she could barely hear through the rush of blood in her ears.

Liam stared at her in shock. "You don't have to—"

"With Madison. My old boss." She'd put her foot in it now, might as well keep going with a story she knew.

"I had to quit the job I loved." She felt both relief and dread when Liam didn't interrupt, leaving her the center of attention.

"We were on a break, but I brought him to the company picnic hoping to reconcile, and he hooked up with Madison."

"Poor love." Roisin patted her hand. "Men. Always thinking with their cocks."

"Roisin! For feck sake," Seamus said. "Watch your language. She's just a wee girl."

"She's not that wee." Roisin gave Daisy an appraising look. "She knows what a cock is or she wouldn't be with our Liam. Isn't that right?"

"Um . . ." Daisy's brain had *cock* on repeat and she couldn't form any words. She'd never heard the word *cock* uttered once in any Patel family gathering. Nor a single swear word. She'd never even had a conversation about sex with anyone in her family, except with Layla.

"Look at her face." Fiona clucked her tongue like a mother hen. "She's only here five minutes and you're already on about cocks. Give her another drink before she faints dead away."

"He's a young man," Seamus said. "You can't blame him for wanting a bit of a rightie. It's a hardship looking as good as Liam and me. The ladies are always wanting a piece of you. Some weekends I had so many, I wore myself out."

"Jesus Christ." Fitz groaned. "We're going to scare the girl away. She'll think we're all crazy."

"You know what's crazy?" Roisin said. "An ayahuasca trip. That's crazy. The first night I took the brew I saw myself floating in Ma's womb. And then I had the purge. In a communal tent. I had to get on all fours because it was coming out both ends and I couldn't reach the buckets. And the force. It was like a fire hose. I ripped a hole in the side of the tent and hit a tree ten yards away. Felt like pure acid. I couldn't sit for a week."

"Why are we talking about Aunt Roisin's crazy ayahuasca trip?"

Brendan raised his voice in frustration. "The bigger issue here is a fraudulent marriage."

Fitz held up his hands palms forward. "It's their relationship, their business. Just like your aunt's psychedelic hallucinated shit is her business even though she has to bring it up in every conversation."

"It was all over me," Roisin continued. "I didn't hallucinate that."

"I thought you just said it was all over a tree ten yards out of the tent." Fitz crossed his arms over his chest.

"That was the second time. The first time I hit the shaman."

Fitz shook his head. "I'm not going to ask what he was doing behind you. Why can't you just get an office job? I would be thrilled to hear stories about accounting errors or missing pens."

"I'm going to get Daisy a drink." Liam pulled Daisy toward the kitchen, although she wasn't in a hurry to leave. His family took bluntness to a whole new level.

"I'm sorry," he said when they were alone in the pretty country kitchen. "They're fine one on one. It's just when they get together . . ."

"I thought my family was very open, but compared to your family they are positively repressed." She glanced up at the door. "Do you think they bought it?"

"Honestly, they wouldn't care except that they seemed relieved I'm not going to turn out like Seamus."

"What about Brendan?"

She heard a snort by the door. "Yeah, bro. What about Brendan?"

"Who the fuck is she?" Brendan swaggered into the kitchen. "I want the truth."

Liam's anger rose quickly, a mix of protectiveness and irritation that their quiet moment had been interrupted. "Get out, Bren. You're drunk."

"Is she some hooker you picked up in the Tenderloin?" He turned to Daisy. "What's he paying you, honey? I'll double it if you get the hell out of here."

Liam had Brendan up against the wall before his brain had even processed he had moved. His hand tightened around Brendan's throat, cutting off his air. "Don't you ever disrespect her again."

"Why? Because it's real? Because you finally found a woman who could put up with your shit and you're in love?" Brendan spluttered, struggling to breath. "This is fraud, and if you insist on playing this out, I'm going to hire a stable of lawyers and destroy you and your damn wh—"

"Fiancée." Daisy slipped her arm around Liam's waist, gently tugging him back. He released Brendan, chest heaving as his blood pounded through his veins. Why was it always like this with his brother? Why could they never get along?

Brendan glared at Daisy. "What did he offer you? I want to know. How much does it cost to destroy a family?"

Liam's vision sheeted red. "You bastard." He moved forward and Daisy grabbed the back of his shirt.

"Wait." She looked up at Brendan. "He didn't pay me anything. Do you really want to turn this into something ugly? He's your brother. Family is what holds us all together."

"Are you fucking kidding me?" Brendan gave a bitter laugh. "You obviously don't know my brother very well, or you would understand why I don't believe this fake engagement in the least. He runs away from everything. His family. His friends. His commitments. There's a reason he's never had a serious relationship. Most women can see through the bullshit to the bastard underneath."

"You don't know anything about me," Liam spat out.

Brendan grabbed one of the bottles from the table. "I know what's going to happen. You'll take the distillery like you took everything from me, and then you'll abandon it and I'll be left to clean up the mess."

"What the fuck are you talking about?"

"It's the story of our lives." Brendan's face twisted in a snarl. "You spent all your time playing happy families somewhere else while I stayed at home, looking after Mom and dealing with all Dad's shit."

"You did nothing to help her." Liam fist connected with Brendan's face, knocking his brother back against the table. Brendan returned the punch, making contact with Liam's nose. Blood poured down Liam's shirt. Eyes streaming from the pain, he slammed his brother's head into the cupboards and received a punch to the gut in return. Moments later, Liam felt hands on his shoulders, pulling him back as Brendan threw fists and knees, trying to get him down.

"Enough, you two." Seamus shoved him toward the back door while Fitz pulled Brendan in the other direction. "Brendan. Go upstairs to your wife and get her to look after those cuts. And Liam, you'd best take Daisy home."

Outside in the cool air, and away from his hotheaded brother, Liam sat on the front step and took a deep breath. What the hell was Brendan on about? He'd never once stood up to their father. It was Liam who had taken the punches and verbal abuse. Liam who had finally gotten their mother away.

"It sounds like your dad really messed you guys up." Daisy sat on the front step beside him, a gentle hand on his shoulder.

Liam rested his elbows on his thighs, dropping his hands between his legs. "He started drinking after he turned his back on the distillery to start his car business. Things didn't go well and he was too proud to ask for help. Money was tight. He didn't want a second kid. When my mom got pregnant he couldn't accept that they'd have to go even further in debt, so he accused her of having an affair. That made me a no-good, worthless burden on the family. It didn't help that I was an energetic kid, always getting into trouble and breaking the rules."

"I can't even imagine how hard that must have been." Daisy pulled a tissue out of her bag and dabbed at the cut on his forehead. "Kids just want to be loved."

"I just wanted him to stop beating on my mother." His heart was still pounding, his control fracturing with each dredged-up memory.

Her expression changed, softened. "It sounds like Brendan wanted that, too."

She was imagining things. This was Brendan, a man who'd watched his dad beat his mom and little brother and never once tried to intervene. "I've got good reasons for doing what I'm doing."

"Wouldn't he say the same? He wants to sell the land to save his company and preserve what he sees as the family business. Maybe you're not so different."

"You don't know anything about my family. I'm nothing like Brendan." He needed to leave. Get on his motorcycle and get away from this house. Away from Brendan. Away from the family who turned a blind eye to the abuse. Away from Daisy and her irritating analytical mind. He had too much to risk to let himself slide back into the past.

As if she could read his mind, Daisy pushed to stand. "You seem to be okay," she said in a clipped tone. "I should get going."

Fuck. Could he mess this evening up any worse? Life had been easier when he'd kept his distance from his family.

"Daisy. Wait." He caught up to her just as she reached her Mini, catching her arm before she could slip away. "I'm sorry. It's just . . ."

She shook off his hand. "I understand, Liam."

"Let me know when you get home so I know you're safe."

"There's no one here." She fumbled in her purse for her key. "You don't have to pretend with me."

Silence filled the space between them, his anger at Brendan fading beneath the weight of regret. Daisy was the only real thing in his life right now. The one person who made sense. He needed her strength, her calm. He needed her to know how much he cared.

"Do it anyway. Please."

"Okay. I will." She opened her car door. Hesitated. "Goodnight, humraaz."

Warmth rushed through him, filling the black hole in his chest. She wasn't just his humraaz. She was so much more.

17

*B*REATHE. *Breathe. Breathe.*

Daisy bent over, arms wrapped around her legs, and tried to focus on drawing air into her lungs. Her anxiety had spiraled out of control after her mother's sudden reappearance years ago and she'd been through three therapists before she found one who was able to help. *Focus on the breath. In for four. Hold for four. Out for four.*

Max had been unresponsive in his basket when she'd arrived to pick him up. While a panicked Mehar Auntie had searched the house for the source of his illness, Daisy had broken the sound barrier to get to the animal hospital, and the vet had taken him in right away. Mehar Auntie had arrived shortly after to let them know Max had gotten into her baking chocolate. Utterly devastated that he'd made himself sick while she dozed on her couch, she'd stayed to keep Daisy company while the vet pumped Max's stomach.

Mehar Auntie rubbed her hair. "He's going to be okay, beta. The doctor said so. Let me take you home, and you can come back in the morning and pick him up."

Her voice caught, muffled by her lap. "I can't leave him, Auntie-ji."

Thick black boots crossed the floor in front of her. She heard the squeak of leather, the groan of the plastic chair beside her, inhaled a whiff of fresh ocean air, and then Liam's face was down beside hers.

"How's Max?"

His unexpected appearance startled her out of her breathing rhythm and she shot up to sitting. "What are you doing here?"

"I thought you might need a friend."

Seven words. They rippled through her body and settled in her soul.

"He's going to be okay." She looked over at Mehar Auntie, who was watching them with interest. "This is Liam. We were visiting his family tonight." After the vet had assured her Max would be okay, she'd somehow managed to send a quick text to Liam, never expecting he'd turn up.

"The fiancé." Mehar Auntie nodded and introduced herself to Liam. "Who is your family? What do you do? How do you know Daisy?"

Daisy's chest tightened as her anxiety peaked again, and she tried to squeeze in a few breaths. "This . . . isn't . . . the time . . . for . . . an . . . interrogation." She leaned forward and felt a gentle hand circle her neck. Warm and soothing, it made her feel curiously safe.

"I'm sorry," Liam said. "I shouldn't have come. I thought you'd be alone. I didn't mean to cause you more stress."

"It was nice of you to come." She sat up, took the tissue he offered, dabbing away the tears. "It's been a long time since I had an anxiety attack. I try hard to keep my life under control."

"I'm not judging." His quiet, rumbling voice was calm and steady.

She nodded, pressing her lips together in case she blurted out something that would let him know that every time he opened his mouth the walls of ice that protected her heart melted just that little bit more.

Mehar Auntie filled Liam in on the details. "The vet told her

Max will be okay and she can go home. He's sleeping now, so he isn't in any pain."

"I can't leave Max." Daisy bent over again, hands fisted against her forehead.

Liam stroked a gentle hand through her hair. "My mom had anxiety issues and it helped when I rubbed her back . . ."

Daisy looked up at Mehar Auntie, who nodded, seemingly pleased rather than disappointed that someone was taking over her job. "Yes, please."

"Pleasure." He put his motorcycle helmet on the empty seat beside him and stroked her back with slow, easy movements of his hand, never stopping, never tiring, until the attack crested and she could breathe again.

"So you have a motorcycle," Mehar Auntie said, her tone slightly curious.

"Yes. It's easier to get around the city."

"What club are you with?" she asked. "Are you full patch? I watched all of *Sons of Anarchy*, so I know what it's about."

"Auntie-ji." Daisy shot up again. "He's not in a motorcycle gang. He just rides for transportation."

"*You* won't be riding for transportation," Mehar Auntie warned. "No Daisy on the motorcycle. If your father were here, he would say the same."

Liam chuckled. "I promise not to take her for a ride unless she asks."

"Can you do tricks?" Mehar Auntie tipped her head to the side. "Ajay Devgan did a full split on two moving bikes in *Phool Aur Kaante*, and then there were all the stunts in *Hero*—standing on the seat, five men on one bike." She hummed under her breath, and Daisy felt a warning tingle in her chest.

"No!"

"Do you know the song 'Ding Dong'?" Mehar Auntie jumped up, singing and dancing to the iconic song, albeit without her usual flair given the limited space.

"Auntie-ji! Sit down. You might disturb people." Daisy shot a frantic glance around the waiting room where photographs of people and their pets covered the bright white walls. A woman with a cat in a carrier sat in one of the colorful plastic chairs and a man with a birdcage was talking to the receptionist. No one seemed annoyed. In fact, everyone was smiling, amused by her aunt's antics.

"She's a Bollywood fanatic," Daisy explained to Liam. "We teach Bollywood dance classes together, and . . ." She gestured to her aunt. "She loves to dance."

Liam laughed, the sound rippling over her skin, easing her tension. He scrolled through his phone to a YouTube version of the song. "Let's help her out."

By the time the last few notes of the song faded away, everyone in the waiting room was clapping along. Daisy didn't know whether to laugh or cry, but her muscles were no longer tight and she could breathe again.

"He's a good boy." Mehar Auntie patted Liam's shoulder. "Maybe I should go home and get some rest since you have extra company."

"I'm happy to stay as long as you need me." Liam placed his hand, palm up, on his knee and Daisy took the invitation. Warm, solid flesh squeezed her hand tight.

"If you're okay with it," she said to her aunt. "I know you love Max . . ."

Mehar Auntie leaned down to whisper in her ear. "He came all this way for you. You don't need an old auntie when you have . . ." She gestured to Liam, her lips curved in a knowing smile as she turned to leave. "This."

"You passed the test," she said after her aunt had gone. "Good call on the music. There's nothing she loves more."

"I aim to please." Liam squeezed her hand. "Do you need anything? Are you hungry? I can bring you something to eat."

She needed Liam to not be Liam but another kind, caring man who would race through the city to sit with a woman in an animal hospital after only three fake dates, a man who would not only humor a Bollywood-loving aunt, but also enjoy her show.

"Avocado and hummus quesadillas."

Liam chuckled. "What about baked tofu fries?"

"*Batata vada.*" Jana Auntie's potato fritters, coated with chickpea flour and served hot with chutney, were one of her favorite snacks.

"How about that crunchy snack food in the red bag that your relatives always bring from India?" Liam put an arm around her and she leaned against him.

"Kurkure Masala Munch?"

"That's the stuff. Loved it. It was an effort not to eat the whole bag."

She couldn't help but laugh. "I appreciate your restraint, but that was your bag. Sanjay never liked it and I had my own hidden away."

He stared at her in mock horror. "You mean I could have eaten it all?"

"Every bit."

She dragged her teeth over her bottom lip, berating herself for falling so easily back into their old banter. It was almost too easy to get comfortable with him, to feel the pull of longing and forget the abject humiliation and the soul-destroying pain. She had rules and she needed to stick to them. Rules kept her safe. Feelings, not so much.

"You don't have to stay." She pulled away from his warmth. "It was nice of you to come, but I might be here all night." She gave a resigned shrug, hoping he would take the hint. "Even if I wanted to go, I can't get up. I think my muscles are locked in this position."

"What if you have to pee?" He moved their clasped hands so he could rest his ankle on one knee, all cool and casual like he hung out in animal emergency hospitals with fake fiancées every night.

"Seriously?"

"I'm very serious," he said. "They won't want you to pee on the floor. It's not hygienic."

"I don't need to pee, Liam."

He raised a dubious eyebrow. "You didn't pee at my grandfather's house, and I'm pretty sure you didn't pee when you picked up Max and brought him here. That's a long time. I have superior bladder function and even I couldn't go that long."

She rubbed absently at her bare arms. Her sweater was still in the car and she could feel the goose bumps on her skin. "I can't believe you're tracking when I pee."

"Just being observant." He rubbed his thumb over her fingers, making it difficult to concentrate on anything but the soothing sensation that fuzzed her brain.

She stared at him, incredulous. "Of pee?"

"Of you."

Warmth flooded her chest, disconcerting in its intensity. She looked away and saw the woman with the cat watching them. "Keep your voice down. I don't want people to hear us talking about pee."

"They'd hear a tinkle. That's for sure."

Her face flamed when the woman snickered. "Fine." She jumped up from her seat. "I'll go to the restroom simply so you'll shut up about it and then you can go."

Liam stood beside her. "Or, since you're standing . . ." He swept her up in his arms like she weighed nothing, although she knew exactly how much she weighed. And why had she stuffed her face with jalebis and *laddu* at Mehar Auntie's house earlier that afternoon at the dance rehearsal? Everyone knew that the weight from sweets you shouldn't eat went on immediately and took at least five days to lose.

"I'll carry you to your car and take you home."

"Liam!" A tingling swept up the back of her neck and across her face. "Put me down."

"I will." He bent to pick up her purse, shifting her weight to one arm. "In your car."

"You guys are so cute together," the woman with the cat called out as Liam carried her through the waiting room. "He's a real catch."

"Did you hear that?" Liam murmured in her ear, his voice amused. "I'm a real catch. You shouldn't let me get away."

"I'm beginning to worry we might not both fit in my car given the size of your ego."

"Daisy?" Still holding her tight in his arms, he pulled open the door.

"What?"

"Don't pee on the seat."

18

NOSTALGIA hit Liam hard when he walked with Daisy up the sidewalk to the bright blue Victorian house that had been his second home. Everything looked the same, from the white picket fence to the tiny front garden, and the porch hidden behind a giant Maidenhair tree.

"I climbed to the top of that tree once."

"I remember." Daisy pulled out her keys. "You and Sanjay threw water balloons at me."

"And then you locked us out of the house and we didn't get our afternoon snack."

She looked back over her shoulder. "Why do all your memories of that time have to do with food?"

"I was a teenager. Food was my life." It had also been a way to connect with Daisy, but that she didn't need to know.

"Do you want to come in for tea while I call an Uber to take you back to your motorcycle?" She flicked on the lights, illuminating the familiar hallway with a warm glow. "And don't even think about calling them yourself. I'm paying and that's all there is to it."

"I can't believe nothing has changed." Liam walked into the living room from the small hallway. "Same drapes. Same couch. You even have the same pictures on the walls." He knew this house better than his own, he realized. The Murphy living room had been a place of fights and violence instead of fun and relaxation, and he'd avoided it when he could.

"Look!" He pointed at a dent in the wall, a thrill of excitement flowing through his veins. "That's from the time Sanjay threw a baseball at me. Your dad had just finished repainting the living room. I think that was the most annoyed I'd ever seen him."

Daisy watched him, amused. "You have more memories of my house than I do."

"What about the kitchen?" He took off at full stride to the small country-style kitchen with its whitewashed cupboards and fading melamine counters. "This is the same, too." He pointed to one of the kitchen stools, the vinyl seat torn and showing its stuffing. "There's my chair."

"It's Priya's chair now. She's my dad's new girlfriend. He was alone for twenty years, and then one day I came home for dinner and there she was. It was awkward at first. It had just been Dad and me for the longest time. But Priya is great. I've never seen him so happy. And since she runs a bakery, we always have treats."

"I'm glad for him. It must have been hard to be alone for so long."

Daisy tilted her head to the side, her forehead wrinkling. "I never thought about my dad being lonely. He had his work, his friends, his family, and us. He never complained. It's one of the reasons I never pursued a serious relationship. If he was content for twenty years without a partner, I could be, too. If you don't get too close, you don't get hurt when people leave."

Liam sat on his old stool. "I made the same decision about relationships, but it was because my parents had such a terrible marriage. I worried that one day I'd turn out to be like my father."

"I don't know all the details of what happened in your house, but I know you," she said quietly. "I can't imagine you hurting anyone that way."

Liam watched Daisy bustle around the kitchen making chai and heating up pastries from the freezer. A deep-seated longing for the past, when things had been easy between them, clogged his throat. How had he screwed up so badly? He missed her, not just romantically, but as a friend.

"The first time I had chai was the night my dad broke my arm." The words spilled out, an attempt to bridge the gulf between them, to reforge the intimacy they had lost. "When my mom brought me to the hospital, I begged her not to tell them what really happened. Every time Social Services got involved, my dad took it out on her. She was afraid to take me back home, so I asked her to call your dad. He'd told me once his door was always open if I ever needed a place to stay."

"I remember that night." She stirred the chai. "You had two black eyes. I'd only ever read about people getting a black eye from being punched. I didn't know it was real."

"Dear old Dad did a real number on me," he said. "It was the first time I tried to stop him from beating on my mom. Brendan wouldn't do it, and I figured that at thirteen I was big enough to take him on. I guessed wrong."

"I can't even imagine how hard it must have been," she said quietly, placing the pastries on a plate.

"I can't imagine what I would have done without your family." He traced a groove in the melamine counter. "I had some of the best times sitting around your table, throwing out math problems for you to solve or talking hockey with Sanjay and your dad." He pointed to the dent. "Do you remember this?"

Daisy put the pastries in the microwave and took down two mugs from the cupboard. "What is it?"

"It's where I dropped a bowl of pakoras when you walked into the kitchen wearing a tight green dress that Layla had bought for you because she was dragging you to a school dance. You were sixteen, and you looked amazing. Your dad and Sanjay went crazy. I think your dad threatened to lock you in your room forever, and Sanjay insisted you wear a winter jacket. Layla had to run interference. That was the day I realized you weren't a little girl anymore and I couldn't treat you like you were."

She dropped her gaze, thick lashes brushing over brown cheeks. "I didn't think you noticed."

Liam chuckled. "I noticed. Maybe too much. But I couldn't say anything out of respect for your family. If the thought of you going out in that dress made them crazy, imagine how they would have felt if I'd asked you out? I wasn't the guy any girl could take home to meet the parents."

She left him in the living room with his tea and pastries and went upstairs to change out of her dress. Liam had just gotten comfortable on the couch when Daisy walked in wearing a tiny pair of worn shorts and a Marvel superheroes T-shirt cut low to reveal the crescents of her breasts.

Liam's mouth went dry and he choked on his pastry. No, she definitely wasn't a little girl anymore, and the things he was thinking were definitely not appropriate for Mr. Patel's worn couch.

"Are you okay?" She sat down beside him and those tiny shorts rode up so high all he could see was a long expanse of beautiful, firm brown thigh only inches away from his hip.

Fuck. He shifted on the couch, trying to hide his growing arousal. Maybe if he focused on the food, or the colorful elephant painting on the wall, or the chai in his hand, or work. Work was a good topic. There was nothing sexy about work.

"I'm good. Great. How's work?" He sipped his chai, savoring the rich spices on his tongue.

Daisy frowned. "Um . . . Fine, I guess."

"Good." Her arm brushed against his when she reached for her mug, sending all his blood rushing to his groin. Liam choked on his chai and quickly put down the cup. "How's it going with Brad?"

"Mia and Zoe think his ideas are out of touch with our target market." She settled back on the cushion. "They came up with a branding proposal last year that focused on female empowerment, but Tyler wasn't interested. It was gritty and real and featured diverse women being strong and fierce. Brad's proposal is almost the opposite of their vision. He has no idea what today's women want."

Well, that dealt with the situation down below. Nothing like a good work discussion to keep things in check. "Did they discuss their proposal with him?"

"They're afraid to lose their jobs." She twisted her lips to the side. "Could you ask him to consider it? Or at the very least just hear them out?"

If she'd asked him to get rid of Brad, he would have done it. He trusted Daisy, trusted her judgment. She was quick, sharp, and fiercely intelligent. If she stood behind her colleagues, then their proposal merited a serious look. "Of course. I'll speak to him first thing on Monday."

Her face lit up with a smile, undoing the effects of the work talk in an instant. Dammit. He was here to support her, not indulge a fantasy he'd had since he was a teen.

"It's strange to sit here with you and not play Xbox." She put her cup on the table. "I don't think we ever sat here together for anything else."

"I'm game if you are." He'd only ever felt her equal when they were on a virtual playing field. And since their work talk was done, it would be the perfect distraction from the sensual curves of her body, the softness of her hair as it brushed over his arm, and the tart sweetness of her perfume.

Daisy stiffened and for a moment he wondered if he'd said something wrong.

"Or I can go," he said quickly. "It's late and—"

"No. I want you to stay." She gently pushed him back. "It's just . . . I'll have to go and get it. We moved the console up to Sanjay's room after he broke the old TV stand." She hesitated. "It happened when my mother came back."

"She came back?" he repeated. "After all those years? Is she around?" Sanjay had rarely talked about his mother, but Liam knew he had been deeply affected by her departure. At the time, he'd figured it was the reason why Sanjay had gone off the rails in high school. He'd tried to help by taking the fall for his friend when he could.

Liam had never regretted his decision. After all, no one expected anything of him, and it was the least he could do for a friend who had opened his home and given him the closest thing he'd ever had to a loving family.

"She came and then she went again." With a sigh, Daisy leaned her head against his shoulder. "It was the year after you left. She'd been gone twelve years by then, and one day she just walked in the door."

"Fuck." He squeezed her hand, although what he really wanted to do was pull her into his lap, wrap his arms around her, and hold her tight.

"Yeah. That sums it up. Sanjay was in the last year of his medical degree and he'd come home for Sunday dinner. We were all in

the kitchen, and suddenly she was there. She'd been in touch spo-
radically over the years—the odd phone call, the occasional birthday card, sometimes an e-mail—but that was the first time we'd
seen her since she left. At first I thought she'd finally come home
for good. And then I thought maybe she finally wanted to build a
real relationship. But she wasn't interested in us. She didn't want to
see my room or hear about my classes or my friends or my dancing.
She didn't seem to care that Sanjay was in medical school. She'd
come for money."

"Jesus Christ." As if she hadn't put the family through enough.

Daisy's voice wavered. "She and dad still owned the house
jointly, and she needed her share. Sanjay lost it. He threw his phone
at the TV stand and broke the glass doors."

"I can't even . . ." He shook his head. "I wish I'd been here for
you both."

She pressed her lips together, her eyes glistening with tears. "It
was terrible. Sanjay walked out. Dad was shouting . . . She didn't
say much to me except to ask if I was still 'weirdly smart.' I ran up
to my room, and when I came down she was gone. My anxiety got
bad after that. It was like being rejected all over again except this
time I knew she'd left because I wasn't normal. That's when Layla
gave me Max, and he's made all the difference in the world."

For a moment, Liam couldn't speak for the fury surging
through his veins. What kind of mother would say that to her
daughter after twelve long years? He didn't like to judge, but hell,
he had no problem judging Daisy's mother and finding her totally
unworthy.

He curved his arm around her to hold her close, rested his
cheek against her head. "Don't ever think there's something wrong
with you," he murmured. "You have gifts that people can only
dream of having. They make you special and utterly unique in a

way that is as far from weird as you can get. You blew my mind when you were a girl. I loved coming here to see what you could do, whether it was solving difficult math puzzles, destroying your dad at chess, memorizing the entire Human section of *The Guinness Book of World Records*, or trying to beat me at video games."

She jolted up, her mouth curving in a grin. "Trying? Seriously? Was there a video game I didn't win?"

Cheer-up mission accomplished, but his ego was taking a beating. "Guitar Hero was never your strong suit."

"Don't even think about challenging me," Daisy warned. "I was a fret-shredding machine."

He gave a dismissive shrug, baiting his trap. "You were young, so Sanjay and I let you win . . ."

She gave him a calculating stare and jumped to her feet. "The guitar is mine."

"The guitar is lame. Drums are where it's at." He picked up the mugs and plates. "Two songs and I'll call an Uber."

"What if we tie? It will have to be the best of three songs and *I'll* call an Uber."

"Are you sure you're up for it?" He watched the gentle sway of her hips as she climbed the stairs. "I don't want you to feel bad when I destroy you."

Daisy looked back over her shoulder and gave him a grin. "You are so going down in flames."

· 19 ·

DAISY awoke as the bright morning sunshine slid through the curtains, her head nestled against Liam's chest, her legs tangled with his. Although she was precariously close to the edge of the couch, she didn't dare move for fear that if she woke him, this perfect, blissful moment would disappear in a puff of smoke.

She closed her eyes, tried to take a mental snapshot—the slow steady beat of his heart, the rhythmic cadence of his breathing, his familiar scent, and his warmth—heat that sank into her bones. His body was hard beneath her, and his arm lay heavy across her back— comforting and secure.

Despite Max's misadventure, she'd had a good time last night. A great time. After countless games of Guitar Hero and a tableful of snacks, Liam had finally conceded her Guitar Hero superiority. Of course, she hadn't told him she'd hacked the game so that no matter how badly she played, she'd never miss a note, but it was fun to watch him try. Liam never got angry the way Sanjay did. He was a good loser, his self-deprecating humor making it impossible to gloat when she won.

After her twentieth straight victory, however, Liam had begun to suspect something was wrong. He had stretched out on the couch with her guitar in his hand to inspect it for tampering, and she had curled up beside him, resting her head on his shoulder. She had closed her eyes just for a moment, listening to the deep rumble of his voice, and then she must have fallen asleep.

Now here she was, living her teenage fantasy—at least, it had been her fantasy until Liam had gone away.

That last thought came and went without leaving its usual sting. The more time she spent with Liam, the more difficult it was to cling to her anger, or to reconcile his actions with a man who could be so callous and cruel. He had pretended to be her fake fiancée at the conference, sat with her at the vet, and suffered through twenty rounds of Guitar Hero simply because he didn't want to leave her alone without Max.

Turning her head ever so slightly, she pressed a kiss to his shirt-clad chest, imagining that this was real and every morning she could wake up in Liam's arms. He stirred, tightening his arm around her. Daisy held her breath, hoping he would stay asleep. Once he was awake, it was back to the world of work and family and a fake fiancé who was becoming more real every day.

Her phone vibrated softly from somewhere on the couch. For the first time, she hated the thought of picking it up and reading all the schedules and notifications, reminders that after their coming sports date they would be halfway through the dating plan—halfway to over.

She snuggled in closer, resting her hand on his shirt over the ripple of his abs. Her gaze dropped below his belt. Had that bulge been there before? It gave her a thrill to imagine she had aroused him as they slept. Maybe she was a little geeky, a bit quirky, slightly emotionally damaged, and she couldn't fit sideways through two blades of grass if she tried, but in his dreams he wanted her despite her flaws. And if he did, what was she supposed to do with that?

She eased her hand down, the tips of her fingers now just below the smooth leather of his belt. The width and length of his erection took her breath away, making her face hot and her pulse quicken. She was suddenly dizzy with her feelings for him—wanting and hating, and yearning, always yearning.

He shifted and she looked up. Sleepy blue eyes returned her gaze, heavy-lidded with desire.

Daisy's eyes fluttered closed as his mouth moved over hers, slow and gentle, his tongue touching, tasting, exploring, like they had never kissed before. Every nerve ending in her body fired at once and she felt nothing but him—the heat of his body, the tenderness of his mouth, the softness of his hair.

With a groan he pulled her on top of him, positioning her so the bulge in his jeans was nestled between her thighs. His kiss grew harder, dark and dangerous, raw with need. It awakened something inside her, jumbling her senses, stripping her defenses, exposing her passion and a longing she couldn't control.

Part of her desperately wanted to believe that she, Daisy Patel, who had once gone four days debugging a program without speaking to another human being, could seduce the man who had been every high school girl's crush. But the other part, the logical, sensible part, knew it just couldn't be true. After all, everyone she cared about had left her, including Liam. What could possibly stop him from doing it again?

Then again, what did it matter? They'd made a plan and she knew how this would end. Why not enjoy the journey?

She wasn't a teenager anymore, tucked under her pink covers, listening to her father bustle around the family kitchen. Nor was she alone in her cubicle at work, deep in her world of code while the rest of the office buzzed around her. The day she'd run through the conference center with an armload of pads, she would never have imagined she'd find herself here—in the arms of the man she wanted and hated with equal passion, only a heartbeat away from making all her sexual fantasies come true, from feeling truly alive.

"You're thinking too loud." Liam's breath was warm against her hair, his quiet voice intruding on her thoughts.

"You can't possibly know what I'm thinking."

"Don't think anything," he murmured. "Just be. Here. Now. With me." His hands slid down her back to rest on her ass. She felt a wave of pure desire, the heat shocking in its intensity. It raced through her body, sending a wave of white-hot fire through her veins.

One word and everything would change. One word and there would be no going back.

But she'd already made that decision when she'd invited him into her home.

"Okay," she whispered. "Yes."

His eyes darkened, and his voice lowered to a pitch that vibrated between her thighs. "When I bumped into you at the conference, I never imagined a few weeks later I would find myself here, back in this house, on this couch, with you on top of me, your lips wet from my kisses, and no knife in your hand. I didn't even think you'd speak to me again."

"I guess there's no turning back now." She twisted her lips to the side. "Although I did leave a butter knife on the table . . ."

His low, ragged growl made the thin cotton of her shorts dampen with her desire. "You're sexy when you threaten me."

"I aim to please."

His eyes raked over her body and he reached for her shirt. "Take this off."

"You're very bossy."

"I've waited a long time to see you. I don't want to waste a second."

"If we're going to do this, we need rules," she said as he reached for the bottom of her shirt.

"What rules?" He eased her shirt up, the tips of his fingers skimming over her bare skin, fuzzing her brain. She grabbed his hand, holding it in place. If she let him touch her again, she wouldn't be able to say what needed to be said.

"It's just one time. No strings. No expectations. No feelings. No long cuddles. It's just sex. Like any other hookup." She released his hand and he tugged her shirt up, exposing more of her skin.

"You aren't any other hookup to me, Daisy, and I won't pretend you are. But I can give you everything else, if that's really what you want."

"It is." Did he sense her hesitation? Hear the lie?

He yanked her shirt over her head, and a giddy feeling of anticipation rippled over her skin at the thought of Liam's hands on her body, of being wrapped in the strength of his arms.

"What the hell?"

Too late, she remembered she was wearing her Iron Man bra, a red and gold mask covering each breast, silver eye slits glaring into the great beyond—or in this case, at the man who had dared take off her clothes.

Liam barked a laugh. "Is that meant to scare dudes away?"

"You know I like the Avengers." She shrugged. "I just wasn't expecting to be . . . sharing the visual."

"So I see." His hands closed over her breasts. "I'm going to cover his eyes. I can't perform if Iron Man is watching."

"Afraid you won't measure up?"

"More like I'm afraid he might break down the door and take me out."

She'd been waiting so long for his touch, imagined it so many times in so many different ways that her breath left her in a rush.

Wild, crazy energy sparked inside her, and she closed her eyes and focused on the sensation, the way he caressed her, the skitter of her pulse beneath her skin, the length of his cock, hard and thick between her thighs.

She wanted him closer, wanted to feel the press of his naked body against hers. She'd never been with a man like Liam—all power and muscle with a force of presence that filled a room. "I think we need to say goodbye to Iron Man," she murmured, opening her eyes.

With a quick flick, he unhooked her bra, releasing her breasts from their confinement. "You are more beautiful than I imagined." He tossed her bra on the floor. "And your skin . . . Christ, it shimmers like gold."

Before she could respond, his mouth was on her nipple, hot and wet and sucking with gentle pulls. She unraveled in an instant, sliding her fingers through his soft hair as she rocked her hips on his cock.

"Fuck, Liam." As a rule, Daisy didn't often use the word *fuck*. With over a million total words in the English language, there were many better ways to express oneself, but when the man of her teenage fantasies was sucking on her nipples while squeezing her ass and grinding his thick cock against her, *fuck* was the perfect word to express both her emotional state—impatient, needy, and flying on an endorphin high—and her hopes for the future.

"Hold on, sweetheart." He released her nipple with a shuddering breath. "I've waited so long for this, I want to take my time." Pulling back, he trailed one finger down her middle. She tensed when he reached her belly, but if he noticed he had to double dip along the way, he didn't seem to care.

"Who am I going to find under here?" He tugged at the waistband of her shorts. "Is Iron Man guarding the Dream Lab?"

The ring of the doorbell startled her, sending her heart into overdrive. Liam froze beneath her.

"Were you expecting someone?"

"No." Daisy jumped up to peek through the curtains, her stomach sinking when she saw four of her aunties at the door. "It's my aunties, Liam. You can't be here."

Liam groaned and threw a hand over his eyes. "You can't be serious."

"I'm very serious." Daisy scooped her bra and shirt off the floor. "I'm a single desi woman. If they found you here like this . . ." She shuddered. "I can't even imagine the fallout."

"I thought you wanted to be ruined." Liam sat up on the couch and pulled on his boots as she raced around picking up the dishes, soda cans, and chip bags from their night of indulgence.

"Not this way. I want to be *properly* ruined."

"Clearly I didn't appreciate the nuance of your ruination." He cocked his head to the side, frowning. "I hear drums."

"They've sent someone to knock on the back door." Heart thundering, she quickly dressed. "You'll have to go out the window in Sanjay's room like you used to do when you two sneaked out at night."

His eyes widened. "You knew about that?"

"You weren't quiet. I used to watch you from the bathroom window, or sometimes I'd go into Sanjay's room and watch you from there."

After a quick check of the room, she raced down the hallway, shouting in the general direction of the door. "Hi, aunties. I'm coming. Just getting dressed."

"I like this view," Liam panted as he followed her up the stairs, one hand caressing her ass. "I was hoping to see more of it, but without the shorts."

"This isn't the time." She slapped his hand away and ran into Sanjay's room.

"It's like he never left," Liam said as Daisy struggled with the window. "I recognize every book, every action figure, every Lego—"

"You can reminisce later," she gritted out. "They're going to break down the door if I don't get downstairs."

"I almost want to stay just to watch," Liam mused, seemingly unconcerned by the danger of being discovered. "Your aunts must be great in a siege."

Daisy shoved open the window and called out to whichever auntie had been sent to do recon in her backyard. "I'll be there in a minute. Meet you around the front."

"I thought I was supposed to meet some of your relatives." Liam straddled the windowsill. "After everyone is inside, I could ring the doorbell and pretend I just arrived."

Daisy shook her head. "It's not in the plan."

"Neither was this morning," he said softly. "And you appear to have survived."

Daisy's face heated. What had she been thinking? Making out with Liam was against the dating plan rules. Her rules. It could complicate an already complicated situation. And yet, her skin still tingled and she ached for his touch. "We can talk about that later."

He lifted his head and a cheeky smile lit his face. "What about a goodbye kiss for being such a good sport?"

With a sigh, she leaned forward, but what was meant to be a quick peck on the cheek became something more when Liam cupped her nape and dragged her closer, his tongue sweeping through her mouth, setting her blood on fire all over again.

Daisy pulled away, panting her breaths, her body tingling in all the wrong places. "You have to go."

Liam stepped out onto the roof and studied the steep incline. "I'm not as young as I was the last time I did this. I need to tell you something in case I don't make it." He drew in a deep breath. "It's about the night of the prom . . ."

"You want to talk about the prom NOW?" She grabbed the window, preparing to tug it down. "I have four suspicious aunties banging on my door. Sharing things about the past was supposed to happen when we were lying on the couch together."

He gave an apologetic shrug. "You know I'm not good with plans."

Daisy leaned out the window as he edged down the roof, following the well-worn trail over the tiles. He'd never looked this unsteady when he and Sanjay had snuck out at night, and her throat constricted

"Liam?"

He looked up, brow furrowed in concentration. "What?"

"Do you want to use the back door?"

"And run the risk of encountering a rampaging auntie?" He shook his head. "I'll take my chances with the roof of doom. Maybe you should take a picture so the police don't think you pushed me when they find my body in the azaleas. If I do survive, it might also be useful to show the trustees. Nothing says 'legitimate relationship' like having to escape down the roof."

Daisy grabbed her phone and took a few pictures as he made his slow, perilous descent. "Liam?"

His head jerked up, fingers embedded in the tiles. "Yes?"

"Thank you for offering to explain about the prom. I'd like to hear it another time."

"Good to know."

"I really appreciated you coming to be with me at the vet," she said quickly. "And taking my mind off Max last night . . ."

Liam grunted when his foot slipped. "Are you thanking me because you think I'm going to die? Not the vote of confidence I was hoping for."

"And this morning . . ." she continued.

"Don't talk about this morning when I'm trying not to fall off the roof. It could prove to be a fatal distraction." He reached for the tree branch he and Sanjay had always used for the last, more precarious part of the descent. Daisy knew every step of their escape route. She had watched them too many times to count.

"But I have to tell you something. It's important."

He froze, teetered on the tiles, his eyes glistening in the morning light. "What?"

"I hacked Guitar Hero. There was no possible way I could have lost."

A smile tugged at the corners of his lips. "I know."

Puzzled, she frowned. "Then why did you keep playing?"

"It made you happy," he said simply. "Same reason I brought you math puzzles, played video games with you when Sanjay wasn't around, tried to guess the after-school snack instead of looking at your meal plan, and offered to take you to the prom when you didn't have a date. I wanted you to be happy, Daisy. I still do."

His sweet words took her breath away. This was the Liam she knew. Kind, generous, selfless, and about to get killed climbing down her roof. "Liam! Wait."

"I'm good." His hand closed around the nearest branch, and her pulse thudded in her ears. A man who would do this for her, who had done so much in the past to make her happy, wouldn't have left so abruptly without a good reason—a reason he'd been willing to share.

"Come back," she called out. "I'll think of something. I'll tell them I'm ill . . ."

Too late. He swung off the roof and the branch cracked, dropping him the last five feet to the grass with a sickening thud.

"Liam!" She leaned half out of the window, her throat constricting when he didn't move. "Are you okay?"

"Daisy?" He pushed himself up, and her knees buckled as relief washed over her.

"Yes?"

"Next time I'm going out the door."

AFTER throwing on some decent clothes, Daisy made her way downstairs and opened the door to Salena, Mehar, Lakshmi, and Taara aunties and poor Hari Uncle, his hands filled with coolers, boxes, and bags.

"Look who is finally here!" Salena Auntie brushed past Daisy and into the house, her bright orange salwar kameez brightening up the curtained living room. "We were worried something was wrong with you. Hari Uncle was going to kick down the door for us."

Hari Uncle shook his head. "No, I wasn't. I have a bad hip. I suggested using the spare key that they keep under the rock. *You* were going to kick the door down."

Salena waved a dismissive hand. "No matter. Mehar told us about poor Max, and you're all alone without your dad so we thought we'd bring you breakfast before you pick him up."

Daisy's skin prickled in warning. Her aunties had always come with dinner when she and Sanjay were young and their dad had been held up at work, but now that she was grown, the unexpected visits usually involved a suitor instead of food.

She peered out the door, trying to find the man they had no doubt brought for her to meet. "Where is he?"

"Who?" Lakshmi Auntie added her shoes to the pile in the hallway.

"Somebody's friend's sister's cousin who just happened to be in town and just happens to be looking for a wife and you just happened to be in the neighborhood and thought you'd drop in."

"It's just us." Taara Auntie held up a Tupperware container. "And my famous Cinnamon Toast Crunch Marguerita Poha." A wannabe chef with two boys at home, Taara Auntie was infamous for her terrible fusion foods.

"Don't eat it," Lakshmi Auntie muttered. "Those are not flavors that go together. I had some this morning and . . ." She held her stomach. "Do you have any antacids?"

"Medicine cabinet in the bathroom."

Daisy followed Salena Auntie into the kitchen and settled on the stool while Taara Auntie took out container after container from her plastic shopping bag.

"We were having dinner at the Spice Mill last night," Salena Auntie said in a tone that was clearly meant to be casual, but was anything but. "Jana said that Nira said that Deepa said that she had helped you find a sherwani for your fiancé who still hasn't met the family. Deepa overheard that you were taking him to the Dosa Palace and she happened to go over there to talk to Amina who said that you had a fight . . ."

Despite being a Patel and growing up in the Patel family, it still amazed Daisy how quickly information got around. You couldn't keep secrets for long when there were family members everywhere and gossip was everybody's favorite hobby. "That was three days ago. Everything is fine now."

"Fighting when engaged is not a good sign," superstitious Lakshmi Auntie said. "Unless you see a brown goat with a white head, fighting early in a relationship portends difficult trials ahead."

Desperate for a way to divert the conversation, Daisy gestured to the cooler bag. "I'm starving. Maybe we should eat."

"Is it just us? Or maybe you have a friend over?" Lakshmi Auntie peered up the stairs.

"Now that you mention it, I do smell something." Mehar Auntie sniffed.

"Nobody is here, Auntie-ji."

They were the right words, but Lakshmi Auntie seemed unconvinced. "A black cat with one green eye and one blue crossed my path three days ago outside a yellow house. It means bad luck on the second floor. Mehar, you should probably go and check it out."

"Be my guest." Daisy waved Mehar Auntie upstairs. "You may also want to check the roof while you're there. Sanjay used to sneak out at night. You wouldn't want to miss anyone who might be hiding there." She couldn't resist throwing out a little dig at her perfect big brother.

"Sanjay!" Mehar Auntie sighed as she headed for the stairs. "Such a good boy. How is he doing?"

"I don't know. We haven't heard from him in months. And did you miss the part where I told you he used to climb out on the roof to sneak out at night against the rules?"

"Such a rascal." Mehar shook her head, smiling.

"You wouldn't say that if it had been me climbing on the roof," Daisy called out.

"You would never have climbed on the roof." Salena Auntie pinched Daisy's cheek. "You're our good Daisy."

Good Daisy. She'd always been good because there had never been an opportunity to be bad. When it had just been the three of them at home, she'd taken over the household chores—all of which made it easier for her to justify avoiding school dances, dating, and parties. If not for Layla dragging her out, she would have been content to stay at home with her schoolbooks and her video games and her online computer world.

"All clear." Mehar Auntie joined them in the kitchen, smiling as if she hadn't just been upstairs checking under beds and in closets for a hidden man. "I haven't been upstairs for a long time. Daisy's room looks just like it did when she was a little girl . . ."

Ugh. Why had she never bothered to redecorate? She was twenty-seven and still living at home in the same room and following the same rules her father had laid down when she was a teenager. If her aunties had their way, she would marry a nice desi boy selected by the family and go straight from her house to her married home.

Daisy grabbed a *bedmi puri* and dipped the crispy Indian bread made of *urad dal* into the *raseele aloo*. Jana Auntie always made it with the perfect combination of spice and tang.

"If things don't work out, Roshan is a lovely boy," Lakshmi Auntie said. "I had your horoscopes done and you're a perfect match. He comes from a good family, and he is an engineer . . ."

Daisy shoved another bedmi puri in her mouth as her aunt extolled Roshan's virtues. Usually she just switched off when her aunties played matchmaker, but today everything they said grated on her nerves. She was a professional with two degrees and a good job. Why did no one even consider that she might be capable of picking a man for herself?

Maybe her perfect match was the kind of man who would propose a marriage of convenience to get her aunties off her back? Or give her a passionate kiss in the middle of the office? Or show up at an animal hospital in the middle of the night after he'd been emotionally flayed by his family?

Maybe she'd stuffed her emotions so deep inside, hidden beneath her lists and rules and lines of code, that she hadn't realized there was a "bad Daisy" waiting to get free.

· 20 ·

Thursday, 8:07 A.M.

DAISY: Confirming Date #4, Thursday 6 p.m. Hockey Game.
SAP Center. San Jose Sharks vs. Toronto Maple Leafs.
Objective: Meet Taara Auntie, Ashok Uncle, and their
boys, Nihan and Imran.

LIAM: Go Sharks!!!!

AFTER messaging Liam, it took Daisy a full thirty minutes to get into her flow state. Even then, a part of her brain was still mulling over their encounter from the past weekend and all the things that could have happened if they hadn't been interrupted. What if they'd actually had sex? How could they continue to have a fake engagement after crossing that line? And what if once wasn't enough? Was she betraying her family by sleeping with the enemy? Or was she putting the past behind her and moving forward?

Only a few short minutes into her flow, Rochelle interrupted with a pop-up message on her screen.

TYLER WANTS TO SEE YOU IN HIS OFFICE.

With a sigh, she pulled off her headphones. Despite the cutbacks, Tyler still wanted to go ahead with their new monthly subscription boxes and a revamped website to reflect the new branding, which meant a whole new level of code.

"What's up?" Mia looked over from her desk. "I thought this was flow time. I've been trying to keep quiet."

"Tyler wants to see me."

"Shh." Josh ripped off his headphones. "It's like you're just sitting there waiting for any excuse to talk, or rip open a foil packet, or sigh, or rustle papers, or . . ."

"Have a donut." Mia offered him a box of fresh crullers from the bakery down the street.

"I know what you're doing," Josh grumbled as he took a donut. "But it's not going to work. I can't be bought with donuts and smiles."

"What about gossip?" Zoe asked, looking up from her computer. "I know something you don't know."

"Is this middle school?" Sarcasm dripped off Josh's tongue. "Are we taunting each other now? Am I going to come to work tomorrow and find a frog on my chair?"

"Fine." Zoe turned back to her computer. "I won't share that Andrew's leaving. Brad is going to hear our branding pitch. Oh, and Hunter asked Rochelle about Daisy. I guess he missed the meeting where Tyler announced she was engaged."

"Hunter asked about me?" Daisy's mouth went dry. If she'd known all she had to do was turn a laptop off and on to get noticed by a guy like Hunter, she would have spent more time volunteering with the Help Desk team.

Josh sniffed. "He probably forgot which end of his laptop was up."

"Or maybe he realized a brilliant, sexy software engineer, who is so awesome she got us an audience with Brooding Brad, has been hiding on the third floor, and he wanted to make his move before anyone else snatched her away," Mia said, snatching the box away. "I can't believe you're jealous."

Josh huffed his derision. "I'm not jealous. I just don't understand why he would ask about her and not me." He flexed both skinny arms, puffing out his chest beneath his *Coding Is Life* T-shirt. "Who could resist this?"

"You're right." Sarcasm dripped from Mia's tone. "Even I can barely hold myself back. How *did* Hunter manage to resist the siren call of your fabulous bod?"

"Exactly." Josh gave a smug smile. "And she's engaged. I'm not."

"Fake engaged." Zoe grinned. "Who wants to let Hunter know?"

TYLER was in a mood.

"What took you so long?" he demanded when Daisy walked into his office.

"I was in the flow." She sat on the chair across from his desk and peered at him over a giant stack of papers. Unlike her tidy workstation, Tyler's office was a sea of paper, coffee cups, pizza boxes, charts, boxes, books, and, curiously, pink paper umbrellas. No surface was clean. Every movement was a study in not knocking something over.

"Brad isn't happy," Tyler said abruptly. "Apparently you convinced Liam to give Mia and Zoe a chance to present the branding pitch that I rejected last year."

Daisy shrugged. "Can he be unhappy and still hear them out? Not one of the women in that room felt that a rebrand of unicorns, rainbows, and scantily clad nondiverse women resonated with them in any way."

Tyler ran his hands through his hair, taking his look from

THE DATING PLAN · 183

slightly crazy to mad scientist in a heartbeat. "I thought you were a behind-the-scenes kind of person."

"It was all an act." Although she'd made the comment flippantly, the words rang true. Although she'd been a high school nerd, she'd never been shy or quiet. At least not until her mom had thrown out a comment that made her wonder if her personality was one of the reasons she'd left. But something had changed in the last few weeks, and it wasn't just the fact that she'd almost slept with her high school heartbreak. She'd made friends at Organicare and discovered a confidence she'd thought she'd lost. She had a passion for the product, and a voice that could help the company succeed.

"Good to know," Tyler said. "Anything else you think we're doing wrong?"

Daisy hesitated. "Is that a trick question?"

"It's an honest one."

She leaned back in her chair, considering. "I'd put people back in their own divisions. Developers in one corner. Marketing in another." She slipped a side eye at Hunter in the glass-walled conference room next door. "Finance could go beside the developers because they're generally quiet."

"Andrew gave his notice."

She startled at the abrupt change in topic, and the skin prickled on the back of her neck. "Yes, I heard."

"Now I don't have a project manager."

"Josh could take over quite easily," she offered. "He worked closely with Andrew."

"So you'd pick Josh over anyone else?"

"He's good at what he does. People like him. He's a bit of a cowboy, but you can easily rein him in."

Tyler studied her for a long moment. "Not you? After all, you came in here and advocated for Mia and Zoe's rebrand, proposed an office reorganization, questioned Brad's vision, and tried to get Josh a promotion. You have the skills and the experience. I think you'd do a good job."

Daisy's mouth went dry. *Project manager?* It was the next step in a developer's career. More money. More prestige. More responsibility. Better work. But on the flip side, it required more commitment. The project manager was the glue that held everything together, and you couldn't be the glue if you weren't prepared to stick around. She had started to find her voice, but it wasn't loud enough to lead.

"No," she said. "Not me."

LIAM'S phone buzzed on his desk. He picked it up and barked a hello. Usually, he enjoyed the rare opportunity to work in the office, but tonight was hockey night. He hadn't seen Daisy all week, and every minute until quitting time felt like a damn hour.

"Your tickets have arrived." His new assistant wasn't fazed by his odd behavior. She'd come from a start-up where the developers dressed and acted as characters from the game they'd created. Even the days when Liam arrived in full riding leathers didn't merit the lift of an eyebrow. "You got the club seats with a center ice view."

"Yes!" He pumped a fist. There was no point going to the game if you couldn't see the sweat on the players' brows. No point making money if he couldn't share one of the few things that brought him joy with his fake fiancée.

He wanted Daisy to know him—the man he was today, not the man who had messed up his life so bad that it took three years on the road and a kindhearted stranger to set him on the right path again. He wanted her to look at him with all the passion and desire he had seen in her eyes when she was a teen, like he was perfect and not flawed, whole and not so utterly broken. And the best way to do that was to show her the things he loved.

Six hours until game time. He drummed his thumb on his desk for a full ten seconds before pressing Daisy's number on his phone. He'd never been a patient man.

"To what do I owe this honor?" Her voice lit him up inside and he instantly forgot all about the accounting systems software pitch deck James had given him to review.

"I wanted to let you know the details of our sports date. I got club seats with a center ice view! It's going to be a great game. I can feel it. One good run and the Sharks will get close to the top."

Daisy sniffed. "A Sharks turnaround that results in a playoff spot is a long shot. There's no point in denying reality."

His breath left him in a rush. Her informed assessment suggested more than just a passing familiarity with the game. Could this day get any better? "You follow hockey?"

"After Sanjay moved away to do his residency, I couldn't let my dad watch the games alone." She sighed. "I can't imagine they'll be able to turn it around. Maybe I shouldn't come. Mia asked me to stay late tonight to help her prepare the pitch for Brad and she wants a second opinion. I also have a program to debug that could use a few extra hours. And Tyler offered me a project manager job but I turned it down and now Josh wants my help after work to transition into the role."

His good mood popped like a birthday balloon. "You aren't coming?"

She laughed and hope swelled in his chest again. "Of course I'm coming. I said I'd come and I love hockey, so I'll be there. I didn't realize it was so easy to wind you up."

"You didn't wind me up," he grumbled. "I knew you were kidding."

"Sure you did."

His heart jumped at her teasing tone. "I'll ask James if I can borrow his SUV. I wasn't going to bring my fan gear but now that I know you're into the game . . ."

"What do you mean by 'fan gear'?" she asked carefully.

He felt a warning prickle on his neck and quickly changed the subject. "Why did you turn down the promotion?"

"I'm not ready for that type of commitment. I don't like to get too involved in the companies I work for so I can keep my options open."

Liam wondered what she considered being "too involved." She had clearly made friends at Organicare—people who trusted and relied on her, and who had inconveniently asked for her help when she had a hockey game to attend. She'd also put her neck on the line to save the company—matchmaking hadn't been enough to convince her to be his fake fiancée, but saving the company had. How much more committed could a person be?

"So you were saying you can't come because you're helping the friends you don't have at the company you don't want to stay at because you don't care?" Was she doing that with him, too? Helping him and pretending she didn't care? When really she did?

Silence. And then, "What time is the game? Your details were incomplete."

"I'll pick you up at six," he said. "And feel free to give me a kiss when I get there because I got such great seats, but do be gentle. I still haven't recovered from falling off your roof."

"I won't," she said firmly.

"You won't kiss me?" He leaned back in his chair, thoroughly enjoying the conversation. "Or you won't be gentle? I'm okay with rough if that's your thing."

Daisy snorted into the phone. "I'm not talking about sex."

"We should talk about sex after what happened the other day." He hadn't been able to stop thinking about it. Alone in his bed at night, he'd imagined the soft press of her body against him, the warmth of her skin, the softness of her hair, her moan when he'd touched her breasts . . . God, she had beautiful breasts.

"It would have been a mistake," she said, without hesitation. "We can't get intimate and have a fake relationship. It doesn't make sense. That's why I made the rules."

"So why do I want to kiss you right now?" He knew just how to throw her off her game, and her sharp intake of breath told him his words had hit their mark. He liked how his strong, intelligent fake fiancée got all flustered when he mentioned anything to do with sex. Daisy's rules made her feel safe and secure. But sometimes you could have the most fun when the rules were broken.

"Because you want to practice for the kiss cam and win free stuff at the game?" she responded after some hesitation.

"Because I like kissing you, Daisy."

Silence. He could almost see her fingers drumming on her desk. "Liam?"

His pulse kicked up a notch and he held his breath, hoping she would tell him she liked kissing him, too. "Yes?"

"What did you mean by 'fan gear'?"

· 21 ·

LIAM was expecting Daisy to be surprised when he arrived at her office building to pick her up after work. After all, not everyone owned virtually every piece of Sharks fan gear ever made, and he'd put a lot of thought and care into which pieces he wore tonight. He was not, however, expecting her to turn and run away.

"Where are you going?"

"No. Stay back." She reached behind her for the building door. "You're one of them."

"One of whom?"

"A crazy fan."

"You don't like my Sharks jersey?" He smoothed a hand over his blue fan jersey, one of dozens he'd collected over the years. "Or is it the hat?" He'd put the foam rubber shark head hat on before he met her so she'd get a good look at its teeth. "I brought a hat for you, too."

Plastered against the glass door, she shook her head. "I'm not wearing a two-foot rubber shark on my head."

Liam felt a sharp stab of disappointment. "What's the point in going if you aren't going to support the team?"

"I can support the team without humiliating myself."

Worried that she might make a run for it across the busy street, Liam approached her slowly and carefully, holding out the gear he'd brought for her to wear in his outstretched hand.

"I'm not a stray dog, Liam," she snapped. "You don't have to creep over to me. I won't bite." Her gaze flicked to his head. "Or maybe I will if you expect me to wear something like that."

"Yours isn't the same." He offered her a small felt hat with a shark fin on top, felt eyes, and long tassels made of white felt for shark teeth. "I thought the rubber might be too much, so I brought you something less aggressive."

She approached cautiously, like he was about to attack her with his foam shark head. "Give it to me."

Liam handed it over and she gave a soft "humph" as she inspected the hat. "It's okay. Actually, it's kind of cute."

"Like you."

Her begrudging smile was all the encouragement he needed. "I brought you a jersey, too." He handed her a smaller version of the jersey he was wearing. "You'd feel out of place if you weren't wearing one. Sharks fans rule." He pumped his fist in the air and shouted, "Go Sharks!"

"Go Sharks!" a passing dude shouted back. "Enjoy the game tonight!"

"Fine." Daisy sighed. "I'll wear the hat and jersey. Anything else?"

"Face paint?"

"No."

"Body paint? You'd have to be naked but I could use a darker blue on areas you'd prefer to keep private."

"Absolutely not."

"I also have flags, banners, pom-poms, blue wigs, a full-size shark costume, giant cardboard teeth, shark plushies, and a few blow-up sharks."

She twisted her lips to the side, considering. "Let's see the blow-up sharks."

He led her to the SUV he'd borrowed from James and lifted the hatch to show her his stash of fan gear.

"This is insane," Daisy said. "It's like a souvenir shop. Do you sell it out of the back of your vehicle at the game?"

Liam's chest swelled with pride. "No, this is all mine. I got most of it when they made the Stanley Cup finals in 2016. I wore the full suit in their last game against Pittsburgh." He lifted the costume. "Come to think of it, I never got it washed . . ."

"I'll take one of these blow-up sharks." She pulled one from the pile. "And maybe a rally towel." Still not smiling, she grabbed a shark plushie. "I want him, too."

"That will be $22.95." He held out a hand, and this time she laughed, the full, delightful belly chuckle he remembered from the past.

"How about I buy you dinner when we get to the Shark Tank instead?" she offered.

"I don't believe that's on our dating plan, Ms. Patel." He pulled out his phone. "Let me see . . . Hmm. It appears that we've already crossed off the dinner option."

Daisy shrugged. "If you don't like their roast beef sandwiches . . ."

"With horseradish?"

"And beer."

Liam stroked his chin as if considering. "Double order of fries?"

"Each."

"And for dessert?" he asked.

"Fried Oreos, of course."

He tucked away his phone. "For you, I'm willing to go 'off plan.'"

AFTER two sandwiches, one plate of nachos, four cups of beer—three for Daisy and only one for Liam since he was driving—one giant popcorn, two candy bars, a bag of fried Oreos, and a 2–1 score as they came up to halftime, Liam couldn't believe he was out with the same woman who had run away from him earlier that day.

"Fear the Fin!" Daisy screamed and shot out of her seat to wave her shark plushie. "Go Sharks!"

"I thought you didn't particularly care for hockey." He nodded an apology to the couple behind them, who seemed to be more amused than irritated by Daisy's enthusiasm. "I thought you only watched it to keep your dad company."

"It's different live." She shoved a handful of popcorn in her mouth. "Also, I've had a lot to drink." Her eyes widened as she stared at the ice. "No. Not Marner!" She slapped her hand on her head as Marner played the puck between his legs and scored with a shot from the slot to tie it at 2–2.

"I thought we could use this time to ask questions so we could get to know each other," he suggested, knowing full well she'd shoot him down. At least she wouldn't be able to accuse him of not sticking to the plan. And really, was there any better way to truly get to know a person than to get them drunk at a hockey game?

"Shh." She slapped his shoulder. "Don't distract me."

There was very little that could tear Liam's attention away from a game, but watching Daisy was far more entertaining than watching the Sharks dominate the Maple Leafs. When halftime finally came, he was almost disappointed.

"Do you want to get something else to eat?" he offered.

"No. There's too much going on." She bounced in her seat to the party music, watching the Zamboni sweep the ice and the Sharks mascot shaking fins in the crowd.

"Anything you want to ask?" he persisted. "This is your chance to get to know the real me. Penetrating questions. Childhood trauma. Friends. Family. Stories from the three years I spent as a nomad biker running errands for outlaw motorcycle gangs and hiding from the law . . ."

That got her attention. "For real?"

"I was twenty-one and had no job and no college education when I left San Francisco. I had to earn money to live. Also, I was pretty messed up at the time."

She poured the last of their Milk Duds in her mouth. "So you turned to crime?"

"It paid well. Most of the bikers were good guys. I'd run errands and they'd give me a place to sleep, something to eat, a little company . . ." He trailed off when her eyes widened. Daisy probably didn't need to know all the details of his wildest days, or how lonely life on the road could be. "There's nothing like being out on a bike. You're part of the world instead watching it go by. The wind in your hair, the sun on your face, the open road in front of you . . . It takes your breath away."

Her lips curved a little, her brown eyes dreamy. "I'd like to try it someday."

Not something he'd ever expected Daisy to say, but he wasn't going to waste an opportunity to take her out on his bike. "It's still on the plan if you change your mind."

"We should go find my relatives," Daisy said abruptly, shaking herself as if caught in a daydream. "I got their seat numbers from one of my cousins who works here as a security guard. We can try to bump into him, too. The only things you need to remember about Taara Auntie are: one, don't eat any food she gives you because she's a terrible cook; and two, praise her boys."

Liam chuckled as they made their way up the steps. "Praise the food; don't eat the boys. Got it."

They walked through the crowd to the food service area outside the section where her aunt was seated. It only took a few minutes of searching before Daisy began to wave. Liam was about to comment on her incredible eyesight, when he noticed two large and two small people in full foam shark suits pushing their way through the crowd.

"I knew I should have worn my suit," he grumbled.

Daisy greeted her relatives with awkward hugs and kisses to their faces, which were visible in the cutouts in the shark costume undersides. Wearing only his jersey, his foam shark head hat, and his fan towel around his neck, Liam felt positively underdressed.

"This is my fiancé, Liam," Daisy said after introducing everyone without taking into account the thickness of Liam's shark head hat. As a result, he missed the boys' names and mentally labeled them Baby Shark #1 and Baby Shark #2.

"So this is the boy." Taara made no effort to hide her perusal, her gaze lingering on Liam's hat. "At least he supports the right team."

Score! Liam fought back the urge to pump a fist at what clearly was a victory in his quest for acceptance.

Taara turned her attention back to Daisy. "Every week I see you. Every week you try my new fusion food. And you told Salena first? I thought I was your favorite auntie."

Emotional manipulation. Liam knew all about it. Every CEO with a failed start-up pitch had a sad story to tell, and he'd quickly learned to harden his heart.

"It was an accident," Daisy said. "If she hadn't bumped into me, of course I would have told you first. You are definitely my favorite auntie. Who else could make me a special engagement celebration surprise?"

Taara's eyes widened in delight. The baby sharks visibly grimaced. Liam sidestepped over to them and slipped a twenty-dollar bill into each boy's hand. "Go buy yourselves something to eat," he whispered.

With a quick, questioning look to their dad, they waddled away, their steps restricted by their shark fin tails.

"If I'd known we'd be meeting you, I would have made something special." Taara handed Liam a clear plastic container filled with brown goo. "But lucky for you, I made extra of our halftime treat. I took all the special foods you can get here—hot dogs, sandwiches, pizza, corn dogs, chocolate, popcorn, Hawaiian barbecue, Dole Whip, nachos—blended them all together, sprinkled on a little cayenne for spice, and some garam masala, and surprise! Shark Stew! You don't have to waste time lining up or deciding what to eat and miss the halftime fun. You can have it all."

Daisy snatched the container out of Liam's hand. "That's so kind, Auntie-ji, but we've already eaten."

"I still have room. I want to try it." Liam took the container and lifted the lid. No noxious smells or odors were released. He took the spoon Taara offered him and had a small sip. Utterly vile. It reminded him of his days as a biker when they would drink every night until they threw up, and then drank some more. Still, Taara looked so hopeful, he didn't want to disappoint. Gritting his teeth, he finished everything in the container, realizing only when he was done that the boys had returned and everyone was staring at him in silence. Liam wasn't sure if that was bad or good. He offered the empty container to Taara. "If we hadn't already polished off a tray of food, I would ask for seconds."

"My God." Her husband shook his head in wonder. "He ate it."

"He likes it. He really likes it!" Taara grabbed Liam's cheeks and gave them a squeeze. "What a nice boy. And such good taste in food . . ."

"Well, weren't you just the fabulous fiancé," Daisy said after Taara and her family returned to their seats. "Am I going to have to take you to the hospital to have your stomach pumped?"

"It was a hard life on the road." Liam cleared a path through the bleachers to their seats. "I had to eat things much worse than that."

"What's going on down there?" Daisy pointed to a food service worker holding two pizzas at the bottom of the stairwell. He was talking with the hockey cam operator and pointing in their general direction.

Liam's pulse kicked up a notch and he pulled down his shark head hat. "They're going to give away free pizzas. We have to draw their attention."

"How?"

"Jump up and down. Shout. Scream. Dance so the camera sees us. Wave your rally towel and your blow-up shark."

Daisy shrank back in her seat. "I can't dance in the seats. People will see us."

He stared at her, incredulous. "You didn't care five minutes ago when you were screaming at Noesen to get the lead out. And I know you have the moves. You are a dancing queen."

"I just don't want to embarrass myself."

Liam wondered how screaming "Fear the Fin" while wearing a shark hat and waving a blow-up shark in the air could be less embarrassing than dancing in front of the seat, but then he'd never understood the inner workings of the female mind.

"I'll take the hit. I'll dance so badly, no one will be looking at you." He jumped up, waving his rally towel in the air as he danced the way her father had danced in front of his television every time the Sharks had scored a goal. "Pizza!" he yelled. "Go Sharks!"

"You're on the big screen!" Daisy jumped up beside him and danced his same crazy dance, waving her shark in the air and screaming, "Fear the fin!" The camera operator swung his camera in their direction, and suddenly they were immortalized on screen in a heart-shaped circle of lights with "Winner" flashing above them.

"We won! We won!" Daisy jumped up and down and threw her arms around Liam, nearly knocking him over as she pressed her lips to his in a delighted kiss.

Her lips were soft and warm and sweet with chocolate. The shock of them short-circuited his brain and for a moment he couldn't breathe. And then he was pressing her lips apart, hungry for her, desperate for more.

She softened against him, sighed. He braced himself for her to retreat, but instead, she tightened her arms around him and kissed him back, her tongue tangling with his as she explored his mouth.

"Pizza!"

She pulled away, leaving him floundering, his brain struggling to understand why someone was shoving a box in his face when all he wanted was her sweet lips and her soft body and her sigh of surrender.

"Pizza selfie." Daisy held up her phone and took a picture of them with the pizza box angled in the corner. She laughed when she showed him the screen. This time he was the one who looked dazed.

Iᴛ was an incredible second half. The Leafs allowed three goals in the third period and lost for the first time in four games, 5–2 to the San Jose Sharks with Radim Šimek scoring on an empty net with fifty-seven seconds left. By the end of the game, Daisy was best friends with the couple behind them, and had high-fived everyone seated in their section. They'd finished the pizza and the rest of the food and shouted themselves hoarse.

"This was amazing." Daisy put her arm around Liam's waist as they shuffled through the crowd. "Much better than a textile exhibition. I never imagined myself in a shark head hat, but I could become a convert."

"Liam! Hey, dude!"

Liam gritted his teeth when he saw the two investment bankers coming toward them. Over the years, he'd wined and dined them countless times, taking them to bars, parties, and various clubs to convince them to invest in his companies. He'd also introduced them to Brendan when his brother took over Murphy Motors, and they'd become good friends. But here, now, with Daisy, they were part of a world he didn't want her to see.

"Business acquaintances," he muttered under his breath. "Tall dark one is Marco. Short one is Dan. They've had a lot to drink. I'll say hello and then we're out of here."

"Are we engaged or just friends?" Daisy asked.

"They know Brendan, so being engaged might help our case."

"Long time, dude." Marco slapped Liam's hand and he made the introductions.

"This is Daisy Patel, my fiancée."

"You? Engaged?" Marco snorted. "To her? Get out of here. Who is she really? A client?"

The skin on the back of Liam's neck prickled in warning. He needed to get Daisy out of there before this went very, very wrong. His shoved a hand in his pocket, feeling for his knife. Not that he needed a weapon, but he needed something to calm him down.

"She's really my fiancée," Liam said, struggling to stay calm. Except for his eyes, he didn't look like his father's side of the family, but he had inherited their Irish temper. "We met eight months ago, and when you know, you know."

"Seriously? Weren't you with that model eight months ago?" Marco frowned. "The one with the legs and the big boobs? Emma?

Or Ella? She invited us to that hot tub party on the top of that hotel."

"The hot tub girl was the one before the one with the legs, and after the one with the boobs," Dan snorted, weaving slightly on his feet. "And I think he had a couple of models in between from the modeling agency start-up that he was considering adding to his portfolio."

"I told you we should have invested in that one," Marco said, making no effort to keep his voice down. "He was swimming in tits and ass." He looked over at Daisy. "Pardon my French."

Daisy gave him a cold smile. *"Quel salaud!"*

Liam didn't speak French, but from the look on Daisy's face he suspected what she'd said wasn't polite.

"So who is she really?" Dan gave him a nudge, keeping his voice low. "I mean, come on, man. You and her?"

"I'm his parole officer." Daisy grabbed Liam's arm and tugged him in the opposite direction. "He's on an escorted day pass. Move aside because I have to have him back in his cell by eleven P.M."

Dan's eyes widened. "No shit? What did he do?"

"He swam in the wrong hot tub." Daisy fixed Dan with a glare. "Next time, check their ID."

· 22 ·

"I'M sorry."

"I know." Daisy bit back a sigh. Liam had apologized ten times since their encounter with his friends. Next, he'd try to explain. Again.

"I should have turned the other way, but they'd seen us and . . ."

Daisy turned to Liam as they pulled into her driveway. "If you say it one more time I'm going to slap you."

"I'm not proud of that time in my life." He turned off the car and they sat in the dark, staring at the blue garage door that had needed a new coat of paint for the last ten years.

"Apparently that time in your life was only eight months ago, which poses a problem since that's when our fake relationship was supposed to have started." Daisy sent a quick text to her neighbor to let her know she was on her way to pick up Max.

"If you hadn't pulled me away, I would have decked them for insulting you." His hands tightened around the steering wheel.

"Insulting me?" She raised an eyebrow. "They were insulting you. Of course someone like you wouldn't be with a beautiful, sexy, curvy, brainiac goddess like myself. How many science fairs did you win in high school? How many math competitions? How many tech companies were beating down your door when you graduated from college with the gold medal? Did you know that the longest

English word is 189,819 letters long? Or that the French word for bastard is *salaud*?"

His lips quivered at the corners. "I knew what you said wasn't polite."

"Not in the least." Daisy chuckled. Liam was much more distraught than she was, but then he'd never been a high school nerd, never been mocked for everything from her intelligence to her clothes. "But they deserved it. Seriously. Who talks like that in front of someone's fiancée? I'm no victim, Liam. I didn't need protecting."

His mouth tightened in a straight line, and he grumbled. "You could have thought of something other than parole officer."

"Are you sulking now?" Her voice rose in pitch. "Because I quickly and elegantly extracted us from an untenable situation? You should be kissing my feet in gratitude."

"You could have been my private jet pilot," he muttered. "Or my personal banker. Now they're going to think I'm incarcerated."

Daisy laughed. "Then it will be a big shock when they see you in a few weeks in your outdoor hot tub draped in glamor models and partying like there's no tomorrow."

"That's not who I am," Liam said. "It's part of the job, but I don't enjoy it."

"Says every man who goes to a strip club." She folded her arms over her chest. "I'm not upset, Liam. I developed a thick skin in high school. But they raised a good point. Maybe we're just not believable as a couple. And if that's the case, we might as well stop this charade. How do you explain going from the type of women you dated before to me? How do I explain going from Orson to you?"

"You developed taste." He preened in the rearview mirror.

She laughed. "And you lost it?"

"I found perfection."

He sounded so serious, she almost believed him. Wanted to believe him. "Always the funny guy. What are we going to do? They didn't believe it. Brendan didn't believe it. Even your aunt said no one believed you the first time you said you were engaged. Will our fake dates be enough to convince everyone this is real? And more importantly, what about my dad? All he's known is that I've hated you for the last ten years. Will we be able to convince him, too?"

"Do you still hate me?" he asked quietly.

She didn't have to think about her answer. "No. I haven't completely forgiven you, but I don't hate you anymore. I've enjoyed our little charade."

"Good to know."

She looked over at him, his hands clenched on the steering wheel, face distant and forlorn. She couldn't send him home to brood. "Do you want to come in and meet Max? Mehar Auntie dropped him off with my neighbor because she was going out for dinner."

Liam sighed. "What if he doesn't like me? You said it would all be over."

"I think he will like you."

"Hmm." He unbuckled his seat belt, his face brightening. "I am very likable."

"You are."

"And I probably should meet him since you are my fake fiancée and he's very important in your life," he continued, his mouth serious but his tone light. "What if he has unusual markings or a strange bark and I get asked questions about him and get them wrong?"

Heat radiated through her chest at the return of his good humor. "It would be terrible. People would know our relationship was a sham, and all this time we've put into setting it up would have gone to waste."

Liam nodded, his eyes sparkling. "I suppose I should meet him if you think it's important for our fake relationship."

"I do."

He reached behind his seat and pulled out a plastic bag with the name of a popular pet store on the front. "Good thing I came prepared."

Daisy didn't know whether to be amused or indignant as he showed her all the dog toys he'd bought for Max. "How did you know I would invite you in?"

"I didn't know." He flashed her a lopsided grin. "I hoped."

Daisy unlocked the front door for him before going to collect Max. Her elderly neighbor stayed up late and was always happy to have a little company.

Max was back to his old self, wriggling happily in her arms and covering her with licks and kisses as she walked back to the house.

Liam was seated on the living room floor when she walked in, the new toys spread around him. "I washed them all." He held out his hand when she put a curious Max on the floor. "I wanted to be sure he was safely bribed."

Max walked over and sniffed Liam's hand, his tail wagging. He gave a happy bark and let Liam give him a rub before turning his attention to his new toys.

"You spoiled him." Daisy crouched down beside Liam when Max brought her a KONG to inspect. "Now he's going to expect toys from every stranger who comes into the house."

"I'm not a stranger." Liam pulled her onto his lap. "You've known me for a very long time."

"I'm beginning to realize that I knew you and didn't know you at the same time." She cupped his jaw, rough with a five-o'clock shadow. "You had a whole life outside of this house that I didn't know much about, except for the year we were in school together when you were either in the principal's office or making out with one of the senior girls in the hallways."

"That's because I couldn't make out with you." He nuzzled her neck, his breath warm on her skin. Max dropped his KONG and jumped on her lap to see what was going on. Daisy gave him a reassuring pat and he went back to inspecting his new toys.

"I would have been thrilled if you had made out with me," she said. "That's all I thought about."

"You were Sanjay's little sister. There was a bro code I couldn't break, and I couldn't get my head around the fact that you were suddenly not a little girl. I had to ask him if I could take you to the prom, and even then he threatened me with all sorts of violence if I did anything more than hold your hand."

"That doesn't sound like Sanjay." She nuzzled his neck, breathing in the scent of him. "He barely knew I existed."

"He had his own issues, but don't think he didn't care about you."

She sat up so she could study his face. "What happened on prom night, Liam? You said you would tell me."

He leaned back against the wall, and pulled her against him, her back to his chest, his arms around her waist, his breath warm on her hair. "My mother gave me the money to buy a tux," he said softly. "I had every intention of taking you. I was looking forward to it."

"Me, too." She watched Max carry his new toys to his basket, one by one, as if he were afraid someone was going to take them away if he didn't have them near.

"I didn't have a car, and I couldn't carry the tux on my motorcycle, so a friend offered to take me to pick it up," Liam continued, his voice growing fainter. "He showed up in a car that I knew wasn't his, but he told me had permission to drive it. We got the tux, and on the way home, he decided to see how fast it could go. He lost control of the car and it hit a lamppost."

Daisy gasped, looked up, but his gaze was far away. "Were you hurt?"

"The airbags saved us, although our faces were pretty banged up. By the time the police got there, we were already out of the car to check the damage. I didn't realize that my friend was high when he picked me up. He told me right after the crash, but before that nothing about his behavior made me think he'd been using. Even the police didn't suspect anything, but then they ran the plate and discovered the car was stolen." His hands tightened around her and she covered them with her own. "He was a good guy, a great friend." His voice thickened. "He didn't deserve to lose everything because of one mistake. He'd done so much for me over the years, I couldn't let him throw his life away."

"Oh, Liam . . ." Knowing what he was going to say, she looked up again, saw his pulse throb in the hollow at the base of his neck.

"Drugs, plus a stolen car . . . it would have been the end of the career that he'd been dreaming about all his life." He let out a ragged breath. "So I told the police I'd been driving. They took me to the station and threw me in jail. I needed my one phone call for a lawyer, or I would have called you."

"All these years I thought you didn't care." Her voice wavered with guilt at the memory of all her unkind thoughts. "You were just being a good friend. I hope he knew how lucky he was."

His voice hitched and he shuddered beneath her. "He's the one who sold his car to bail me out two days later. The owner of the stolen vehicle was someone he knew and he convinced the dude not to press charges. I got off without a record. He even gave me back the tux. But I couldn't come and see you."

"I would have understood, Liam. Dad and Sanjay, too. You made an incredible sacrifice to save a friend. No one could fault you for that."

He dropped his forehead to her hair, squeezing her so tight she almost lost her breath. "I felt sick at the thought that I'd hurt you, and I was ashamed I'd been in jail. You were smart, beautiful, and ambitious and you had your whole life ahead of you—an incredible future with an amazing career and a partner who could give you the world. And I was everything my dad had said I was. No direction. No motivation. No prospects. That night I got a taste of my future, and I didn't want you in it. I didn't want to drag you down. I thought it was better if I left with you hating me than if I came to say goodbye."

Tears welled up in her eyes as she relived the emotions of that night, knowing now that he was nothing like her mother, that he'd left because he'd thought he wasn't good enough and not because she wasn't good enough for him.

Turning in his arms, forcing him to release her, she pulled his head up, framing his face with her hands. "Thank you for telling me. It doesn't take that pain away, but it makes all the difference now that I understand."

Sensing her emotional distress, Max squeezed in between them, tail wagging, up on his hind legs, pawing at her shirt with his forelegs, trying to lick her tears away.

Liam gave him a rub. "I wish I'd had a Max back then."

"He's the best." She gave Max a reassuring cuddle and reached for one of his new toys. "He also won't leave us alone now. Emotional Daisy usually gives him a lot of attention."

"We could . . ." He jerked his head toward the stairwell. "Go upstairs."

"Hmmm." She pressed a soft kiss to his lips. "I was planning to seduce you here, but it might be easier without Max watching."

He smiled, and the last of the shadows that had darkened his face slid away. "I am delighted to be seduced anywhere by you."

Daisy took Max to his basket in the kitchen with all his new toys and gave him a good-night cuddle. Liam was waiting at the top of the stairs when she was done. He dragged her against him and captured her mouth, devoured it, holding her so close she could feel his heart pound.

Sliding her arms around his neck, she walked him backward, reveling in the feeling of being in control. "Prepare yourself. Nothing has changed in my bedroom since I was a teenager."

He slid one hand down to squeeze her ass. "I don't plan on spending a lot of time looking at the décor."

"The rules still apply," she said. "One time. No obligations. No feelings. No expectations. No sleeping over. This is my make-up-for-prom fantasy. It's all I want."

Disappointment flickered across his face so fast, she wondered if she'd seen it. "I'll take you any way I can get you." He gave her a slow, sensual smile. "But I promise, one night with me won't be enough."

"We'll see about that." Once in her bedroom, she backed him up to her bed. Daisy had never had a man in her room before. It was her sanctuary, the one place she could truly be herself. Over the years, she'd traded the princess décor for shabby chic, but the white country-style furniture remained the same.

"What do you think?" she asked.

"I like the contrast of Avengers posters on pink walls." He nodded at the bed. "And the pink cover is very . . . girlie."

Daisy laughed. "I've never been able to bring myself to change it. My mother decorated it for me before she left. I didn't realize it was because she was planning to say goodbye. I kept it the same way hoping she'd come back. And when she did, she wasn't even interested in seeing it. I should have redecorated it then, but I couldn't be bothered."

"Time for a change." Liam sat on the edge of her bed. "Wipe the slate clean."

"I've never seduced a man before." She closed the door in case a curious Max came looking for her. "How am I doing?"

Liam gestured her forward, then pulled her into a straddle over his lap. "You've got me on the bed. I'd say you are ninety-eight percent there."

"I want to see you." She tugged on his Sharks jersey, and he obliged her by pulling it over his head.

Daisy licked her lips as she took in the hard planes and angles of his broad chest, the ripples of his six-pack and the narrow trail of hair leading below his belt.

"Sweetheart . . ." His voice dropped to a husky growl. "If you keep looking at me like that, you won't have to seduce me. All you'll have to do is take off your clothes."

Daisy lifted an eyebrow. "You'd like that, wouldn't you."

"Very much."

She ran her hands possessively over his chest. "You'll have to wait. I'm enjoying my prom fantasy."

"You might enjoy it more if you took off my jeans."

"Don't make me laugh. I'm trying to concentrate." She leaned forward and nuzzled his jaw.

"You want serious sex?" He reached for her shirt, but she gently knocked his hands away.

"No touching."

Liam groaned. "You're killing me."

"I know." She pulled the shirt over her head and grinned when his eyes widened.

"I see I have some competition." He studied her black bra with the Hulk's face printed on each cup. "Is that a challenge? Because not even the Hulk is going to stop me now that I have you on the bed."

"The Hulk is pretty strong," she teased.

"I've got something he doesn't have."

"What's that?"

He moved quickly, grabbing her around the waist and tumbling with her back onto the bed. "You."

They wrestled for control, but he finally pinned her with the weight of his body, his breath fanning the side of her neck. "How should I pleasure you first?" he mused, amusement dark in his voice. "I need to make you feel so good you'll never make me climb over your roof again."

Desire flushed through her veins, heating her skin. Why did she react this way to him? It was like her body was tuned to his frequency, tingling at his every touch. "You already make me feel good. I can be myself around you. I don't have to worry about being too serious, or too odd, or sharing weird numerical facts, or making plans and lists, or having a sense of humor that no one seems to get."

His mouth took hers, firm and hot. Pressed against him, she could feel the power of his hard body, the rumble of his pleasure.

"I get it." He rolled to the side. Desire flushed deep in his face, softened his lips. "I get you, Daisy. And the things you mentioned are what I like most about you." His hand dropped down over her stomach to unbutton her jeans.

Daisy lifted her hips so he could slide them down and help her kick them off. "Your turn."

A growl lumbered from him. "Promise not to move. I love you like this, spread out on the bed for me like a delicious treat."

Laughing, she nodded. "I promise." She had no interest in moving when Liam stood and unbuckled his belt. He had a magnificent body. She drank in every defined ridge, every powerful muscle, as he dropped his jeans to reveal a pair of black boxers and an erection so thick and hard everything below her waist tightened. She licked her lips and his blue eyes darkened.

"Temptress." He climbed up beside her and tapped his fingers right above her mound, where the Hulk's face was prominently displayed. In anticipation of something happening tonight, she'd worn a matching bra and panty set. After all, it never hurt to be prepared.

"This dude . . . watching me . . ." Liam shook his head. "He has to go. There can only be one alpha in this bed."

"Jealous much?" She pushed up to press a soft kiss to his chest.

With a groan, Liam stretched out on the bed and pulled her into a straddle over his hips. Almost giddy at the prospect of taking control, she let her mouth roam, slicking her tongue over the ridges of his muscles, delighting when his hard, powerful body quivered beneath her. He was so strong, he could easily unseat her, but the restraint he showed as she worked her way down to the waistband of his boxers made her smile.

"Kisses go here." Liam stopped her when she reached his belly button and pointed to his lips.

"What about here?" She flicked her tongue over the hard bulge in his boxers.

"Fuck." Liam groaned, head falling back on the pillow.

"Not yet." Daisy grinned and eased his boxers over his hips. "I believe the plan was to make you feel so good you would never want to go."

"That was *my* plan." He slid his hand through her hair, tugged her head up. "And there's only one place I want to go right now."

"Impatient." After stripping off his boxers, Daisy settled between Liam's legs and licked the length of his shaft, ripping another groan from his throat. Heat radiated from him, his skin hotter than normal.

"I liked it better when I was on top," he grumbled, his hand tightening in her hair.

"I'll go slow." She took him in her mouth, marveled at the heady masculine taste of him, the power she could exert just by tightening her lips or stroking with her tongue. His body went rigid, the powerful muscles of his thighs taut beneath her. She stroked and licked until he was rock hard, but before she could take him to the edge, he gently eased her away.

"I want this. Fuck. I want this. But I want you more." He didn't wait for an answer. A heartbeat later she was on her back on the bed, wrists pinned over her head in his strong hand, her body at the mercy of his mouth.

Still, he took his time, brushing kisses along her jaw and down to the hollow of her throat, then over her sternum to the crescents of her breasts. Despite his tight hold, she arched to rub up against his chest, her nipples hardened to tight buds.

"Let's get rid of the competition." He released her hands to strip away her bra. His rumble of pleasure as he revealed her breasts vibrated between her thighs.

Liam's demanding mouth captured her own and she opened to the wet heat of his kiss. Groaning, he moved down her body, his lips heating a trail from the hollow at the base of her throat to her breasts, where he proceeded to lick and suck her nipples until she was writhing on the bed.

She reached between them, stroked along his hardened length.

"Not yet." He gently moved her hand away. "I made you a promise that I intend to keep." Kissing his way down her body, he hooked his fingers into her panties and tugged them off. "Hulk's gotta go."

Warm hands held her firm as he settled between her legs. His warm, wet tongue drew lazy circles around her sensitive flesh, so gently at first, she hovered between pleasure and pain, and then harder, faster, until the ache inside her blossomed into edgy need. He slid one thick finger into her wet heat, and then another, a sensual intrusion that stole her breath. And then his lips closed around her aching nub.

She cried out, throwing back her head, hands fisting his hair, pleasure cresting and flooding through her veins, trickling out to her fingers and toes.

With a low growl, he pushed up and sheathed himself with a condom he pulled from his pocket. On instinct, she rolled her hips, wrapped her legs around his hips to pull him close. Liam grabbed the edge of her headboard with one strong arm and plunged inside her.

She gasped at the exquisite sensation and tightened her legs around him. Need pulsed beneath her skin.

"Move, Liam. Please. I won't break." Her body took over, hands gripping his thick biceps, hips rocking, taking him deeper.

A strangled groan escaped his lips and he gripped her hip so hard she knew his fingers would leave bruises. Braced against her headboard, he pulled out and pushed in deep and hard, shoulders straining as he gave in to her demands, filling a need she didn't know had existed, taking her outside of herself, beyond control.

The bed squeaked, swayed. The headboard hammered against the wall in time to the rhythm of his thrusts. Need coiled inside her, tighter and tighter, until finally she peaked. Her spine arched, her orgasm sweeping through her body in a tidal wave of pleasure, filling her with heat.

Liam growled her name, corded throat tightening, muscles going rigid as he followed her into oblivion.

The sound of wood splintering startled her, made her heart jump. Liam dropped down, covering her with his body as the headboard split in two and crashed down on top of them.

"Oh my God." She panted beneath him. "We broke the bed. Are you okay?"

Liam heaved the headboard up so she could slip out from underneath him. When she was safely away, he lifted it onto the floor and gave a satisfied growl. "Now, that was good sex. Where's my phone?"

"You are not posting a picture of this." Daisy's heart pounded as she surveyed the destruction. "What if someone in my family saw it?"

"It's just for me." He grabbed his phone and snapped a quick picture. "But if anyone did see it, they'd be jealous that you are with a fucking sex machine who is so powerful he ripped your headboard in half." He curled his arms, popped his biceps. "The Hulk is no match for the power of these pythons."

"I see another python is also proud of the fact that my room is destroyed."

Liam cupped his semi-erect length and gave a manly tug. "The desk is next. Or should we do it on your dresser? You've got a weapon of mass destruction at your beck and call. Just point me in the right direction."

Laughter bubbled up in her chest. She loved this playful, joyful side of Liam. Maybe he'd never really had a chance to embrace that part of his personality when he was growing up, but he was definitely making up for it now.

"Are you seriously comparing yourself to a weapon of mass destruction?"

"Look at this room." He opened his arms wide. "We rocked the fucking world."

Daisy made her way across the broken shambles of the bed. It didn't look girlie anymore. They'd managed to knock off the pink duvet, and all the fluffy pillows, and tangle the delicately flowered sheets in a heap.

Definitely time for a change.

"Where are you going"—he growled—"wiggling that sexy little ass at me?"

Daisy looked back over her shoulder and smiled. "You said something about a desk?"

· 23 ·

Friday, 3:30 A.M.

DAISY: Are you awake?

LAYLA: I am now.

DAISY: I had sex with Liam.

LAYLA: Is that your idea of a joke? It's too early in the morning.

DAISY: We broke my bed and my desk and my collection of Disney princess teacups.

LAYLA: OMG. I can't even . . . Are you CRAZY?!!?

DAISY: Maybe.

LAYLA: He's supposed to be your FAKE fiancé.

DAISY: It was just a onetime thing. I'm about to send him home. He's sleeping on my collection of stuffed pigs because there are splinters in my sheets.

LAYLA: What are you going to do when your dad comes home?

DAISY: Tell him I had a nightmare.

LAYLA: I hope it's a nightmare and Sam is going to wake me up and I'll be in my bed not texting you in the middle of the night.

DAISY: It was soooooo goooooood.

LAYLA: Stop. You're hurting my eyes.

DAISY: He's waking up.

LAYLA: We need to talk about this. Send him home now. Don't do anything stupid.

DAISY: GTG. He wants MORE!

SUNDAY morning, Liam drove up the narrow lane leading to the distillery, with Jaxon bouncing excitedly in the back seat behind him. He couldn't remember the last time he'd been to visit but he was shocked at the state of disrepair. The white wooden fences were gray and worn, the low stone walls crumbling, and the cobblestone drive was bumpy with holes. Looking at the run-down buildings and rusted barns, he wondered if Daisy would think their arrangement wasn't worth the effort.

He'd spent a lot of time during the last couple of days wondering what she thought. What would she do if he texted her before their next date for no reason other than to see how she was doing? They hadn't made a rule about texting, but they did have a rule against developing feelings. It was a stupid rule and he was stupid for agreeing to it, especially because the feelings were already there. And now that he'd slept with her, he was even more certain that the feelings he was having were going to get him into trouble, and there was nothing he could do about it.

"Go faster, Uncle Liam. I want to see the horses."

"Sorry, bud." He caught Jaxon's gaze in the rearview mirror. "This is your mom's car, and I don't want the gravel to chip the paint. She might not let us go on any more adventures together."

A few minutes later, he rounded the final bend of the long road and parked outside the visitor center alongside Joe's blue pickup truck. As soon as he stepped out of the car, he could smell the grains cooking, the scent of slightly sour bread. It was a smell he associated with his grandfather, and he felt a sudden pang of sadness in his chest.

Jaxon ran across the gravel to see the horses in the neighboring field as soon as Liam helped him out of the car, stopping briefly to say hello to Joe who had come out to greet them.

"I wasn't expecting to see you out here." Joe wiped his hands on his coveralls before shaking Liam's hand. At seventy-five, he was slightly stooped, his dark hair thinning and gray, but he was still strong and fit, his mind as sharp as it had ever been.

"It's been a while and I've been wanting to stop by. When Lauren asked me to look after Jaxon today, I thought we'd make a day of it."

Joe sighed. "Good idea, since it's all coming down in a couple of weeks anyway."

"No one is tearing it down," Liam said firmly. "Your job is safe, Joe, and the jobs of the other employees here, too."

Joe lifted an eyebrow. "So that girl you told us about at the will reading . . . She's real?"

"Very real. Her name is Daisy. She's the sister of an old friend. She knows what it's all about and she's okay with it because the arrangement benefits her, too."

"I thought she hated you." Joe leaned against the faded white picket fence that surrounded the visitor center.

"I think we may have worked that out." He wasn't sure how Daisy felt about him, but after the other night, he was pretty sure hate wasn't at the top of her list.

"Well, good for you. I won't say anything. As far as I'm concerned, you've known her forever."

"I have known her forever, but we've gone on dates to make it seem more real." He pulled out his phone to show Joe the pictures of him and Daisy at the clothing store, the restaurant, the hockey game, and the one he'd taken when he'd declared her the winner of their Guitar Hero marathon.

Joe gave Liam a quizzical look. "You sure it's fake? Looks like you two are having fun."

Liam stared at the picture they'd taken at the hockey game. She'd kissed him, not the other way around. And it hadn't been for show. He'd seen something in her face—something soft and raw and real. And then, just when he'd thought it was all over, when his past had come back to haunt him, she'd shown him just how strong she really was, and made him want her even more.

"It's *supposed* to be fake." He frowned, disconcerted by the question. "It *has* to be fake. She wants it to be fake."

"What do you want?" Joe asked.

Liam shrugged. "I don't do relationships. As you know, I didn't have a good role model in that department." He waved Jaxon over, and they walked together to the visitor center.

"You're not your old man," Joe said. "You're your grandfather's boy. I saw it in you then, and I see it in you now. That core of goodness. Inner strength. Selflessness. And the sheer Irish stubbornness that meant that no matter how many times you were knocked down, you kept getting back up. Your dad saw it, and he hated you for it. He knew he would never be half the man you were at thirteen. You were everything his father had wanted him to be. Your grandfather was so damn proud of you. He kept tabs on everything you did right up until his last days."

Emotion welled up in Liam's throat, the pain and grief he hadn't allowed himself to feel when his grandfather died threatening to rip a hole in his chest. He pulled out his knife and closed it in his fist. "I lost all those years with him." His voice cracked, broke. "I couldn't forgive him for not helping my mother. I couldn't forgive any of them. It was only when he got sick . . . when I knew I was going to lose him . . ."

Joe clasped his shoulder. "No one knew how bad it was with your mom. She didn't tell anyone, and you boys didn't say anything. You kept your secrets. We only found out about the abuse after your father died and your uncle Fitz called your mom in Florida to see if she wanted to come to the funeral. That's when she told him the truth. Fitz and the others decided not to tell your grandfather. His health was already bad and they didn't want to cause him any stress."

No one knew. He couldn't even begin to process what Joe had told him. All those years of thinking his family had turned a blind eye to the abuse, when they didn't even know. And he was partly to blame. He'd kept his mother's secrets, just as he was keeping secrets now. Secrets destroyed relationships. He didn't want to make the same mistake again.

He left Joe to his work and took Jaxon for a tour of the malt house, one of three large warehouses where the whiskey was made, then went to the mash tun to watch the malt and water being stirred by giant paddles. They followed the liquid wort as it was passed into the old wooden wash back tanks where the yeast was added and fermentation began, and then walked into the stillroom.

"Look down here, Jaxon." Liam squatted beside one of the oak casks where the whiskey was aging. "This cask came all the way from Ireland. This is where all the Murphy men leave their mark." He pointed to the last name on the list. "That's me. My grandfather gave me a knife to cut my name there when I told him one day I wanted to run the distillery."

Jaxon squatted beside him. "Where's Dad's name?"

"Your dad and your grandfather were busy with the car business and didn't have time to run the distillery."

"I want to run it. I'm a Murphy man." Jaxon stood up tall. "Can I put my name there?"

"Sure you can." Liam pulled out his knife, and together they carved Jaxon's name beneath Liam's in the soft oak, and then blew out the sawdust for luck.

They had just started a game of hide-and-seek when Joe appeared in the doorway, his face creased with worry.

"You'd better come quick. There are a couple of contractors here. They say Brendan hired them to do site prep for tearing down the distillery. They're planning to bring the demo crew out next week."

His good humor faded in an instant. "What the f—" He cut himself off just in time. "Take Jaxon and give the estate lawyer a call. I'll talk to them."

He found the contractors in the visitor center, checking out the display of whiskey bottles in the tasting area.

"What the hell is going on?" His boots thudded over the worn, dark wood floor. The exposed beams in the ceiling had been painted to match, contrasting with the dingy, whitewashed walls covered in framed pictures of the Murphy distilleries over the years.

Usually the familiar scent of whiskey calmed him, but today it reminded him of everything he could lose.

"Just doing a site survey for the demo next week." The taller of the two, a heavyset dude with thick arms and broad shoulders, held up a hand, palm forward. "We were hired by Brendan Murphy. I've got a work order in my truck. Do you want to see it?"

"Brendan doesn't have the authority to sign anything," Liam spat out. "The distillery is being held in a trust, administered by the law firm Abel & Ashford. Only they can sign off on a survey."

"That's who signed off," the contractor said. "Brendan Murphy hired us but the name on the work order is Ed McBain from Abel & Ashford."

"Christ." No doubt Brendan had taken advantage of Ed's inexperience. The junior lawyer had messed up big time.

Liam shoved his hand in his pocket and curled his fingers around his penknife. "I'm going to have to ask you to leave. I'll get in touch with the lawyers and sort this out."

The contractor scratched his head. "We've been paid to do a job, and it sounds like the right people signed the work order, so we need to get the work done. It's just a survey. Nothing's coming down today."

"You walk anywhere other than to your truck and—"

"Liam!" Joe appeared in the doorway. "Let them do what they have to do. We'll sort this out the right way. Don't let Brendan send you down a path that will compromise everything you've built. Knowing him, he might have set this up to do exactly that. Think of Daisy. She's got a stake in this, too."

Liam gritted his teeth, taking deep breaths to try and slow the ragged throb of his pulse. *Think of Daisy.* No doubt she would be fiercely angry on his behalf, just as she had been when they'd met his investment banker friends at the hockey game. He could imagine her tossing out cutting French insults that no one could understand, or making everyone's head spin with esoteric facts and the rules of law. She'd been sympathetic and understanding when he'd told her about his previous arrest; however, she might not be happy if he wound up in jail again. He couldn't take that risk. Daisy was fast becoming the most important thing in his life. He didn't want to lose her again.

"Get the hell out." His voice was as sharp as the knife in his pocket, and the contractors scurried away.

After they'd gone, and Jaxon had been settled in the back office with a soda and a snack, Liam sat on the worn bench by the door, his head in his hands.

"What was Brendan thinking?" he said to Joe, who had come out to join him. "It's three weeks to my birthday. If I'm not married by then, the distillery is his, free and clear. I introduced him to Daisy and he didn't even believe our relationship was real, so what's the big rush?"

Joe leaned back on the bench beside him, his arms folded under his head. "He was here the other day with Lauren. She told me his company is in big trouble, and the news is going to hit the papers in the next few days. Apparently, the IRS found some anomalies during an audit and reported them to the regulators, who started an investigation. Turns out your dad and four of the directors— friends he'd appointed to the board—were involved in some kind of fraud that affected the shareholders. I don't understand the legal stuff, but it's big, Liam. We're talking tens of millions of dollars. Lauren says Brendan didn't know anything about it. That he's barely been keeping his head above water just trying to fix the mess your dad left when he died. The regulators have frozen the company's assets. He can't pay his employees . . . It's a mess."

"So he thought the solution was to sell the distillery out from under me?" A knot of bitterness tightened inside him. "He's no better than my dad."

Joe shrugged. "Desperate people do desperate things. You're planning to marry a girl you don't love. Are you any different?"

"Yes." He stared out over the sea of wildflowers dancing in the green fields around them. "I do love her. I always have."

· 24 ·

Wednesday, 8:00 A.M.

DAISY: Confirming Date #5. Thursday 6 p.m. The Rose &
Thorn Pub, The Mission District. Objective: mix with
colleagues, meet your cousin, Ethan, and your bar friends.

LIAM: What do you mean "mix with colleagues"? I thought
it was a date.

DAISY: It's a date with friends.

"LEFT hand like it's moving to the side and right hand like you're combing your hair. Bend your leg to the side and then turn." Daisy demonstrated the Bollywood dance routine for twenty eager young dancers in front of the mirror. Twice a week after work, she taught Bollywood dancing at the neighborhood recreation center with Mehar Auntie. It was always the highlight of her week.

"My turn," Mehar Auntie said. "Cue the music."

Daisy walked to the side of the room to adjust the sound system and spotted Layla in the doorway.

"I'm beginning to regret asking Mehar Auntie to teach Sam and me a few routines for our sangeet after your class," Layla murmured. "She always steals the show."

Daisy laughed. "I'm always surprised she lets the girls dance at all."

"You haven't answered my messages for the last few days."

Daisy practiced the next few steps of "Dola Re Dola," the dance she was teaching next, turning away so Layla couldn't see her face. "I've been busy at work. I stayed late a few nights helping Zoe and Mia put together their pitch for a rebrand. Josh still isn't sure about the project manager promotion, so I've been going over Andrew's planning sheets with him. And Tyler wanted someone to go with him to meet investors in case this thing with Liam falls through, and then—"

"I know what you're doing," Layla said. "Your feeble attempts to distract me won't work. Do you think I'm not going to mention the fact that you had sex with Liam? Your FAKE fiancé?"

"Oh." Daisy sighed. "That."

Layla folded her arms across her chest. "Yes, that."

Daisy twirled around, as much to practice her dance steps as to avoid Layla's stern glare. "You could be a little more supportive. I had a dry spell after Orson, and the sex with Liam was amazing. AMAZING. I've never had sex like that before. In fact, I don't even think what I was doing before was actual sex because no furniture got broken, I never came multiple times, and the things he can do with his tongue . . ."

Layla held up a warning hand. "I'm sure you could have found someone equally skilled. You didn't have to sleep with the man who broke your heart."

"First, my heart was bruised, not broken," Daisy said. "Second, there is no way I could have found someone with that level of talent. And, third, sadly, it was just the one time. I told him the rules and he agreed to them."

Layla slapped a hand to her head. "When has Liam ever followed the rules?"

"He's doing pretty well with the dating plan," Daisy offered. "Well, except for when he showed up at the clothing store before our date and bought a sherwani and a sword. And also when he showed up at my office, but that was part of helping out the company. Oh, and then he went off-plan when he came to the vet clinic after Max ate the chocolate, and then again when he played Guitar Hero with me until the early hours of the morning so I wouldn't be alone." She brightened. "But other than that, he's followed the dating plan for our last three dates."

Layla didn't look convinced. "I just don't want you to get hurt."

"I know you don't. I don't want to get hurt, either." She twisted her hands, making the shapes of wolves and flowers as she went through the arm motions of the dance. "That's why I invited everyone from my office to our Irish pub date tonight. We had a rule against sex and we broke it, but we agreed on a new rule that it would be just once. There will be no chance I'll get drunk and want to sleep with him again when my work colleagues are around."

"Seriously?" Layla's tone dripped sarcasm. "You need an entire office staff to help you restrain yourself when he's around?"

"It was very intense and I don't want to take any chances." Daisy danced a few steps. Sometimes her cousin could be way overprotective, although thinking back, she'd acted the same way when Layla had gotten together with Sam. "Maybe it was just old feelings resurfacing and I was still back in high school crush mode thinking 'Oh my God, Liam Murphy is taking me on a date,' 'he's kissing me,' 'we won a free pizza,' 'he's sitting in my car looking like a lost puppy,' 'he likes me and Max likes him,' and then my brain exploded and no more thinking went on."

Layla shook her head. "Get out now. Forget about the aunties. It's not worth it. Roshan is a catch. I met him and you know I wouldn't steer you wrong."

"I can't get hurt if it isn't real," Daisy said lightly. "Even his friends didn't think it was real—which is highly problematic for the success of our charade, and I have yet to properly think it through."

"It sounds real." Layla followed her across the floor to keep up the conversation.

Daisy dropped to a crouch and sprang up again. "It's not just about me anymore. It's about saving jobs and helping my friends at Organicare. I can't let them down."

"And I can't watch you go through that again," Layla said. "Liam was bad news before and he's bad news now. I just can't see a happy ending to this fake relationship."

Daisy fought back her anger and disappointment at not getting the support she had expected from the woman who was as close to her as a sister. Her new friends at work were much more enthusiastic.

"I can handle this without getting hurt. I know what happens when I care too much. And I know the things that make me special are not the kinds of things that would make me . . . desirable—my mom made that pretty clear. And that's okay. I'm good with it."

"I used to hate Liam with all my heart," Layla said, her jaw clenching. "But now I realize the hurt he caused you was nothing compared to what your mother did. I wish I could wash her words out of your head, or at least make you see them for the bullshit they really are."

The music stopped and Daisy looked back to see Mehar Auntie waving her over. "I have to go. Don't worry about me. I've got my rules and I'm sticking to them. Trust me."

"I do trust you," Layla said. "But I don't trust him."

"WHAT are you doing over here when your girl is over there?" Rainey took a bottle of whiskey down from the shelf.

"I was sent for refills. Three pitchers of draft, four vodka coolers, and two pink lemonade martinis." Liam gestured to the Organicare crowd who had taken over all the tables in the back corner of the bar. "Not exactly what I had in mind when I suggested Daisy and I come here for our date."

Rainey laughed. "Errand boy. I like it. I'll give you a free shot because it means I don't have to go over and serve. I'm trying to conserve energy for my weekend race."

Liam took a seat at the bar. "Death Race?"

"Nah. Just a marathon. But I'll be wearing a ten-pound bag of flour on my back, so that should make it more interesting." She grabbed two empty glasses from the rack.

"Did Ethan get the box of Murphy whiskey I sent over?" Liam asked. "I found a few extra cases in the visitor center and since we're not getting many visitors, I thought he could use it."

"Ethan!" Rainey yelled down to the end of the bar. "Did you get Liam's cases of Murphy whiskey?"

Liam winced. "You could have just told me he was there."

"Then I couldn't have annoyed him. He hates it when I shout."

Ethan joined them a few moments later with a scowl for Rainey and a handshake for Liam. "Thanks for the bottles. That must have been a good year." He looked over at the Organicare table. "So, which one is the fake fiancée?"

Liam pointed out Daisy, who was wearing a layered green dress, the skirt just skimming the bottom of her ass, neckline diving down so low he could see the soft swells of her breasts. She'd taken off her quirky green hat when she arrived at the bar, and the yellow feather that had adorned it was now tucked behind her ear.

"She's not really your type," Ethan said, leaning against the bar.

Liam bristled. "You don't know what my type is. Maybe I've just been killing time, waiting for a woman like Daisy who is beautiful, fiercely smart, funny, kindhearted, loving, and totally dedicated to her family. She's organized and efficient, and she created an entire spreadsheet with a plan to make this marriage authentic. She's got it all under control. And she's going to kill it at quiz night tonight because she has an incredible memory for trivia. She knows how many tamales people ate in San Francisco in 1890."

Rainey and Ethan shared a look.

"He slept with her." Rainey poured a shot of Murphy's into Liam's glass.

"I didn't say that."

"You're not saying a lot of things." She smirked. "Usually you're the most talkative customer at the bar."

Daisy looked up just then and smiled, making him feel like he was the only person in the room. She started toward him and he tried to rearrange his face so he looked cool and casual when inside he felt anything but.

"You hungry?" Rainey offered Liam a napkin. "You've got a bit of drool on your chin. Or is that for the girl who's walking this way?"

He snatched the napkin from her hand. "Don't you have other customers to serve?"

"Are you kidding?" She grabbed a towel and wiped down the counter. "I am dying to meet this woman who has you all tied up in knots. Have you told her how you feel?"

"There's nothing to tell." He toyed with the knife in his pocket, running his thumb over the smooth wood surface.

"I think there is," Rainey said. "And you'd better do it before it's too late."

"Do you need any help with the drinks?" Daisy joined him at

the bar, leaning forward so he could see a soft portion of the curve of her breasts over the low-cut top of her dress. "We're going to need two more martinis and another pitcher." Her smile widened. "Hunter is here!"

Liam's skin prickled in warning. He looked over to the Organicare crowd, where he saw a golden-haired, broad-shouldered Thor lookalike pulling up a seat at Daisy's table. "Who's Hunter?"

"He's the CFO. I fixed his computer for him a few weeks ago." Her lashes swept over her cheeks, and her voice softened. "Zoe heard he was asking around about me."

Liam hoped Hunter had asked about her because his computer had broken down again, and not because he was looking for a different kind of fix.

Rainey hummed the theme song to *Jaws* while Ethan snickered beside him.

Liam made the introductions, letting Daisy know that Rainey and his cousin knew the true nature of their relationship.

"I love the bar," Daisy said to Ethan. "It's got a great atmosphere. So cozy and lively. It's exactly how I imagined a pub in Ireland would be. I love that you've shown off your Irish heritage with cultural memorabilia, especially that Celtic cross on the wall." Her gaze fell on Rainey and she studied the bartender's ink. "That's an interesting tattoo on your forearm. *Timshel*. It's a quote from John Steinbeck's novel *East of Eden*."

Rainey looked momentarily taken aback. "You know it?"

"It means 'thou mayest'—a reminder that people always have a choice."

A curious sensation filled Liam's chest. It took a moment for him to identify it as pride. "I told you she was smart."

"Good thing you brought her on quiz night," Ethan said. "Maybe you'll win the grand prize."

"Quiz night?" Daisy's eyes widened. "You brought me here on a quiz night?"

Secretly pleased by her delight, Liam shrugged. "I thought you'd enjoy it."

"Yes!" She threw her arms around him, pulling him off his stool. "I've never been to a pub quiz. What a great idea!" And then she was hugging him, and his arms were around her, and she smelled of wildflowers and sunshine, and she was soft against his chest, but he hoped she would stop jumping because "highly aroused" wasn't a good look for him in a public place.

His lips found hers and he kissed her softly and thoroughly. When she trembled in his arms, returning his kiss with passion and abandon, a rush of something sweet and innocent flooded his senses. He'd kissed dozens of women and none had ever affected him this way. None had ever tasted of sunshine. None had made him question what was real.

Drawing in a ragged breath, Daisy pulled away. "That was . . ."

"A good show," he said quickly. "People were watching."

Her face smoothed to an expressionless mask and she patted down her dress. "Right. Yes. Good idea."

After they had collected the drinks and returned to the tables, Daisy organized everyone into teams for the quiz. Their team included her friends Mia and Josh, as well as Hunter, a declared trivia buff who plucked the yellow feather from Daisy's hair and tucked it into his own "for luck."

Daisy and Hunter dominated the game from the start. After the first round, Mia and Josh gave up trying to answer and got busy drinking and flirting. Liam quickly realized that if he didn't distract Daisy with a congratulations kiss after each right answer, she would lean across the table to high-five Hunter, whose attention was never focused on her face.

"How did you know that was a Wim Wenders film?" Hunter asked after Daisy answered yet another obscure question, and he'd beat Liam to the win with a high-five salute.

"I went to his retrospective at the Roxy last year."

"I heard about that." Hunter stretched in his chair, his T-shirt riding up to reveal what appeared to be a twelve-pack of toned abs. "He's definitely earned his place among the pantheon of postwar European auteurs and reinvigorated German film in the seventies."

Liam ordered two shots of whiskey from a passing waiter while Hunter regaled Daisy with amusing anecdotes from Wim Wenders's best art house films. He drank them one after another and ordered three more.

"What are you doing?" Daisy whispered after Hunter excused himself to talk to his friends at a nearby table. "You're going to get wasted."

Liam wasn't drunk, but getting close. His brain was fuzzed and it was getting more and more difficult to keep his emotions under control. "What's the deal with this dude? Why is he so interested in postwar European auteurs, and why does he keep looking down your dress?"

"He isn't looking down my dress." Daisy's eyes widened. "Are you jealous?"

"No. Look at me. Utter magnificence. Why would I be jealous? I could take him down with a pantheon of punches."

She quirked an eyebrow. "Why would you need to take him down? Mia says he's interested in me, and you and I are in a fake relationship."

"It didn't feel fake to me when I broke your bed." He puffed out his chest. "How many men have given you that kind of ride?"

"Liam!"

"So, are you going home with him tonight?" He swallowed hard, trying to keep his anger in check. "Are you going to watch Wim Wenders films and share interesting trivia facts while you—"

"Do not even go there," she warned.

"I think the waiter was held up at the bar." He pushed his chair away. "I'll get Rainey to set me up. Do you want anything?"

"I want you to stop drinking." She stood beside him. "I'm going to tell her to cut you off."

"Be my guest."

Rainey was busy talking to Hunter at the bar. The dude was like a snake, slithering all over the place, sticking his nose where it didn't belong. Or was it a tongue? How did snakes smell? He opened his mouth to ask Daisy, but Hunter got to her first.

"Hey, babe." Hunter smiled. He'd obviously had dental work. No one's teeth were that perfect. "I was just ordering some food for the table. You want anything? I'm vegetarian, but—"

"Daisy likes meat," Liam said abruptly, throwing an arm around Daisy's shoulders. "We went to an Indian restaurant and she pounded back an entire plate of *rogan josh* like she hadn't eaten in weeks. She attacked it like a piranha. I didn't think a pound of meat could disappear that fast."

Daisy pushed his arm away. "What's gotten into you?"

Hunter's gaze flicked from Liam to Daisy and back to Liam. "Hey, man. I don't want to step on any toes. I heard you two were in some kind of fake relationship, but if it's real . . ."

"It's not," Daisy said.

Liam leaned against the bar, arms folded across his chest. "We have a plan. Daisy is all about plans. And then we didn't follow the plan. But now it seems the part of the plan where we can see other people is still on the table." He looked over at Rainey. "Any hot tub parties going on tonight?"

"Ethan's got a bead on something going on after the bar shuts down."

"Great." His gaze fixed on Daisy. "Tell him I'm in."

"YOU'RE going to a hot tub party?" Daisy glared at him. "On our date?" She could just imagine him in a hot tub surrounded by women. They would be all over him like leeches.

"Our date was over when you invited the whole office along," he said in a tone lined with frost.

"I think I'll go wait for the food at the table." Hunter turned from the bar. "Let you guys talk it out."

Daisy watched Hunter cross the room. He was a nice guy. Definitely a ten in the looks department. Sociable, friendly, and fairly normal. He was an accountant, a trivia machine, and he liked art house films. They had a lot in common. She should have been over-the-moon thrilled that he was interested in her, and five weeks ago she would have been. But something was missing. Something that was staring her in the face.

"I invited them because we need people to see us out together," she explained. Partially true. But the real reason was that she'd been worried she wouldn't be able to keep her hands off Liam after a few drinks. And now, after discovering he'd set this date up on a quiz night and watching him glare at Hunter every time the dude even looked in her direction, it was clear she'd been right. It was taking all her effort not to throw her arms around him and drag him away.

"What good does it do if you tell them our relationship isn't real?" Liam spluttered.

"I didn't tell him. Mia did. She knew I liked him, and she heard that he'd asked about me . . ."

"Is that 'like' as in 'like as a friend'?" His petulant tone made her lips quiver with a smile. "Or 'like' as in 'I think I like him, too'?"

Daisy cupped his face between her hands. "Don't do this," she said softly. "We had rules, a plan."

"I can't help it. The dude is trying to get into your pants." He covered her hand with his, gliding his fingers slowly over her skin. She felt his touch as a shimmer of heat through her body that coalesced into a throb between her thighs. It took only seconds, and yet she felt like they'd just spent hours between the sheets. She couldn't move, couldn't think, couldn't breathe. She wanted the feeling to go on forever. She wanted to understand this curious connection and how that simple touch could set her body on fire.

"Maybe I wanted him in my pants." She leaned closer, brushed her lips over his.

A soft growl rumbled in Liam's chest. "Are they as pretty as your dress?"

"They would be if I were wearing some." Rules be damned. She wanted him. Now. And it was clear he wanted her, too.

Liam raised an eyebrow. "I didn't think you were that kind of woman."

"The kind of woman who would come to a bar without her pants? Or the kind who would mention it?" Her pulse kicked up a notch when he slid his arm around her waist. "And why would you care about my pants since you're going to a hot tub party?"

"I only care if they're going to get in my way." His free hand slid up her thigh and under her skirt.

"Get a room." Rainey threw a set of keys on the counter. "Back office. You have fifteen minutes, and you'd better give me a good tip."

Liam grabbed the keys and within moments they were in a

dingy office with a metal desk, a worn chair, and a few half-empty shelves.

She didn't know who moved first. One minute they were tumbling in the door, and the next she was in his arms. His mouth crashed down on hers, his hands sliding down her back to her ass, pulling her tightly against his hips. Her mouth opened for the kiss, fingers threading through his soft, thick hair.

Their tongues touched and electricity zipped through her body like a bolt of lightning, firing every nerve ending. Drunk on a cocktail of lust, alcohol, and the adrenaline rush of quiz night, that one touch made it impossible to pull away. Instead, she pulled him closer, pressing her breasts against his chest, shameless in her desire to feel every inch of his body against hers.

A groan rumbled from his chest, and he lifted her against him. Her legs wrapped around his waist and she rocked against the bulge beneath his jeans. The world faded away and she was lost in a sea of sensation—the taste of whiskey on his tongue, the rock hard muscles beneath her hands, the pure heat of his body against hers, the sound of their panting breaths, the glimpse of the Liam she remembered beneath the hooded eyes.

"Condom?"

"Got one." Still holding her with one strong arm, he dug into his back pocket.

"Door?"

"Locked."

"Belt?"

"I've run out of hands." He released her and she jumped down and yanked on his belt.

"I hope you weren't lying about wearing no pants." He lifted her dress and groaned. "Captain America? Couldn't you have gone for someone less wholesome?"

"I wasn't planning on sexing it up in the back room of a bar when I got dressed this morning."

Liam leaned down and nuzzled her neck. "Anytime you're with me, you should expect to be ravished. Come prepared. Leave the Avengers at home."

"What happened to just once?" She yanked open his fly and slid her hand inside his jeans to stroke his shaft beneath his boxers.

Liam hissed in a breath and gently pulled her hand away. "Once at home. Once at the bar . . ." He dropped to his knees, his warm hands slipping under her dress to ease her underwear over her hips. With one hand offering her support, he helped her step out of them like the gentleman ravisher he was.

"We have ten minutes and thirty-seven seconds," she whispered as he rolled on the condom.

"You're sexy when you keep time in your head." Still on his knees, he pressed her legs apart. "Open for me, my timekeeping seductress."

"We don't have . . ." Her words died away when she felt the heat of his mouth, the slow, sensual strokes of his tongue, the rub of his unshaven jaw against the soft skin of her inner thigh. Her pulse hammered and she sank her fingers into his scalp, holding him in place.

He took his time, stoking her desire with a steady seduction, licking, teasing, his tongue everywhere except where she needed it to go. She sank against the door, gave herself over to the long, liquid wave of pleasure, the firm grip of his hands on her thighs, the exquisite sensation of his tongue sliding over her most sensitive spot.

When he slid a thick finger deep inside her, and then another, she moaned, certain the ground was quaking beneath her feet. His mouth went from light and gentle to hot and demanding, and she rocked her hips against him, trying to soothe the wicked ache between her thighs.

She came in a rush, fisting his hair, her vision narrowing, breath lost to the exquisite pleasure of giving her body over to pure physical sensation.

Liam surged up as she rode the aftershocks of ecstasy. Wrapping his arms around her, he lifted her, bracing her back against the door. She locked her legs around his hips and crushed her mouth to his in a fevered kiss.

This was what she wanted, these wild sensations, frenzied need, liquid fire in her veins. She wanted to lose control, to stop thinking, to do nothing but feel.

He savaged her throat with hungry kisses, ground his hardened length against her slick, wet heat. Her pulse pounded in her ears, throbbed at the juncture of her thighs. She arched against him, rocked her hips, demanding his possession.

"Liam. Don't tease."

With a low, guttural groan, he shoved his boxers down and positioned himself at her entrance. "Say my name."

She knew instantly what he wanted. Not his name. Their name. Their secret. "Humraaz," she whispered. "My humraaz."

With a satisfied growl, he pushed inside her, one hand under her ass, the other braced against the door beside her head.

"Oh!" Daisy tilted her hips, allowing him to sink deeper with every thrust. She was flying, high on being bad, on breaking the rules and loving it, on following Liam into the abyss and knowing she would survive.

"Ask me for it." His brow furrowed, his face a mask of concentration as his body moved in a timeless rhythm. "I want to give you everything."

"Fuck me." Dirty words. Filthy words. But this time there were no better words in the English language to tell him what she wanted.

Sweat beaded his brow and he hammered into her, his warm breath rasping against her cheek. She came without warning, without realizing she'd tipped over the edge until she heard her own voice cry out, the sound echoing in the empty room.

Liam kept moving, pressed her against the door, his groans intensifying with his thrusts, body tensed and straining. He followed her over the edge, holding her tight, his shaft pulsing deep inside her.

He collapsed against her, his forehead resting against hers. "How's our time?"

"I don't know," she said with wonder. "I wasn't keeping count."

His lips brushed lightly over her nose. He seemed in no hurry to release her, so she drew him closer, languid in his arms.

"I think I'm ready for that motorcycle ride."

He looked up and grinned. "I can hardly wait."

"Liam?"

"Yes?" He nuzzled her neck.

"You won't be going to your hot tub party. I'm changing the rules. No dating is allowed. Your amended dating plan will be in your inbox by morning."

"Daisy?" he whispered her name.

"Yes?"

"The only person I'd want to be in a hot tub with is you."

· 25 ·

Saturday, 8:00 A.M.

DAISY: Confirming Date #6. 9 a.m. Visit motorcycle shop to
buy gear then motorcycle ride. Objective: ??

LIAM: Who gets up at 8 a.m. on a Saturday?

DAISY: I had to take Max out and I'm making you breakfast.

LIAM: Very noisy. Trying to sleep. Need to recover from
night with sex-crazed fake fiancée.

DAISY: What's our objective on this date?

LIAM: This is for us. Shared experience. Photographic
evidence of you in leather.

DAISY: Confirming Date #6. 9 a.m. Visit motorcycle shop to
buy gear then motorcycle ride. Objective: Shared
experience, pictures of Daisy in leather.

LIAM: Did you seriously just do that?

DAISY: Don't pretend to be surprised.

LIAM: Where's my breakfast? Was supposed to be asleep.
Now hungry.

DAISY: Stop complaining or you'll have to make it yourself.

LIAM: Are you going to bring it to me in bed?

DAISY: It's no longer a bed; it's just a mattress.

LIAM: Are you going to bring it to me on the mattress?

DAISY: Yes.

LIAM: Naked?

DAISY: You want a naked breakfast?

LIAM: Is there any other kind?

HAMISH had been on the road again. Liam could tell as soon as he walked into McCallum's Motorcycles; the familiar scents of diesel and leather were overpowered by the rich tang of barbecued ribs.

"You trying to drive the customers away?" He held the door for Daisy, and the bell tinkled behind them.

"I *wish* I could drive them away," Hamish said. "I've got so much work I've barcly got time to eat."

"You clearly had time to ride. I thought the doctor told you to stay off the bike and eat healthy. Heart surgery is no joke."

Well over six feet, with thick arms and a few extra pounds on his belly, his long brown hair streaked with gray, Hamish was the best motorcycle mechanic in the city and Liam's first employer. He'd been approached by no less than five outlaw motorcycle clubs hoping to lure him away, but Hamish loved his shop—an old garage in the Theatre District—and his freedom. He also loved the gossip his biker customers shared about themselves and each other.

"Don't give me a hard time about my food," Hamish said. "Life isn't worth living without ribs. I got my friend Lucas to bring me ribs the day after my surgery. Puked them all up and sent him out for more." His steely blue eyes zeroed in on Daisy. "You gonna introduce me to your friend?"

"This is Daisy. My fiancée."

Hamish wiped his hand on his *Ride or Die* T-shirt. "You ride, sweetheart?"

"No, but—"

"Didn't think so."

She gave an affronted sniff. "What's that supposed to mean?"

"Means there's some people who live to ride and some people who live to hide." He lit a cigarette and took a slow, considered drag.

"It's illegal to use those indoors," Daisy said. "Smoking can kill."

"But it's fantastic after a morning ride along the coast, followed by a good fuck with a pretty girl, and an amazing three-course Korean barbecue." He blew out a smoke ring, and Daisy coughed.

"Daisy is going to ride pillion on my bike," Liam explained, before Hamish could share any more details of the story he was clearly dying to tell. "We came to get some gear."

"So you finally got yourself an old lady." Hamish took another puff.

"'Old lady'!" Daisy huffed. "I'm not old."

"That's what we call the girl who sits behind her man." Hamish wheezed out a cloud of smoke.

"What if the woman's riding and the man's on the back? What's he called?"

"A pussy." Hamish made a rumbling sound, a laugh that shook his belly.

"We'll also need a pillion seat and pegs," Liam said quickly. Hamish's sense of humor wasn't to everyone's taste.

"You'll need a grab bar and backrest, too, if you're gonna take a newbie out on your XDiavel." Hamish blew another smoke ring. "You're lucky I've got some time. I can get it ready for you right away and you can be on the road in an hour." He pointed to a rack at the back of the store. "Ladies' gear is over there."

Daisy dodged the drifting cloud. "I'll go check it out."

"So what's the deal with her?" Hamish took another drag of his cigarette as he opened the small door that secured the cash area. "Seems a little uptight. You sure she's the one?"

"It's complicated."

Hamish made an amused noise. "Nothing complicated about getting a hot piece of ass on the back of your bike. Still waters run deep, my friend." They joined Daisy beside a wall of leather jackets. Hamish grabbed a metal hook and lifted a jacket from the top row.

"Try it on." He handed the jacket to Daisy. "See if it fits. Elbow, shoulder, and back armor are built in. If you don't like the leather look, you can still get good protection with a GORE-TEX jacket with integrated armor, but I wouldn't recommend it. My friend Chains bought his old lady a GORE-TEX jacket for a bike trip to Montana. He took a curve too sharp and they went straight down the side of mountain into a ravine. Chains was wearing leather and got off with a couple of broken bones, but his old lady . . ." He sucked in a rattling breath. "Jacket shredded like paper and her skin was sheared right off her. She paid for the skin grafts out of the divorce money."

"I'll take the leather." Daisy pulled it on, her shoulders rounding with the unfamiliar weight.

"I knew you would." He shot Liam an amused look. "Cool on the outside. Hot on the inside." He reached for the zipper. "Just like you."

Liam's hackles rose, a surge of jealousy flooding his veins. What the fuck was wrong with him today? Hamish, twenty years older, with his shirt stained and his breath reeking of smoke, was hardly a threat, but some long dormant possessive instinct didn't care.

With a soft growl he batted Hamish's hand away and took over zipping up the jacket.

"This one has the most aggressive riding fit," Hamish said,

seemingly unaffected by Liam's posturing. "It protects your spine and vital organs in the event of a crash. My friend Skeeter wore one of these. He was knocked off his bike by a transport truck, flew thirty feet through the air, landed in a ditch, and after three years of physical therapy he can now lift a hand to drink a beer. If he'd been wearing GORE-TEX, he would have had no arms left."

"Do you actually sell anything with that pitch?" Daisy walked over to the mirror. "Or do most of your customers run away screaming?"

"Only the pussies." Hamish handed her a pair of leather pants. "You'll need these, too. They'll protect your legs. I got this friend Wheels. He was pinned between two transport trucks. Doc said if he'd been wearing leathers, he might have had legs today . . ." He trailed off, his eyes growing misty. "We don't call him Wheels anymore 'cause he doesn't ride. We call him George."

"Give her the heaviest leathers you've got with the strongest armor," Liam snapped. "Full steel if you've got it. I want her to be safe."

Daisy disappeared into the changing room. Liam could still see her through the three-inch gap left by the ill-fitting curtain. With a growl of annoyance, he stood in front of the curtain, blocking the view of anyone in the store. What the fuck was wrong with him today? It was like someone had flicked on a protectiveness switch and he was seeing danger in every corner.

His phone buzzed and he checked the message. He had to read it twice before the words sank in. Kevin Mah, one of Evolution's senior partners, wanted him to return to New York to discuss partnership. The day had finally come. It was what he'd been working toward since he'd joined the firm. It was the culmination of a dream. Proof that he wasn't the failure his father had always thought he would be.

Moments later, the curtain rattled open and Daisy strode out, a vision of hotness in head-to-toe body-skimming black leather. She'd taken out her ponytail and her hair lay loose and wild around her shoulders.

"I'm badass," she whispered, staring at herself in the mirror. "Look at me."

He was looking. And he was wanting—wanting with a ferocity that took his breath away.

"Hamish! Quit gawking at my girl." He had a decision to make. But right now, all he knew was that he had to follow his heart, and his heart was strutting in front of the mirror, wrapped head-to-toe in black leather.

Hamish snorted a laugh. "I don't think what you two have going on is complicated at all."

PLASTERED against Liam's back, her hands tight around his waist, the motorcycle rumbling between her thighs as they raced south on Highway One along the beautiful Pacific Coast, Daisy wondered what the hell she'd been thinking when she'd agreed to the ride.

The fastest she'd ever gone on the San Francisco streets was the day her family had taken Sam to Oracle Park to propose to Layla. Jana Auntie had pulled her Giants hat down low and raced her van through the busy streets to get him there on time. But even that stomach-churning ride was nothing compared to the total and utter lack of control she had as a pillion rider, or the sheer terror of being perched on a wedge of suede-like material about the size of a fluffy breakfast pav.

With zero space between her seat and Liam's, her chest was pressed firmly against his back. Not a problem when they were cruising through the city streets at 15mph. Romantic, even. But when they hit the open road and he applied the acceleration, she couldn't hold on tight enough, terrified of toppling backward into the exposed giant rear wheel, despite the little backrest Hamish had installed for extra security.

Although her riding leathers provided protection from the wind and flying bugs, it was lacking armor where it really counted. Between the endless bumps and the relentless vibration of the Testastretta DVT 1262 engine, Daisy could only wish for a new, more padded ass.

Forty minutes into the ride, they stopped for gas in Half Moon Bay. Liam helped Daisy off the seat and she grimaced when her feet partially hit solid ground.

"She's a beast!" Liam grinned. "Are you feeling it?"

Oh, I'm feeling it. There was no point worrying whether they'd have sex ever again because she couldn't feel anything below her waist.

Daisy nodded, not daring to speak in case the stream of invective running through her head came out of her mouth.

"You need help with the visor?" He flipped up the visor for her and she drew in a breath of cool, fresh air. With her hands frozen into claws from holding on so tight, there was no way she could have opened it herself.

"What do you think?"

Daisy thought a lot of things, none of which she could share with Liam, who was so overjoyed that she had come with him that he couldn't stand still. Since she couldn't lie to him convincingly, she fell back on the next best thing. "Wow—156 hp. I never imagined how that would feel. It's like a street-legal rocket ship."

"More than any bike on the road." His eyes crinkled at the corners as he unlocked the gas tank. "Are you doing okay?"

"Just a little stiff." She forced a smile through the mind-numbing pain shooting through her thighs and ass. Was it supposed to hurt this much? Although she wasn't a fitness freak, she kept in shape with running and dancing, and once she'd joined an intense kickboxing class with Layla where the former drill sergeant instructor took it as a personal affront if they didn't work hard enough to puke.

"The place I want to take you for coffee is another half hour or so through Redwood Park. Then I thought we could go up through Woodside and get back on the 92." His smile faded the tiniest bit. "Or we could go back . . ."

"Go back? Are you kidding?" She pumped a fist with feigned enthusiasm. "I'm all in." Her feet tingled as the feeling came back in an excruciating wave of pins and needles. "I'll just hit the restroom and I'll be good to go." Gritting her teeth, she forced her feet forward, one after another, riding leathers creaking, inner thigh muscles quivering when she tried to force them together.

"Daisy? You sure you're okay?"

She waved over her shoulder. "Peachy. I'll be back in five."

Alone in the restroom, she pulled out her phone and searched for blogs about the XDiavel's pillion ride. All the glamorous black-and-white promotional images featured thin, beautiful smiling women in skintight leather, perched high on their miniature seats, looking relaxed and happy as their hair—unfettered by the inconvenience of a lifesaving helmet—fluttered in the breeze.

Maybe that was her problem. She had too much ass.

THIRTY minutes of pain and suffering later, they pulled up in front of a small wood building that looked to be a cross between a mountain chalet and a log cabin. Worn wooden steps led up to a sunny deck that overlooked the road, and carved wooden statues flanked the front door. Motorcycles filled the parking areas along the sides and on the street out front.

"Everyone comes here." Liam pulled off his helmet, his eyes dancing with delight. "Families, bikers, hikers, equestrians, writers, musicians, Silicon Valley entrepreneurs, locals—"

"Mmm-hmm." Afraid to open her mouth in case the tooth-rattling ride had broken her crowns, she pried her fingers off his jacket, and contemplated how she was going to get off the seat. Pain had morphed into agony only five minutes into the second leg of their ride, and instead of enjoying the scenery, she'd shifted her focus to staying alive.

Using force of will alone, she managed to get off the bike. Far from being a relief, standing was worse than sitting, her muscles protesting the change of position, thighs locked apart in the indelicate pose of appearing to have wet her pants.

"Let me help you with that." Liam parked the bike and helped her take off the helmet. Fresh mountain air rippled through her sweat-soaked hair.

"Liam!" A tall woman in tight black leather walked toward them, striding along all easy and loose, sleek dark hair fanning behind her like she hadn't just done the same tortuous ride in a five-pound frizz factory helmet. Her thighs came together when she stopped in front of them, like normal thighs were supposed to do. She gave Liam a hug, murmuring something in his ear that made him chuckle. Daisy could have sworn she'd been in the promo picture for the XDiavel.

"This is Tanya Weber," Liam said. "She and a friend founded Empower Ventures. Their venture team focuses on investing in female-focused industry disruptors. We've known each other for years."

"In every sense of the word." Tanya gave him a nudge and they shared another laugh.

In every sense of the word . . . Daisy felt a cold stab of jealousy at their intimate moment. It didn't make sense. Her relationship with Liam wasn't real. But the more time she spent with him, the more the line blurred and she didn't know where she stood.

"Daisy is a senior software engineer for an exciting new start-up that's focused on menstrual products," Liam said. "She's in line for a promotion to product manager. The company couldn't run without her."

Daisy grimaced. "I think that's a bit of an exaggeration."

"Take the compliment," Tanya said. "Liam doesn't throw many around . . . At least, he didn't use to."

At least, he didn't use to . . .

Was the bitch purposely trying to goad her with little reminders about her shared past with Liam? Daisy's teeth gritted together. Well, she got the message. Tanya was a cool, bike-riding, smooth-haired venture capitalist ex who clearly wasn't suffering in any way after her journey. She was probably so tough she didn't need any padding in her seat. Maybe she just sat on a board or the bare steel frame.

Liam ran a hand through his hair, ruffling the dark waves into a sexy tangle. Was he subconsciously grooming himself for Tanya? Or was he just too warm? "What are you riding now?"

"Triumph Street Triple 675. I got rid of the Ninja. Not enough power."

"You like the naked styling?" Liam asked.

Tanya smirked. "Naked is my thing, as you know too well."

Naked is my thing . . . *As you know too well* . . .

Daisy tried to shut off the snarky voice in her head, but something about Tanya set her possessive teeth on edge.

"Do you want to join us inside?" Liam asked. "We're going to have a coffee before we finish the loop."

Say no. Say no. Say no.

"Sounds good." Tanya took a few steps and looked back over her shoulder. "Do you need a hand, Daisy?"

Only to slap you.

"I'll loosen up a bit and meet you there." She forced a smile, rocking her hips from side to side like she rode pillion every day.

By the time she'd lurched her way to Liam and Tanya inside the café, her back was covered in sweat, her jaw ached from gritting her teeth, and her muscles were trembling. Thank God she'd made the effort. Tanya was standing a little too close to Liam for comfort, and she had a hand on Daisy's man.

"Have you found a table yet?" Daisy put her arm around Liam's waist, pulling him into her side and forcing Tanya to drop her hand from his shoulder.

"It's not looking good." He put his arm around her shoulder. "I'll have to get you a motorcycle as a wedding present and we can ride out here together when it's not as busy."

Daisy bit back a smile. Liam knew what was going on and he'd just made it clear where his loyalty lay.

Tanya's gaze flicked from Liam to Daisy and back to Liam. "You two are engaged?"

"Best decision of my life," Liam said, pressing a kiss to Daisy's sweat-covered temple.

"What happened?" Tanya's smile faded. "I thought you didn't do relationships."

Another squeeze. "I just hadn't met the right person."

Daisy gave Tanya a smug but sympathetic smile.

"Congratulations." Tanya's face smoothed to an expressionless mask. "It doesn't happen for all of us." She looked over Liam's shoulder. "I see a table. I'll go and grab it."

Still walking like she'd wet her pants, Daisy held Liam's arm as they followed behind her. "She seems nice," she said lightly. "I take it you two were together at some point."

Liam chuckled. "Briefly."

"It seems like she wants to be together again." She nodded at the people who were throwing amused glances their way. So what if they were laughing? They'd all been in her position once upon a time.

"Are you jealous?" he asked in a teasing, slightly hopeful tone.

"Of course not. Don't be ridiculous." She tossed her hair. "She doesn't look half as good in her leather pants as I do, and she's only got half the ass."

Liam slid one hand down and squeezed her bottom. "Damn right. You're the sexiest woman here."

"You just like me in leather."

"I like you out of leather more." His smile faded when she lurched to the side. "Why didn't you tell me you were so stiff? You can barely walk."

"I walked over here just fine."

"Because you were jealous." A slow smile spread across his face. "Of Tanya."

"Don't be ridiculous."

His eyes softened and he turned, pulling her against him. Leaning down to brush his lips over her mouth, he said, "You care."

"Maybe I fake care because we're fake engaged." Her pulse kicked up a notch as he nuzzled her neck.

"Maybe you really care even though we're fake engaged."

Feeling bold and brave in her biker leather, she said. "What if I did care? What would you do about it?"

"I'd take a shortcut home," Liam murmured. "And then I'd take advantage of the fact that you can't close your legs."

It was everything he had imagined and more. Sunny day. Blue sky. Open road. His bike purring between his legs. And Daisy on the seat behind him. Arms wrapped around his waist. Legs tucked up against his hips. Chest resting against his back. He wanted it to go on forever. Not just the ride, but them.

She was his humraaz and he was hers, but he didn't want to keep secrets any longer.

It was time to tell her how he felt. He loved her. He loved her quirks and eccentricities. Loved her eclectic clothes and fancy shoes. Loved her schedules, lists, and plans. He loved her passion for trivia and all things Marvel, the fact she could hack a game and own it, and that she was the smartest woman he knew. And he loved how dedicated she was to her family, how she adored and respected them, but wanted her independence, too.

He heard the high-pitched rev of an engine behind him. Tanya shot past, a blur on her red Triumph. If it had been any other day, he would have hit the throttle and chased after her. But he had Daisy with him, and he wasn't in a hurry to get home. This was their last date, and that meant they were almost at the end of her dating plan. Only one thing remained—the meeting with her family. And one huge obstacle—her dad.

He had a speech all planned out. An apology. A partial explanation. He would show Mr. Patel that he'd turned his life around. That he wasn't the man who had disappeared in the middle of the night. That he loved Daisy. And it wouldn't be a lie.

He could only hope she loved him, too. That when their fake relationship ended, she would want to start something real.

Or maybe they already had.

He rounded a corner and saw a truck barreling toward them, trying to overtake a vehicle in the oncoming lane.

Heart pounding a frantic beat, he made a split-second decision and drove onto the shoulder, pumping his rear brake as they hit the gravel. The bike skidded, heading for the concrete retaining wall. Liam released the handlebars and, in one fluid motion, he twisted, grabbed Daisy, and threw them both off the bike. His body hit the ground with a teeth-rattling thud. He rolled and rolled until the world began to fade. He reached out his arms, but Daisy was gone.

· 26 ·

LIAM had no idea how long he'd been sitting on the chair outside Daisy's hospital room. It could have been an hour or a day or a week. All he knew was that he couldn't leave. Not until he knew she was okay. Not until he'd said goodbye.

Bent over, elbows resting on his knees, head down, he stared at the floor. He was vaguely aware of people going in and out of Daisy's room. Old and young, family and friends, nurses and doctors. Her family had rented a function room somewhere in the hospital where they could gather and support each other, sending people two at a time to her room so she wouldn't be alone when she awoke. He figured they must have brought enough food to feed an army. Every hour or so, someone would offer him a plate, but he couldn't eat. Daisy couldn't eat. Why should he?

He heard a rustle beside him, caught a glimpse of a bright green tunic, felt a hand on his shoulder. Although he just wanted to be left alone, he looked up. Just in case. Good news or bad, he needed to know.

It took him a moment to recognize Daisy's aunt Taara without her shark costume. She was shorter than he'd thought, older, her dark hair swinging around her shoulders.

"I made this for you." She handed him a clear plastic container, her face creased in a frown. "Layla said you haven't eaten anything in three days. It's your favorite. Shark Stew. I went to the SAP arena to get the authentic ingredients. All your nutrients are there."

"Thank you." His voice, unused for so long, was so hoarse it was almost unrecognizable. "That's very kind."

They had all been kind. Her family had treated him as if he were one of them. It made no sense. Daisy was in that hospital bed because of him, because she had been on his bike, because he had asked her to ride.

"Taara, what are you doing?" Daisy's aunt Salena reached for the container. He remembered her from the conference center, although they had only shared a few words. "He survived the crash. We don't want to kill him now."

"He likes it." Taara handed him the container. "I gave him some at the hockey game and he ate it all. Every bit."

"Did he now?" Salena gave Liam an appraising stare. "He must have a cast-iron stomach. Or maybe he's missing his taste buds. Or maybe . . ." Her voice softened. "He has a good heart."

"He has a broken heart." Taara patted his shoulder. "But it's going to be okay. Daisy is going to be fine. The doctor said so. No broken bones. No internal injuries. Not even skin abrasions. She was well protected in her motorcycle suit. She just needs to wake up, and it will all be good."

Liam pressed his lips tight together and nodded. It wasn't going to be fine. He was his father's son after all, causing pain to everyone he loved.

Time passed. Deepa stopped by his chair to tell him his sherwani was ready, and she'd found him a bigger sword. Amina had a new recipe for a not-so-spicy pork vindaloo. Sam had arranged for Hamish to pick up his motorcycle and take it to the shop. Mehar, who had snuck Max into the hospital in Daisy's Marvel tote bag, put Max in Liam's lap for a quick hug.

Someone sat beside him and he tensed, hands clenching into fists as he prepared to be assailed yet again by love. He couldn't even imagine having a family like the Patels. A family that would hold him up, instead of tearing him down. A family that would rent a room in the hospital so he wouldn't be alone.

"Even I think this is too much," Layla said, tugging on his shoulder until he was upright. "You had a concussion, too. You were supposed to go home and rest."

"I am resting."

"You're brooding," she said. "And you're blaming yourself for something that wasn't your fault. I talked to the police. They had the dash-cam footage of the car behind you and witness statements of the drivers on the other side of the road. The guy in the truck was drunk. He'd been driving dangerously before the accident, trying to get ahead of a long line of traffic. He tried to pass on a blind corner on a double yellow line and was directly in your path. There was nothing you could have done to avoid a head-on collision other than go off the road. Not only that, you saved her. The police officer said what you did was heroic. If you hadn't jumped off the bike with Daisy, you both would have hit the retaining wall and no amount of body armor could have saved you."

Emotion welled up in his chest and he pressed a palm to his forehead. "She was on that road because of me."

"She wanted to be there," Layla said. "She texted me before she left. She was excited, Liam. Not hesitant. Not afraid. She didn't feel pressured in any way. It was her choice." She patted his arm. "Go home. Take a shower. Eat something. Have a rest. I promise I'll call if she wakes up."

"I'm not leaving." Not yet.

"It's not your fault."

But it was. He'd hurt her. Just like before.

• • •

IT was time. Liam took a deep breath, bracing himself for what he had to do. Daisy had been awake for twelve hours. She'd had visits from doctors, police officers, reporters, and her relatives two by two. Layla had assured him that she was going to be fine and they were discharging her in the morning. The crowd had finally dwindled. Visiting hours were coming to a close. It was his turn to see her but he still didn't know what he was going to say. Lost in thought, he was jolted back to reality by a sharp intake of breath.

"Liam? My God, is that you?"

His head jerked up at the sound of Nadal Patel's deep voice—a voice that meant home.

Except for some thinning of his hair and a little gray on the sides, Daisy's father looked almost the same. Lean and slightly stooped, dressed in his favorite outfit of short-sleeved checkered shirt and pants one size too big, he was so familiar it made his heart ache. How many evenings had he sat at the kitchen table listening to Mr. Patel's stories about his extreme adventures? Or having his confidence bolstered by Mr. Patel's encouragement and advice?

"You know Limb? Daisy's fiancé?" Standing beside Daisy's father, Salena frowned. "Poor boy. He was driving the motorcycle when they were run off the road."

"I know Liam." His face tightened. "Very well."

"It's nice to see you again, Mr. Patel." Liam held out his hand, but Daisy's father didn't reciprocate.

"What's wrong, Nadal? Shake his hand." Short and slender, with a sweet heart-shaped face and a bob of salt-and-pepper hair, the woman on his right gave him a nudge. When he still didn't move, she introduced herself as Priya.

"Priya is Nadal's . . . girlfriend. They were in Belize together," Salena said with a hint of disapproval. "They flew back when they got the news."

"I'm sure Belize wasn't the same when you left," Liam said, trying to break the ice.

Priya laughed but Mr. Patel still didn't smile.

Puzzled, Salena frowned. "Nadal, are you going to say hello or not?"

"Not." He folded his arms across his chest, his mouth pressed into a firm line.

"Nadal!" Priya's shocked expression was a reflection of Liam's feelings. He'd tried to predict how Mr. Patel would react to seeing him again, but if he'd had to guess, abrupt dismissal would have been the last thing he would have expected from the gentle man who had welcomed him into his home.

"It's okay," Liam said. "I can understand how difficult it must be to see me again after how I hurt Daisy, and now this—"

"It wasn't just Daisy you hurt," Mr. Patel said, his voice uncharacteristically abrupt. "It was Sanjay and me. You were a part of our family." He made a sweeping gesture with his arm. "If you had a problem, you should have come to us instead of running away."

"I left because of my family," Liam retorted. "I wasn't part of yours."

"Every day you came to my house." Daisy's father waved his hands around, as he had always done when he was agitated. "You were a friend to my son. You made my daughter smile. You said your jokes and made me laugh. You sat at our table and ate our food. And always you were fixing things in the house. You helped us. We helped you. That's family. And then you just left. No explanation. No goodbye. Not even a phone call to let us know you weren't dead."

Words failed him. He had never even considered that Daisy's father would care what happened to him after he'd hurt his daughter. His own family didn't care. They hadn't even tried to find Liam when his father died. He'd found out only when an estate lawyer had contacted him to let him know he had been cut out of the will.

"I didn't think you would want to hear from me."

"After almost eight years of being part of our family?" Mr. Patel's voice cracked, broke. "We all make mistakes, Liam. How could you think I wouldn't care? What kind of man do you think I am?"

"Mr. Patel . . ." Emotion rose in his throat, choking his words.

"And now you show up and want to be part of my family again?" He was trembling, his lined face twisted in a scowl. "I thought I knew who you were when you came every day to my house. Even that night of the prom, I thought your reason for what you did would be a good one. You would explain and we would make things right. But you didn't come. For ten years you didn't come. No e-mail or letter. Now, I don't even know who you are."

Liam's face heated and he willed the ground to swallow him up. Her father did know who he was. He'd been unworthy then and he was unworthy now. A delinquent in all but name. Even if he accepted the partnership at Evolution, he would never be good enough for Daisy. She was surrounded by a warm, loving family. They wanted her to be happy, to have a family of her own with a good man who would love and care for her. How could he take that away from her? How could he continue to deceive her family into believing she'd found a partner who truly loved her? How could he betray Mr. Patel yet again?

He wanted to be worthy. He wanted to walk into the room and hold his head high. The Evolution partnership was a step in that direction. And so was releasing Daisy from the bargain he never should have made.

• • •

Daisy had been awake for exactly twelve hours, twenty-eight minutes, and forty-three seconds when Liam walked into her room. She'd seen twenty-six relatives, including her dad and Priya, two nurses, one police officer, two reporters, two doctors, and one excited Max hidden in a tote bag. She'd had two naps, swallowed four pills, drank six glasses of water, traded three terrible hospital meals for plates of food snuck into her room in oversize handbags by aunties who were worried she'd lose weight, and she'd been cleared to leave in the morning.

Salena Auntie, on her way out with Priya and her father, had told her that Liam had been sitting outside her room for three days. She'd also heard about the altercation with her father and had received an earful for not telling Salena Auntie who Liam was. She didn't know what she'd expected when she finally saw him, but it wasn't a man who looked so utterly destroyed.

"Daisy . . ." His voice cracked, broke, and in that moment she knew with gut-wrenching certainty exactly what was going to happen, play by play, as if it were a movie she'd seen before.

Act I: Liam Blames Himself

"Liam, don't you dare." She folded her arms across her chest and mentally willed him not to say what he was about to say.

Misunderstanding, he stopped five feet away, a frown creasing his brow. "How are you feeling?"

"I'm fine. Just took a while to wake up. Probably because I wasn't getting enough sleep . . ." Her joke fell flat. He didn't even smile. "Are you okay? Layla said you had a minor concussion. Why didn't you go home?"

"You were here." He moved to the foot of her bed, a pained expression on his face. "I couldn't leave."

"Well, you can go home now," she said gently. "As you can see, the body armor did its job. I didn't wind up as one of Hamish's gory stories."

He drew in his lips, and she felt a prickle on the back of her neck. "I'm sorry. If I hadn't taken you out . . ."

Daisy held up her hand. "Don't even start. This wasn't your fault. The police officer told me what happened. Layla told me what happened. All my aunties and uncles told me what happened. You saved me, Liam. You were a hero. Most people wouldn't have thought to pull us off the bike, or to roll so you cushioned my body. You saved me. The end."

Still no smile. Instead, he shook his head. "Most people wouldn't have thought to put you on the bike in the first place." She could feel his tension rising, see his anxiety ripple under his skin.

"It was my choice, and except for the fact that your pillion seat is the most uncomfortable thing I've ever sat on in my life, and that's even with all my extra padding, I loved being out there with you. It was fun and exciting and it took my breath away. I'm not saying I'll be jumping on your motorcycle the minute I get out of here, but—"

"The bike was totaled in the crash, and I'm not sure if I'll buy another one." He hesitated, and the part of her mind that had detached from her emotions sat back and called the next scene of this train wreck of a breakup as her pulse pounded in her ears.

Act II: Liam Justifies His Self-Delusion

"I can't do this." His voice was a hoarse whisper, the creak of a door in a silent room. "I can't pretend anymore."

Daisy frowned. "What do you mean, you 'can't do this'? I

haven't told anyone that we're not really engaged. The dating plan isn't done. We still have to meet my family for the big interrogation, and then the marriage at city hall . . ."

"I should never have asked you to get involved," he continued. "I was so focused on my family and saving the distillery, I never really thought about how we would be misleading your family, too. And now that I've met them, and seen your dad again, I just can't—" His voice caught, broke. "He was like a father to me. And your aunties . . . I can see that they could be . . . difficult to handle, but they love you. They just want to find someone who will make you happy, someone worthy of you. And it's clear, that's not me."

Dread slid icy fingers along her spine. She wanted to run, to hide, to sink back into the oblivion of unconsciousness where her nightmares couldn't come true. Unbidden, her mind took her back to the day her mother left. They'd put the last touches on redecorating her bedroom, coordinating the bedspread and pillows with the bright pink walls. A kiss. A hug. And then her mother packed up the car and drove away. At seven years old, Daisy hadn't understood it was forever. She'd sat at the window for hours waiting for her mother to come back until Sanjay had come home and read the note on the kitchen table. Even then she couldn't wrap her mind around it. For two weeks, she returned every day to the window, waiting for her mother to come home while Sanjay shouted and raged, and her dad sat on the couch and cried. Little had she known that in ten years, she'd be sitting at that window again, waiting for someone else to come back to her. Had she not learned her lesson? Why had she put herself in this situation again?

"So after everything, you're just walking away?" She stared at him, incredulous. "What about Organicare?" It wasn't the question she wanted to ask, but the words wouldn't come from her lips.

What about me?

Liam frowned. "I've done everything I said I would do. Once

Brad finishes the rebrand, I'll make sure it gets to the Evolution partners for consideration with my full recommendation. I've been called back to New York to discuss partnership, but because of the conflict of interest I won't have a vote—"

She stared at him, aghast. "You're moving back to New York?" She hadn't seen that one coming.

Act III: Liam Pulls a Devastating Hat Trick

"I hadn't decided if I was going to accept the offer, but I made my decision today." His gaze dropped to the floor and he shrugged. "It was my dream. I wanted to show the world that a guy with nothing and no college degree could make it to the top."

Her face fell. It was happening too quickly, spinning out of control. Caught in a maelstrom of emotion, she could barely breathe. "And what?" she demanded. "That's it? You're just walking away? What about the distillery?"

What about us?

Liam shrugged. "My dream of saving the family legacy was just that . . . a dream. I never really thought it through. But you've shown me I need to be practical. I need a plan for my life moving forward. I can't run a distillery from New York. What you have—people who love you, who care about you, who made sure you were never alone—that's a legacy. What am I really trying to save?"

Us. But there was no *us.* It was a game. A charade. A made-up relationship. It wasn't real, and it was never meant to be. He had been honest about that from the start. She just hadn't expected it would end so soon.

She had rules about getting too close and she'd broken them. She had a life plan and it didn't include relationships with motorcycle-riding bad boys who had once broken her heart. She had learned her lessons about love and yet she'd made the same mistake again. Except this time, she had a chance to do it right, to say what she wanted to say, to answer the question that had haunted her the two times she'd been left before: What if they knew?

Act IV: Daisy Throws Herself on Her Sword

"I love you, Liam." Tears misted her eyes. "I have always loved you, except for the ten years I hated you. But then you came back and I fell in love with you all over again. I don't care about partnerships or careers or inheritances or distilleries. I care about you, and the kind of person you are." She drew in a shuddering breath, twisting the sheet in her fist. "I wish you could see yourself the way I see you. You're a good person, a kind person, someone who makes me laugh and feel good about myself and who I looked forward to seeing every single date. You are funny and sweet and generous, protective and strong. You made me feel both normal and special at the same time. You followed my rules but you also made me break them. You encouraged me to step outside my bubble and be the best person I can be. I like who I am with you. Somewhere along the way, this became real to me." Her voice trembled. "I want it to be real."

"God, Daisy . . ." His face crumpled. "Please . . . don't . . . You can't love me." He crossed the room in two steps and took her in his arms. She clung to him, buried her face in his chest, breathed in his scent one last time as she soaked his shirt with hot, wet tears.

Act V: The End

"I love you, too," he whispered as he released her, and his words tore a hole in her chest. "I will never stop loving you. That's why I have to go."

· 27 ·

"BETA! I've brought more ice cream."

Layla pushed herself off the couch, patting Daisy on the knee. "Move those bowls of candy out of the way and I'll go get it from your dad. One carton or two?"

"One. And tell him to be quiet. I'm starting *Iron Man 2*. This is the one where the palladium core of the arc reactor that protects Iron Man's heart is starting to break down. He's in an impossible position—either he slowly lets his body be poisoned or he dies by the shrapnel piercing his heart."

"Very apropos."

"Isn't it, though? If it were me, I wouldn't have even built an arc reactor." She tucked her pink princess blanket around her. "Then I would have saved myself the pain of being slowly poisoned by someone I knew I shouldn't get involved with in the first place."

"I thought Iron Man was poisoned by palladium."

"Liam. Palladium. Same difference."

Layla sighed. "Sometimes I wish you could just watch tear-jerking rom-coms when you're sad instead of forcing me to sit through Avengers movie marathons and stuff myself with candy. If you keep this up, I won't fit into my wedding dress. What's wrong with *The Notebook*? It's only about two hours long. You watch it. You cry. And then it's out of your system."

Daisy ripped open the bag of Kurkure Masala Munch that Mehar Auntie had sourced from a friend who had just returned from India and shoved a handful in her mouth. *Take that, Liam.*

"I need to see all the movies to really cry at *Avengers: Infinity War*. It doesn't have the same emotional impact if I skip any of the films."

Max snuggled beside her in solidarity with her decision to check out of the world for a few days and lose herself in junk food and movies. He had been more than content to spend hours with her on the couch watching superheroes saving the universe.

"Is Liam really worth all this?" Layla raised her voice over Daisy's loud crunching. "His crisis of conscience was too little too late and very ill timed. I mean, seriously, he tells you all this when you're in the hospital? Who does that?"

"I was fine. I was being discharged. They were keeping me overnight as a precaution. And it's not about *when* he said it; it was *what* he said. I thought I was the broken one in our relationship, but now I realize it was him." She tossed a few gummy bears in her mouth to counteract the spicy taste of what had been Liam's favorite snack. "Was Sam worth eating a pot of dal and puking all over your mother's restaurant floor?"

Layla laughed. "Point taken. But after that I pulled myself together. After one more weekend, I expect the same from you."

Daisy sank back into the cushions. "That's not enough time for a full MCU movie marathon if I have to eat, sleep, and visit with people. I've only been watching for four days. The hospital signed me off for a full week of medical leave."

"Promise me," Layla said. "This weekend will be the end of the Avengers and the last pity food you'll consume over Liam. You have to move on." She returned a few minutes later with Daisy's ice cream and two spoons, and settled on the couch beside her. Layla loved movies, and although the Avengers weren't her favorite, she watched them just to keep Daisy company.

"How can I move on?" Daisy stabbed at the ice cream—mint chip; her dad always knew what she needed. "I miss him. I feel like a part of me is gone. It started out as a game but somewhere along the way it became real and I . . ." She drew in a ragged breath. "How can two people love each other and not be together?"

Layla scooped up some ice cream. "Because one of them is a hot, broken mess. He was already gone when he walked into that room. He'd made his decision. Do you really think three words could have changed his mind? If he really loves you, he'll come back, and if he doesn't, it was never meant to be." She grinned, the teaspoon half in and half out of her mouth. "I read that on a coffee cup once. I've waited a long time to use it."

"Great. I'm getting advice from a coffee cup." Daisy turned up the volume. "I need some Iron Man catharsis."

"What happens at the end of this one?" Layla curled up on the couch. "Does he die by poisoning or shrapnel?"

"You'll have to wait and see."

SILENCE greeted Daisy when she walked into the office on Monday morning. Two months ago, she wouldn't have given it a second thought, but now that she was used to the sounds of people talking, phones ringing, printers humming, chairs creaking, and papers rustling, the silence felt oppressive and wrong.

She carefully placed her coffee cup three inches to the left of the desk separation so Mia didn't knock it over when she arrived. Her bag went underneath instead of on top because Zoe needed the extra space for her designs. And she pulled her chair close to her desk so Josh wouldn't bang into her when he leaned back to talk.

Once her headphones were on, and her screen flickered to life, she was ready to work. She stared at the lines of code, trying to remember the bug fix she'd thought of last night. But it was too quiet. Now used to the distractions, she couldn't focus despite the music in her ears.

Zoe arrived just as she decided to hit the coffee bar and catch up on gossip. Daisy edged over to give her more room, but Zoe didn't unload her portfolio as usual.

Daisy pulled off her headphones. "Where is everyone?"

"You didn't hear?" Zoe slumped into her seat. "I thought Liam would have told you. We pitched the rebrand. Brad didn't like it. He went ahead with his unicorns and rainbows. Tyler sent the revised pitch deck with Brad's rebrand to the Evolution partners. They rejected it, so Tyler had to make some more cuts. Thirty percent in every department."

Daisy's heart leaped into her throat. "Oh no. I can't believe it."

"Mia's gone." Zoe's eyes glittered with tears. "Tyler asked for volunteers and she didn't want me to get cut because I have Lily, so she said she'd go. I feel sick about it. Josh was furious. He said there were lots of incompetent people in our department for Tyler to choose from and there was no reason for Mia to throw herself on her sword. He went to talk to Tyler about reinstating her and wound up handing in his notice."

Nausea roiled in Daisy's belly. She should have been here. Instead, she'd used her post-concussion medical leave to wallow in self-pity when her friends needed her the most. "Why didn't anyone call me?"

"We thought you knew because you and Liam . . ." She trailed off when Daisy shook her head.

"We ended our arrangement."

"I'm so sorry." She leaned over to give Daisy a hug. "I know you said it wasn't real, but when I saw you two together, I kind of thought it was."

So did I.

An hour later, Tyler called her to his office. Slumped in his chair, back to rumpled shirts, missing ties, and unkempt hair, he looked even worse than she'd felt at the end of her MCU movie marathon.

"You heard?"

"Yes. I'm so sorry, Tyler." She fisted her skirt in her lap. "I had hoped it would work out with Evolution."

"They said we weren't a good fit." He swallowed hard, his face flushing. For a moment, Daisy thought he was going to burst into tears. "It wasn't just the product. They were looking for something more cutting-edge."

"Were they talking about the branding?"

Tyler nodded. "I watched Mia and Zoe's branding pitch. It was fantastic. I could see the boxes on the shelves, the ads, the website. It was Organicare. It was our original vision. I couldn't believe that Brad rejected it." He scraped a hand over his face. "I called Liam, and he told me Brad was the only expert he could find who was even interested in working with our products. He agreed that Brad's ideas weren't in line with current market trends and he had no problem if we wanted to cut him loose, but . . ." He shook his head. "Brad had three times the experience of the most senior members of our team, a big name in the industry, and so many successful campaigns—"

"But not with this kind of product," Daisy pointed out. "And not in this political climate. That's probably why he had the time for us in the first place. He was out of touch and no one wanted to hire him."

"I was just too afraid to let him go." Tyler buried his head in his hands. "Too afraid to go with Zoe and Mia's ideas instead of his. I've made so many mistakes. I was afraid to make one more, even though my gut was telling me that Brad's ideas wouldn't resonate with our target market."

"You did what you thought was best for the company," Daisy said softly. "Everyone knows that."

"I failed them." His shoulders heaved and he let out a ragged sob. "I failed our team, our company, the customers who loved our products, and all the girls we could have helped through our outreach program. I was afraid to trust my instincts. I was afraid to take a chance, and now everything is gone."

"CONGRATULATIONS. Welcome to the partnership."

Liam felt like he'd been waiting a lifetime to hear those words. As he shook hands with the managing partners, Eric Davis and Kevin Mah, he imagined his dad looking down on him, and gave a mental finger to the old man who had never thought he'd amount to anything.

"We were impressed with your work," Eric said. "You have the largest portfolio of any senior associate, great industry contacts, and a history of sound investment decisions. Finding and working up companies like Organicare is exactly the kind of initiative that has made you so valuable to the company. If we hadn't just shut down our consumer products portfolio, they would have been worth another look, even with their branding redesign disaster."

Kevin handed him a folder. "That's the partnership agreement. You don't have the same academic qualifications as the other partners, but we were willing to bend the rules because of your value to the company. Take a look through the documentation, and come back to us with any questions. We'll need your answer by the end of the week. It means a permanent relocation to New York. I trust that's not a problem."

"Of course not." It was what he'd always dreamed about. Making it to the top. Proving to everyone who had ever thought he was nothing that he was worthy. His sense of elation was somewhat diminished by the reminder that he would always be less and not equal because he had no letters after his name, but he couldn't have everything. Life didn't work that way.

"We'll need you in San Francisco until we find someone to run the West Coast office," Eric said. "Then you'll be back here making the day-to-day decisions that keep the business running smoothly. As a junior partner, you'll be handling the largest share of the admin, but after a few years, you'll be back to spending most of your time out in the field. There will be a buy-in, of course . . ."

Between his savings and his inheritance he had more than enough for the buy-in. There were benefits to not owning property or having any expenses other than his bike and the gear to go with it. But he'd never really considered the admin side of partnership. He wouldn't be out looking for new opportunities, meeting new people, or helping start-ups grow. For the first few years, he would be in an office behind a desk fighting to keep his portfolio alive. But he'd be a partner. In New York. It was what he'd always wanted.

UNICORNS sucked.

Liam held Organicare's pitch deck over the recycle bin. In anticipation of his acceptance, the partners had cleared out a corner office, and he was packing up his things to make way for the new associate they'd just hired. Eric and Kevin had rejected the pitch outright, and he didn't blame them. He'd done his best to help Tyler come up with ideas for restructuring and refinancing, but the rebrand to something so overtly feminine in the current market had turned the partners right off. Daisy had been right about her colleagues' cutting-edge proposal, but Tyler wouldn't bite. He was too afraid to take the risk. Liam had seen it before. Good inventors weren't always good businessmen. Sometimes they needed someone else to run the show so they could get back to doing what they did best.

His phone buzzed on his desk and he glanced at the screen. Brendan again. *Christ.* His brother had called six times this morning, no doubt to harass him about the distillery. Still trying to process his promotion, and the implications of a life in New York, he just couldn't deal with Brendan right now.

The pitch deck thudded into the recycle bin, and he stared through the glass window at the gray, overcast city. When he'd left San Francisco on his motorcycle ten years ago, he'd never intended to wind up on the East Coast, but it seemed that no matter how long he rode, he couldn't get far enough away. A chance encounter with well-known venture capitalist Tom Robertson in a biker bar in Oregon had decided his fate. He'd helped the weekend warrior repair his motorcycle, shared his opinions on several start-ups, and the next thing he knew, he had a job as an assistant at Evolution.

Tom was a self-made man, with only a high school diploma, who had started Evolution in his garage and turned it into a multimillion-dollar venture capital company. He believed Liam had an instinct for the business and liked his risk-taking nature and unconventional attitude. He'd taken Liam under his wing and the investment paid off. Although Liam was the only associate at Evolution without an MBA, or even a college degree, he was now an Evolution partner. He had it all. An office in the clouds. The title on his business cards. The respect of his colleagues. The achievement of a lifetime goal. He could finally stick it to his old man.

Except the old man wasn't around to see it.

No one was around. He had a few casual friends in New York, but no family. No one who really cared. There were no aunties beating down his door so he wouldn't be alone. No cousins warning him that "extra hot" meant raging inferno. No families dressed in shark suits trying to poison him with home-cooked meals. No sly relatives overcharging him for giant swords. No one had come to the hospital to see him.

But then, he hadn't told anyone he was there.

He'd always blamed his family for not reaching out, but he had never reached out to them. He thought they hadn't helped his mother when, in fact, they hadn't known about the abuse she suffered. Not a day had gone by after the night of the prom that he hadn't thought about Daisy and her family, but he hadn't even considered getting in touch. Secrecy had been such a huge part of his childhood that it had become ingrained in his life.

His phone buzzed again and Brendan's name appeared on the screen. He might as well get the call over with. Once he officially accepted the offer, he wouldn't be in a position to run the distillery. And even if he was, he couldn't meet the terms of the trust. There was only one woman he wanted to marry, and he'd left her behind.

"Liam! Thank God." Brendan let out a loud breath. "Lauren!" He shouted. "I've got him. He answered the phone."

Liam's pulse kicked up a notch at Brendan's frantic tone. "What's going on?"

"I've been trying to get you all morning," Brendan tripped over his words. "We went to the hospital and your apartment building. I didn't have the address for your new office so I called New York and the receptionist was new and she said you worked in San Francisco, and she just gave me the same number . . ."

"Did something happen to Jaxon?" His pulse kicked up a notch. If Jaxon was hurt, and he was thousands of miles away . . .

"Jaxon? No, he's fine. He's playing out in the backyard. We were worried about you. Lauren saw something in the news about a motorcycle accident, and they mentioned your name. They said you were a hero and you'd saved Daisy, but no one we talked to knew where you were or if you'd even survived. When we couldn't get in touch . . ." He let out a ragged breath. "Where are you? Are you okay? They had pictures of your bike and it was destroyed."

Liam swallowed past the lump in his throat. This wasn't Brendan. He didn't care. He hadn't been there for Liam when they were young. Why would he want to be there for him now? "If you're worried about the distillery . . ."

"The distillery? Fuck the distillery," Brendan said. "I'm calling about you. I was an ass the last time we met, and then Lauren read about the accident, and all I could think was that you were gone and that was the last time I would have seen you . . ." He choked up and Liam heard Lauren's soothing voice in the background. "Why didn't you call us?"

Liam rubbed his chest, trying to relieve the tight feeling. Was this a joke? He couldn't remember the last time he and Brendan had had a civil conversation, other than their brief interactions when he would pick Jaxon up or drop him off. It was a big leap to even contemplate that his concern was real. "Why would you have expected me to?"

Brendan let out a long breath. "I deserve that. I've not been the best brother, but then neither have you. Ten years is a long time to stay away. If not for Jaxon, we probably wouldn't have seen you until the funeral."

Very true. Until Jaxon was born, Liam had never even considered calling Brendan when he was in town for conferences and meetings. Lauren had been the one who invited him to meet his new nephew, and after that first meeting, he hadn't been able to stay away.

"I didn't think you'd care," he said honestly. "But I'm fine. Minor concussion. Nothing serious. I'm back in New York now."

"He's fine," Brendan called out, his voice slightly fainter.

"What about Daisy?" Lauren's voice was muffled in the background. "The article said he saved her."

"Is Daisy okay?"

"She had a more serious concussion," Liam said as his heart squeezed in his chest. "But she's good."

"She's okay," Brendan called out. Then to Liam, he said, "So, you're still together?"

Ah, now the truth came out. As he had suspected, it was about the distillery after all. "Don't worry, Bren," he snapped, his blood heating to a boil. "You can have the damn distillery. I've been offered partnership at Evolution so I'll be staying in New York. There's nothing for me in San Francisco." He had to force the words out. "Daisy and I aren't together anymore. So, I can't meet the terms of the trust."

Silence.

"It was real." A statement. Not a question.

Part of Liam wanted to just hang up the phone and be done with the whole damned conversation, but another part, a pathetic, sad, and lonely part, still wanted to believe that Brendan cared, that he'd called because he had genuinely been worried about his brother. Liam hadn't talked to anyone about Daisy, or the accident, or how badly he had messed things up. The temptation to open his heart to someone who actually knew him was almost overwhelming.

"It's complicated, but yes, in the end it was very real."

"I'm sorry," Brendan said. "I'm sorry about Daisy, and the accident, and the fight at Grandpa's house, and . . . fuck . . ." He cleared his throat. "I thought you were dead. It kind of puts things in perspective."

Still trying to process the unexpected show of emotion from his brother, Liam had no words.

"When you're in town again, maybe you could come over for dinner," Brendan said. "Jaxon would love to see you."

"Brendan!" Lauren's voice was louder this time, her admonishing tone clear.

"Christ," Brendan muttered. "At least now you know who wears the pants in this family." And then louder. "*We'd* like to see you."

They chuckled together, and Liam realized for the first time that they shared the same laugh. He didn't really know the man his brother had become. What else did they have in common, other than the secrets they'd kept about their family?

"Come home," Brendan said, his voice laced with amusement. "Please. She won't leave me alone until you do. That story was one hell of a wake-up call."

Home. He'd never thought of San Francisco as home, but everything that truly mattered was there.

"SURPRISE!"

Daisy froze in the hallway. She'd just picked Layla up from work to have a quiet dinner at home with Priya and her dad. Forty relatives, Bollywood music blaring through the house, kids running everywhere, and the scents of an Indian banquet weren't what she'd had in mind.

"Your father invited us over," Mehar Auntie said. "And look who is here! Roshan!"

Daisy smiled at the pleasant-looking man beside her auntie. She barely remembered Roshan from the conference. He was a few inches taller than her, his hair dark, thick, and glossy, curling into the collar of his blue shirt. He had a neatly trimmed beard, and his eyes, rich chocolate brown behind designer glasses, were warm and sympathetic.

"For the record, I was opposed to another sneak attack," Roshan whispered under his breath. "But your aunties are very persuasive."

Daisy smiled. "I have a feeling you're being overly kind. Knowing my aunties, I wouldn't be surprised if they'd knocked you unconscious and dragged you here against your will."

Max came running over to her and she lifted him for a cuddle. He sniffed at Roshan and turned away, burying his head in her arms.

"This is Max. He's usually a bit friendlier. Do you like dogs?"

"My family is allergic so we've never had one." He gave Max an awkward pat. Max sniffed and gave him the doggie equivalent of a cold shoulder. Quite right. Roshan wasn't even a candidate if Max couldn't be around his family. Not that she was looking. There was only one man she wanted, and she'd pushed him away.

"I'm sorry I didn't get a chance to talk to you at the conference." Daisy put Max down so he could charm her relatives into giving him treats.

"No problem." His lips turned up at the corners. "I could see you were otherwise occupied. Are you still together?"

Her first kiss with Liam. It felt like a lifetime ago.

Daisy sighed. "No. It didn't work out. My dad didn't approve."

"When it comes to marriage, family knows best."

Daisy didn't know if family always knew best, but a few days in the office with hardly anyone around had made her realize she didn't truly want to be alone. She missed the chatter around her, the chance to use her family connections to help people out, and the support that she got from her friends. There was no way she could go back to a job where she congratulated herself every day for the number of hours she'd gone without human interaction. She needed people. And she liked being needed in return.

"Why don't you help yourself to some food?" she suggested. "I'm just going to find my dad and see what's going on. This was supposed to be a quiet family dinner." She left Roshan with Layla and pushed her way through the crowd until she found her dad stirring dal in the kitchen with Priya.

"Beta! We were waiting for you and Layla to get back. Now, everyone is here and the announcement can begin!"

"Why is Roshan here?" she asked bluntly, agitated past being polite. If he planned to announce her engagement to a man she barely knew . . .

"The family talked it over. We thought, since you are clearly interested in a relationship, you should meet Roshan properly, and since we organized this party to announce our engagement, it was the perfect time."

"Wait . . . what?" Her eyes widened. "You and Priya are getting married?"

"I just popped the question," her father said, grinning. "All this talk of marriage made me realize there was no time to waste. I was going to propose either on a sailing holiday from Florida to the Azores, or during a deserted island survival adventure in Panama, but then this morning, I was eating leftover samosas for breakfast, and I had the idea."

"What idea?"

He grinned. "The proposal idea."

"Day-old samosas in the kitchen are better than proposing in the middle of the ocean?" Daisy stared at him, incredulous. "Or on a tropical island full of white sandy beaches and coral reefs?"

"Priya doesn't need those things," he said. "She's a modern woman and I'm a traditional man. I wanted something that would bring the two together."

Priya gave him a dreamy smile and kissed him on the cheek. "He's so romantic."

Daisy liked samosas, but had never thought of them in a romantic way. Maybe she'd been missing out. "So, what happened?"

"I bit into the samosa," her father continued. "And I knew. It was a sign."

"A sign that you were hungry?"

He laughed. "No, beta. A sign that this was it—the idea I'd been waiting for. So I shoved the ring into the samosa and I called Priya downstairs and I said . . ." He trailed off and turned to Priya. "Tell her what I said."

"He said, 'Taste this samosa.'"

"Those are exactly the words I used." Her father grinned. "She remembers them." He put his free arm around Priya and gave her a squeeze. "Tell her what I did next."

"He sat down," Priya said.

Daisy frowned. "Were you not feeling well?"

Her father grimaced. "I wanted to get on one knee but I twisted it when we were cave tubing down the Caves River in Belize."

"You twisted it when we were on the ATV jungle tour and you went too fast around the corner and the ATV fell on you," Priya said gently. "You knocked yourself out when we were cave tubing because you took off your helmet after they told you not to."

"I had to take it off," he protested. "I felt a sting. I thought it was a scorpion."

"Did you scream?" Daisy asked.

"No."

"Collapse? Have a seizure? Swelling? Did the guide give you antivenom?"

"No. I just had a small itch right here." He tapped his right temple.

"Then it wasn't a scorpion," Daisy said dryly. "And also, you are banned from any more extreme holidays. Next year you're going to sit on a beach in Maui."

"Actually, we just signed up for a training camp because we're going to tackle Mount Everest," Priya said. "It's for our honeymoon."

"You two are made for each other." Daisy shook her head. "But please don't encourage him. He gets into enough trouble as it is."

Daisy looked from Priya to her father and back to Priya. "Or . . . did you guys maybe bring something back that you weren't supposed to? Something you might have been smoking this morning?"

"She thinks we're high," her father said to Priya. "And we are. High on life. Tell her the rest of what I did when I proposed."

"He told me to take a big bite of the samosa," Priya said. "But I guess the bite was too big, because I swallowed the ring and almost choked to death."

"I Heimliched her," Daisy's father said. "Grabbed her around the waist and almost broke her ribs, but we saved the ring. She coughed it up on the floor. And the samosa, too."

Priya sighed. "Such a waste of a good samosa."

Daisy's father's eyes misted. "Then I brushed off the peas and the potato filling and—"

"He told me he'd been waiting twenty years to find love again and he'd found it with me." Priya wiped away a tear. "And he asked me to marry him."

"And she said yes!" Daisy's father pumped his fist in the air. "Can you imagine? She wants to be with an old man like me."

"You're not old, Dad."

"Not anymore. Priya makes me feel young again."

Daisy shot Priya a sideways glance. She didn't look like she felt she'd been shortchanged on her proposal. She was smiling and leaning against her dad's shoulder like almost choking to death on a ring-stuffed samosa had been the best moment of her life.

"We're getting married next Friday," he said. "Just something small. Maybe five hundred people or so. Salena is organizing it all. We're not getting any younger so we didn't want to waste time. Then Layla's wedding is next, and you and Roshan can get married after that. We will have a year of weddings!"

"I'm not marrying Roshan," Daisy said. "I'm happy being single. I tried the dating thing and it didn't work out for me. I'm the kind of person who does better on my own." They were the same words she'd always said, but for the first time they didn't ring true.

"Get to know him." Her father patted her back. "He's a good boy. He'll look after you. And if you don't like him, I have a file of marriage résumés for you to see. Lots to choose from. Tall, small, intellectual, sporty, beard or no beard, glasses or no glasses, likes dosas, hates dosas . . . You tell your old dad what you want and I'll get him for you."

"We're talking husbands, Dad. Not takeout."

Her father handed the spoon to Priya and pulled out his phone. "How about this one: Jamil. Age forty-two. Fitness trainer. Paleo. Gardener. Entrepreneur. Inventor. Breeds ocelots. Cat lover . . . Seeks fit, healthy, garden-loving meat-eating woman who is not squeamish."

Daisy leaned against the counter and folded her arms. "Is this a joke?"

"Which part didn't you like, beta?"

"He's a cat person. Max would hate him." She bent down and lifted Max into her arms. "You hate him, don't you Max?"

Max barked his disapproval of the aging ocelot-breeder who had failed the basic test of loving dogs.

"How about someone younger," her father suggested. "Chetan. Age thirty-six. Grew up in the Bay Area. Two masters degrees and two Ph.D.'s. Enjoys art house films, walks in the park, electronics-free dates . . ."

"Yawn."

Her father lifted an eyebrow. "Is that a no?"

"I've never seen an art house film that I actually enjoyed. And four degrees means he's spent his life in school and knows nothing about the real world. I'll bet he's never ridden a motorcycle or been to a hockey game."

"One more," her father said. "Sunny. Age thirty-two. Dog lover. Go Sharks. Appeared on *Dancing with the Stars* in 2019. Loves dosas. Male model. Marvel producer . . ."

"Marvel?" Daisy flew across the kitchen. "He produces Marvel films? Are you serious? Let me see his CV."

Her father shook his head. "You're right. He's not a serious prospect. He has no degrees. He didn't even finish high school because he went into the movie industry. I'll just delete that one."

"No! Dad!" She grabbed for the phone, only to see a smile spread across his face.

"Gotcha." He grinned. "I knew you didn't want to be alone. You are just waiting for the right man."

"You're not funny," she huffed.

He scooped some dal from the pot and put it into a bowl. "But I'm right."

Daisy pressed her lips together and glared. "Maybe I've already met the right man and no one else measures up."

"What man is that?" Priya asked.

"Someone who makes me laugh," she said. "Someone who can enjoy himself and doesn't care what people think. Someone who can take me out of myself and make me do wild and crazy things, but who needs me to make sure the boat doesn't capsize."

"Roshan is wild and crazy," her father said. "Did you see his pants? I didn't think they made corduroy anymore. And he has a big nose. You can laugh at him."

"I don't think that's what she meant," Priya said gently. "I think she wants to laugh with him."

"You want a clown?"

"I want Liam." There. She'd said it. And she could tell right away her father didn't approve.

"There are so many men out there, beta. Men who will stay and deal with a problem instead of taking the easy path and running away."

"I don't know if that's always true," Daisy countered. "In the developer world, we say 'disconnect to reconnect.' It means that sometimes you have to walk away to figure out a problem so you can come back and solve it."

He tasted the dal and frowned. "You think he'll come back?"

"I don't know, Dad. When he told me he'd been offered a position in New York, I panicked. I said all the wrong things and none of the right ones. But in the end, I told him I loved him. I told him I wanted what we had to be real."

"What wasn't real about it?"

Daisy twisted her skirt in her hand and told him everything from the moment she'd seen Orson and Madison together at the conference to the day Liam had walked away—minus the R-rated moments, of course. "I fell in love with him," she said finally. "And then the accident happened, and . . . well . . . now he's gone."

"I think you should sit down, Nadal." Priya took the spoon from her father's unnaturally still hand and gently helped Daisy's silent father to a chair.

"Too much," he mumbled.

"I know." She patted his hand. "I'll get you a cup of chai."

"He was like a son to me, and then poof, he was gone." He swallowed hard. "Just like your mom."

"She left because she didn't want us," Daisy said tightly, sitting in the chair beside him. "He left the night of the prom because he thought he wasn't good enough, because he thought I would have a better life if he wasn't around to drag me down."

"Ah, then they are not the same." He hugged himself, rubbing his arms. "Your mother said we were holding her back from the life she wanted to live. She was a free spirit. I think I always knew she would leave, but it didn't hurt less when she did."

Daisy bit her bottom lip. "I thought she left because I wasn't normal, because I wanted to do math puzzles and science experiments instead of playing dress up and dolls. When she came back, she asked if I was still 'weirdly smart.' I thought that was the reason she didn't want me."

"Who is the normal one?" He was agitated now, hands waving in the air. "The mother who leaves her family to find herself, or the woman who works hard, achieves success, finds love, and stays to look after her father so he isn't alone?"

Priya handed him a cup of chai and he kissed her hand. "I always thought I'd done something wrong, too," he said. "Maybe I didn't tell her I loved her enough. Maybe I wasn't kind enough. Maybe I spent too much time at work . . . She told me it had nothing to do with me—or you or Sanjay. She said she just wasn't cut out for marriage and motherhood, but I refused to believe her. All those years I wasted, blaming myself, afraid to love again, and every day I was going into the bakery café near my office, and I would see Priya. I would have my treat and my coffee, and her smile would make my heart sing, and I wasn't listening to the song."

"Tell her about the rappelling," Priya said. "I love that story."

Daisy's father grinned. "Do you remember the day I rappelled down the Hilton in Union Square? Forty-six stories! An old man like me."

"I remember begging you not to go," Daisy said dryly.

"Well, I went, and when I got to the bottom—"

"You had an epiphany?"

"No, beta. I had a hunger pain. All that adrenaline used up the sugar in my body and I craved a pastry from Priya's bakery, the chocolate ones with the chocolate inside and swirls of chocolate on the top." He licked his lips. "I drove all the way there, and when I walked in the door, I almost slipped in a puddle of spilled coffee."

"I was about to clean it up," Priya said. "It had just happened."

"And that's when I knew," he said. "Life is short. One moment you are pulling out your wallet to buy a pastry, and the next maybe you are lying with your head cracked open on the bakery floor, blood and brains oozing out everywhere. I knew then that I had to ask her out."

"He did it when I bent down to pick up the cup." Priya pressed a kiss to his forehead.

Her father smiled. "I didn't stand a chance when I saw that luscious—"

"Dad!" Daisy stood so quickly the chair wobbled. "No. Please. Just. No."

"My point is," he said, "if you want something, go after it. Don't let fear hold you back. Take your chance. Live a life of no regrets. And don't blame yourself if it goes wrong. People have their own journey and it has nothing to do with you. If he comes back to you, then maybe I will talk to him and hear his story. If he doesn't, then the world will not end. You have survived this before, and you will survive it again because you are my beautiful, clever, brave, strong, sweet Daisy and you have the strongest heart of anyone I know."

· 29 ·

"THIS invention is going to revolutionize the world." Barely out of his teens, and dressed not to impress in a pink T-shirt and a pair of oversize board shorts, the blond surfer-dude inventor flashed a megawatt smile. "I introduce you to . . . Pot-ee. The first edible cannabis underwear."

"Could you bring us a couple of samples?" Liam called out. "Any flavor will do." Turning to James he lowered his voice. "First impressions?"

"He'd be a good face for the company," James offered.

Liam was back in San Francisco tidying up loose ends while the partners searched for a new branch manager. James had good instincts, but he needed more experience to handle the pressure of running an office. In the week Liam had been away, the work had piled up, and the dude still couldn't distinguish a good pitch from a dud. Today's pitch session at a small tech con was Liam's last chance to guide him in the right direction.

"We can hire actors if we want a pretty face," Liam said. "What about his personality? Can you work with him? What do his clothes tell you about his attitude toward business? Would he take direction well? Would he work hard? Is he committed?"

"He seems relaxed," James whispered. "Do you think he's stoned?"

"I would hope so, since he's selling edible cannabis underwear."

"Seriously?" James gave him a questioning look.

"No, James. Not seriously. Do you want to work with someone who's always stoned? How much work is he going to get done? Is he going to be out pounding the pavement looking for distributors or is he going to be chilling in his office chewing on his Y-fronts?"

"That's kinda disgusting."

"And that's the conclusion you should have come to when he told us they came in banana."

Twenty minutes and twelve flavors later, he gave the inventor the usual send-off. "Thanks. We'll be in touch."

"Cool! Keep the samples."

"Will do." Liam had no idea what he was going to do with avocado-flavored cannabis Y-fronts, but maybe one day . . . "What's next?"

James looked down at the schedule. "The Heash. A human leash so dogs can walk their owners."

"This should be good. Bring him in." Liam already knew the invention wouldn't sell, but after a difficult week sitting at a desk staring at screens of financial reports and pressing Daisy's number only to hang up before the call went through, he needed something to smile about. When the dude walked in with a giant dog collar around his neck, Liam almost felt like himself again. This was what he loved to do. Meet new people. Share their enthusiasm. Help them succeed. And, in the case of unfortunate inventions like the Heash, have a laugh. He just wished Daisy were there to share the moment. James was a nice guy but he didn't have her biting wit or her sense of humor, or maybe it was just that nothing seemed as funny without her.

"We walk dogs. Why shouldn't they walk us?" Heash-dude whistled and an immaculately groomed toy poodle walked in holding a leash in her mouth. She dropped it as his feet and barked.

"Beast loves to walk me." He clipped one end of the leash to his leather collar, and the tiny dog took the other end in her mouth and bounded across the room to where James and Liam were seated, dragging the inventor behind her.

"I've met tons of dog owners who thought this was a great idea, so I thought I'd start my own business. I'm looking for fifty thousand dollars for a twenty-five percent interest in my company." He handed sample Heashes to Liam and James.

Liam took care to give the invention a thorough inspection while Beast walked the inventor back and forth across the room. It was basically a human-size studded leather collar, complete with a D-ring closure. James put his on and snapped it closed just above his shirt collar.

"How do I look?"

"Fifty shades of ridiculous."

James tugged on the Heash, but it wouldn't open. His face reddened and sweat trickled down his temple. Liam dropped his head to his hand to stifle a laugh. "Never try a product that is going to get stuck, humiliate you, choke you, or make you gag," he muttered under his breath. "You may think you're doing them a favor, but really, they want to look up to you and they can't do that when you've got a human collar fastened around your neck."

"Get it off."

"Are you sure? The Texan bartender I introduced you to at the Rose & Thorn would be absolutely delighted if you showed up in a collar and leash."

"It's a Heash," James said, struggling with the clasp.

Liam fought hard to repress his laughter. "I don't think she'd care what it was called if it meant she could walk you down the street."

Liam tried to imagine Daisy's face if she saw James with a collar around his neck. Likely no one would be able to tell what she was thinking, but he would know from the quirk of her left eyebrow, or the tiniest lift of the corner of her mouth. She also would think it wouldn't sell, and he had to agree. Why not let the inventor know that up front so he could pursue other options?

"It's an interesting product, but I think you're looking at a very niche market," he said at the end of the presentation. "Unfortunately, it's not one that would fit our portfolio."

Beast led the inventor out of the room, as if she understood the dismissal.

As soon as they were gone, Liam unfastened James's collar and placed it on the table between them. "What the hell were you thinking?"

"I met him at a club." James rubbed his neck. "He said he'd had ten thousand dollars' worth of online sales in the first month alone."

"Did you check his financial statements and sales records? If he did move that much product, I'm pretty sure it wasn't to the dog-loving community."

When James didn't answer, Liam sighed. "What's next?"

"Liquefied ocelot poop for gardens. They call it 'O Crap.'"

"Why ocelots?"

James shrugged. "Their poop is special?"

"Is that a question? Are you asking *me* if ocelot poop is special? Pass. Anything else or did I fly here from New York just to kill time?"

"Cougar Catcher. A drink that makes men irresistible to women of a certain age."

James seemed to have an uncanny ability to find the worst inventions on the planet. He was worth keeping around just to know where not to invest. "What's in it?"

"A secret blend of known aphrodisiacs including asparagus, oysters, chocolate, baked beans, figs, and sparkling apple juice."

A smiled tugged at his lips. It sounded like one of Taara's concoctions. He'd disposed of the Shark Stew in a biohazard bin at the hospital, but he still had the container at home, reminding him that even though the smell had almost knocked him unconscious, it had been made with love.

"I don't think even a real cougar would want to be near you if you drank that." He waved a dismissive hand. "What the hell have you been doing while I was gone? You've spent twenty thousand dollars wining and dining these entrepreneurs and you don't have one solid lead."

James shifted in his chair. "They all seem so convincing. It's only when you're sitting here that I realize they aren't as good as I thought they were. I just find it hard to say no."

"We can't say yes to everyone," Liam said. "And sometimes that 'no' can make the difference between success and failure. Some of my most successful clients pitched hundreds of times, learning from each rejection until they got it right. Sometimes it meant just tweaking the product or the marketing strategy, but sometimes it meant going in a totally different direction, maybe even starting over, or getting focused on a plan."

It was the same advice Tom had given him at the start of his career, and yet he wasn't following it himself—personally or professionally. Did he really want to sit behind a desk, pushing paper, reading financials, and running a company with people who didn't think of him as an equal? Was his self-worth so intrinsically tied to his job that he couldn't walk away without feeling less of a man? Was he really going to give up the woman he loved because he couldn't accept that she wanted him just the way he was?

The bottom line was that he loved Daisy. It hit him suddenly

and painfully, that he wanted, no needed, Daisy in his life, with her
plans and lists and charts, her trivia facts, her kind heart, her big
family, and her dry sense of humor. Not just as a girlfriend, or a
fake fiancée. He wanted her in his bed and in his home and in his
heart forever. And if that meant giving up a partnership to be with
her, then that's what he would do. Besides, James wasn't going to
make it on his own. Unicorns weren't found in ocelot poop or
Heashes. Just as love wasn't found when you were hiding in New
York.

He needed a plan to get her back. Or maybe he already had one.
He pulled out his phone to check Daisy's spreadsheet. Dates #7
"Family" and #8 "Wedding" were still outstanding.

After all they'd been through, it would be a shame to leave
things undone.

"I THINK I might have a way to save Organicare." Daisy pushed
Tanya's card across Tyler's desk, trying to ignore the butterflies in
her stomach. It had taken her a full hour to work up the nerve to
leave her cozy workspace and meet with Tyler, and that was after
the sweat-fest that had been the telephone call to Tanya that pre-
ceded it. But she believed in Organicare, and more than that she
believed in herself and her ability to make a change. Her father had
told her to go after what she wanted. She wanted Organicare to
survive, and she had the tools to make that happen.

"Empower VC." He studied the card. "Never heard of them."

"They're an all-female venture capital company that invests in
diverse female-run businesses. I met Tanya on a motorcycle trip. I
called her this morning and asked if she would be interested in
hearing our pitch."

"It may have escaped your notice that I am neither diverse nor do I identify as a woman." Tyler leaned back in his chair, making no move to take the card. "How do you get over that hurdle?"

"Restructure and bring on some female executives. Convince Kristina to come back." She had spent the night on a group chat with Mia, Zoe, and Josh, talking things through. Mia and Josh were still interested in helping the company, especially if it meant they might be able to come back.

Tyler shook his head, apparently not convinced. "I don't think—"

"You've run yourself ragged trying to do everything," she continued, cutting him off. "I read Evolution's report. They recommended hiring an executive team so you could step into a chief development officer role and focus on product development, which is what you love to do. Over ninety-eight percent of Organicare's employees are women. You have a good pool to choose from." She handed him a document folder. "I made a plan for a revised pitch. I also e-mailed you a spreadsheet with . . ." She trailed off when Tyler leaned his elbows on the desk and dropped his head into his hands.

"I can't handle any more."

She stared at him, aghast. "What are you talking about?"

"Hope." He sighed. "Every pitch, every meeting, every day I kept hoping things would work out. And just when I had given up, Liam walked in the door. When even that didn't work out, I resigned myself to the fact that this was the end. Now you're asking me to hope again, and I just can't do it. I can't stand up and give the pitch again because I'll be wondering how I'll make it through when it fails."

"You won't have to do it," Daisy said, thinking quickly. "Get your new executive team in place and they'll handle it for you. It doesn't have to be a one-person show."

"I thought you were a one-person show." He rubbed the back of his neck. "Come in. Do your work. Slip out the back. Don't socialize with your colleagues . . . I was surprised you weren't the first one out the door when things started to go wrong. When I hired you, I knew you never stayed in one place for long. It worked for me because things here were so uncertain, but now . . . What's changed?"

"I've changed," she said. "I was afraid to commit to anything, afraid to open myself up to making friends or become involved in the companies I worked for. I was afraid of getting hurt if things didn't work out. But over the last few months, I've been forced to step outside my bubble. I met people who invited me into their lives and their hearts, who believe in me and like me for who I am. They made me realize that I have a lot to give besides being a coding genius." She grinned, and Tyler responded with a halfhearted chuckle.

"I've realized that being 'weirdly smart' doesn't make me less; it makes me more. I want to help Organicare be all it can be, and I'm willing to take risks to make that happen. And if it doesn't work out, I know I'm strong enough to move on and keep taking chances. Because that's how I'm going to live my best life, and that's how you can live your best life, too."

This wasn't just about work, she realized. It was about acceptance and forgiveness. It was about love.

"That's quite the speech." Tyler pulled the folder toward him and flipped through the pages. "And this is quite the proposal. But there's one big problem." He sucked in his lips, ran a hand through the tangle of his hair. "Kristina won't come back. She's totally committed to the work she's doing to raise awareness in third-world countries."

"You could hire a new CEO."

He stared at her for so long, she shifted uncomfortably in her seat. Had she gotten this wrong? Overstepped? Or maybe he'd already sold the company and . . .

"Why would I do that when the perfect person is sitting right in front of me?" He leaned back in his chair, his eyes warm with approval. "You pitched with me at the tech con. You brought Liam to help save us. You pushed for Mia and Zoe's proposal. And now . . ." He tapped the folder. "You've done this, when it would have been easy for you to walk away. Those are leadership qualities, and right now the company needs a young, dynamic female leader, someone with the passion, drive, and commitment to see this through. That's you."

If anyone had told her two months ago that one day she'd be asked to lead a pitch to save Organicare as the company's CEO, she would have laughed. But two months ago, she'd been stuck in the past, nursing old wounds, afraid to embrace her life and move on.

She wasn't that woman anymore.

· 30 ·

LIAM parked his motorcycle in the distillery parking lot. He wasn't surprised to see gleaming yellow backhoes, dump trucks, and wrecking balls lined up side by side. He'd met with Ed McBain and explained that since he wouldn't be able to meet the terms of the trust, there was no point wasting time. Ed had authorized the demolition, and today the distillery was coming down.

"Thought you ran away to New York to become a big shot partner at your firm." Joe blew out a puff of smoke from his favorite seat at the top of the front steps. He was smoking again, but at seventy-five years old he'd earned the right not to quit.

"I did, but I had to come back to deal with some loose ends." Liam joined him on the step and they looked out over the parking lot and the green fields beyond.

"Was this one of them?"

"Brendan invited me to come and take one last look around."

"You still have a week left before your birthday." Joe gave him a hopeful look. "What about that girl you brought to meet the family?"

Liam sighed, feeling empty inside. "Didn't work out."

"I've got a niece . . ."

"Thanks, Joe, but there's only one woman for me."

After a few quiet moments with Joe, he headed into the visitor center, where Brendan was talking to the contractor. Jaxon saw him walk in and jumped up to greet him.

"Uncle Liam!" He ran over to give him a hug. "Can we go see the distillery again? Can we see my name and fly a plane in the stills?"

His throat tightened. "I don't think so, bud."

"Joe's outside," Brendan told Jaxon. "He'll take you around if you want to have a last look."

Jaxon pushed open the door and ran outside calling Joe's name.

"Lauren's working today and I couldn't leave him at home," Brendan said, watching Jaxon go. "I thought he'd like to see the heavy equipment at work, but's he's more interested in flying his plane in the field."

"I would be, too, if I had this much wide open space." Liam looked around at the polished wood bar that their great-great-grandfather had shipped over from Ireland intact. "Should we have a last drink?"

"Sounds good." Brendan turned to the contractor. "You can get started. The paperwork is in order and we're ready to go."

"So that's it." Liam poured from one of the open bottles. He thought he'd feel sad or even angry with Brendan, but he was numb inside. "The end of an era."

"Or the beginning of a new one. It depends how you look at it." Brendan took his glass. "I know you were worried about the employees. I'll make sure they're all taken care of. There will be more than enough money after the sale to be generous."

"I appreciate it. Some of them have been around for over twenty years. I can't even imagine how it felt to hear the distillery was shutting down. It must have been quite a shock."

"Kind of like finding out your brother left town with your mom without telling anyone what was going on," Brendan said with a hollow laugh.

Whoa. Liam's breath left him in a rush. *Where did that come from?* He'd come home thinking maybe there was a chance he could repair his relationship with his brother, and giving up the distillery had been a big part of that, but it was clear Brendan still carried a lot of resentment. "You didn't see her that night."

"I was at college over thirteen hundred miles away."

Liam drained his glass, one hand fisted on his knee. "I didn't have time to call you. She was in bad shape. And it was my fault. She'd given me money to rent a tux to take Daisy to the prom and—"

"Daisy?" Brendan froze, his hand on his glass. "That story about knowing her in the past was legit?"

"Yes. We reconnected at a tech conference. She's Sanjay's little sister." Now that Brendan was actually talking to him, he didn't want to share that it had started exactly as Brendan had suspected, because it was *now* that mattered, and *now* that was real.

"Stuff happened the night of the prom that meant I didn't get the tux back to the rental place in time," he said. "They couldn't get in touch with me, but the owner of the store knew Mom, so he called the house. Dad answered the phone . . ."

"Oh Christ." Brendan's jaw tightened.

"He went ballistic because she'd given me the money without asking him." His voice wavered, cracked. "Bren, I can't even tell you what it was like to walk into the house and see her like that, lying in a pool of blood." His hand closed around the glass, squeezing it so hard his knuckles turned white. "I thought she was dead."

"Jesus." Brendan muttered under his breath. "She was always doing things like that, always trying to help us out when she knew she would suffer for it."

"He wouldn't have known about it if I'd returned the tux on time." Liam's shoulders slumped under the weight of his guilt. "That was the last straw. I wasn't going to let him touch her again.

I told her she had to leave because the next time I saw him it was going to be him or me, and I didn't want to spend my life in jail. I think she knew the next time would be the last. She agreed to go. We packed up the car and I drove her to a hospital out of state and arranged for Aunt Jean to come from Florida to get her. Then I came back for my motorcycle and got the hell out of the city while he was still passed out." His chest heaved, and he poured another drink. There wasn't enough whiskey in the whole damn distillery to erase his memory of that night.

"I didn't know it had gotten so bad," Brendan said quietly. "Mom called to tell me you'd helped her get away. I was so relieved she was finally free of him, but I have to admit I resented you for doing what I couldn't do, and for getting out when I knew I'd have to go back and help him run the company, and you and mom wouldn't be there."

"Since we're sharing . . ." Liam drew in a shuddering breath. "I resented you for doing nothing to stop him when we were young, and then for blowing out of there for college and leaving me alone with a man who thought I was a worthless, no-good piece of shit."

Brendan's breaths came faster, heavier. "I'm not you, Liam," he snapped. "I don't have your strength—facing him down at thirteen was something I didn't have in me. But I did what I could. I hid his bottles, watered down his liquor, and took his keys. I'd ask Mom to take me shopping just to get her out, or I'd take you to the playground. I would ask him to watch a game, throw a ball in the park, or I'd just try and talk him down, even though spending time with him was the last thing I wanted to do."

Liam's glass slipped from his fingers, thudding softly on the bar as he tried to process everything Brendan had told him. After all these years of thinking his brother had been sucking up to their father, he'd been trying to protect him and their mom in his own way. He took a deep, pained breath and closed his eyes. "Bren . . . I didn't know."

"I know you didn't," he said, not unkindly.

When Liam opened his eyes again, Brendan was staring into space, holding his glass loosely in his hand. "I tried to protect you, but you didn't seem to need me. All the verbal abuse he threw at you just rolled off your back."

"If it had, I'd be with Daisy right now." Liam's voice was thick and hoarse. "I heard every negative word he said about me. I felt them. I carry them with me, and I can't let them go."

"He didn't think you were worthless, Liam. Just the opposite."

"What the fuck are you talking about?" He didn't want to hear a story about his dad that wasn't exactly like the one in his head. He'd spent too long hating the old man, too long trying to prove something to someone who didn't care.

"He envied you because you were everything Grandpa had wanted him to be, and you were a constant reminder that he'd let his father down. You were smart, strong, brave, loyal, and honest. Not only that, he couldn't control you because you didn't put up with his shit. When he couldn't break you with his fists, he tried to break you with his words. Grandpa told him once that you were a better man, more worthy of his legacy at thirteen than he would ever be, and he intended to leave the distillery to you. That's what set him off the night he broke your arm."

Worthy. Because of who he was, and not what he'd done. The goal he'd been pursuing all his life had been inside him all along.

Emotion welled up in his chest. They'd never been an affectionate family so the closest he could get to a hug was to clap Brendan on the shoulder. "Thank you for telling me. For everything."

"And you." Brendan turned away, but not before Liam saw his eyes glisten.

"They're starting now," Joe called out from the door. "Bulldozer is on its way to the rickhouse. You want to watch?"

"Tell Jaxon I'll be right there," Brendan said.

"He's not with me." Joe stepped inside, frowning. "I haven't seen him since Liam arrived."

Brendan's breath hitched and he rose quickly from his seat. "I sent him out to see you."

"I'll take a look around," Joe said.

"You don't think he would have gone into one of the buildings?" Brendan made his way quickly toward the door with Liam close behind.

"Jaxon's not like me," Liam assured him. "He doesn't break the rules. He might just be playing nearby—probably in the field with his plane . . ."

"Liam . . ." Brendan's voice trembled.

"We'll find him, Bren." Nausea roiled in his belly and he feigned a confidence he didn't feel in the least. "Don't worry."

Ten minutes later, after a quick search of the parking lot and the distillery grounds, they met up with Joe.

"I checked the malt house, the mash tun, and the stillroom. He's not there."

"I need to call Lauren." Brendan pulled out his phone, his hand shaking.

"You'll just scare her," Liam said. "It will take her over an hour to get out here and she'll be totally panicked when she's driving. Let's look again. If we don't find him in the next ten minutes, then give her a call. I'm sure we'll find him. He's only five years old. How far could he go?"

A tremendous crash startled him and he looked over just as the wall of the rickhouse crumbled.

"Jesus Christ. Didn't anyone tell them to stop?"

All the blood drained from Brendan's face. "What if he's inside?" His voice rose to a panicked pitch. "I can't lose him. I didn't think after Dad I could love anyone, but Jaxon and Lauren, they're everything to me."

Liam had never thought he could love anyone, either. Family had meant only pain and hurt, betrayal and disappointment. But then Jaxon had been born and his walls had started to crumble. After his dad died and he'd reconnected with his grandfather, a sliver of light had reached his heart. And then he'd met Daisy again. She hadn't measured his worth in the amount of money he had, or the number of letters after his name. She liked him for who he was and how he made her feel. She had opened him up to a world of love and laughter, hope and happiness. And he had let her slip away.

"You won't lose him. Not if I have anything to do with it." Heart pounding, Liam ran over to the bulldozer and waved at the driver to stop. He told the contractor to stand his men down and raced into the partially fallen building.

Despite the gaping hole in the wall, the room was cool and quiet, the empty casks still standing in rows. Now, more than ever, it reminded him of the inside of a Spanish galleon, and he remembered telling Jaxon how he'd played pirates here when he was a boy. He looked down the longest row to the wall at the back and knew in an instant where to find his nephew.

"Brendan!" He shouted over his shoulder. "I know where he is."

Together, they ran to the back of the rickhouse and found Jaxon crouched behind the old Murphy cask with a sharp stick in his hand. Biting back a sob, Brendan hugged Jaxon to his chest.

"What were you doing here?" he scolded, although his voice was shaking. "We were looking everywhere for you."

"Your name was missing." Oblivious to the panic he'd caused, Jaxon pointed to the cask that bore the names of all the Murphy men. "I wanted to carve it into the wood. I thought if your name was there then you wouldn't knock the distillery down and when I grew up it could be mine."

Brendan stroked Jaxon's hair, and sighed. "I'd like to save it, too, but the distillery is old and falling apart, and we need to sell the land to save our company."

"Can't we fix it?" Jaxon asked. "You and me and Uncle Liam could work together. We could keep just this piece. I want to be a Murphy son."

Brendan met Liam's gaze over Jaxon's head, and his lips pressed together in a slight grimace. "I'd like that, bud. I was always jealous that your Uncle Liam got to spend his time here with your great-grandfather. But he's going to be living in New York, and I have the car business to look after . . ."

"But I can help." Jaxon's lower lip quivered. "I know all about the distillery. Uncle Liam showed me. And you hate your work. I heard you tell Mom."

Liam ruffled his hair. "Sometimes adults say things they don't mean."

Brendan sat heavily on the old wooden floor. "And sometimes they mean what they say. He's right. I hate it. It's not what I wanted to do with my life. I joined the company to help Dad create a new family legacy, but in the end . . ." His voice quavered dangerously. "It was an empty shell. He'd taken everything of value and destroyed it."

Until this moment, Liam had always thought Brendan was happy to follow in their father's footsteps. It had never occurred to him his brother had dreams of his own. He touched Brendan lightly on the shoulder. "What about making this your legacy? Sell the company and get the distillery up and running again?"

"You don't know how many times Lauren and I have talked

about walking away . . ." Brendan shook his head. "But I couldn't do it alone. It's too big of a task."

Liam's pulse kicked up a notch as an idea formed in his mind. "What if I joined you?"

"You?" Brendan's voice rose in disbelief. "What about New York? The partnership?"

"You've made me realize that I won't find my self-worth in a partnership title if I haven't found it first in myself. And I think that journey for me begins here with you and Jaxon and Lauren and Daisy." He pulled out his grandfather's knife and handed it to Brendan. "Jaxon's right. There's a name missing."

Brendan took the knife, ran his thumb over the worn wooden handle. "Jaxon had a good idea about selling off some of the land and keeping the distillery. We could use the money to partially fund the refurbishment . . ."

We. A small word with so much meaning. It meant forgiveness, love, and acceptance. It meant closing old wounds and moving forward.

It meant home.

"SURPRISE!"

Daisy groaned as she closed the front door. *Not again.* She'd been looking forward to a quiet dinner with her dad and Priya before spending the evening preparing a revised pitch deck for Tanya. With Mia and Josh back in the office and a huge list of new responsibilities, it wasn't easy to get any work done.

She dodged Layla's nieces, who were chasing each other through the house, picked up two stray squeaky toys and put them in Max's basket, tidied the enormous pile of shoes in the hall, and picked up three plates of half-eaten jalebis to take to the kitchen.

It was chaos as usual.

Jana Auntie was at the stove cooking pork vindaloo, and Lakshmi Auntie was rolling naan on the counter. Taara Auntie was stacking plastic containers of brown soup in the fridge, and Salena Auntie and Hari Uncle were arranging plates of appetizers while Mehar Auntie practiced dance moves in the hallway.

"Is this party for Dad and Priya's wedding?" The sangeet was in two days, but she hadn't heard about any planned get-togethers before then.

"Make way!" Priya wrestled a giant pink bakery box through the back door. "I've got another dessert. I've been trying new piping techniques, so this cake might be over the top for a meet-the-fiancé night, but I don't think anyone is going to complain."

"'Meet the fiancé'?" Daisy racked her brain, trying to think which of her cousins were on the marriage market.

"I'm back!" Layla walked into the kitchen with Sam behind her. "Who needed the cayenne?"

"Over here." Jana Auntie held out a hand. "I heard he likes his vindaloo extra hot."

Vindaloo? Extra hot? Daisy's skin prickled in warning.

"This is so exciting!" Mehar Auntie clapped her hands and spun around, almost knocking the box from Priya's hands.

"Mehar! Go outside and dance with the girls," Jana Auntie said. "They're rampaging through the house. I think they might have broken the furniture in Daisy's room. When I went in there to find them, everything was in pieces." She gave Daisy a sympathetic look. "We'll make sure it's all fixed up for you. They must have been jumping on the bed. I can't believe they would be so naughty."

"It's okay, Auntie-ji." Daisy grimaced. "I was trying to redecorate, and it . . . all came apart." She looked around the kitchen. "Where's Dad?"

A smile spread across Priya's face. "Out for coffee with your fiancé."

"*My* fiancé?" Daisy's knees trembled and she grabbed the counter. "What are you talking about?"

"Limb!" Salena Auntie pinched her cheeks. "Limb is coming to meet the family."

LIAM trusted his instincts. Growing up with an abusive alcoholic meant that he had learned to read the subtle signs of impending danger. A tense phone call. A heavy footstep. A raised voice. He knew all the triggers, and he knew when to make himself scarce.

His instincts had screamed at him to make himself scarce before he'd walked into the small café around the corner from the Patels' house. But one smile from the man who had been like a father to him, and he knew he'd made the right decision when he'd called Mr. Patel the previous day and asked for a chance to explain.

Mr. Patel stood to shake Liam's hand. "I was glad to hear from you. I owe you an apology. My behavior at the hospital wasn't good. I should have heard you out, but it was all such a shock."

"You don't have to apologize," Liam said. "I'm the one who was in the wrong. Daisy was on my motorcycle."

"And you saved her." Mr. Patel shook his head. "There will be no more talk about it."

A waitress came to take their order, and they talked briefly about Mr. Patel's trip to Belize and Liam's work as a VC until they'd been served. Liam sipped his coffee, unsure how to begin.

Taking pity on him, Mr. Patel gave an encouraging nod. "So, you wanted to tell me what happened the night of the prom . . ."

Liam poured out his soul, telling Mr. Patel the full story about the accident and his decision to leave San Francisco. He left nothing out except Sanjay's involvement. He'd made a promise, and that part of the story was Sanjay's to tell.

He didn't know what he'd expected when he'd walked into the café, but tears, spilled coffee, and Mr. Patel jumping up to pull him out of his seat for a hug wasn't it.

"Liam . . ." Mr. Patel choked on his words. "I knew you were a good boy. I knew you had an explanation. I won't say I wasn't hurt, or that my heart didn't break for Daisy, but now I understand." He pulled away, still holding Liam by the shoulders, his teary eyes intense. "What you did . . . the sacrifices you made . . . I couldn't be prouder of you if you were my own son."

Liam swallowed past the lump in his throat. *Christ.* Where were the damn napkins? Why had he agreed to meet Mr. Patel in such a public place?

While Mr. Patel apologized to the server who had come to mop up the table, Liam sank into his seat, grateful for the chance to gather his thoughts. Beyond his wildest dreams, he'd been offered forgiveness, sympathy, and understanding. He was worthy. It should have been enough. But there was one more thing he needed.

"Daisy told me all about your distillery problem, your fake engagement, and your dating plan." Fully recovered from his emotional outburst, Mr. Patel wasted no time as soon as he was seated at the table with a fresh cup of coffee.

"I'm sorry." Liam's hand tightened around his cup. "I didn't mean to hurt anyone. I shouldn't have asked her to—"

Mr. Patel cut him off with an abrupt wave of his hand. "The time for that is past. The question is, what are your intentions?"

"I love her," Liam said quietly, grateful for the opportunity to discuss Daisy without having to bring it up himself. "I always have. I want to marry her, if she'll have me. I want to spend my life trying to make her happy." He caught his breath when Mr. Patel frowned. "If you approve . . ."

"Hmm." Mr. Patel's lips quivered at the corners. "You would have to meet the family."

"Of course."

"Lucky for you, I asked them all to get together at the house this evening." He finished his coffee in one swallow and pushed out his chair. "Let's see what they have to say."

Friday, 6:16 P.M.

LIAM: Confirming Impromptu Date #7. Patel residence.
Objectives: Beg Daisy's forgiveness, meet Daisy's family,
eat delicious food.

Liam's palms began to sweat as soon as Mr. Patel pushed open the front door. He needed to get a grip. He'd sat through meetings with some of the biggest venture capitalists and CEOs in the business. How bad could one family dinner be?

"I just got your text. What are you doing here?" Daisy accosted him in the hallway between piles of shoes. If she hadn't been wearing a curve-hugging gray minidress printed with Marvel superheroes and a pair of naughty schoolgirl knee socks, he might have been able to give her a coherent response, but all he could do was stare. One week seemed like a lifetime, and he drank her down like he was dying of thirst.

"Answer me," she demanded, her forehead creasing in a frown.

"Beta, no need to shout." Her father kissed her cheek. "Liam asked to meet me to explain what happened in the past. And since you're engaged, I thought it would be a good time for him to meet the family. He's as surprised as you are."

"We're not engaged," she said, dropping her voice low. "I explained that to you. It wasn't real."

"Your aunties and uncles think it's real. And Liam has just declared his intentions."

Daisy's eyes narrowed. "What intentions? Our arrangement is over." She turned on Liam. "You said so yourself just before YOU LEFT."

Heart drumming in his chest, Liam looked to Mr. Patel for help, but Daisy's father just smiled.

308 · SARA DESAI ·

"I'll get everyone together in the living room and let you know when we're ready." He walked away, humming along to the music that was blasting through the house.

"Why are you doing this?" Daisy asked, leaning against the wall. "I thought we were done. Is it the distillery? I thought you'd decided to give it up when you moved to New York."

There was too much to say, and this wasn't the place for a heartfelt talk, especially after he'd just been set up for an interrogation by ambush. Maybe if he appealed to her logical side. "I like to finish what I start. Seeing a plan through to the end, even a dating plan, is just good business."

"Business?" She glared at him. "You think this is business? I love you, Liam. That's not business. That has to do with my heart. And you broke it. Again."

She loved him. She loved him still.

"We're all ready." Mr. Patel waved them into the living room and gestured Liam to one of the kitchen chairs that had been placed in the center of the room.

Liam's mouth went dry as he took in the overwhelming number of people crammed into the small space. The furniture had been pushed against the walls, and it was standing room only for all but the elderly.

"He's very pale," someone said when he settled in his seat. "Maybe he's hungry."

Taara pushed her way forward and handed Liam a plastic container and a fork, a smile on her face. "This one is new, but I made your favorite. Five containers. I put them in the fridge."

Mehar groaned. "What are you doing, Taara? We need him alive to answer questions."

"Why are you always making fun of my food?" Taara blocked Mehar from snatching the container out of Liam's hand. "It's my new fusion dish, spaghetti fish pickle masala oat surprise. My boys loved it."

"I thought one of them had to go to the hospital to get his stomach pumped."

"It was a virus." Taara patted Liam's arm. "And Liam likes my food. We saw him and Daisy at the hockey game, and he ate a whole container of Shark Stew."

A murmur of awe whispered through the crowd.

"He also ate an entire dish of extra hot pork vindaloo at the restaurant." Amina gave Liam a shy smile. "He finished every bite."

Nods. Smiles. So far so good. He could always kill it when it came to food.

A lean man in a blue pullover cleared his throat. "I heard you were Sanjay's friend. Are you a doctor, too?"

"I'm in venture capital."

"Business." The man sniffed, and Liam's confidence slipped a few notches. *No.* He wasn't going down that road again. He'd worked hard to pull himself out of the hole he'd dug in high school, and he was proud of his accomplishments. Daisy loved him even though he was *just* a businessman.

"What about a house?" An elderly man asked. "Do you own a house?"

"No, I rent."

"Renter?" The man looked at Salena, standing beside him. "No house. Where will the children live?"

"Maybe he doesn't want children." Salena cocked her head to the side. "Do you want children?"

Liam had never thought about children, but as he sat in the midst of Daisy's warm, loving family, he realized he desperately wanted a family of his own. "Yes. Very much."

"Very good." The elderly man smiled, and hope swelled in Liam's chest. Daisy should have warned him that meeting her family would be an emotional roller coaster ride.

"What about a car?" A boy of around fourteen shouted to be heard. "What do you drive?"

"I had a motorcycle . . ." His breath caught, and suddenly he was back on the road, the truck bearing down on him and nowhere to go. His pulse kicked up a notch. Sweat beaded on his brow.

"Liam?" Daisy knelt by his side, her face creased with concern. "Are you okay?"

"Yes." He shook himself, pushed the memory away. He'd been so busy blaming himself he clearly hadn't fully processed the trauma, and this wasn't the time. "Any other questions?"

Wrong thing to say. The questions flew thick and fast.

Liam shared his views on politics and religion, his passing familiarity with baseball, and his predictions for the Stanley Cup. He was lauded for visiting Daisy at the vet clinic, buying an expensive sherwani from Nira's store—*he didn't even haggle!*—and for sitting outside Daisy's hospital room for three whole days. But he was also grilled on his ten-year absence from the city, his lack of college education, and his distant family.

Finally, they were allowed to eat. Daisy laughed when she saw his plate. "You'll get brownie points for having a good appetite."

"I'm trying to drown my sorrows in food. I kept hearing Roshan's name every time I turned around. I'm not sure if that means I failed the test."

"He's your competition and every desi father's dream." She scooped some butter chicken with a piece of naan. "They gave him the two thumbs-up of approval."

Liam felt a stab of jealousy at the thought that a man, pre-vetted by the family, was waiting in the wings to snatch Daisy away. No doubt, he had an acceptable degree, a house and car, and all the things a family could want in a husband for Daisy.

But Roshan didn't love her.

And she didn't love him.

"Why are you here?" She asked after they'd finished their meal. "I thought you were moving back to New York. What about the partnership?" She fiddled with the belt around her waist, the soft gray tassels flicking through her fingers.

"They gave me a week to decide, but I don't need the time." He balanced his plate on his knees and reached for her hand. "What I want is right here. I love you. I wanted to tell you the day of our motorcycle ride, and then the accident happened, and I couldn't forgive myself for hurting you again."

"Just like before," she murmured.

"This time was different." He rubbed his thumb over her knuckles. "I'd told you all my secrets, opened myself up, and instead of rejecting me, you told me you loved me. It changed everything for me. It made me realize what was important in my life. It gave me the strength to reconcile with Brendan and to discover the truth about my father. I don't need the partnership to be worthy. It comes from in here." He brought her hand to his heart. "I didn't need fake dates and a spreadsheet to fall in love with you because I've always loved you. I just needed to believe in myself, before I could accept that you loved me, too."

Friday, 11:00 P.M.

LIAM: Re: Date #7. Were objectives achieved?

DAISY: Forgiveness objective still under consideration.

LIAM: What are you doing right now?

DAISY: Sleeping.

LIAM: Your light is on.

DAISY: How do you know?

LIAM: Still waiting outside for an Uber.

DAISY: It's cold. Maybe you should wait inside.

LIAM: On my way. Make room in the bed.

DAISY: Very presumptuous. You have not been forgiven.

LIAM: Will do whatever you want. Walk on bed of hot coals. Whip self with cat o' nine tails. Eat five containers of Shark Stew. Fly to India to buy you Kurkure Masala Munch. Grovel and kiss your pretty feet.

DAISY: Come to me.

LIAM: Front or back door?

DAISY: Sanjay's window.

DAISY sat by Sanjay's window and watched Liam try, for the fifth time, to climb the tree beside the house. He was definitely not as spry as he used to be. Back when they were teenagers, he and Sanjay had made the climb with practiced ease, gaining momentum by running across the lawn and jumping to grab hold of the thick branch that brushed up against the porch. From there, they had swung to a higher branch and then crawled onto the roof. So far, Liam had fallen from the lower branch three times, missed it twice, and once, he had run right into the trunk of the tree. He was covered in cuts and bruises, but he still hadn't given up.

This time he started farther back, ran faster, hit the garden, then leaped into the air. The crash was spectacular. His landing audible. Only the thickness of the rosebush saved him from serious injury. But *oh*, those thorns.

He was fading by the time he finally managed to get on the first branch. There were no swings or acrobatics. No grins or funny antics. He climbed slowly and steadily to the second branch, then shimmied onto the roof. Sweating and bleeding, his shirt torn, thick hair now a tangled mop, he crawled up the steep incline until he reached the window.

He knocked.

She lifted the window the tiniest bit. "Yes?"

Puzzled, he frowned. "You asked me to come."

"Oh." She shook her head, feigning confusion. "That was ages ago. I'm about to go to sleep."

"Daisy." His head dropped back and he groaned. "Please."

Taking pity on him, she opened the window and let him in. "You can clean up in the washroom," she whispered. "But be very quiet."

By the time he returned, she'd positioned herself on her mattress wearing only a Marvel Universe T-shirt featuring all her favorite Avengers. Liam collapsed on the bed beside her, seemingly oblivious to the fact that she had nothing on underneath.

"What's wrong?" She snuggled against him, head on his chest, listening to the pounding of his heart.

"I can't move." He groaned again as he pulled her into his side. "Everything hurts. My hands are covered in cuts. I have thorns in places thorns shouldn't be, and bruises in places I don't want to think about."

"That's too bad." Daisy took his hand and placed it on her bare bottom. "No Avengers protectors down here today. I guess you won't be able to take advantage."

He squeezed her ass, a low, contented rumble vibrating in his chest. "I'm starting to feel better."

"What if I do this?" She tipped her head to nibble kisses along his jaw, rough with a five-o'clock shadow.

"Why aren't you whispering?" Hard hands pulled her over his

body, sliding under her shirt until his thumbs skimmed the sides of her breasts.

"Why would I?" She turned her face into his throat, drawing in the scent of him.

"We don't want to wake your dad and Priya." He parted his legs, forcing hers to follow, leaving her vulnerable to the exquisite sensation of his hard shaft pressing against her beneath his fly.

"They aren't here." Her breath was already coming too fast, her body going liquid. She'd wanted to control this encounter, but the minute he touched her she couldn't think.

Liam froze, his hands mere inches away from her breasts. "Then why didn't I come in the door?"

"Because you left me and broke my heart," Daisy said. "And I liked watching you climb more than I would like to see you grovel or eat five containers of Shark Stew."

"Wicked woman." With one hand fisted in her hair, he pulled her down for a kiss. His tongue met hers, lighting a fire inside her. Pushing herself to sit she tugged his shirt over his head. Her mouth watered at the sight of his chest, firm and lean, taut with muscles. Running her fingers down the trail of soft hair to his belly, she reached for his belt.

"Christ, Daisy." He gently pushed her hand away. "It's been so long and I've missed you so much. You can't imagine how much I want you, but if you undo my belt, I'll finish before we even start." He slid his hands under her shirt and pushed it up. She helped him pull it over her head and he cupped her breasts, thumbs rubbing over her nipples.

Her blood turned to lava in her veins and she moaned in desperation.

"You're killing me, sweetheart," he murmured. "I love to hear how much you need me."

His arms wrapped around her and he pulled her down to kiss her again, deeper and harder, forging an unbreakable connection between them. Without warning, he rolled, pinning her to the bed with the weight of his body. Once settled between her legs, he kissed his way down her neck to her breasts. She threaded her hands through his hair as he closed his mouth around her nipple, her back arching at the sheer pleasure of his warm, wet mouth.

"Take off your clothes," she demanded. She could feel his hard length beneath his jeans, the rough fabric a delicious burn against the sensitive skin of her inner thighs. But she didn't want to wait anymore.

Liam pushed up in one fluid movement and peeled his jeans off, stealing the breath from her lungs. Even with all the cuts and bruises, he had a beautiful body, a dark sensuality that called to her soul.

When he returned to the bed, she drew his mouth to her breast, holding him to her as he electrified every inch of her skin with gentle nips and deep sucking pressure. Her body melted into the bed, as he kissed her all the way down, parting her legs with his broad shoulders to bare her to the magic of his tongue. He knew just where to touch, where to lick, and what she needed to send her over the edge, shattering her world into heat and light and wrenching pleasure.

"I want to be inside you." His low, gravelly whisper sent erotic tingles over her skin.

Languid with release, yet desperate for more, she answered him with a kiss. He rifled in his pocket for a condom and deftly rolled it on.

"Are you hot for me?" He pushed a thick finger inside her and the delicious sensation made her arch off the bed.

"Yes." Her words came in a breathless rush. "Now. I want you now."

"Say the magic words."

Her desire raged, fuzzed her brain with lust. "Please?"

"No."

Daisy groaned. "No games."

"Say my name."

This time there were no secrets between them. This time she wanted him for who he was.

"Liam," she murmured. "My Liam."

His heated gaze never left her as he drew up her legs and thrust deep. Molten heat streamed through her veins, threatening to incinerate her. She cupped his neck, pulling him forward. "Don't stop."

"Never." With long, powerful strokes he drove into her, stoking her passion. When her legs began to shake, he took her mouth in a hot, wet kiss, and then he hammered into her, arms corded, hips rocking, sweat beading on his brow. She grabbed his shoulders, caught his rhythm, tension spiraling inside her until she was swept away in a tidal wave of sensation, her insides clenching in a deep, pulsing rush of pleasure. Liam threw his head back, his body going rock hard as he joined her in release.

He collapsed over her, pressed his face into her neck as she panted her breaths beneath him. His hand found hers, and he brought their twined fingers to his rapidly pounding heart.

"Feel what you do to me, sweetheart."

She felt him, knew him, opened herself to the love he offered, and gave her love in return.

· 32 ·

HAMISH had closed for lunch. The shades were down and the store was quiet when Liam walked in. A vast array of unhealthy foods littered the counter, takeout boxes open to reveal almost everything the doctor had told him not to eat.

"Are you trying to kill yourself?" Liam had come for a distraction. Two days of not hearing from Daisy was killing him. Had he been accepted or not? Did her family approve or had they decided Roshan with the two-thumbs-up five-star rating was the better option?

Liam had already told Brendan that if things didn't work out with Daisy, he would have to leave the city. Brendan had assured him he had no issues at the prospect of Liam becoming a long-distance partner in their new distillery business. He'd already stepped down from his position at Murphy Motors, and with the pressure off, he was a changed man. They'd spent the previous day together playing with Jaxon's new drone, watching hockey on TV, and then being shouted at by Lauren for keeping Jaxon up late.

With a hamburger in one hand and forkful of ribs in the other, Hamish laughed. "Can you think of a better way to go? My friend Duke pounded back six burgers and four pounds of bacon a day and he was as healthy as a horse. Only reason he's not here is because he got caught in the crossfire when two rival MCs started shooting at each other at a burger bar in Montana. He died doing what he loved best."

Liam groaned. "You've now put me off burgers for life."

"Too bad. When you called to say you were coming, I bought you a birthday surprise."

"My birthday isn't for two days."

Hamish handed him a cardboard container. "But you're here today, and this is one of the best burgers in town. It's a serious half pound of grass-fed beef topped with cheddar, bacon, pineapple, pickles, special sauce, and onions on a homemade sesame-seed bun."

Hamish delivered as promised. The burger was delicious. They talked bikes while they ate and Liam shared his fears that the panic attack he'd had at the Patels' might mean he would never ride again.

"You need to get back on the road." Hamish wiped his mouth with the back of his hand. "Best way to get over that kind of trauma. Take it from me. I've had so many accidents, I can't even count. You gotta push through it. What you want is on the other side of your fear."

Liam walked around the store, checking out the gear while Hamish cleared off the counter. "So what are you saying? I should buy another bike?"

"I got a big shipment in the other day," Hamish said. "Maybe you should take a look at the new XDiavel. I can grab the keys if you want to take it for a test drive."

Liam walked through the gleaming rows of bikes in the showroom to the outdoor lot. Although dark clouds had rolled in, threatening rain, the XDiavel gleamed in the fading light.

"If you've got the cash, I'd say this new model is worth serious consideration."

It was beautiful. Sporty. A devil of a machine. But something was missing. "What about the pillion seat?"

"It's still really meant as a solo ride," Hamish said. "I wouldn't recommend that bike if you're planning on taking Daisy out on a regular basis."

"I don't know if we'll be together." Liam's voice caught and the words tumbled out before he could catch them. "Her family wants her to marry someone else. He doesn't know her. Not the way I do. He's not going to understand when she starts putting lists and schedules all over the house, or doodles math problems on every surface. He won't know she likes martinis, or that her favorite restaurant is the Dosa Palace, or that her room looks exactly like it did when she was fourteen. He's not going to understand what it was like for her to grow up without her mom. He won't know that she can scream 'Go Sharks' loud enough to win a free pizza. And he won't know that Max is a very special dog."

Hamish studied him for a long moment and then wound his way through the motorcycles until he got to a monster bike, a blue and black Honda Gold Wing Tour. "It's not about the ride, it's about who you've got in the pillion seat, and it sounds to me like you're done with the XDiavel." He patted the massive black leather seat. "I think this might be what you're looking for. The new four-valve six gives you 125bhp and it's got a full suite of electronics. But the reason people buy this bike is the pillion seat. We're talking super plush and super safe. It's got armrests, a heated seat, electric screen, you name it. It's a lounge chair for the open road. Any pillion will rightly feel like a queen."

It was hands down the biggest, heaviest bike Liam had ever seen. There would be no pep to that motor, no leaning into corners, no zipping in and out of traffic. It lacked the style and sophistication of his XDiavel, the racetrack-ready sport bike feel. Far from being maxi-naked like the XDiavel, the Gold Wing was fully clothed—a motorcycle made for two.

"That's the bike," he said. "I'll take it, but I need it now." He wasn't going to sit around and wait to be chosen. He wasn't going to let fear stop him from going after what he wanted. He was going to Daisy's house and he would show her family that no one was more worthy than him.

"I'll put a dealer plate on it and you can take it for an extended test drive while I do the paperwork." Hamish handed him the keys. "You need any gear?"

"Full armor. The best you've got. And helmets. For two."

LIAM had it all planned out. He would park his new Gold Wing outside Mr. Patel's house. Daisy would be waiting on the front step. There would be hugs and kisses. Tears and congratulations. Mr. Patel would come out to shake his hand, telling him it had never really been a choice. They had always wanted Liam, and welcome to the family.

The first part of his plan couldn't have gone better. The dark clouds parted as soon as he left Hamish's shop, and a sliver of sunshine lit his way to the Patels' house, where he found a parking space right out front. He eased the bike to a stop and turned off the engine, his gaze flicking to the porch to see if Daisy was there. That was when he noticed the decorations.

Paper lanterns, streamers, flowers, and shiny twirling spirals dripped from the overhang above the front door. A birthday perhaps? Or maybe an anniversary? After securing his helmet, he rang the bell. No answer. He knocked on the front door and sent Daisy a quick text. When she didn't respond, he took a quick peek through the windows and felt the first stirrings of concern.

There could be many reasons why the furniture had been removed to make way for long tables covered in colorful tablecloths, each with a centerpiece of brilliant flowers. Or why there was a pile of presents in the hallway, wrapped in paper decorated with wedding bells and cartoon brides and grooms. Maybe they were hosting a relative's wedding celebration. Or opening a party shop. Or maybe he'd won the battle, but lost the war.

He heard a bark and saw Max playing fetch with an elderly woman in the adjacent yard. He walked over and introduced himself as Daisy's friend, then crouched down to give Max a pat.

"Any idea what's going on next door?" he asked the neighbor. "Looks like they're having a party."

"I think it's the wedding." She smiled down at him. "Nadal was so excited. He was swinging Daisy around and they were dancing on the driveway. She looked so beautiful in her dress. Poor Max wanted to go with them, but they don't allow animals at the Golden Gate Club."

Fear slid icy fingers down his spine. Was he too late? Had they picked Roshan?

Thunder boomed overhead and the sky darkened, the sliver of sunlight disappearing beneath the rolling clouds.

Hand shaking, he pulled out his phone and texted Daisy. Maybe her neighbor was mistaken. Maybe there was another explanation. How could his plan go so wrong?

Max stood on his hind legs and pawed at Liam's chest, tail wagging, furry face nuzzling until Liam stood and lifted him into his arms. Max licked his face and Liam's tension eased.

He won't know that Max is a very special dog.

"He sure likes you," Daisy's neighbor said. "He's not usually that friendly with strangers."

"I'm not a stranger."

He doesn't know her. Not the way I do.

Daisy loved him. She was his humraaz, the light in his soul. There was no way she would marry Roshan.

He gave Max one last cuddle. And then he got on his bike to find his queen.

As expected, Mehar Auntie had hogged the dance floor at Daisy's father's sangeet.

"I can't believe her." Layla crossed her arms and glared at Mehar Auntie as she tore up the dance floor at the Golden Gate Club with an overly rehearsed version of "Galla Goodiyaan." "It's supposed to be a family dance. She should have saved her solo performance for something like 'Tamma Tamma Again.'"

"We could join her," Daisy suggested as she loaded her plate from the buffet. "Once we start dancing, everyone else will come."

"But then she won't speak to us for weeks. How will you run the dance class with her?" Layla's brow creased in a frown. "I'll tell you right now, she better not do that at my wedding. I want everyone on the dance floor."

"Don't worry. I have a plan. You've given me lots of time to prepare. Unlike my dad." Her father was smiling and clapping his hands, oblivious to the amount of stress he'd caused Daisy by deciding to have a quickie wedding. Even with Salena Auntie's contacts and the entire family pulling together, she'd struggled to get everything organized in time. But that was her dad. Even his wedding had to be extreme.

"Where's Liam?" Layla added a samosa to her plate. "Sam wanted to compare sword sizes with him. After he found out Deepa had given Liam a bigger sword, he went to trade his in. At this rate, there won't be room for me beside him at the wedding."

"I didn't invite him." She scraped her teeth over her lip and looked down. "Sanjay is coming and I didn't want to ambush him and possibly cause a scene when this is supposed to be a celebration. I thought it might be better to wait until after the party so I can break the news gently. He never talked about how he felt about Liam leaving, but I'm sure he was just as devastated as Dad and me." She still felt guilty about ghosting Liam for the last two days, but how could she explain she was organizing a party to which he wasn't invited when, for all intents and purposes, he was her fiancé?

Layla shot her a curious look. "So does that mean your dad gave his approval? I hope so, because all the aunties and uncles loved him, and after he saved your life, I definitely hate him a little less."

"He said he wanted to talk to Sanjay first." She checked her watch. "He should be here any minute. He'd made arrangements to take leave when he heard about my accident, and then Dad and Priya announced their engagement, so it was perfect timing."

After they finished their plates, they headed to the bar and Daisy introduced Layla to her new favorite drink, a pink lemonade martini. Rainey had made it for her as a postcoital refreshment at the Rose & Thorn.

"I see nothing has changed," a deep voice said behind them. "The two of you are still stuck together at the hip and gossiping like aunties."

Daisy whirled around, her eyes widening when she saw her brother standing behind them. "Sanjay!" She threw her arms around him. "I was getting worried you wouldn't make it."

Tall and lean, with wide cheekbones in a sculpted face, his shoulders slightly stooped like their father, and his dark eyes streaked with gold like their mother, Sanjay was a perfect mix of their parents both in temperament and form.

"Are you kidding? I wouldn't miss this for the world." He released Daisy and gave Layla a quick hug. "Congrats on your engagement, cousin. I heard you're marrying a doctor. I'm looking forward to meeting him."

"He took some getting used to," Daisy murmured. "But now that he's part of the family, he's mellowed."

Sanjay ordered a beer and they moved to a quieter corner to chat about his posting in Somalia and his plans to stay in the city for the next eight months to do a fellowship in emergency medicine. "It's like I haven't been away." He laughed as he checked out the room. "Mehar Auntie is up to her old tricks, Hari Uncle is already drunk, the kids are running wild, and the *rishta* aunties are trying to set people up like it's a game." He gave Daisy a nudge. "I'm surprised they aren't over here with someone for you."

He'd given her an opening. Should she tell him? Daisy looked to Layla for help, but her cousin just shrugged. "I . . . met someone."

"Do tell." His eyes widened with interest. "Who has managed to capture the heart of our fair Daisy?"

Daisy put down her glass and took a deep breath. "Liam Murphy."

Sanjay froze, his glass halfway to his lips. "Liam? My old friend Liam? He's here?"

"Not *here* here," Layla said. "He didn't come to the sangeet. But he is in San Francisco."

Sanjay ran a hand through his dark hair. "I can't believe it. He's back. And . . ." His forehead creased. "You're together?"

"Not just together. They're practically engaged except for the pesky matter of your dad's approval." Layla grinned. "But you know what the two of them are like. They can't get out of their own heads. It took a broken menstrual pad dispenser, a chance encounter, an inheritance, a failing company, a distillery, a rishta auntie, a hapless suitor, a spreadsheet, seven dates, a sword, extra-hot pork vindaloo, an Irish brawl, a sick dog, endless games of Guitar Hero, a hockey game, Shark Stew, a broken bed, a walk of shame, a quiz night, back-office shenanigans, a jealous ex, a motorcycle crash, a crisis of conscience, a break up, six pints of ice cream, four pounds of gummy bears, a partnership offer, a heart-to-heart, a family interrogation, a grovel, and a death-defying midnight climb to get them together. And now, apparently, it's all up to you."

"Me?" Sanjay folded his arms across his chest. "Why is their happiness suddenly in my hands?"

"Because they're still afraid."

Still reeling from Layla's all-too-accurate description of her relationship, Daisy bristled. "That's not true. Dad said he wouldn't approve the engagement unless he talked to Sanjay. He wants Sanjay to hear Liam's side of the story, like he did."

Sanjay stilled, his voice thickening. "Liam told you what happened?"

Layla took Daisy's glass and discretely backed away. "I'll go get you a refill and let your dad know Sanjay is here."

"Not everything," Daisy said after Layla had gone. "He didn't tell me the name of the friend who was with him that night."

But she knew. Now that Sanjay was standing in front of her, guilt and regret etched in every line of his familiar face, the pieces all came together. When Sanjay had come home the night of the prom, his face had been battered and bruised. He'd told their father he'd been in a fight, but she'd known he was lying when he came into her room, an emotional and physical wreck, to babble a semi-coherent apology that Liam hadn't been able to take her to the prom.

"It was you," she whispered. Her brother wasn't so perfect after all.

"He saved me, Daisy." Sanjay's chest hitched, his throat bobbing as he spoke. "You wouldn't believe how many times he pulled my ass out of the fire over the years. What he did that night . . . what he sacrificed for me . . . I wouldn't be where I am now if not for him. I'm the reason you had no date for the prom. I'm the reason he had to leave town. If I hadn't been so stupid . . ." He took a deep, pained breath and closed his eyes. "My actions that night hurt so many people. I wanted to make it up to Liam, but he'd disappeared and I couldn't find him. I decided to use the gift he'd given me—the chance to go to medical school—to help people in desperate need. I try to save lives to make up for all the pain I caused in the past."

He looked haunted, so broken that Daisy wrapped her arms around him and squeezed him tight. "Don't be so hard on yourself. Everything worked out in the end. He was able to get his mother out of a terrible situation. He found his passion and joined a venture capital firm in New York. And I dated all the wrong guys so that I knew the right one when I found him."

"Liam." He pulled away and smiled. "I can't think of a better man for you. I would be proud to have him as part of our family." He looked around. "Why isn't he here?"

"I didn't want to ambush you at the sangeet. I didn't know what you would think."

Sanjay frowned. "If he's your fiancé, he should be here, regardless of what Dad or I think. Do you really love him? If we didn't approve, would you let him walk away?"

Daisy's mouth opened and closed again. "I haven't really thought about it properly. In the beginning our relationship wasn't real. We pretended to be engaged and went on a series of dates to legitimize a marriage of convenience that would help him get his inheritance, save my company, and get the aunties off my back. The family introduction was the final step in the plan. I told him I wouldn't go through with the fake marriage unless the family approved . . ." She trailed off as something that had been niggling at the back of her mind suddenly became clear.

Sanjay saw it, too, and his voice softened. "You gave yourself an out. But don't use the family as an excuse. If you really love him, it doesn't matter what anyone thinks. This is your life, Daisy. I know you've been hurt and it's made you afraid of commitment, but of all the people I've met, Liam is worth the risk."

He was right. Of course he was right. She'd told Liam she loved him, but some part of her had been afraid to take that final step—going off-plan and committing to something real.

"I'll text him right now." She pulled out her phone and saw the messages she'd missed while she'd been busy at the party.

Saturday, 11:06 A.M.

LIAM: Confirming Date #8 in expectation of family approval. Sunday, June 24, 3 p.m. Las Vegas. Objective: Wedding.

Saturday, 12:15 P.M.

LIAM: At your house. Couldn't wait any longer. Not much time to get sherwani and book flights. Not taking no for an answer.
LIAM: If no, will steal you away so we can elope.
LIAM: Max can come, too.

Saturday, 12:25 P.M.

LIAM: Paging Humraaz. Where are you? What about the plan?
LIAM: Joking about Max. Dogs not allowed in chapel.
LIAM: I chose an Elvis song: "Can't Help Falling in Love."

Saturday, 12:36 P.M.

LIAM: Talked to your neighbor. You're getting married. All
Shook Up.

Bile rose in Daisy's throat when she read the last message, and she stared at her brother, aghast. "Oh God, Sanjay. Liam went to the house to see me, and our neighbor told him this was *my* wedding! He thinks I'm marrying someone else." Her heart pounded so hard she thought it might explode. She called and messaged, but Liam didn't answer his phone. "What if he goes back to New York?" Her voice shook as panic took hold. "I have to find him."

· 33 ·

DAISY checked her phone again as she ran down the road to her car. Liam hadn't responded to her messages. Where was he? She had his work address, but she had never been to his apartment. Would he have gone straight to the airport? Would he have stopped at Brendan's place to say goodbye? She knew all about his plans to fix up the distillery with Brendan and his dream of starting his own venture capital company after he turned down the Evolution partnership. Snuggled together in the dark after he'd climbed over the roof to be with her, they'd shared their hopes for the future and their regrets about the past. Would he give up his dreams to go back to New York? Maybe he'd just gone for a drink at the Rose & Thorn . . .

She reached the corner of Sheridan and Montgomery just as the heavens opened. Across from an open field, with only the grand Presidio buildings behind her, she was totally exposed. Her salwar kameez, a lavender faux georgette pantsuit with jewel-tone beadwork and an embroidered floral pattern, provided little protection from the downpour. With no umbrella and a ten-minute walk ahead of her, she wrapped her dupatta around her and raced for the nearest bus shelter to wait out the storm.

Fists clenched, fingernails biting into her palms, she paced in short spans, willing the rain to stop before it was too late. An engine rumbled in the distance. She poked her head around the glass and saw the silhouette of a motorcycle inching slowly through the rain.

Unlike Liam's sleek and sporty XDiavel, this motorcycle was a monster, slow and steady, the mechanics encased in shiny blue, black, and chrome.

The motorcycle rumbled to an unsteady stop at the curb in front of her. She recognized Liam even before he pulled the helmet off his head. Who else would find her at a bus stop in the rain?

Her heart lifted in her chest, filling her with light, her voice with wonder. "You came."

Liam parked the bike and joined her in the shelter, pulling her into his arms. Her light clothes were instantly soaked, but she didn't feel anything but the warmth in Liam's eyes.

"I hope you're not married to Roshan because I'm going to kiss you." His voice was rough and tender at once. "And then I'm going to challenge him to a fight. No one can beat an Irishman in a brawl."

She drank in the slightly mussed dark hair, the clear blue eyes, the cocky smile. "I'm not married."

"Thank God." He let out a shuddering breath. "I'm still bruised from climbing onto your roof." He framed her face between his warm palms and met her gaze. Everything inside her clicked into place. She was exactly where she needed to be.

"I thought I lost you once," he said softly. "I'm not going to lose you again."

She melted against him, her lips yielding to his passionate kiss.

"Tell me this is real," Liam murmured, nuzzling her neck. "Did your dad say yes?"

"I don't need anyone to tell me what I know in my heart." She slid her hand around his nape and pulled him close. "I love you. I want you and only you. So, yes, Liam. This is real."

Liam dropped down to one knee and clasped her hand. "From

the first day we first met, I knew I needed you in my life. You took the chaos and made it calm. You lifted my heart with your smile and awed me with your brilliant mind. I kept every secret valentine, every scribbled note, your stuffed rabbit, and the answer to every math question I gave you. I hoped one day to be the kind of man you could love, a man who would hold and cherish you, a man worthy of you, and who would protect you with the sword you are going to allow him to have at our wedding." He fumbled in his pocket. "I didn't really plan this . . ."

Daisy laughed. "Of course not."

"I did try, but it wasn't me, and if I had, I would have missed this incredible opportunity to turn the ultimate cinematic symbol of uncontrollable passion upside down and make the fantasy of a love so intense that nothing else matters into something real."

Her face softened. "You remembered all that?"

"I remember every moment I spend with you." He pulled out a silver ring with a Sharks logo on top. "I keep my fan gear in Hamish's warehouse. I grabbed it when I left with the bike, just in case." He slipped the ring on her finger. "Daisy Patel, my humraaz, love of my life, will you marry me?"

Her happiness bubbled over and she punched her fist in the air. "Go Sharks!"

"Is that a yes?" He looked up, frowning. "It's a little less romantic than I had anticipated . . ."

"Of course it's a yes." She pulled him up and kissed him, her body pressed against his, their hearts beating as one.

"So . . ." Liam pulled back. "Date #8. Wedding. If we want to finish the dating plan in the allotted time, we'll need to pick up my sherwani and sword and book our flights to Vegas."

"Is that what you want?" Plans and lists and schedules were the furthest thing from her mind now that her heart was so full.

"I want you to be happy, and if finishing the plan the way we wrote it makes you happy, then that's what I want to do."

"Plans can be changed." Daisy shrugged. "Rules can be broken."

"I think I might have proposed to the wrong woman." His lips whispered over hers, and he followed the touch with a long, soft kiss that scrambled her brain.

"It would be a terrible waste if you only wore your expensive sherwani for a ten-minute wedding." She ran a finger along the edge of his jaw. "And that sword. No one would see it but me and Elvis. Not even Sam."

Liam sighed. "That would be a terrible tragedy."

"What if we amended the plan to change the date?" She feathered kisses along his jaw. "And maybe instead of Vegas, we could have it here, and invite your family, and my family, and there would be music and dancing and lots of food."

Liam twisted his lips to the side as if considering. "Pork vindaloo?"

"Extra hot."

"Jalebis?"

"Of course."

"I want all the food we had at your dad's house the other night and at the Dosa Palace, plus Priya's cake."

"Done."

"And no Shark Stew."

"I'll do my best."

"What about the crunchy treats?"

"Kurkure Masala Munch? You'd be the groom. You could have as much as you could eat."

He lifted an eyebrow. "I can eat a lot."

"You won't be disappointed."

He rubbed his lips with his finger. "I suppose just this once I can agree. I'll expect the amended spreadsheet by the end of the day."

Daisy pressed up against him, sliding her fingers through his damp hair. "How about we go to your place and amend it together? Our fake wedding day starts at midnight, and I want you naked in a bed that isn't broken to celebrate the end of the plan."

"Spreadsheet birthday sexy times." He gave a satisfied growl. "I'm in." He turned, gesturing to his bike. "Whenever you're ready to ride again, your chariot awaits. It has the highest pillion seat safety rating and I've bought you head-to-toe body armor to go with it."

Daisy laughed. "Seriously? Is that your new bike?"

"It will be as soon as I sign the paperwork. I finally understood something Hamish told me."

"What's that?"

"It's not about the ride. It's about who is in the pillion seat."

· 34 ·

"LIAM!" Daisy's eyes widened when she saw him in the mirror behind her. She'd slipped out of the tech conference to smooth down her hair before her pitch session. "What are you doing in the ladies' restroom?"

"I have to show you something, and I thought I'd get arrested if I pulled it out in public."

Her gaze dropped below his belt, and he laughed. "I always knew you had a dirty mind." He opened his sports bag and pulled out a sword. "I'm talking about this."

"Oh my God." Daisy groaned. "You picked up your sherwani, didn't you? Our wedding is six months away."

"Deepa called to say it was ready, and Sanjay wanted to see it. I couldn't wait." He beamed, and Daisy knew it wasn't just about the sword. After a long conversation, Sanjay and Liam were as tight as they'd ever been. When they were all together at her father's house, joking around and throwing snark, it was like time had stood still.

Liam held the sword up to the light. "The outfit is in my new SUV, but I was afraid to leave the sword in case someone stole it." He lunged forward, thrusting at the menstrual pad dispenser. "*En garde.* I will protect my lady's honor with my life."

"If you keep that up, you'll get a sword full of pads."

"Don't you need them for your pitch? A few strokes and I can fell the evil machine and you can have all the pads you want." He lifted an admonishing eyebrow. "Or do you prefer to steal them?"

"I did not steal them," she huffed. "And I'm not Tyler. I had all my product samples packed and ready for the pitch three days ago. I have backups and backups for the backups as well as three copies of all the documents, and I've practiced my pitch so many times I could do it in my sleep." When she hadn't heard back from Tanya, she'd assumed the worst, and had arranged to attend the Vizio Tech Con to try and find investors for the new, streamlined Organicare, with its cutting-edge branding.

"I would expect no less." Liam slashed with the sword. "And if you get rejected, I'll pay them a little visit in the middle of the night."

Her lips quivered as she fought back an amused smile. "Your lady has a pitch to give, so how about you put the sword away and give her a kiss for luck?"

With a soft growl, Liam grabbed her around the waist and pulled her into his chest, grinding his hips against her black suit skirt. "How about we exchange this sword for another?"

"You also have work to do at the conference today," she said, trying to maintain the dignity and professionalism of a CEO while her very hot, very sexy, very real fiancé stoked the heat of her desire. "There are a dozen excited young entrepreneurs waiting to pitch to your new company and I think they might be put off if you showed up with any kind of sword."

He gave a satisfied rumbled of pleasure. "Brendan and Jaxon are going to love it. I'm going to take it out to the distillery tomorrow and show them some moves after we check the new wash back tanks. Are you sure you can't come?"

"Layla's wedding is only a few weeks away, but I'm sure you could convince Sam to join you for a sword fight." Sam and Liam had, of course, become sword-toting besties, while alternately sneaking into Krishna Fashions every week to slip Deepa a few dollars to ensure she knew who to call if she found a bigger sword.

Liam's shoulders slumped, and he tucked his sword back in his sports bag. "How about I take off your fancy new suit and sheath my non-lethal sword somewhere that will make you scream my name in pleasure?"

Biting back a laugh, Daisy tried to put on a stern face. "Because I might have all the Avengers protecting me today."

His face brightened with interest. "Let me see. I have a surprise that would make the imminent destruction of the Avengers worthwhile."

"A surprise in you pants?"

"No, a surprise in the mail." He laughed when she gave him a puzzled frown. "Aunt Roisin sent us an early wedding gift before she left for her ayurveda retreat in Sri Lanka. She gave us my grandfather's house. It was part of her inheritance, but she said she doesn't need it. She's decided to live a life free of worldly goods, so she transferred the title to us."

Daisy's hand flew to her mouth. "A house! Oh my God, Liam. We're going to have a house!"

"Which means I'll pass the last two Patel tests: house and car." He licked his lips. "Now can I see under your skirt?"

"No way." She turned to face him, licking her lips. She'd already made her decision, but she didn't want him to think it was that easy. "The minute I lift my skirt, you'll do that thing you do, and suddenly it will be 12:50 P.M. and I'll be running down the hallway to my pitch session with my hair mussed and my clothes half off, and no one will believe I'm the CEO of Organicare."

"I'll believe it." His hand stroked over her hair, and she felt his touch as a throb at the juncture of her thighs. It was always like this with Liam. She couldn't get enough.

After her father's wedding, and knowing Priya would take good care of her dad, she'd decided to move out and start living her own life. She'd found a dog-friendly apartment near work and they'd furnished it together, starting with a king size bed with a solid wood frame and an even more solid headboard. They'd also bought a large dining table to entertain their families. Her dearest wish was to help bring Liam's family together. For appearance's sake— her father was still a traditional man—Liam kept his small apartment, but they spent all their time at her place, rarely in their clothes, christening each piece of new furniture they purchased.

"Tanya believes it, too," he continued. "I just bumped into her at one of the VC sessions and she told me the good news."

Daisy's ears perked with interest. "What good news?"

"You got your Series B funding!" His blue eyes sparkled. "She was going to let you know after your pitch sessions. A second investor would make things a lot easier so she didn't want to tell you until you were done."

"Oh my God!" She jumped up and down in his arms. "I have to tell Mia, Josh, and Zoe. They'll be thrilled. Organicare is saved."

"Because of you. My fiercely determined, superintelligent, hot CEO."

A smile touched her lips. She still couldn't believe it. Even without a business background, she'd managed to run the company for the last month without any hitches. Hopefully, when their funding finally came through and a proper board was appointed, they would vote for her to stay permanently in the job.

"You think I'm hot?" She gave him a slow, sensual smile.

His hand dropped to her hip and he tugged her skirt up. "So hot, I think I need to do you over the sink."

When he looked at her that way, with heat and desire in his eyes, she couldn't deny him anything. "Did you lock the door?"

"Of course."

"Condoms?"

Liam sniffed. "I knew you were going to be at the conference. Did you think I'd come unprepared to service your needs?"

"We'll have eleven minutes for the good stuff. Three to clean up. Two to fix our clothes. Ten to get to our respective conference rooms. Does that work for you?"

Liam spun her around and yanked up her skirt. "I love it when you schedule our sexy times. It turns me on."

"That's good because I planned for this in advance and left the Avengers at home."

"DAISY! I've been looking all over for you." Madison caught Daisy as she exited the restroom, one minute later than scheduled, giving her only nine minutes to get to her pitch.

"I'm actually just on my way to a—"

"Oh. Liam." Madison cut her off, smirking when Liam walked out of the restroom behind her, still adjusting his tie. "Nice to see you again."

Totally nonplussed, Liam smiled. "Madison."

"Men's room closed?"

"Not at all." He put an arm around Daisy's shoulder and pressed a kiss to her cheek. "Just needed a little alone time with my fiancée."

Madison's smile faded. "You're still engaged?"

"Yes, we are." He held up Daisy's hand to show off the diamond ring he'd bought her to replace the Sharks ring he'd given her at the bus stop. "When you meet the woman you want to spend the rest of your life with, you don't let her go."

Daisy slipped an arm through Liam's. "How's Orson?"

"Orson?" Madison frowned as if she had no idea who Daisy was talking about. "Oh. He's gone. Maybe New York?"

"I'm sorry to hear that."

"I was sorry to hear that Organicare was going under." Madison's smirk returned. "I was wondering if you were interested in coming back to work for me. I need a senior software engineer and——"

"Organicare isn't going under," Daisy said. "We've given the company a total overhaul and we've just secured our Series B funding. I've had interest from other investors and I'm here to meet some of them right now. So, if you'll excuse me . . ."

"She's the CEO," Liam said, beaming. "She saved the company and now she's running the whole show."

"Congratulations." Madison's voice was flat as she checked her watch. "You're right about the time. I've got a meeting in five minutes. I'd better go."

"You didn't have to do that," Daisy said to Liam. "It was a little bit petty."

"You enjoyed every second of it."

Her lips tipped in a smile. "Okay. I did. She was like every mean girl in high school who mocked me, and now the tables have turned and not only am I running a company, I got the coolest guy in school."

Liam put an arm around her shoulders. "My fiancée thinks I'm cool."

"I think you're hot, but we'd better not go down that road again because we'll be late." They walked down the corridor, and she couldn't help but remember the last con they'd attended together. This time there were no aunties chasing her with suitors in tow, no heartbreaking moments listening to her ex-boyfriend making out with her boss, no fumbling with boxes of pads as she quelled her fear at the thought of helping Tyler with the pitch . . . but there was Liam. Always and forever Liam.

"I was worried she was going to ask us how we first met." Daisy leaned into his side. "Maybe we should have a plan."

"We don't need a plan," Liam said. "We'll tell them the truth. We met when we needed to meet. We found each other when we needed to be found. We fell in love because it was meant to be. And you became mine at a bus stop in the rain."

Acknowledgments

Writing often starts as a solitary endeavor, but it takes a team to bring a story to life.

To the entire Berkley team, including Tara O'Connor, Jessica Mangicaro, Marina Muun, Katie Anderson, and especially my fantastic editor, Kristine Swartz, who can make a story shine with one stroke of her virtual pen, and tempt me with delicious recipes that I have yet to be able to replicate.

To my agent, Laura Bradford, for her tenacity, faith, and ability to talk me through the highest highs and the lowest lows.

To my friends Anne and Andrea, for enduring my endless talks about writing and the woes of editing, sharing my highs and lows, and keeping me sane.

To all my desi readers who wrote to me after reading *The Marriage Game* to share their enthusiasm, support, and encouragement. I will keep writing if you promise to keep reading.

To Sapphira, who encouraged me to write a different kind of hero, and talked me through the twists and tangles of the plot. May your world be filled with the strong, smart, empowered women you inspire me to write.

To my parents, Joe and Marie, and to Sharon, Rana, Adele, and Tarick, for supporting my dreams and for thinking I am the world's best writer.

To John and my girls, for your endless patience, love, support, and attempts at cooking. I wouldn't be where I am without you.

Photo copyright Linda Mackie Photography

Sara Desai has been a lawyer, radio DJ, marathon runner, historian, bouncer, and librarian. She lives on Vancouver Island with her husband, kids, and an assortment of forest creatures who think they are pets. Sara writes sexy romantic comedy and contemporary romance with a multicultural twist. When not laughing at her own jokes, Sara can be found eating nachos.

CONNECT ONLINE

SaraDesai.com